Berkley Sensation Titles by Renee Bernard

Obsession Wears Opals

RENEE BERNARD

BERKLEY SENSATION, NEW YORK

THE BERKLEY PUBLISHING GROUP
Published by the Penguin Group
Penguin Group (USA) Inc.
375 Hudson Street, New York, New York 10014, USA

Penguin Group (Canada), 90 Eglinton Avenue East, Suite 700, Toronto, Ontario M4P 2Y3, Canada
(a division of Pearson Penguin Canada Inc.) • Penguin Books Ltd., 80 Strand, London WC2R 0RL,
England • Penguin Group Ireland, 25 St. Stephen's Green, Dublin 2, Ireland (a division of Penguin
Books Ltd.) • Penguin Group (Australia), 250 Camberwell Road, Camberwell, Victoria 3124, Australia
(a division of Pearson Australia Group Pty. Ltd.) • Penguin Books India Pvt. Ltd., 11 Community
Centre, Panchsheel Park, New Delhi—110 017, India • Penguin Group (NZ), 67 Apollo Drive,
Rosedale, Auckland 0632, New Zealand (a division of Pearson New Zealand Ltd.) • Penguin Books
(South Africa) (Pty.) Ltd., 24 Sturdee Avenue, Rosebank, Johannesburg 2196, South Africa

Penguin Books Ltd., Registered Offices: 80 Strand, London WC2R 0RL, England

This is a work of fiction. Names, characters, places, and incidents either are the product of the author's
imagination or are used fictitiously, and any resemblance to actual persons, living or dead, business
establishments, events, or locales is entirely coincidental. The publisher does not have any control over
and does not assume any responsibility for author or third-party websites or their content.

OBSESSION WEARS OPALS

A Berkley Sensation Book / published by arrangement with the author

PUBLISHING HISTORY
Berkley Sensation mass-market paperback edition / December 2012

Copyright © 2012 by Renee Bernard
Cover art by Alan Ayers. Cover design by George Long.

ISBN: 978-0-425-25981-8

BERKLEY SENSATION®
Berkley Sensation Books are published by The Berkley Publishing Group,
a division of Penguin Group (USA) Inc.,
375 Hudson Street, New York, New York 10014.
BERKLEY SENSATION® is a registered trademark of Penguin Group (USA) Inc.
The "B" design is a trademark of Penguin Group (USA) Inc.

PRINTED IN THE UNITED STATES OF AMERICA

10 9 8 7 6 5 4 3 2 1

ALWAYS LEARNING   PEARSON *continued . . .*

"What a refreshing new take on two people who from first sight are determined to detest each other . . . I was immediately engrossed with the fiery, witty dialogue and the curiosity of how this couple, who loathed each other upon their meeting, would come full circle to a beautifully shared love in the end."
—*Fiction Vixen*

Revenge Wears Rubies

"Sensuality fairly steams from Bernard's writing. This luscious tale will enthrall you. Enjoy!"
—Sabrina Jeffries, *New York Times* bestselling author

"If you're a fan of spicy hot romances mixed with a bit of intrigue and set in Victorian London, don't miss this one!"
—*The Romance Dish*

"Galen's journey from emotional cripple to ability to love is a captivating, erotic romance."
—*Fresh Fiction*

More praise for the "grand mistress of sensual, scorching romance."*

"Sinfully sexy . . . Wickedly witty, sublimely sensual . . . Renee Bernard dazzles readers . . . Clever, sensual, and superb."
—*Booklist*

"Scorcher! Bernard debuts with an erotic romance that delivers not only a high degree of sensuality but a strong plotline and a cast of memorable characters. She's sure to find a place alongside Robin Schone, Pam Rosenthal, and Thea Devine." —**RT Book Reviews*

"Very hot romance. Readers who enjoy an excellent, sizzling Victorian story are going to thoroughly enjoy this one."
—*Romance Reviews Today*

"Shiverlicious! A captivating plot, charismatic characters, and sexy, tingle-worthy romance . . . Fantastic!" —*Joyfully Reviewed*

"Crowd-pleasing."
—*Publishers Weekly*

This book is for every woman who had the courage to go when she needed to and stood up for herself, and for all the women who are waiting for their chance to escape. You are not alone.

To Geoffrey and my girls. Almost there. Keep on swimming. I love you.

Acknowledgments

Memo to me: Happier acknowledgments please. No one wants to read about the dreary slog of my life or how anyone living in the twenty-first century cannot for the life of her manage not to fall further behind every time she tries to "upgrade" her technology. Seriously, I must be doing it wrong. If there's an "easy" button outside of that commercial, I've lost mine.

I want to thank Eric Ruben for being more than my agent. He's become my true friend and a pseudo-sibling. I have to thank Kate Seaver for being such a patient and wonderful editor and for fighting for me. My thanks to Sheila English at Readers Entertainment for making me part of the team and to Megan Bamford and the Aussie Crew for introducing me to red frogs, new varieties of Tim Tams, and the opals (Oh, goodness! The opals!). My thanks to everyone at RT for their amazing love and support. I have to mention Anne Elizabeth, who is so dear to me as a friend and advocate that there just aren't words. I'll never be able to repay her for all her advice and support—if having a loving heart was a sport, Anne would be a world champion.

I want to acknowledge Carolyn Follett for all her hard work and her attempts to keep me from leaving a trail of personal belongings in my wake at RT Chicago. Also a huge thanks to Michelle Drew, Lindsey Ross, and Josie Cusumano; I couldn't ask for a better cheering section or nicer friends. And I didn't forget you, Ms. Pierre. You're in the next book, so brace yourself. You went waaaay past a mention and accidentally landed yourself in the finale of the Jaded Gentlemen series, so make sure you're sitting down!

A special thanks to Danny Kemp of *The Desolate Garden* for reassuring me that British men are, in fact, the most fabulous things walking and worthy of all their fictional following—but also that their heroic worth has nothing to do with their social standing and everything to do with their hearts. Married to the love of his life, Danny is the measure of a truly good man and I want to thank him personally for his friendship and support.

And to Judi McCoy. If you'd lived to be a hundred, it still would have been too soon to lose such a bright and funny star in the skies. You were always yourself and that was the best lesson any mentor could teach. I love you and I'll think of you every time I see a dog, hear someone talking about *American Idol*, or God help me, step into a hotel bathtub. (And, yes, you snored. We'll argue about it later.)

It isn't a book until I tell my mother how much I appreciate her and adore her. We talk almost every day, which I secretly fear qualifies as stalking, but she's still my best friend and who else would put up with me? The pact we made together when I was a child has held through the years and will outlive us both. We swore to back each other up and dream big, ignore the worst of it, and keep our eyes on what mattered most. She probably didn't know it at the time but it's the lifeline that has kept me afloat. I love you, Mom. (Don't tell Dad, but if I win the lottery I'm whisking you off to Australia next year . . . rumor has it, they've got *opals* there!)

Hello, Dear Readers!

Thank you for all your wonderful notes and messages. It's a bit of a cliché to admit that writing is ultimately a solitary task and it's easy to feel isolated sometimes. But you've made sure that I never felt alone, and I've loved creating the Jaded Gentlemen for you and I appreciate the reception they've received! I try to answer every e-mail and note that I receive because it means the world to me to have that opportunity to connect with readers.

Obsession Wears Opals has been a labor of love, and as a true nerd, I confess I've always had a secret crush on the smart, shy guy in glasses. So who's to say my sexy Darius can't prove that intelligence can win over brawn, and win a few readers' hearts along the way? Just to avoid any confusion if you've been following the series, note the timeline. Darius is in Scotland while Josiah is meeting his match in London and so these stories *start out* concurrently—so if Darius isn't yet aware of his friend's romantic fate with Eleanor Beckett, it's because he hasn't gotten the news in Edinburgh, where this story takes place. And naturally, if this is the first book you've discovered in the Jaded Gentleman series, welcome and don't worry! You can enjoy this one without having read any of the previous books in the series. I promise.

So, it's still January 1860, and while Josiah Hastings is battling his shadowy demons, here is the answer to Galen's question, "Damn it, what is keeping Darius in Scotland?"

Enjoy!

Renee Bernard

The minute I heard my first love story
I started looking for you,
not knowing how blind that was.
Lovers don't finally meet somewhere.
They're in each other all along.

—RUMI

Chapter

1

Edinburgh
January 1860

Somewhere a drum was beating.

Isabel groaned in frustration at its insistence, at its intrusion on the numb, cold peace that had finally overtaken her. She'd lost track of time. She didn't know how far she'd ridden, but the gallop of yesterday had long yielded to a slow crawl through the night, and Isabel couldn't remember seeing the sunrise. She had ridden until exhaustion and the wintry lash of wind and icy rain had woven together into a tapestry of deadly quiet.

Except for that infernal drumming.

The rhythm was steady and slow. But loud enough to draw attention, she thought, because now there were voices. Someone was screaming and then there was an exchange, distant and anxious. Hands were touching her with muffled questions she couldn't understand. And then someone was lifting her from the frozen wet ground.

I was on the ground? Did I fall from the saddle? How is that possible—Samson would never let me fall. . . .

Isabel's anxiety bloomed at the thought that something had happened to her faithful stallion, that she'd ridden him beyond the limits of his strength, but then her ankle was being freed from the stirrup where it had caught, and she was being pressed against someone and cradled in a man's arms, wrapped in a coat and blankets. She struggled to open her eyes, aware for the first time that she must have closed them.

The voices were closer, the vibration of the deep timbre of his speech touching off a spike of agonized fear that jolted her back to reality.

The drumming was my own heartbeat.

God help me, I was praying for it to stop.

Numbness fell away in a single breath and Isabel cried out at the cruel loss. She didn't want to feel—anything. Not the fiery bite of the sleet against her cheeks or the warmth of his frame against hers; or the horrible return of memory and terror that had driven her to try to escape.

"I've got you," the stranger said softly, and something in her ached at the gentleness but despised the pain that it evoked.

You have me.

And what would you say if I just begged you to leave me as you found me?

There was a flurry of activity and Isabel became more and more aware of what was taking place as her weightless state gave way to sodden skirts and labored breathing. A woman was hovering behind them and making an awful keening fuss as they crossed the threshold and the warmth of the house enveloped them all. "Is she dead? Oh, God! A dead woman in my winter garden! I'll be haunted all my days!"

"She's *not* dead." He shifted her carefully and began to make his way toward the heart of the house. "Calm yourself, Mrs. McFadden. Fetch Hamish and ask him to ride for Dr. Abernethy at once."

"No," Isabel croaked barely above a whisper, wincing at the agony of speech, but her terror overrode everything.

"P-please, I beg you. N-no . . . a-authorities . . ." She looked up at him and tried not to cry as desperation bled into her words. "P-please, sir. I c-cannot . . . go back."

"What's that she's saying?" the woman screeched from the kitchen doorway.

Isabel held her breath, praying for mercy in an unmerciful world, and nearly broke when she saw the flood of compassion and comprehension in his green eyes.

"Forget the doctor," he amended, raising his voice slightly and turning back to his housekeeper with authority. "Tell Hamish to tend to that horse and make sure the upstairs blue bedroom has enough firewood. Our guest will recover there, but for now, I'm taking her to the library where it's warmest. And hot broth, blankets, and dry clothes, Mrs. McFadden, as soon as you can manage it, please."

"Yes, Mr. Thorne."

Her terror retreated slightly as the threat of a doctor faded and she was carried through another doorway into a small library. He knelt and then, with his free hand, yanked the cushions off a nearby chair to make a nest for her in front of the fireplace. His hands were efficient as he rolled her gloved hands in his to warm the leather enough to peel it from her fingers, and he spoke pleasantly as if they were experiencing an ordinary introduction.

"My name is Darius Thorne and you must forgive my housekeeper, Mrs. McFadden, for her reaction. I must be such a dull man that she's grown unused to any excitement at all." He laid the gloves aside and then sat back on his heels to address the jet buttons on her riding coat. "Pardon my familiarity, but if we don't get you out of some of these soaking wet clothes, then I won't be able to keep my word and will have to send for Dr. Abernethy after all."

She nodded, weakly trying to help him with her jacket but failing as her fingers refused to obey her commands. "Thank you. Sh-she has every right to complain. P-people r-rudely landing in her k-kitchen g-garden." Isabel's teeth chattered as she spoke. "I—I'm ruining these cushions, t-too."

He smiled, apparently ignoring that she'd not offered her own name in return. "No worries. I'll make sure she knows I'm to blame since I've long disliked that chair with its embroidered scene of some idiots cavorting about and shooting deer." He undid the last button and drew the sodden coat from her shoulders, replacing it with the blanket that had fallen off as a temporary aid to ward off a chill. "Let's get your boots off."

Her extremities had begun to warm, and with the return of her circulation, her skin began to burn as if pricked by a thousand needles. She winced as he pulled off her boots and forgot modesty as he made quick work of her stockings to toss them on the stone hearth.

"Damn," he muttered beneath his breath and, without preamble, began to vigorously rub her feet and calves.

"It hurts!" she protested but stopped when she saw the pain in his face.

"I'd not hurt you for all the world, but we must get your blood flowing to ease your injuries. Please forgive me." He returned grimly to his task and she nodded slowly, acquiescing to his good sense. But there was more to it.

Isabel paid no heed to the tears on her cheeks as she studied her rescuer for the first time. The sincerity in his face was a strange balm that removed her from discomfort. By the firelight, his wire-rimmed spectacles gleamed like copper and his handsome features were accented by the glow. He had the soulful look of a poet, with arched eyebrows and sweet eyes, but his face was chiseled as if nature had hoped to fashion him for war. He was calm and careful as his strong hands gently worked over her flesh until the pale skin finally began to glow pink and become pliant to his touch, and when he looked back up at her, Isabel's breath caught in her throat.

"Better?" he asked. "No frostbite, I'd say."

He'd said he'd not hurt her for all the world and it made no sense in the world she'd experienced to believe him. But there she was, sitting in front of his fire with her bare feet tucked into his lap, half frozen and miserable—and inexplicably feeling safe for the first time in months. It was impossible but she wanted to trust this man.

She nodded and opened her mouth to answer him but a crisp knock at the door ended the spell.

"All's prepared upstairs, Mr. Thorne. I've a roaring fire going and a tray of hot broth and fresh pastries to follow, but I thought I'd see her up and settled first."

"Yes, brilliant, Mrs. McFadden." He stood, unfolding from the floor, and Isabel winced out of habit at the sudden movement. "Are you unwell?"

She shook her head. "N-no. I don't think so."

"Here, let me help you." He lifted her up effortlessly as if she were a small child and made his way toward the doorway and his impatient housekeeper. "Lead on, Mrs. McFadden."

Isabel closed her eyes and swallowed any protest she might have made. Pride urged a lady to insist that her legs worked and that she couldn't allow him to exert himself on her behalf, but a small practical voice inside of her won the day by noting that she couldn't really feel her toes, that every part of her ached, and that the room was starting to spin.

The haze of exhaustion reasserted itself as they moved up the staircase, and Isabel fought to stay alert in his arms. The transition to his guest bedroom was smooth and well choreographed by the firm instructions of Mrs. McFadden as he set her down on an upholstered couch at the foot of the bed. The room was as warm as toast, and while Mr. Thorne waited dutifully outside the door, Mrs. McFadden saw her out of every stitch of her wet clothes and into soft woolen stockings and several layers of an old flannel nightgown. And then Mr. Thorne returned and lifted her up to carry her to bed as Mrs. McFadden tucked in a heated brick wrapped in cloth to serve as a bed warmer and turned back the covers.

Ensconced under mounds of bedding, Isabel sank into the feather mattress and lost the battle to keep her eyes open.

"There you are," he said softly, before he retreated. "Safe and sound."

Safe and sound.

Isabel slid into the darkness that opened up around her, welcoming oblivion before one last thought bubbled up.

I'll never be safe again.

* * *

"She's English," Mrs. McFadden noted, her lips pressed into a thin, worried line.

"Yes." Darius headed down the stairs with his housekeeper on his heels.

"And that's no maid run off from service!"

"No." At the bottom of the staircase, he encountered a very surly looking Hamish blocking their path.

"It's a crime, I tell ye! Anyone who'd take a bit of horseflesh like that and ride him into such a state!" Hamish, his driver and houseman, crossed his arms, openly furious. "If you don't take the gentleman out that did this and beat him bloody, I will!"

"Hold, Hamish!" Darius had to take a deep breath to keep his own emotions in check. "First of all, no one is beating anyone for anything or speaking out of turn! Whoever the lady is, she is in need of our help and our sympathy. I'm sure she never meant to harm her horse and will thank you when she recovers for your skilled nursing of the animal, Hamish, and your care for him."

"L-lady?" Hamish asked, looking appropriately chastised. "The harridan there didn't say a word of it, sir. Naturally, I'll see to the beast and have him set to rights."

Mrs. McFadden gasped at the insult and glared at her nemesis with an unspoken promise of dirt in his next bowl of porridge.

"Thank you, Hamish." Darius spoke deliberately, dismissing the man so that he could have a private word with Mrs. McFadden.

Hamish turned and went back to the stables, and Darius invited Mrs. McFadden into the library, where the woman immediately busied herself by picking up the soggy cushions from the floor.

"Mr. Thorne. What are ye thinking?"

"I'm thinking that nothing matters but her health and comfort."

Mrs. McFadden dropped the cushions onto the chair. "I think that woman's in some trouble. Ye should've sent Hamish to fetch the constable."

"No." Darius turned back to his housekeeper. "We're not sending for anyone until she requests it."

"This isn't a stray cat we've plucked from the snow, sir, if you don't mind me sayin' it!" Her thin faced was pinched with disapproval and unhappiness. "Poor thing!"

For Darius, everything ground to a halt at her words. His instincts had been raging ever since he'd laid eyes on the woman, and when she'd pleaded for him not to contact the authorities, a part of him had guessed at the truth. "How bad is it?"

Mrs. McFadden averted her eyes but dutifully answered. "It's the worst I've ever seen. Her back looks like she just took a serious flogging. Whoever it was used a cane, I'd say, but somehow managed not to break any of her ribs. It's . . . it's a horror, sir."

Shit.

"We'll keep ourselves to ourselves, Mrs. McFadden. Tell Hamish to keep that horse out of sight, and when the lady is ready, I shall offer her whatever assistance she needs. But under no circumstances are you to tell anyone of her presence here. If it's what we suspect, then the authorities will provide no relief." Darius ran a hand through his hair, wincing at the taste of rage in his mouth at the man who would inflict such harm on a woman. "Do you understand?"

She nodded. "Yes, but—"

"No. No, Mrs. McFadden. I told her she was safe and sound, and by God, I mean to do everything in my power to see that she is. Are we clear?"

"Yes, Mr. Thorne. Not a word to anyone." She bobbed a curtsy and withdrew, leaving him alone with his books and papers.

Darius waited until the door closed behind her and the startling realization that he had an unexpected houseguest sank in. He bent over to retrieve all the notes he'd scattered in his rush and tried to reorder his thoughts.

The shock of it wasn't lessening and so he gave up for a minute and sat down at his desk. When he'd seen her lying in the snow, his heart had stopped. Her horse's saliva had frozen into a wreath on his bridle from laboring for so long, and his sides shimmered with frost. The beast had apparently failed to clear the garden's low stone wall and then stood over his mistress unsure of where to go.

At the first scream, Darius had instinctively grabbed a decorative sword from over the fireplace and launched from his study, prepared for anything. Tossing the useless sword from his hands, he'd slid on the icy path to kneel next to her, praying her neck wasn't broken. But she'd been intact. Ice cold and nearly frozen to death, but intact. Pale blond hair and skin almost as white as the ground around her, she was ethereally beautiful with fine, delicate features so perfectly formed it was like stumbling onto a life-size porcelain figurine.

She was so slight and frail that he'd worried that her spirit might have already departed, but when she'd cried out and then struggled against him, his relief had been palpable.

Alive.

He'd been carrying her inside when she'd opened her eyes and begged him not to send for the surgeon. One look into her eyes and he'd simply known.

He'd known that Mrs. McFadden would find bruises.

He'd known that nothing would ever be the same.

And not because she's English and well-off. Her riding coat was velvet, her jacket tailored, and the buttons were carved jet. Even her boots bespoke privilege, not to mention that horse—not that I'm gifted with Galen's eye for horse-flesh, but that wasn't a common pony.

She's the loveliest thing I've ever seen, God help me.

She's a lady of high quality and she's in trouble.

No need to ask who hurt her.

Because the beautiful lady with blue eyes like white opals had a band of gold on her left hand. Darius had seen it when he'd removed her gloves.

What have I gotten into?

His guest was married.

Chapter
2

Isabel awoke slowly as layers of her nightmarish dreams shifted into more tangible forms of discomfort. Her back ached and the pain of the bruises made even breathing a little daunting. She squeezed her eyes shut tightly, wondering if she could will herself back into a dislocating sleep and claim a few more hours of temporary respite. But she abandoned the notion as the gray light stole into the room and opened her eyes to try to gauge where she'd landed. Of her arrival, she remembered very little.

Except for *him*.

There'd been a man—a stranger with kind green eyes and wire-rimmed spectacles who'd given her his name—Darius Thorne. A man with a handsome face and gentle hands who'd lifted her from the snow. She'd begged him not to send for a doctor or alert the authorities and he'd said he wouldn't. But words were meaningless things and Isabel knew it.

The constable's probably downstairs waiting—or Mr. Jarvis.

The image of her husband's man lurking somewhere

nearby was enough to propel her into action, terror setting pain aside.

Isabel struggled to sit up, biting the inside of her cheek to keep from crying out, but she managed it by pressing back against the pile of pillows for leverage and pushing out with her legs. Finally, she'd propped herself up, though without any grace by her own reckoning, to at least get a better view of her situation.

The bedroom was comfortable and well-appointed and the corner grate was blazing cheerfully with a fire that warmed the room. She touched the lace and flannel around her throat and absorbed the details of a borrowed nightgown, unfamiliar woolen socks, and the lack of her own clothes.

A large wardrobe against the far wall beckoned as a possibility.

I can hardly run or make much of a case for myself if I'm wearing nightclothes.

But Isabel's heart began racing at the stupidity of her flight.

She pushed back the covers and slid her feet over, wincing at the protest her back was making. A smarter woman, she chided, would have had a plan. Or even thought to take some of her jewels from her bedroom and tucked them away into her pockets before . . .

Before mindlessly running away.

This was the first time she'd allowed herself to stop and think. Only because it had been sheer folly to bolt as she had, and by the time her initial panic had faded a little, she'd been too far to turn back. The impulse to just *go* had been replaced by a greater terror: the knowledge that she'd defied her husband and that the punishment he'd repeatedly promised was now fast on her heels.

Even if she limped back and threw herself on his nonexistent mercy, Isabel feared she'd supplied Richard with exactly what he needed to justify shutting her up in an asylum or imprisoning her in a new hell of his design. Her husband was a powerful man and a peer of the realm, and she'd naively played directly into his hands.

He'll kill me—or worse. Make me wish I were dead while I'm chained to a wall somewhere in a mental ward.

The firm surface of the wooden floorboards against her feet brought her back to the present. She glanced down to learn that the thickly knitted, nearly manly socks she wore were a reddish orange that almost made her smile, but Isabel's attention returned to the wardrobe.

She stood on unsteady legs and made her way toward it, as quietly as she could, wary of creaking floorboards or any sound that might give her away. But when she pulled open the large carved doors, they revealed bedclothes and a single flannel robe.

Where are my riding clothes? My boots?

A wintery wind blew outside the window, the lonesome sound of it framing her thoughts. *No escape. There's no escape today.*

"Aaah!" A woman's screech of surprise made Isabel wheel around, instinctively holding up her hands in defense.

"P-please . . ." Isabel gasped, miserable at being startled and caught out of bed like a naughty child.

The woman who approached was a forbidding-looking thing, with her thin frame and hair pinned back so tightly it made her narrow face appear even more wraithlike. But the impression was softened almost immediately by the sight of a tray laden with steaming dishes in her hands, and her words. "Bless you! Out of bed, poor mite! I thought I was seein' a ghost over there and I've lost a slice of my soul from the fright!"

She set the tray down on a table by the door and came over to Isabel with her hands out—as if she were approaching a wounded animal. "I'm Mrs. McFadden and you—are going to catch your death, madam, if you roam about wearing nothing but a nightgown, yes?"

Isabel nodded. "Yes, I remember you. I don't . . . mean to . . . be any trouble, Mrs. McFadden. I'm very sorry."

"Of course you don't! Trouble comes where it wishes without anyone's permission so no need to apologize. I should say it's a pleasure to have a guest." Mrs. McFadden put her hands on her hips and assessed Isabel's lack of progress back toward the sanctuary of warm bedclothes awaiting her. "Now, to bed."

Clearly, Mrs. McFadden was a woman used to being obeyed without argument.

Isabel reluctantly released her hold on the wardrobe door and made it only one or two steps before her hostess intervened and offered a gentle hand to steady her and guide her back to her nest. "You're too kind, Mrs. McFadden."

"Never!" Mrs. McFadden smiled. "I'm a terror. That's what I've got 'em believing anyway, so I'd appreciate it if you kept my secret." She settled Isabel and readjusted the thick goose-down-filled coverlet. "I made you a hearty breakfast, madam. You're too thin. Bad enough I can't get the professor to eat when he should, but I'll not have you starving under my roof!"

"The professor? Is Mr. Thorne a professor?"

Mrs. McFadden's look of mortified shock melted away to amusement. "Mr. Thorne is my employer and the owner of the house and I suppose . . ." The housekeeper's brow furrowed. "Professor's a bit of a name I've given him since he's apparently got more degrees and education than sense, if ye ask me. Any man that can speak ten languages and sleeps in his library should remember where he put his hat!"

"If I lose things, I'm sure it's to make you feel appreciated, Mrs. McFadden," Darius interjected from the open doorway.

Isabel's eyes dropped to her hands. He'd caught her prying into his business and she hated the bite of fear that whipped through her. But when she looked up, he was smiling at his housekeeper and cheerfully standing in the doorway. "May I come in?"

"She's to eat! So you can visit for a minute or two or I'll blame you if she's forced to eat a cold meal or faints for lack of it!" Mrs. McFadden growled. She turned back to Isabel and whispered, "You'll ring the bell if you need a thing and I'll pretend to complain but I'll come as quick as a wink. All right?"

Isabel nodded, unable to stop a smile. "Yes, Mrs. McFadden."

Mrs. McFadden withdrew and Darius stepped inside, politely leaving the door open. "She's all show," he said. "Like a kitten that spits and hisses but has no claws."

"She's—remarkable," Isabel agreed. "I should thank you. For . . . I'm not even sure how I came to be here, but . . ."

"There's no need. I have a firm long-standing policy of harboring anyone who lands in my garden and consider it my sacred duty to keep any women who attempt to freeze to death from succeeding in their efforts," he said, his tone light and teasing.

"It happens often, then?" she asked.

"Oh yes." He nodded and pulled up a chair to sit next to the bed. "It's practically a weekly occurrence, so I'm going to have Hamish just put in a wider gate and set up fairy lights to help more lost souls find their way a little easier."

The man was a puzzle to her, but not an unappealing one. "I'm grateful to you, Mr. Thorne, and I have no intentions of . . . rudely intruding on your life any longer than necessary. I'm sure I can be on my way by tomorrow morning to—"

He leaned forward, the intensity of his gaze alone ending her declaration to depart. "I'd rather you didn't."

Anxiety seized her by the throat. "Wh-why?"

"Because you're safe here." He waited patiently as if aware of the internal war waging inside of her.

"Not because you'd like me to wait for the constable to arrive once the weather has passed?" she asked, the words like bitter copper on her tongue.

He shook his head. "I honor my promises and my word is not something I give lightly. I sent for no one. There is no one coming."

No one is coming.

Isabel nervously rearranged the crocheted edges of her nightgown's sleeve. "Thank you."

"Will you tell me your name?"

And there it was, the inevitable question that would open

a floodgate of inquiries and obligations, that would force him to break his word or make him regret his promises. Isabel's eyes filled with tears and her throat cinched closed at the pain of it.

Such a simple question, really. I tell him my name and then it all changes and whatever safety I'd started to feel evaporates like mist in the sunlight.

"It's understandable," he spoke.

She lifted her head and stared at him through her misery, uncomprehending.

But he went on. "To go through such a traumatic fall and endure that cold, it would rob anyone of their senses or their memory. It's understandable if some of your history is lost to you. It's a temporary state, I'm sure, and nothing to worry about."

She nodded, wary but oddly relieved at the path he was deliberately laying out at her feet.

"Amnesia. The loss of memory can be so profound that a person doesn't even remember their name or anyone associated with them." His gaze was steady and sincere. "It must be very distressing, am I right?"

"Yes."

"Then you should have all the time you need to heal and to remember when you can. Unless—" He sighed deeply but there was no judgment in his eyes. "Can you recall that there was somewhere you were specifically trying to get to? Someone who was waiting for you? A rendezvous with a friend?"

She shook her head, the tears spilling down her cheeks unheeded. "No. There is no one. I don't think I have . . . anywhere to go."

He pulled a silk handkerchief from the pocket of his wool coat. "Here. The answers will come, and in the meantime, there is a hot breakfast to be seen to. Claws or no, I'd like to avoid the fiery dressing-down when Mrs. McFadden's authority has been thwarted."

She took the handkerchief from him and dried her eyes. "Is Samson all right? My horse?"

"Hamish is spoiling him back to health and I'm sure he'll recover. He's lame, but if anyone can see him set right, it's Hamish. He has a way with horses." He stood and retrieved the tray, bringing it to her bedside table. "I'll leave you alone to sample your breakfast at your leisure."

"Mr. Thorne?"

"Yes."

"I want to say thank you, but it seems a paltry way to repay you for—all of this."

He smiled. "It's more than enough."

As he set the tray down, he knocked the bell from the narrow stand over onto the floor, and within seconds, Mrs. McFadden was in the doorway, breathless and unhappy.

"A minute or two, Mr. Thorne! You overstay and you'll wear her out!" she scolded, bustling in to take over. "How can she eat if you keep her? And aren't you expected in town?"

He gave Isabel a sheepish look of apology and she smiled back, sharing an instant alliance. "I lost track of the time, Mrs. McFadden."

"The weather's not getting better, so you'd best head off now." Mrs. McFadden's hands landed on her hips, and even with their acquaintance being so new, Isabel recognized the signs. The man had his orders.

"It seems I'm off." Darius bowed slightly before heading out the door. "I'm meeting an old friend in town, but I'll be back before nightfall. Mrs. McFadden, if you would?"

The housekeeper followed him out and Isabel was alone again, left to marvel that the impact of Darius Thorne's presence wasn't diminished by the light of day.

* * *

Every soldier in the front ranks sat precariously awaiting the trumpet's notes that would herald their fates and the White King surveyed the battlefield and held his breath. Here was the moment when the line would either hold or yield. A kingdom would be won or lost.

Sweat glistened off the horses' ebony flanks, their hides twitching with tension as their riders reined them in with brutal hands. The line seemed impenetrable, and the look of swarthy confidence on each carved face drove home the point that here was a formidable army not to be taken lightly.

And then it was on.

A chaotic dance ensued of clashes and cowardice, minor victories and wretched sacrifice, all choreographed by the kings behind their lines.

The White King waited patiently until he saw the Black King smile as momentum appeared to carry the day—and the black line broke just as the white general had predicted. Arrogance drew them out and the white lancers he'd hidden from sight swept in to inflict a brutal justice and deliver conquest into the White army's hands.

The White Queen rushed to his side, protected and safe, and the king savored the sweetness of her presence and—

"Thorne." His opponent sighed, knocking over the ebony king in defeat. "It's extremely annoying when you beat a man effortlessly at chess and appear to be daydreaming all the while."

Darius Thorne snapped back to the realities of the small game room above the coffee shop. He'd lost himself in a ridiculous fantasy of war and strategy and felt a bit embarrassed at the easy win, and the indulgence of including a pale queen in his mental gambit. "I apologize, Professor Warren. I assure you, I was engrossed entirely in the game."

"Not over there calculating ancient stone arch angles and conjugating Chinese verbs?" Warren asked kindly, beginning to put away the black carved pieces in a wooden box. "You can confess if you wish."

Darius smiled. "I may be guilty of such feats, but generally it's only during academic teas or—"

"Mrs. Warren's forays into musicales?" the older man interrupted with a laugh. "God, I'll never forget the look on your face after an evening of impromptu performances! You were so young then, but already, I could see that mind of yours working away while the rest of us suffered through three renditions of my wife's butchery of songs about nightingales."

"I'm sure she wasn't that bad," Darius said. He laid his own ivory pieces in the box in orderly lines, enjoying the brush with a gentle nostalgia that held no judgments or dark nightmares. So much of his recent past wasn't anything he wanted to recall, so an afternoon with an old colleague seemed a welcome balm to his nerves. "As I remember it, she was very . . . enthusiastic."

"What a diplomat you'd have made, Thorne! My darling Hattie is many things, but gifted with the ability to sing a single clear note, she is not." Professor Warren closed the box and slid it across the table toward Darius. "I'd missed our regular games."

"You were a good teacher."

"Apparently so, if my student has learned to play better than his mentor ever had." The older man lifted his warm pewter mug filled with mulled wine to ward off the chill of a Scottish winter's day. "I'm glad I ran into you in Edinburgh. But so far from Oxford! I'd have expected you to have won a permanent position at Trinity College and been mentoring young minds of your own by now."

Darius shook his head. "My life has taken a few unexpected turns, Professor. But with all due respect, I'm still determined to win a place despite my lack of pedigree. If not at Oxford, then—there's time yet for my studies to garner some notice and secure me a position somewhere."

"Well, if it's the University of Edinburgh you've set your sights on, then say so. I have a few contacts and could—"

"On my own merits, Professor Warren. I'll list you as a reference and request a letter if the opportunity arises, but I want my own work to open the door. I'm here to eventually look at the archives of the historical society and glean what I can for a few theories I possess. But for now, I have personal business in Edinburgh and in London that takes up most of my time, so any serious academic pursuits will have to wait."

"You've not abandoned your original thesis on ancient civilizations and their architecture, have you?"

"No," Darius conceded, reaching for his mug of spiced tea. "I'm too stubborn to quit."

"What few notes and drawings you've shared from your travels to Asia and India have been most impressive. You'll publish, of course!"

Darius smiled at the older man's confidence. "Of course. Even if it's a dozen copies at my own expense, I shall be sure to send you one for your library."

"You're too humble."

"And you're too kind, Professor." The words rang with a genuine sincerity that ended the friendly debate. Warren had been like a father to him, encouraging a young Darius to see beyond the limiting spheres of his origins and family. Somehow he'd seen something worthwhile in Darius, who had suffered a crippling shyness in his youth. The professor had determined that his quiet charge had a keen intellect and an open and curious nature that had outshone his peers. Professor Warren had nurtured him without any signs of judgment and unofficially fostered him as his own. Even Mrs. Warren had never objected to Darius's presence at her table or the long hours he had, for all intents and purposes, taken over their library for his studies and kidnapped her husband for endless debates into the night.

"So long as you're working, Darius." Professor Warren drained his cup. "These are difficult times, and if you need anything while you finish your thesis, I hope you'll remember that Mrs. Warren insists on keeping a room ready for you."

Darius had to swallow the lump that formed in his throat. He couldn't remember any of her off-key tunes, but he recalled every instance where she'd found him at his studies and brought him a warm bit of tea or gently reminded him to eat. "I've been remiss in my correspondence, Professor. Please tell her—I will make a point of visiting as soon as I can. If only for some of her wonderful marmalade cakes."

Professor Warren pretended to wince. "She's making me fat, Darius! Her baking's gotten more and more enticing over the years, and I warn you, if I tell her your message, you'll be swimming in cakes before the summer."

Darius laughed. "And where is the threat in that? You'll

be spared gaining another stone and I'll be the envy of every bachelor I know."

Warren smiled but then the sound of freezing rain striking the windowpanes interrupted their merriment. "It's been an afternoon well spent but I should go before this delightful Scottish weather improves and makes the roads impassable."

"So should I. My housekeeper will be standing watch by now." *Not to mention my own need to look in on my house-guest and reassure myself that she's still safe.* Darius stood to help his friend to his feet and handed him his rosewood-handled cane. "Shall we meet again for a rematch?"

Warren shook his head. "I'm to return home in the morning. I'm presenting my latest theorem on the correlations of education and prosperity next week, that is, if the dean of the college doesn't hang me first."

"He wouldn't dare. You're too beloved a revolutionary, sir."

"I'm a pain in his backside, but let us hope you're right. Besides, I've gotten craftier in my old age. It's all hypotheticals and carefully hidden metaphors so he can't openly accuse me of championing the Irish or spitting on our beloved aristocrats' toes."

Darius helped him with his wool coat, before shrugging into his own. "Who knew that a doctorate in economics could be so politically treacherous?"

"True. You were wise to avoid following in my unsteady footsteps too closely, Thorne." Warren took his arm as they headed down the narrow staircase. "But if I can offer one last bit of advice—for old times' sake . . ."

"Of course," Darius said. "I value any advice you care to share."

"Don't wait too long, young man."

"Don't wait?"

Warren sighed as they reached the doorway of the shop. "Don't wait for positions or your fortunes to improve or the completion of studies or any of the endless excuses a man can make to materialize before pursuing your own happiness. You isolate yourself too much. You always have, Darius.

Marry while you're young and seize the chance to live among your fellow human beings and experience all that life has to offer."

"I'm not isolated." Darius saw the look in the professor's eyes and amended his claim. "I'm not *as* isolated as I once was, Professor Warren. I have good friends to ensure I am exposed to more experiences than I ever thought possible, and my fortunes have vastly improved. India was . . . life changing." It was an understatement, but even speaking to Warren, he didn't think he could find the words to explain what it was like to be in the circle of the Jaded.

Over a year in the black of a dungeon in Bengal had forged a brotherhood without equal and redefined each man's character in unexpected ways. The name of their club had been a jest at first, but it had held. Darius doubted the name was appropriate, considering that for half their number, cynicism had given way to a woman's gentle influence. He, Josiah Hastings, and Michael Rutherford were the last bachelors standing. It was easy to imagine Hastings, the sensitive artist, succumbing to romance, or even Rutherford, the surly giant, losing a battle to love—but he had no such hopes for himself.

Even when fate throws a beautiful woman in my path, she is definitely out of reach, which is probably Providence being kind. Better to enjoy my friends' happiness from a safe distance. Better for all.

The words sounded hollow in his head and plaintive, and he hated it. A lifetime of self-discipline redirected his thoughts away from the painful edges of his loneliness and back to Professor Warren and the conversation at hand.

Darius forced a smile. "I'm not waiting, sir. I shall make the most of my opportunities."

"You do seem more confident than I remember. And more strikingly fit! Where did that skinny, frightened boy go?" Warren teased as he pulled on his gloves. "You have the build of a prizefighter rather than a professor, sir."

"My friend, Rutherford, was a soldier, and I admit, he's been a strong influence in ensuring that I can hold my own."

Darius searched his pockets for his own leather gloves. "Not that I'm planning on any physical contests."

"No man does, but a wise man is prepared for anything," Warren said. "I like Mr. Rutherford already for it. You must bring him by when next you are at Oxford and we shall engage him in a rousing debate on the stratagems of war."

Darius hid a smile at the impossible image of the massive Michael Rutherford uncomfortably perched on one of Mrs. Warren's chintz chairs enduring a "rousing debate" on any subject. The man loathed conversation for conversation's sake, and Darius knew Michael wouldn't thank him for the invitation. But then again, the chance to see Rutherford trying to evade the Warrens' hospitality might be worth the price.

At last, both men were armed with layers of outerwear for the weather and farewells were made. Darius saw his mentor safely up inside his carriage and then made his own way to his brougham and signaled his driver, who'd been waiting under the cover of the stables.

"Sorry to head out in this, Hamish."

"What, this? A wee bit of wet?" The Scotsman dismissed the freezing rain with a wave of his hand. "I enjoy a brisk drive, sir!"

Darius shook his head. The weather was bone-crushingly cold and the damp served to give it sharper teeth, as far as he could perceive. But the locals appeared to take pleasure in pretending to enjoy it and poking fun at the misery of unprepared visitors. He was getting used to the elements after weeks in Edinburgh, but there was no possibility of him describing it as "a wee bit of wet."

"Let's get home, then." Darius climbed up inside the carriage and firmly shut the door. The brougham pulled away from the inn almost immediately, and Darius leaned back and tried to reorder his thoughts for the two hours or more it would take to reach his house.

He'd told Warren that his life had taken a few unexpected turns, but the woman was a twist he'd never seen coming. He'd deliberately said nothing of her to Warren. Every fiber of his being felt protective of her, unwilling to think too far ahead of his improvised plan to simply provide her a haven until she'd recovered and a better solution could be found. Darius lost time staring out of the windows at the icy land-scape and imagining what his friends would make of his "rescue." Her pale beauty was distracting and unsettled him. He was determined to keep his appointments and make no outward changes in his household for her safety, but already he could sense that his mental landscape had suffered a vast shift.

I could anonymously set her up somewhere but—where? How far is far enough to guarantee her safety? I can just hear Ashe now. He'd say something witty about the geo-graphical reach of marital discord and offer a—

The brougham lurched as one of the wheels caught in the mud, but Hamish's skilled driving kept them upright and moving. Darius wedged his foot up against the sidewall of the upholstered compartment and tried to steady himself against the jostling. He closed his eyes and gave in to the distractions of all the tangled mysteries in his life. Between sacred treasures, hidden enemies of the Jaded, and damsels in distress, Darius was fairly sure he'd a plateful. Darius began picturing all the events and pieces of the Jaded's puzzle until he'd created a vast map of tenuous threads and unique symbols that oscillated and danced on a wall of mirrors inside his head.

It was an old trick and a skill he'd honed to a razor's edge in the dark of that dungeon. As Darius indulged in the escape his interior world provided, the long drive home evap-orated.

"Ye're home, Mr. Thorne." Hamish's voice was the first sign he had that the carriage had stopped and he'd arrived at his house.

"Oh yes, thank you, Hamish." Darius put his hat on before climbing out to make the short run under the eaves of the front door, where he could scrape the mud from his boots before entering. It was a lovely two-story stone home with a thatched roof and walled garden that had long since gone to seed. It was Darius's idea to find a place convenient to Edinburgh for the city's famed gem traders and to benefit all the Jaded, since their windfall from India had consisted in jewels. He'd secured the house after returning to England without even seeing it because the real estate agent had mentioned that it came with a library of abandoned texts. "Floor to ceiling, all leather-bound nonsense from what I can discern," the man had confessed. "Man died without much family except a distant nephew who cares nothing for it and says you're free to burn the lot for kindling if you wish."

The previous owner had been an eccentric and a reclusive scholar who'd spent whatever money he had on books, and Darius had experienced an instant kinship with the spirit of the man. If there was any solace or joy to be found in life, Darius was sure it was inside books. He'd bought the house without asking a single question about the state of its foundation—and been extremely lucky to end up owning a home with a sound roof and spacious rooms to go with the books in his new library.

The collection had turned out to be very valuable, and a delightful mix of classical reference books in Latin and Greek, French and German history texts, and even a few Russian books on horse breeding and training. The subjects were a mash of science and art, with a few bits of rare poetry and practical home guides tossed in. Whatever cataloging system the deceased collector had used was a mystery, and so even now, Darius took delight in making discoveries on an upper shelf or uncovering a first-edition collection of John Donne tucked into a pile of penny novels.

The door opened and Mrs. McFadden stood in the archway, her thin face pinched in concern. "You're late! It's nearly dark and I was sure Hamish had overturned that carriage and killed you both!"

"He's as safe as a church mouse," Hamish protested before climbing back up into the driver's seat. "And mind you're the one jawing away and keeping him in the cold! You'll freeze your precious Englishman to death complaining about my driving, witch."

Darius ignored them both, tucking his gloves back into his pockets as he kicked the worst of the mud off his boots. Their bickering was all flash and no substance, and he'd come to appreciate the subtle affections between the pair. His widowed housekeeper preferred to openly despise his driver, but he knew better. Hamish MacQueen never went hungry, had his clothes repaired, his socks darned, and his laundry fresh and folded—all without a single word. And Mrs. McFadden never had to lift anything heavier than a pot of stew, had fresh flowers for her table, was chauffeured on all her shopping trips, and was never without a certain Scotsman nearby to allow her to fuss to her heart's content. They were a match.

"How is she?" Darius asked without preamble.

"Better off than you! Come in, then!" Her cheeks stained pink in uneven patches as she held the door open a little wider to allow him to pass. "That's kind of you to keep the muck out but that idiot's got the right of it. We should have you in by the fire, Mr. Thorne."

"Thank you, Mrs. McFadden. Did she rest, then, today?" He handed his hat, coat, and scarf over to her.

"When I looked in on her last, she was still abed, sir. I've got a good poultice recipe that's nearly ready and was going to see to her back once she's awake." Mrs. McFadden's hands fisted at her waist. "There's naught for you to do, except stand there and catch a chill. To the library with you!"

Darius's intense desire to see his guest again was temporarily overridden by his housekeeper's practicality. He retreated to his favorite room if only to give Mrs. McFadden time to prepare her poultices and see to the lady's comfort before he stopped in to finish their conversation.

As promised, the fire in the library was already blazing merrily, awaiting his arrival, and the papers spread out over his desk remained just as he'd left them. Darius returned to his chair and surveyed the texts, settling in out of habit and almost immediately taking up the thread of his thoughts from the previous day. The afternoon with Warren had refreshed him and he was pleased to rediscover the lines of his logic in the middle of chaotic piles.

As the sun set and the winter storm gained strength, Thorne's mind took him away to the stifling heat of an Indian summer. He disappeared into the labyrinth of spice-scented market stalls on his way to the mapmaker's, retracing his steps and seeking the moment where random exploration gave way to fate's marked path.

The best puzzles are the ones that look wretchedly complicated but turn out to have a singularly simple solution. Which means I'm either overthinking it or I'm not even looking at the correct pieces. . . .

Or the answer is right in front of me and I don't want to see it. Because we may not have the sacred treasure the villain's after—and how do you bargain with something you don't have?

"Mr. Thorne!" Mrs. McFadden hailed him from the doorway. "Please come! I think something's terribly wrong with her!"

For the second time in so many days, Darius found himself vaulting around his desk and praying that he would reach her in time.

Chapter
3

She'd been looking out the bedroom window over the desolate, icy garden in its wintry, neglected tangle and watching the clouds dampen the last weak light of the day. Isabel had marveled at how raw and bleak it all looked when the memory of another garden view had seized her.

Another garden. Another window. Another season.

A spring day when she'd looked out through glass panes and imagined that every happiness was ahead of her. Isabel had been a bride awaiting her husband's arrival. Their courtship had been a whirlwind of tender gestures and romantic persuasion, a fairy tale that had left her breathless with the giddy speed of it.

The last of the guests had finally left and a quiet had descended when she'd stopped to take in the view from her new bedroom window and absorb the immense change she'd undergone. Isabel hadn't even pulled the flowers from her hair.

From girl to wife.

At any moment, Richard would arrive to take her into

his arms, at last. He would soothe her fears and remove her nervous apprehension of what might be involved with what her mother had alluded to as "the price of marital contentment." From what few chaste kisses and sweet lines of poetry he'd offered her, Isabel longed for his arrival. They would be truly alone for the first time, and her beloved Richard would set aside her childish fears and kiss away the icy flutter that had settled against her ribs.

Isabel had looked out over the blooming flowers in the garden of her new home, and for a few minutes, she'd been nothing more than a nervous, happy young bride.

And then he'd been behind her.

Before she could turn to greet him, he'd whispered an obscenity in her ear, the warm hiss of it against the shell of her ear like a whip across her psyche, the smile on her face freezing in shock—because the dear, sweet man who'd said he would worship her for all her days would never say such a thing. He would never use such language—never—would never even have known those words.

And then he'd said it again.

She'd gasped and started to turn to him in protest and he'd gripped the back of her neck so hard she'd thought she might faint. He'd pressed her against the window, transforming from a romantic hero into some obscene monster at her back.

"How dare you think to look at me, you stupid cunt! You'll submit and stand there as I please. I am your husband and your master now. You'll stand there with that pert little pig nose of yours pressed against the glass until that empty space between your ears has determined that defiance and stupidity are no way to start out a marriage, Isabel."

"B-but I . . ." she whispered, but he'd cut her off with a squeeze of his fingers. The pain was unfathomable to her and she'd cried out against it.

"You shut up, cow!" he growled behind her, the horrifying misery of his hold increasing as he ground his fingers against the tender base of her skull. "You shut that mewling! I am your husband, you stupid, stupid slit! Shut up!"

She'd forced herself to be quiet and she'd stood.

She'd stood in her wedding finery and watched as her view of the world shattered and shifted. She'd stood while the monster she'd married just hours before whispered vile and unthinkable profane curses into her ears.

She'd stood for what felt like hours.

Until her knees ached and she was shaking so badly she wasn't sure she could prevent herself from falling—and when finally she started to break from the pain and the strange onslaught of his venomous insults, Isabel had tried to lean back against him for relief. But his viselike hold on her neck began to tighten and she'd panicked.

She'd struggled uselessly until he had demonstrated his mastery over her. He'd released her only to slap her hard across the face, then wheeled her about to face the window again.

"Why? Why, Isabel? Why must you make me punish you? You've done this. All I ever wanted was to begin properly. Is that so much to ask? A small gesture of submission for you to demonstrate your love and your obedience, but you defy me from the start, Isabel. Is this how you intend to begin, you worthless, ungrateful, useless slit?"

She shook her head, crying silently.

"You are unschooled when it comes to pleasing a husband, Isabel. But I'm going to give you the lessons you so desperately need. And you will learn, my dear. And when you've proven yourself a proper wife and shown me that you can be obedient, we shall get along beautifully, you and I. You will be the envy of every woman in England, Isabel." Richard's hand returned to the back of her neck. "But for now, we must get your punishment out of the way, mustn't we? You must get what you deserve for sniveling and trying to strike me, my darling."

Her knees began to buckle, but his grip and the pressure of his body behind her kept her upright. With his free hand, he began a new assault that she simply wasn't prepared for. The endearment my darling *was followed by a brutality Isabel hadn't imagined in her sheltered existence. He'd lifted her skirts, bunching up the fabric to push apart her thighs, and raped her.*

He'd raped her, pressed against a window overlooking a beautiful spring garden.

Isabel experienced humiliation that had nearly undone her sanity. To be so exposed in full view as her senses were assaulted so completely at the strange invasion and violation of her husband's body and the burning agony it invoked—it was unreal. Isabel was trapped in a cascade of bruising pain, but she'd been too weak to scream.

At last, he'd let out a strangled crow of triumph behind her, and as he'd slipped out of her body, Isabel's thighs were splashed with the warm slime of his climax. Richard had laughed at her. "There. That's a good wife. You stay right there until I return."

And he was gone.

She'd sagged against the drapes and stood there, too frightened to move, sure that at any moment he would return and punish her for her disobedience if she crawled across the floor to her bed. Terror and shock gripped her so tightly that she lost control of her bladder, and Isabel accepted the ultimate in shame as she remained in her place.

Ruined. Soiled. Destroyed.

"—ice, dear!"

Isabel couldn't move. She recognized the woman's voice behind her as it finally penetrated the waking nightmare that was robbing her of will.

"Madam?" Mrs. McFadden spoke again, her voice fraught with caution and concern.

But Isabel was afraid to move from the window. It made no sense. Richard wasn't there. It was all just a memory, but her knees were locked in place and her hands were shaking.

The housekeeper retreated without another word, her footsteps banging down the stairs. All Isabel could do was try to use the solitude to quickly recover her wits before the woman brought the rest of the house into her bedroom.

This is ridiculous. It's a different window and a dead garden.

"It's been months since that day," she whispered, and the glass fogged from her breath. "Please." *I should be numb from all of it and Richard isn't lurking behind the door to—*

The sound of heavier male footsteps running up the stairwell and down the hall unnerved her. A logical part of her knew that it would simply be the groomsman or even Mr. Thorne, but logic held no power against the panic that gripped her.

She waited, either for the worst to be over and for the specter of her husband to round the corner, or for Mr. Thorne to begin to pose all the well-meant questions she couldn't answer. Her horror was complete—because no one's compassion extended far enough to harbor a madwoman who clung to windows without explanation.

No one.

"Samson misses you." Darius's voice was level and calm as he took a seat on the end of her bed. "For a destrier, he's very docile."

The topic was unexpected and Isabel's breath caught in her throat.

"Although his appetite is very worthy of a warhorse, at least once he was coaxed to eat," Darius continued as if it were as ordinary as rain to speak of horses with a woman clutching window frames. "He was too worried about you."

"S-Samson said as much, did he?"

"According to Hamish, it was practically a conversation. I don't think he has any complaints about the accommodations, but Hamish swore he was pouting this morning. I can only guess it's because he fears for your safety."

"Or he's craving his treats." Isabel nodded, aware that she'd managed to let go of the windowsill.

"Mrs. McFadden sacrificed a jar of molasses to mix in with his oats since Hamish guessed he might have a weakness for sweets," Darius said. "The only thing he's craving now is his mistress's company."

Slowly and carefully, she turned to face him, her face flushed with mortified embarrassment. "I'm not insane, Mr. Thorne. I . . ."

"No one thinks you are. Mrs. McFadden was merely concerned and—you look to me like a woman who was just lost in thought."

It was all she could do to hold her place without bursting into tears. "Yes, I was . . . lost."

"When you're ready, perhaps in a day or two, you can come down to the stables." Darius's gaze was steady and without reproach. "But I have a favor to ask first."

"A favor?" Instantly, anxiety lapped at the edges of her control. "What sort of favor?"

"You must let me give you a name, even if it is temporary and foolish. It would be a favor to me, because I'm afraid my social skills are rusty enough as it is." Darius sighed. "But referring to you with pronouns and improvised terms is bound to get me into trouble sooner or later."

"Oh." Isabel smiled. The man continued to surprise her. "Please do then."

"I'm going to call you . . ." He tipped his head to one side. "Helen."

"Helen?" she asked.

"Because I think you're as beautiful as Helen of Troy must have been and it suits you." He stood slowly. "Is that all right?"

She unconsciously stepped away from the window, slipping from the grip of her memories at the distraction of his smiles. "I like Helen very much."

"Then Helen it is." He stooped to retrieve the knitted shawl she'd dropped and held it out to her. "I'll ring Mrs. McFadden if you'd like. I'm sure she has a dinner at the ready."

Isabel took the soft knit from him and started to throw it over her own shoulders, only to wince as her bruised back protested.

"Here, allow me." He helped her to draw it over her back and then stepped back. "There, that looks warmer."

"I am *not* frail." She faced him again. She wanted to reassure him but also herself. She'd survived this long and had just started to wonder what her choices would cost her. "I . . . I am stronger than I appear."

"Of course you are. The hovering and fuss is for our benefit more than yours."

"And how do you benefit?" she asked.

"Well, for one, Mrs. McFadden's attentions are almost entirely centered on you, which leaves me free to do as I wish. I can wear mismatched socks, leave windows open, or dine sitting on the floor in relative quiet."

Isabel laughed. "You desire to do those things?"

"What man doesn't?" he countered, the mischief in his eyes contagious.

"And Mrs. McFadden's boon?"

"A guest always makes life more interesting. So, there you have it!" he said, clapping his hands together.

Isabel started, stepping back defensively at the sound—instantly upset that she was acting more like a rabbit than a woman. Her fear was palpable and Darius froze in place.

"That was stupid of me," he said softly, his stance wary like a woodsman confronting a fawn. "I'm sorry, Helen."

"No, of course not!" Isabel deliberately lifted her shoulders. "I'm the one who's . . . being difficult. It was nothing and I . . . It was *nothing*!"

He nodded.

"Mr. Thorne," she said as she crossed her arms. "I would very much like to get out, for a meal or a walk."

"Then you will," he answered. "Whenever you wish, but for my sake, please wait until the morning. You're not a prisoner, Helen, but it was just yesterday that you came to us and it's a miracle you're alive."

"No, not a prisoner." She repeated the phrase and savored the words.

"If you'll excuse me, I have some work downstairs in the library and I really should leave before—"

Mrs. McFadden's voice was rusted nails in a pan. "What's this? I've a poultice ready for madam's back and it's not doing her any good at all so long as I'm standing out here in this drafty hall!"

Isabel found herself smiling as Darius gave every impression of a schoolboy caught off bounds.

"I was just leaving," Darius said as he retreated.

The housekeeper swept in with her tray. "As you should. How can I do anything with you constantly underfoot?"

Darius gave Isabel a wink and then bowed before leaving.

She sighed at his departure. "Mrs. McFadden, please be kind to him."

Mrs. McFadden's cheeks reddened. "I snap too much. He's as gentle a man as any I've seen and as thoughtful as a poet, even if he does have to be reminded to wear a coat in a snowstorm. But that's not our concern! Let's see to your back. . . ."

Isabel submitted as stoically as she could to Mrs. McFadden's care, grateful for the poultice's numbing effects on her bruises—but it was Darius's face she couldn't get out of her mind, or his assurance of her freedom.

I'm free . . . until my husband finds me.

* * *

Darius retreated as quickly as he could to the library and sat down to put his forehead onto the cool surface of his desk. A groan of frustration escaped his lips.

Helen was as vulnerable a soul as any he'd encountered, but there was so much more to her than her circumstances. The flash of spirit in her eyes and the brief demonstrations of her good humor made her all the more appealing.

Helen of Troy.

Damn.

Such an apt name for a woman of such astonishing beauty, but that's not all. Darius sat up to let out a long, painful exhale. He'd picked the name as deliberately as a surgeon selecting a scalpel. Because Helen of Troy wasn't just lovely. She was also the wife of a jealous king and stealing her had led to the tragedies of the Trojan War and the downfall of many a hero.

It's a good lesson to remember. For this Helen is a woman I intend to protect, but God help me if I fall in love.

Chapter
4

"How far do you think he was ridden?" Darius stroked the stallion's velvet black neck, admiring his firm lines and the proud way the animal tossed his head as if to shirk off a mere mortal's uninvited touch.

"Too far," Hamish grumbled, refilling the hay bin. "Too fast, too hard, too far. That's all I can tell, but if ye were hopin' for a report in miles—he's not talkin'."

The morning light cut through the stable door and Darius leaned back against the rough wall. His breath fogged out in front of him in the crisp air, so cold it made his chest ache. "Will the leg heal? I may have . . . promised the lady that you would set him to rights."

"Did ye now?" Hamish looked up with a wry grin. "Any other promises I should know of?"

Darius ignored the question. "Can you mend him?"

"I can mend any animal that's got limbs still attached," Hamish said. "I've wrapped his knees and he's to rest. I'm going to try warm blankets on his back with a good mint rub, twice a day if he'll allow it. But he'll mend. He just needs time. Two or three weeks of babying and then I'd ease him back. If it's rushed, you'll ruin him sure! You tell her that!"

"Thank you, Hamish." Darius left the groomsman to his work and began to cross the small yard to the house, only to be arrested by the sight of Helen in the doorway. She was bundled against the cold in a brown wool coat. He could see Mrs. McFadden's hand in the warmer elements and the green morning dress. Darius smiled at the joy on Helen's face. She strolled forward to meet him in the middle of the yard.

"Good morning, Mr. Thorne." She managed a playful curtsy. "I have escaped the confines of the sickroom!"

"Good morning," he said. "Does your keeper know or should I make an attempt to distract her while you stretch your legs?"

"She knows."

"Did she approve?" he asked with a stifled laugh.

"Of course not!" Helen readjusted her knitted scarf. "Which means I'm apparently on a strict time schedule to avoid pneumonia and certain death, Mr. Thorne."

"Then there's no time to waste! Samson is waiting." He held out his arm and escorted her across the muddy yard, noting that the lady was wearing her riding boots. As they entered the stable, he called out, "Hamish!"

The surly groomsman's head popped up, his expression instantly changing from open annoyance at the intrusion to shock at the sight of Samson's owner. "Oh . . . he's . . . there," he said gruffly before ducking back down.

What a world! My fearless bear of a driver is shy of one small Englishwoman.

The stallion lurched against the boards keeping him from her, and Helen moved toward him calmly and quickly, removing her gloves to stroke his nose and muzzle. She whispered soft assurances and the beautiful hulk lowered his head to bury his nostrils in her hair and nuzzle her neck. "Samson, dearest, there, now. I'm here. You did it! We are away, my warrior, we are away," Helen whispered.

Darius tried not to stare but it was as intimate and lovely

a moment as any he had ever witnessed. The beast was so dark and she was so fair, it was a striking visual portrait. The bond between them was as tangible as the ground beneath him, and Darius caught sight of his stable master equally astonished and impressed as he peered back over the stall's low dividing wall.

Helen and Samson gazed into each other's eyes and Darius looked off to study the carriage tack for a few moments, wondering if it was a normal occurrence for a man to be jealous of a horse.

At last, she turned back to Darius, her eyes shining with unshed tears. "He'd have run to the sea if I'd asked him."

Darius nodded. "Without question." He moved closer to join her but kept a wise distance from Samson's reach. It was one thing to be permitted a pet or two, but another to insert himself between a devoted animal and his mistress during their tender reunion. "Hamish has him in good keeping."

"Will he be sound enough to ride again?" she asked.

"In time." Darius glanced over to see if Hamish would weigh in, but the stubborn Scot retreated up the stairs to his loft and living quarters above the stables. "It will be at least two or three weeks. He'd be willing now, but you risk making his injuries permanent or more severe and losing him altogether."

"Too long, I fear." She sighed. "Too long, but I cannot lose him."

"Too long?" Darius watched her closely. "Helen—"

"I cannot impose on your hospitality for long, Mr. Thorne. I cannot—risk it." She cut him off, her anxiety apparent.

"Helen, you cannot risk running without a plan and alone. . . ." Darius took a deep breath, deliberately keeping his voice steady. "A woman is easier to track if she is traveling alone. People are more likely to take note of her, as it is unusual, and with your refined manners and singular beauty, even more so. They will wonder where your maid is or why you have no chaperone—and every question marks your steps like ripples in a pond."

Her eyes widened in new terror and he quickly continued. "I say this not to frighten you, but you must use your head. Solving puzzles is my specialty and I pride myself on the belief that, if given the facts, there is nothing that cannot be accomplished."

She managed a tenuous smile. "Am I a puzzle, Mr. Thorne?"

"Yes, and a very challenging one." He smiled in return. "So, let's see what we have. You are safe here and you can stay here for as long as you wish. The two members of my household are sworn to keep your presence a secret, and Samson has every chance of recovering under Hamish's care. But if you can tell me what pursuit you expect or what encounters you may have had on your journey here, then we can anticipate it and take measures to prevent your discovery."

Her smile evaporated. "I am not sure."

"Then let us start with an easier question. Do you know how far you rode, Helen?"

"It was . . . a blur. It was midmorning when I set out. We rode all that day and then into the night. The snow and the cold made it hard and it was—afternoon when we landed in your garden? Is that right?"

"Late afternoon, yes." Darius readjusted his glasses. "You could have covered a vast distance in that time. But did you come from the city? Did you ride through streets and towns, Helen?"

She shook her head. "It was fields and forest . . . and more than one country lane. We jumped so many walls that I lost count. I was so—frightened. I confess I tried to avoid civilization, Mr. Thorne. But as to distance, what if I was riding in circles?" She caught at his sleeve as she gave voice to her fear. "What if I didn't get very far at all? He—he could be right behind me!"

He took her bare hands into his gloved ones to warm her fingers and center her attention on his words. "No. You are safe. I don't care if the man comes with an army of thugs, Helen. For here is the real Troy. I want you to imagine it.

Great, vast, impenetrable walls that no one can breach and, even better, no one who will admit that you reside within."

She shook her head. "Didn't the walls of Troy fall?"

"Ulysses and the wooden horse," he admitted with a shrug. "That was a literary version of Troy. You must trust me when I say if anyone puts a giant statue of a pony on my doorstep, I'll have Hamish crack it open and turn it into firewood before we roll it into the garden."

"If *he* comes . . ."

"In a worst-case scenario, he'll find Samson but that's all he'll find." He gently squeezed her fingers. "And I'll offer him vast sums to keep Samson just where he is, all right?"

She started to cry and for Darius it was a singularly horrifying moment as he had to resist his first instinct to pull her into his arms. A part of him dictated that she would fit against him perfectly and that nothing in his experience would match the sensation. But discipline won the moment and instead he pawed through his pockets until he found his handkerchief and handed it to her.

"Thank you, Mr. Thorne." She took the plain cloth from him and dabbed at her eyes while he forced himself to count the odd and even stitches on a nearby harness hanging on the wall to maintain his composure. A coil of heat warmed his spine and he began to pray for colder resolve.

"I'm . . . ruining your handkerchief, Mr. Thorne." Her voice was muffled as she spoke with her face buried in the white linen.

"Tears can't hurt it, Helen."

"Why are you so kind?" she asked plaintively. "No one is this kind."

Darius had to swallow hard, marveling that any man existed who had the indecency to hurt such a creature. All he could think to do was attempt a bit of humor. "If I were truly kind, I'd have offered you my coat sleeve or thought to bring more than one handkerchief."

She leaned back and wiped her cheeks with a fresher

edge of the cloth. "I swear at this pace it's going to be impossible to convince you that I am capable of more than weeping, Mr. Thorne."

He held out his arm. "No need. I'm already certain that you are accomplished and strong."

"Why is that? All I have 'accomplished' is falling off my horse in your garden, Mr. Thorne," she said. "As for strength . . ."

"These things are measured in countless ways. Sometimes it takes courage to simply walk away." He watched the shadows threaten her composure and decided a new subject was in order. "Here, let's make the most of your last few minutes of freedom before Mrs. McFadden comes out to scold us in from the cold. Would you care to take a turn in Scotland's most untidy garden, madam?"

She smiled as she tucked a hand into his elbow. "Yes, that sounds lovely."

They walked back across the muddy courtyard and through the stone arch entrance into the house's unkempt yard.

"May I ask what you do for a living, Mr. Thorne? Are you a tutor or a writer?" she asked.

"I'm merely a scholar," he admitted. "I aspire to teach at a university but my own research has taken me far afield in recent years. I spent some time in China and then more recently India, but that adventure took quite a turn."

"Were you there during the rebellion?"

Darius noted that the small tremble of alarm in her voice on his behalf was nothing short of delight in his ears. He had a strange urge to tell her all the wretched details if it meant she might sigh and fuss on his behalf.

I'm turning into an idiot.

"I was. In Bengal, in fact, and as my friend Dr. West would say, it was an ill-timed plan. I was so interested in ancient architecture and filling my notebooks, I don't remember giving imperial politics a single thought. By the time I realized there might be trouble, I was standing in a dungeon

in chains and studying a very different kind of architecture."
He shrugged. "A lesson learned, Helen."

"Oh my! You were imprisoned in India?"

"Along with a small gathering of Englishmen as potential
hostages, but it is my theory that the raja who had us was so
insane that he simply forgot us, as we were there for almost
two years, long after the worst of the uprising. Some of the
locals had whispered of his cruel unpredictability before I
was taken and apparently"—he smiled as he continued
on—"they weren't exaggerating. So his nature worked to
our advantage, led to his downfall in a little rebellion of his
making and to our escape."

"You speak of it so calmly!"

"Because I am here. I am alive and out of it." Darius
kicked over a frozen, muddy root ball. "The brothers I made
in that terrible place are more dear to me than any I've
known, and I'm a better man for being one of their company.
I choose to focus on the boon of it and not the price."

"Well, there you have it, Mr. Thorne."

"What do I have?"

"Irrefutable proof that you are anything but boring as
you'd claimed." Her steps slowed and she let go of him to
reassess the tangled dead vines as they clung to the outside
walls of the house and garden around them. "Did you inherit
this home, Mr. Thorne?"

He shook his head. "I accidentally became something
unheard of—a *wealthy* scholar, but that's another story. I
bought it after acquiring a bit of a windfall on our journey
home. The solicitor said it had a stocked library and I sent
the contract before I'd even seen it. I love books."

"Y-you bought a house for its . . . books?"

"It seemed reasonable at the time." He eyed the wide,
desolate garden and the cracked stone fountain at its center.
"Although, now that you say it in that tone, I wonder if I
shouldn't have asked a few more questions."

"You are a remarkable man, Mr. Thorne."

"I am an ordinary man, a bit too common in my tastes

and horribly troublesome as I'm prone to flights of distracted thought that lead me to lose track of almost everything— time, meals, and undoubtedly, hats. Mrs. McFadden is a very tolerant and understanding woman."

She gasped at the outrageous lie. "She's a bit of a tyrant!"

"I didn't say she was soft-spoken but—" He stopped in his tracks at the unexpected sight of a sword sticking up from the ground in the midst of a hedge. "Ah, that's where that went!"

Helen spied it and laughed. "Shall I pull the sword from the stone and earn a crown?"

"Please leave it." It was an impulsive request, but the instant he'd spoken he meant it. It was the weapon he'd thrown aside in his haste to reach her that fateful night and he'd forgotten it in all the chaos. The blade gleamed in the wintry sunlight, defiantly beautiful in the miniature winter's landscape.

"But someone might think you hate rosemary."

"Or that I'm daft out here trying to murder garden fairies and gnomes and keep them from my garden." He chuckled. "Well, as I'm English I can see that rumor sticking with the locals but let's leave it all the same."

"Are you certain? It will be rusted and ruined by the weather before long."

He nodded. "When Mrs. McFadden sounded the alarm, I grabbed it on my way out and then cast it aside when I saw you. It's a tiny residual of your arrival and I like it."

She looked away from him, suddenly shy and quiet.

"Helen, why don't you plan on eating downstairs with me this evening? It is not much of a change of scenery, but if you would like some company . . ." Darius suddenly felt unsure of the rules of etiquette. He'd probably shattered at least a dozen firm social commandments already by sheltering her and inviting her to cry on his coat lapels. *Hell, at least a dozen commandments . . .*

"Yes."

It was a small victory but he took it. "We should go in. For once, I would like to comply with my beloved housekeeper's orders *before* she utters them."

Helen laughed, a true, unrestrained melodic peal of laughter that demonstrated just how far she'd come in the brief span of time that he'd known her. For one moment, she looked like any other young lady, unhindered by the cares of the world or the strains of a dark past.

Just as she should be.

Chapter
5

Isabel nervously touched her pale blond hair to make sure it was in a respectable chignon. Her hair was fine and forever eluding the hold of combs and pins. It was the habit of a lifetime to try to dress for dinner and make a good showing for her host. Mrs. McFadden had brought her two dresses that morning from the housekeeper's own wardrobe, both plain and ready-made, but Isabel was thrilled to have them. For shoes, Isabel had kept her riding boots since the women did not share a common shoe size.

Mrs. McFadden had tried to apologize for the drab gowns, but Isabel didn't mind and had praised the fashions as if they'd come directly from a couture house in London. She'd abandoned a closet of satin shoes and fripperies, and as she studied her reflection wearing simple green gingham, she couldn't remember feeling happier. Mrs. McFadden was slightly taller, but the women had solved the puzzle with a decorative belt to hide the folds that temporarily hemmed the skirt to a better length.

The dark green made her look even more pale than usual,

but Isabel was grateful to be out of a nightgown. She pinched her cheeks to try to add a little color and then gave up on the enterprise.

I'm acting like a ninny. This is no time to be primping and I'm not a woman in a position to worry about what Mr. Thorne thinks of the lack of color in my cheeks—or to invite him to notice.

Even so, Isabel leaned in closer to the glass, drawn to her reflection. She studied the familiar sight of her own features and looked to see what traces the last few months may have left there. But there was almost nothing. Her cheeks were thinner, along with the rest of her, but other than the anxiety in her eyes, Isabel saw nothing to betray her experiences. Not a single scar or sign of Richard's games marred her face.

It was a hollow miracle that made the nightmare of her life even more surreal.

But then she thought of Mr. Thorne's handsome face and the agile light in his green eyes. Surely he had also suffered in that Indian prison, horrors he wasn't sharing. But she would never have guessed it from his warm countenance and generous manners.

"If he can be brave, so can I."

Yes, but his monsters are a world away and mine—could be anywhere. If Richard has hired agents to search or—

Isabel set the framed little mirror abruptly over on the table, banishing her reflection and ignoring the hysterical bubble of fear that was threatening to ruin her hard-won composure. "Troy," she whispered. "This is Troy and I am safe within these walls."

She left the room and headed down the hall to the staircase, wincing at the sound her riding boots made on the wooden floors. It was hardly the ladylike approach her mother and governess had always required, but even this small and necessary rebellion made her feel stronger.

The dining room table was set with covered dishes at its center for an informal meal. Mrs. McFadden was adding cutlery and putting out the serving spoons. "Ah! There you are! I've yet to pry the professor from his books but perhaps you can fetch him for me."

"Are you sure he wouldn't come at the bell?" Isabel was hesitant to interrupt her host if he was busy. "H-he might be cross at the intrusion."

The housekeeper laughed. "He wouldn't hear a church bell above his head if he's got his nose against a page of that heathen scribble—and that man *never* barks. Though he comes at a cry of distress, I'd rather not give him a heart attack over beef pie. Besides, if we don't interrupt, he'll have a cold supper for the kindness."

"Of course," she said and dutifully went to the library to seek out Mr. Thorne. The door was closed so she knocked softly. But when there was no answer, she opened it slowly, ready to apologize at the first indication of protest.

But there wasn't any. She looked to find him at his desk, but instead was captivated by the sight of him sitting on the Oriental rug on the floor, surrounded by maps and papers. Darius had his back to her as he shifted leafs of parchment and picked up a small note to study it, mumbling a bit as he went.

She stole a selfish moment to watch him in his element and admire the man. The light from the fireplace made his brown hair look auburn and set off his broad shoulders. She caught a glimpse of his profile as he spread out a map and her breath caught in her throat at the masculine beauty of him. Kneeling, he evoked the image of a man at prayer, his strong, slender fingers so careful with each sheet he touched as if they were sacred texts.

How is it you have no wife, Darius Thorne? How can you be as wonderful as you are and still be alone?

"Mr. Thorne?" she asked.

He made no indication he'd heard her.

She cleared her throat and tried again, with a bit more volume. "Mr. Thorne."

He didn't move and Isabel lifted the hem of her skirt to attempt to approach him without stepping on any of his papers. It was a tricky business but she smiled a little as she tiptoed across the ivory mosaic. Isabel touched him gently on his shoulder, braced for him to jump in case her presence startled him from his scholarly reverie.

But he didn't jump. Darius looked up slowly like a man waking from a dream. "Helen! Were you . . . ?" He sat back on his heels and glanced behind her. "Did I miss the dinner bell?"

She shook her head. "Mrs. McFadden insisted it wouldn't work and asked me to come get you for the meal while it is still warm."

He smiled and gathered up a few papers to create a cleared path from the circle. "She's right. I was—transported in thought." He stood, brushing off his pants and straightening his long wool jacket. "Were you there long?"

"No," she lied. "Not at all."

"It's one of my terrible failings, you perceive now, to shut out the world when I'm working, but I'm glad you're here." Darius held out his arm to her. "Shall we see about dinner?"

"Yes." She took his arm and they returned to the small dining room.

"It smells wonderful, Mrs. McFadden," Darius announced. "You're a culinary genius!"

"I'm as plain a cook as any." She deferred the compliment, flustered at the attention. Mrs. McFadden filled their cups with warm spiced cider. "I'll be back with the bread, but don't wait to start."

Isabel smiled. "She took that well."

Darius pulled out Isabel's chair for her and the two settled in without ceremony. "I never know what to say to please her. She seems to think I don't eat enough but . . ." Darius eyed the numerous dishes with a wary eye. "I don't think the British army could finish off meals to her satisfaction."

"Perhaps she's used to providing for a larger family."

"That must be it. She's told me more than once that bachelors make for terrible employers. So I've tried to be as little trouble as possible, but your theory makes me wonder if I've been coming at this all wrong." He began to uncover the dishes to allow them to sample the fare. "I might have to come up with an experiment or two to test out the idea."

Isabel pushed away a silly image of Darius deliberately attempting any kind of "trouble" for his housekeeper. "What is your usual area of study, Mr. Thorne?" she asked.

He hesitated. "I would rather not put you to sleep at the subject, Helen."

"I am very interested, Mr. Thorne. Please."

"Normally, it would be my theory on the reflective and universal truths that can be deduced about a culture simply by looking at an example of its architecture. But these days, it seems to be a more narrow chase involving sacred Hindu objects and Indian relics." He took a healthy serving on beef pie onto his plate and sighed. "Although it currently doesn't feel very narrow. I'm not getting anywhere! It feels more like wearing a blindfold and having cloth sacks on my hands while trying to learn to embroider."

Isabel struggled not to laugh. "What a fantastic metaphor!"

"I didn't mean to speak so colorfully," he said as he lifted out a ladle of thick creamed vegetable soup.

"From architecture to sacred objects; what is the connection, Mr. Thorne?" Isabel added food to her plate as she spoke.

"A tenuous one at best." He sighed, but the turn in the conversation inspired him. "Every thread worth tugging takes me back to India these days. Men have spent decades there and been less entangled than we were in that brief span in the dark. Isn't that odd? That I might live to be a hundred but still be defined by one small slice of time."

"Not defined, Mr. Thorne." Isabel shook her head. "By *we*, you mean your friends and yourself?"

"The Jaded," he intoned. "A misleading name our informal club achieved after a jest at a party in London. An outsider noted that we appeared to be very exclusive and dreary without realizing our origins. There are only six of us altogether who survived the experience, and it's probably made us a bit too serious to participate in frivolous dances and salon conversations. We prefer to keep to ourselves."

"What a horrible name!" she exclaimed.

He shrugged. "It is apt in many ways. India changed us, Helen, and the trappings of society aren't an easy mantle to put back on without some skepticism. A man can be hardened by survival."

"You don't seem hardened, Mr. Thorne, or the least bit dreary."

"Opinions are subjective." His face reddened and Darius adjusted his glasses.

"And how is it that you are in Scotland, Mr. Thorne, looking for Indian artifacts and not in Bombay?"

"Ah!" Darius set down his fork and knife. "It turns out that—"

Mrs. McFadden entered with a small basket of fresh rolls. "Are you entertaining her, sir?"

"I am hardly qualified, Mrs. McFadden," Darius said. "Are you sure that's the custom?"

The housekeeper came round to him to hand over the bread. "You've a guest and it's your duty to do so. Don't think I've time on my hands for parlor games and nonsense!"

Isabel's back stiffened. "Mr. Thorne is wonderful company."

Mrs. McFadden nodded. "Good, then. I'm sure you've no need of a chaperone. I can attend to cleaning the kitchen and not worry about having to stand about and encourage small talk." She turned and left so quickly that Isabel had to swallow a hiccup of surprise.

"She is very . . . abrupt with you," Isabel said. There wasn't a maid in her mother's house that wouldn't have been packing her bags after such an exchange. Isabel's cheeks warmed at the thought, but somehow Mr. Thorne made it seem perfectly sweet that his housekeeper was so outspoken.

"Always." Darius held out the basket to her. "She thinks I read too much and am addled as a result, which, of course, is partially accurate. But she was attached to the property and knew the previous owner and it seemed appropriate to keep her on. The apothecary in the village told me that she

was widowed at twenty and never forgave the world for it."
He sighed. "I love the way she keeps the house, and for all
her noise, she makes the place less . . . quiet. I've asked her
to hire a girl to help but the suggestion wasn't well received.
It was cold soup for three days."

Isabel selected the smallest roll. It seemed Mr. Thorne
truly did have a policy of rescuing women. "You are not fond
of quiet, Mr. Thorne?"

He shook his head. "It has its place."

"Well, your housekeeper is wrong about one thing."

"Is she?"

"It falls to *me* to provide entertainment as a good guest
to repay my host for his hospitality," Isabel said. "Do you—
have a pianoforte?"

"No, I'm sorry."

"Harp?"

"This is going to lead down a meandering path of disappointment, Helen." He sighed, then brightened. "You can
read aloud to me! I'd love to hear someone else reciting some
poetry for once. My own voice is gravel in my ears."

Isabel nodded. "If you wish."

"Or . . ." Darius's voice trailed off in thought.

"Or?" she prompted him gently.

"I think I have a better idea. Do you play chess?"

"A more direct path to disappointment, Mr. Thorne. I'm
afraid I don't."

"Would you like to learn?"

Isabel sat back and considered it. There had been several
chess sets throughout her parents' large house, but she had
never been invited to touch them. Even her husband had possessed an ornate board in his study. But Richard had never
played and she'd never asked.

"It's a man's game, isn't it?"

"Not at all. It's a game of strategy and of battle, but it is
a mental game, which doesn't limit it to either gender."
Darius put his elbows on the table, his countenance changing
as he was swept up, making his case. "Two sides face each
other and the goal is conquest."

Her brow furrowed. "I have no interest in war."

"Perhaps not, but chess is an elegant reduction of conflict and many things. It is the art of defense and offense, of tactical planning and patience. Like dancing, there are choreographed moves and predictable patterns, as well as surprises."

She smiled. "You are obviously a great fan of the sport."

"You should learn chess, Helen."

"*Should* I?" she asked, mystified at his persistence.

"For one more reason I've yet to mention."

"And what reason is that?"

"Because the most powerful piece on that board isn't the armed knight on horseback or the brute soldier or even the solemn-looking fellow wearing the crown."

"No?" She held her breath, drawn in by the light in his eyes.

"It's the queen. The singular female on the field has more power and freedom to move than any other piece." He lowered his voice conspiratorially. "Imagine it, Helen. She is the strongest element on the board and every other piece is either struggling to make sure she is safe or to stay out of her way."

"Oh my!" Isabel let out the breath she'd been holding. "Really?"

"Here, I'll show you. Bring your plate of food!"

She almost gasped in shock at the outlandish suggestion, but when he stood from the table, she followed suit. They abandoned the dining table with their stolen plates and hurried like mischievous children back to the library, where Darius quickly rearranged the chairs in front of the fireplace and set out a table between them for the board and their dinner plates.

Isabel was given the White army to champion and almost immediately discovered what a great teacher Darius was. He patiently explained each piece's strengths and moves but added a story with the figurines so that by the time they were ready to begin a game, she was heartily attached to each of her little soldiers, fearful of their safety, proud of her brave knights, and impressed with the haughtiness of her bishops and the righteous indignation of her royal couple at the cheekiness of their rivals' impending invasion.

Especially my queen.

The tiny feminine carved face was calm and unyielding, her lips in an eternal imperial pout. Isabel liked the look of her with her ivory crown and robe encrusted with dots of paint that resembled pearls. Here was a woman who was powerful and unafraid.

The first game was less a battle and more a series of lessons on how a battle unfolded and the consequences of every choice she made. He held his Black army in check, never striking aggressively against hers but advising where he *could* have, letting her retrace her steps and weigh out her moves. The first loss of a knight made her almost tearful, but Darius walked her through the realities of a necessary sacrifice to achieve a greater goal.

"You must try to see all the pieces as part of a larger entity, all working together." He turned the board just a few inches to the left. "Take a deep breath. Sometimes I like to imagine that my men are all eager to do their duty and consider sacrifice a great honor—especially when I promise to resurrect them for the next battle."

She laughed. "Such absolute power!"

"Heady, isn't it?" He squared the board again between them. "When you play chess, nothing happens on the field without your command."

"But I'm not commanding you." She eyed the intimidating lines of his pieces. "And your men don't look happy about dying just to please me!"

It was his turn to laugh. "True! The Black army seeks only to please their dark queen, but let's see if you cannot outwit them."

"I will do my utmost to make her rage in frustration." Isabel bent her head in concentration, trying to see the board as he did. Her poor knight stood forlornly next to Darius's hand—a captured piece. "But only if you sign a treaty not to mistreat any of my men who fall into your hands."

"Agreed." Darius solemnly held out his hand. "I shall be merciful."

"Good." Isabel took his hand to shake it, her bare palm pressed to his and the warmth of his firm touch enveloping her slender fingers. It was meant as a jest, her proclamation of the articles of their little war, but the spark of sensation she experienced drained her of humor. There was nothing funny about the seductive pull of the heat shimmering across her skin. Isabel knew it was forbidden, this pleasure, but suddenly—it was hard to accept why.

I'm married—and already so far down a path to scandal that I may never recover. But this—God, how is this even possible? When I thought never to want any man's touch again for as long as I lived?

"And you?" he asked, still holding her hand across the board. His gaze was steady, the green in his eyes deepening as the contact between them lingered.

"M-me?" Isabel tried to regain her mental footing and ignore the sweet fire curling up inside of her.

"Will the White Queen also pledge to be merciful? My army stands ready in either case, but a gentleman must ask if the treaty is to be balanced."

"Of-of course." Isabel conceded, then reluctantly let go of his hand. "I'll serve them jam and biscuits while they wait for you to pay their ransoms."

"Very kind of you." He dropped his hand too quickly and clumsily knocked over his rook and two pawns. "Whoa! Disorder in the ranks!"

Darius reordered his pieces and Isabel took the opportunity to catch her breath and press her cool fingers against her cheeks. *Mutiny abounds and I should take care that my growing affections for him don't add to the mess I've made of my life. I'll have caused Mr. Thorne enough trouble without abusing his offer of friendship.*

* * *

Darius silently cursed his clumsiness, praying she hadn't noticed the way her touch derailed his thoughts. The game was meant to be a diversion but not like this. He'd hoped to teach her something new and cheer her. In the firelight, she'd transformed her ethereal beauty into a feminine figure of fey glory, and her quick grasp of the game and willingness to play along with his fanciful stories had humbled him. He'd never revealed to anyone else as much of the odd workings of his mind. Chess was a serious game but Darius had never played it without folding in a bit of drama.

Instead of laughing at him, Helen had openly approved, proclaiming herself enchanted, and revealed that her imagination outpaced his. Even now, she took his breath away as she announced, "My lone knight is melancholy to think of his lost twin, Mr. Thorne, but I warn you, he is getting a fireside speech from his comrades to rally his spirits. They've reminded him of our cause and inspired him to avenge his brother!"

Darius was entranced—a man held in thrall. "No less inspiring than the cries of my generals to my battered men-at-arms. He is promising extra rations of ale and a parcel of land to the first common man to take down one of your bishops."

"How wicked!" she exclaimed, her eyes gleaming. "The White army needs no such bribery."

"Well"—he leaned in conspiratorially—"they do need one thing."

"And what is that?" she asked, her attention instantly diverted to the board, her expression anxious. "Is someone in danger?"

"No, not necessarily," he conceded. "But the White army does need the lady ruling the White Kingdom to make her next move, or my wicked forces will start to conclude that she has forfeited."

"Oh yes, of course!" Helen bit her lower lip, her gaze narrowing as she concentrated. She touched her rook, but hesitated. "Hold on to the tapestries, gentlemen, for we are moving."

She slid the rook forward to plant it boldly just out of

reach of a pawn, an unsubtle threat to his knight, and lifted her fingers. "There!"

Darius winced playfully and reached for his chest as if he'd been struck. "My scouts have betrayed me!" He let out a slow deep breath and then reassessed the board. "I'll retreat and see if I can't turn the tide."

The game continued with mourned losses on both sides and celebrated advances, but Darius deliberately made sure she had an opportunity to ultimately win. The fierce joy on her face after her careful trap sprang on his weakened court and yielded a kneeling black king at her queen's feet was priceless.

Hell, I may never win another game, for she makes losing such pleasure.

"Checkmate!" she exclaimed.

"You are victorious," he said, ritually knocking his king over with a flick of his forefinger to formally surrender. "I am yours."

Mrs. McFadden cleared her throat as she entered with an empty tray to collect their half-empty plates with a fleeting look of disapproval. She said nothing as Darius met her gaze openly, daring her to spoil the evening's fun.

"Thank you, Mrs. McFadden," he said calmly.

"Yes, thank you, Mrs. McFadden," Helen added, her expression anxious. "We . . . didn't mean to be a bother."

The housekeeper's stern look softened. "No matter. I'll serve your dinner here in the future if you'd rather and save myself a few steps. But you should mind the time, Mr. Thorne. It's getting late and the lady should be resting."

Darius looked over at the clock on the mantel, amazed at how they'd lost track of the hours. "So it is!"

Helen stood and he immediately did the same. "I'll retire if only to allow me to withdraw while I'm victorious. It was a wonderful evening, Mr. Thorne. Thank you for being such a patient teacher."

"We'll have a rematch tomorrow night and see if you're as graceful in defeat as you are in triumph," he teased her.

"You *let* me win this first time but I'm enjoying it all the same, sir!" She curtsied and left the room with the carriage of a queen.

Darius forgot his housekeeper and simply watched Helen go.

Best game of chess I've ever played!

Mrs. McFadden cleared her throat again and Darius sighed. It was too much to hope for that she'd keep her opinion to herself for very long. "She's not a kitten come in from the cold."

"Why? Was I offering her milk and discussing the vermin population in the stables to give you that impression?"

She ignored him. "I've said nothing of her arrival to anyone and have no intentions of betraying my promises, but have you decided what you're to do?"

"I'm already doing exactly what I should be doing. I'm letting her heal and recover until I can come up with a good plan that doesn't put her in jeopardy." He walked over to the center of the room, collecting papers from the chairs and various surfaces as he went. "Besides, Hamish said her mount won't be fit for at least another three weeks, so there's no need to rush."

"I don't see that her horse has anything to do with anything. There are other means of travel in this world! You've a good carriage of your own and—"

"I'm not packing her off until I know that she has somewhere to go."

Mrs. McFadden grunted her disapproval. "I'm getting fond of her, so don't you dare misunderstand. It would be impossible not to melt a bit, but it's no harmless game for you. You're a bachelor and it's all kind of scandal, this! If her husband finds her here . . . in your company . . ."

"He won't and we've broken no law taking her in from the cold." Darius started folding away his maps. "But I'll be damned if I—"

Darius didn't allow himself to finish the thought. What threat could he make? He'd vowed to keep her safe, but if her husband appeared and demanded her, if Helen herself agreed to return to him—it could be a lost cause. It made no sense for her to forfeit her hard-won freedom, but he'd experienced firsthand the deadly, illogical turns of abuse. Helen was terrified enough of her husband to run from him.

But nothing was certain.

Darius sighed. "I don't care what the risk is. If things turn ugly, then I'll be sure to proclaim your and Hamish's innocence in all of it. It was my decision and I'll take the blame."

"It's not really myself or that brute I was worried about. She's so pretty," Mrs. McFadden said more quietly. "Mind you don't lose more than a chess game in this nonsense!"

"You're the one encouraging entertainments!" Darius's temper gave way at last. "Mind your manners, Mrs. McFadden. I'm not a schoolboy in need of a chaperone and you are not a relation to be so familiar and so unkind! Helen has done nothing wrong and I . . . I will be responsible for my own actions. I am a gentleman and a scholar; and there's an end to it!"

He braced himself for a waspish reply but none followed. He'd never chided her before but he couldn't take it back.

"I see." Her hands fell away from her hips. "Are you to town tomorrow? It'll be Tuesday."

There's an unexpected show of mercy!

"Yes. Let Hamish know we'll make the rounds in Edinburgh as usual." He laid the stack of maps down haphazardly on his already cluttered desk. "And, Mrs. McFadden, please determine what things our guest needs and I'll try to acquire them as discreetly as I can in the city."

Mrs. McFadden pressed her lips together in a thin line but nodded. "Yes, sir."

She closed the door firmly behind her as she left with her tray, and Darius sat down slowly behind his desk.

Helen was a lady of quality and good breeding. He knew he was in denial of just what level of quality he might be contending with.

Could she be the wife of a recently elevated man? Some self-important baron or squire, God willing! Please, God, be willing!

He abandoned his chair and began to pace the room.

And what if he is a baron? My logic's flawed. As if being some country gentleman means I can afford to buy out his wounded pride or that he'd be more easily persuaded to release his wife or be less stubborn. A small terrier can be worse than a deerhound, and I've known enough village bureaucrats and university officials to know that even a small dash of power can transform men into tenacious vipers.

But even vipers have their price.

The Jaded already possessed one unknown enemy, and Darius wasn't oblivious to the fact that by complicating his own situation, he could inadvertently add to everyone's troubles. But he knew there wasn't a man in the Jaded who wouldn't have done the same to protect a woman in need—and not a single man who would advise him to set her out.

He pulled the heavy curtains back from the window, rewarded with nothing more than his own reflection in the glass. The sight interrupted his thoughts. He'd never been a vain man. Darius had spent a lifetime more focused on his internal landscape and the capacity of his mind than anything else. Ashe Blackwell had chided him more than once in their friendship for ignoring fashion or forgetting to savor the finer things in life. But he'd never seen any value in peering at one's own skin.

He wondered how a woman saw him.

How Helen sees me . . .

His gaze narrowed as he assessed the man in the glass. His features were well-defined but Darius thought them a bit too sharp. The eyes were unremarkable, in his opinion, and his coloring hardly exotic enough to evoke the prose that ladies seem to favor. He was paler than he liked but knew he had himself to blame for all the days spent indoors with his books. He was tall and lean, broad in the shoulders, but not overly athletic.

Darius leaned forward, pressing his hot forehead against the icy glass, and closed his eyes. *What does it matter if she thinks I'm a bespectacled troll or an Adonis?*

I'm forgetting my place in the world.

He didn't possess the pedigree to aspire to marry even the second cousin of an impoverished country squire. He knew the worst of his past, and before he'd put on his first pair of long pants, he'd determined to live alone and it wasn't just because of the simple stains of poverty. *They say blood will tell. Why am I dwelling on it now?*

He'd vowed to protect her. It was a flimsy excuse for keeping her.

Mrs. McFadden is right. I'm in danger of losing more than a chess game.

He crossed his arms defensively and turned back to survey the room. "Perspective, Thorne. One puzzle at a time."

He worked late into the night, reading texts from other travelers to Bengal and from local sources until the words began to swim on the pages and Darius conceded his efforts. He retreated to a wide couch to fall into a deep, dreamless sleep, where the tangle of the Jaded and his fears for Helen disappeared.

Chapter
6

❋

The dining room was set for a party downstairs, the long gilt mirrors glittering with the reflection of dozens of candles. She knew it even though she was standing in a dark closet. She could hear the muffled sounds of the guests' conversations and laughter through the door. Somewhere music was playing and she wondered if there would be dancing.

The earl was having a house party.

His wife would not be attending.

He'd told everyone she was ill, and they had sighed in sympathy, pouting at the young lady's misfortune. They'd hoped to meet the new mistress and catch a glimpse of her famed beauty, but poor Richard had apparently married a sickly thing, for she was never seen in public since the wedding.

"What a shame!" The words echoed and echoed and Isabel struggled not to cry.

She could hear Richard's voice downstairs and she was glad. That meant he wasn't nearby. That he might enjoy his party and drink too much and forget where he'd put her for—

"Punishment," he whispered behind her, and in the logic of dreams, it made terrifying sense that he was there. That she could hear him laughing in the dining room but feel his hot breath at the back of her neck.

Even in a dream, she knew not to fight him.

She wasn't allowed to attend the party because she'd angered him that morning at the breakfast table. She couldn't remember what she'd done or said, but he'd struck her hard across the face.

Richard almost never hit her where the mark would show to a casual observer.

But his rage had been so great that he'd forgotten his own rule.

And so it was her fault.

To have angered him so and spoiled her looks before his grand party.

She'd earned another punishment and he'd locked her in the upstairs hall closet until he'd decided what it should be.

And the demon in the dark began to touch her and Isabel screamed.

She awoke to the sound of her own distress, already on her hands and knees in twisted bedding as if she'd meant to crawl her way out of the nightmare. Isabel's skin was damp with sweat and she shivered at the lingering memory of Richard's hands around her throat.

And then Darius was in her doorway, his handsome face illuminated by the candle he was carrying. He was still dressed for dinner, but his shirt was unbuttoned and his hair was mussed as if from sleep. "Helen?" he asked. "Are you unwell?"

She shook her head, her voice thick with shame as she pulled the lace of the nightgown up to cover her throat. "It was—just a dream. I'm fine."

"Here, let's get you resettled. Mrs. McFadden isn't awake but I think we can manage things without disturbing her." He stepped forward and set his lit candle down on the table next to the bed. "I shall avert my eyes and allow you to get back under the covers, if that helps. It's almost five in the morning, but there's time yet to rest."

She smiled. The man was a marvel to worry about her modesty at such an hour, but her feet felt like ice and she was grateful for the kindness. She climbed back under but sat up against the pillows. "I'm back where I belong, Mr. Thorne."

He didn't turn right away and she almost repeated herself in case he'd misheard her, but then Darius shifted back around to make quick work of readjusting the feather comforter, his movements brisk and efficient. "Let's get something for your shoulders."

He located the knitted wrap that Mrs. McFadden had left at the end of the bed and brought it over to her. "Here we are."

"You'd make a remarkable ladies' maid, Mr. Thorne."

It was his turn to smile. "I will make a note of it, and if my next work fails publication, I'll make inquiries." His smile faded and he reached out to touch her cheek with the back of his fingers. "You're soaking wet and icy to the touch."

"I . . . The night terrors are . . ."

"You'll catch your death if the chill takes hold," he said. "Damn, the fire's gone out."

"I'm fine!"

He didn't bother to argue. He stood from the bed and immediately began to reset the little fireplace with kindling and wood and started a blaze. Within just a few minutes, a cheerful warmth began to radiate from the hearth and he'd rearranged the screens to direct its heat toward her.

"Mr. Thorne," she said.

He stood, his back to her. "There. That's better."

"Mr. Thorne," she repeated, making a firmer bid for his attention.

He turned and her breath caught in her throat.

There it is again. That flutter in my stomach when he looks at me. That same sensation as when he took my hand . . . She could see the bare skin of his throat and a few tantalizing inches of skin across his chest to reveal the dark brown swirl of hair there. He emanated an attractive masculine power that confused and excited her. On the heels of her nightmares, instead of being frightened by his strength, Isabel was drawn to it.

"You're still wearing your clothes, Mr. Thorne. Did you never go to bed?" she asked.

He reached up to touch his jacket collar, as if just discovering his state of dress. "I fell asleep in the library again. Another terrible habit."

Isabel pulled the soft shawl more tightly around her shoulders. "It doesn't seem like such a horrible flaw. There are worse sins."

He drew closer, standing to one side at the foot of the great bed. "There are." Darius's fingers traced the scrollwork on the carved bed's columns. "After . . . India, when we'd returned to England, I had nightmares every night. I think I deliberately got into a habit of working late to the point of exhaustion to try to outpace them, but it only made them worse."

"Do you still have them?"

"No." He tipped his head to one side, shy at the topic. "Because I finally confessed about them to Ashe. I told him about the dreams and—it helped. I'm not sure why, but when I named my fears, they lost their power over me. And if"—he looked back at her before going on—"you ever wanted to talk about what happened or describe your nightmares, I'm a good listener."

"You truly are, I think." Isabel took a deep breath, wondering if she could be that courageous and speak the unspeakable. Shame and embarrassment threatened to drown out reason, but looking at him, Isabel could remember only how sweet he'd been and how he'd not once pressed her for answers or spoken out against her impulsive escape from her commitments. "I don't believe I could bear it if you thought less of me, Mr. Thorne."

"My opinion of you could never lessen, Helen, no matter what you say." He sat down gingerly on the edge of the bed, a respectable distance from her but still within reach. "Unless you're about to tell me that you value Roman philosophies over the Greek schools of thought—a man must draw the line somewhere."

The jest surprised her and made the moment more real.

"Marcus Aurelius's writings are unparalleled for their common sense, are they not?" she challenged him quietly. It was truthfully the only Roman philosopher she could summon to mind as his nearness worked against her wits.

"Marcus Aurelius?" He pretended shock. "But where is the elegance? He dictates the answers when Socrates would seek to ask questions." He sighed. "You're a master of redirection."

"As are you," she said. Isabel took a few moments to study her hands on top of the coverlet and gather her courage. But it eluded her. "It's all so . . . vile and . . . demeaning. I can't speak of it. Please don't ask me."

He said nothing and she risked a glance to see if he might be frowning in disappointment. But his expression was kind, his concern apparent. "Another time perhaps."

She nodded, but Isabel wasn't sure if she ever wished to give voice to any of it. If she even knew how to describe the horrors that marriage had brought her—or admit to her worst fear, her fear that she had somehow earned her punishments by some great inherent failing of her own. Richard had made it clear that she was a disgrace, not good enough to be a proper wife. He'd said that she'd forced him to treat her harshly so that it was all he could do to make an effort to salvage happiness from his disappointment.

On their "best" days, he'd looked almost sweet expressing his regret that their marriage was so tumultuous and that she was so dispassionate. He would buy her a gift or allow her to go for a ride on Samson to coax her into hoping that the worst was behind her.

She'd seen so many other women positively glowing with the pleasure of a good match and marriage. Richard blamed her, and after hearing it a thousand times a day, Isabel wasn't sure that he wasn't right.

Perhaps all of it was my fault.

Which would make my escape even more groundless and stupid.

Or my complaints of any of it sound like the whining of a child.

Darius shifted off the bed and added one more piece of wood to the fireplace. "There, that should keep until dawn and Mrs. McFadden comes up to check on you. I'll be gone at first light on business, but I expect to be back in time for dinner and our chess game."

"You're going?" she asked, a stab of distress at the news choking her.

"Just into the city for a few hours. I'll hurry the matter, Helen, no need to fear." He retreated to the door with an awkward bow, leaving the candle behind with her. "But for now, I should get to my own room and get some sleep. I'm at the end of the hall, and if you're in any distress, I'll return right away."

"Thank you, Mr. Thorne."

He ducked his head with a smile and left, and Isabel lowered herself to settle under the covers. The ghost of her husband was held at bay as she watched the fire dance and considered the changes in her fortune.

And finally fell asleep just as the first tendrils of light touched her window.

Chapter
7

"You've come again!" Mr. Errol Craig greeted Darius as he entered the shop, the silver bell above the door jangling to herald his arrival. "You are welcome, naturally, Mr. Thorne, and I'll admit I always look forward to your visits."

Craig & Cavendish were one of the most reputable gem dealers in Edinburgh and famous for the skill of their cutters. They'd been a reliable contact for him as he'd begun the discreet business of trade for his friends far away from the gossip of Town. Also, the Scottish dealers were a good source of information since the bulk of treasure coming into the country passed through their hands. Darius wrestled with the meaning of *sacred treasures* and where an Englishman would look for such a thing.

London would have been the obvious choice to start to look for exotic treasures, but if the East India Trading Company was part of the equation, it made no sense that they'd not have found it already if it were in the capital under their noses.

Their unknown enemy had accused the Jaded of possessing a sacred object that they wanted back at any price. But whatever it was, they hadn't openly asked for it. Instead it had been a ridiculous game of cat and mouse with threats made and cryptic notes. Darius had dismissed it as troublesome but it was *troublesome* only until someone had tried to poison Ashe Blackwell and nearly killed his beloved bride.

Now there was no time to lose.

His friends were relying on him to use his contacts in Edinburgh and his knack for puzzles to help them solve the mystery and rid themselves of their nemesis. Unfortunately, his progress was slow and Ashe's last letter from London had indicated that he wasn't willing to wait any longer. The Jaded would be making a move soon. Ashe had asked him to consider returning to London and forgoing his inquiries. Blackwell clearly didn't care what their enemies wanted anymore. Ashe just wanted revenge against whoever had poisoned his wife.

The game is changing fast.

But it's still chess, and how do we effectively plan a strategy when we can't see the whole board?

"You are too kind, Mr. Craig." Darius removed his hat as he approached the counter. "I trust business is good these days."

"I cannot complain, Mr. Thorne." The dealer pulled aside the black velvet covering the glass-enclosed display just in case his customer was in a buying mood. "Was there something in particular you wished to find, sir?"

Darius surveyed the offerings, newly impressed with Mr. Cavendish's goldsmith skills. The fashion of the day was ribboned chokers and embellished pendants that called for a creative and steady hand at the jeweler's bench. He was about to politely defer when an elaborate piece caught his eye. It was from India, by the look of it, layer upon layer of worked gold with empty settings held aloft by the eyes of burnished peacock feathers recreated in the metal. It was as if nature had been reshaped and even improved by the goldsmith's hands, and Darius wondered if there weren't a cheat in it.

Did he just dip the feathers into some sort of molten gold? The detail's too fine to be handmade, isn't it? Hell, you can see each fiber in those feathery eyes. . . .

There were no stones in the open settings. Instead the necklace awaited the tastes of its buyer.

My God! Helen would be glorious in that with white opals to match her eyes.

"You have a good eye, Mr. Thorne." Mr. Craig lifted the necklace from the case and set it atop the now folded black velvet. "And I know better than to try to sell you any stones for it."

Darius smiled. He'd sold a few of the Jaded's stones in Edinburgh and made good trades with the dealers whenever his friends needed funds. The jewelers welcomed him for it and were always eager to see if he had anything else to sell. He lifted it up, expecting it to be as light as the feathers it portrayed, but the cool weight of the metal made him gasp. "Where did you get it?"

"A foreign gentleman, sir. Gambling debts, I fear, have led him to shed a few of his family's heirlooms. But more than that, I cannot say."

"Not even to tell me what stones were originally in the piece?" Darius asked.

Mr. Craig smiled and shrugged. "Stupid bits of glass, if you can imagine it! I took them out, Mr. Thorne. I cannot have things below my standard in the shop, and as a gem cutter, my reputation is at risk if anyone mistakenly thought I was passing them off as if they had value."

"You are an honorable man."

"And a sentimental one! A smarter man would have melted this necklace down for the gold, but I couldn't do it. Even Mr. Cavendish said he couldn't recreate it if he'd cared to try. . . ." Mr. Craig sighed. "But it does not sell."

"No interest?" Darius asked, a bit surprised.

"Too garish I think for the region, sir, and buyers are wary of the cost of setting it, I'd say." Mr. Craig stopped and gave him a hopeful look. "Takes a bit of imagination, does it not?"

Darius laughed. He was in no position to be buying jewelry, and while the pleasant notion of being able to shower women with expensive gifts had its appeal—there was only one woman in his thoughts today. Last night, he'd felt like a clumsy fool trying to do anything in his power to comfort her without actually touching her. He'd fussed with the fireplace and rattled on about drafts because his palms had burned to caress her cheeks and smooth out the look of terror that still clouded her eyes. He'd been dreaming about her when she'd awoken him, and the tenor of his dreams had nothing to do with polite reserve and gentlemanly etiquette.

She was like quicksilver in his arms, all silken heat and yielding—unafraid and bold, like the White Queen should be when she took her full measure in victory.

So he'd ended up bumbling about and then standing against the wall outside her room, waiting for his composure to return and for his blood to cool, embarrassed at how easily a man could forget his place and dream of touching a woman he couldn't have.

"—wouldn't it?" Mr. Craig said.

"Pardon, I was . . . distracted for a moment." Darius gave himself a quick mental shake, impatient at his own lapse. "What were you saying?"

"The necklace. It complements your interests, doesn't it?"

"It might. The foreign gentleman. It was a family piece, you say? Can you tell me what region of India they resided in?" Darius turned the necklace over in his hands, looking for a maker's mark or symbol, but there was nothing.

Mr. Craig shook his head. "I didn't ask. He offered that it was charmed, of course, but as you and I have spoken often, what piece from that part of the world isn't, according to the seller?"

"Charmed?" Darius looked up from the necklace. "How?"

"It's to do with vanity." Errol folded his hands behind his back, warming to the topic. "The claim, which we at Craig and Cavendish do not guarantee, was that a lady with a sweet spirit may wear it and her outer appearance will reflect the loveliness of her heart. But if a vain, worthless woman makes a try at it, she'll look a fool and the world will see the ugliness of her heart."

"And it hasn't sold?" Darius teased him dryly.

It was Errol's turn to laugh. "Cowards! I can't see why. . . ."

Darius reluctantly set the piece aside. He was far too aware of the social rules prohibiting the act of purchasing necklaces for married women. "I know a very worthy lady but perhaps another day, Mr. Craig. I shall think about it."

"Anything else, then?"

Darius nodded. "My quest continues. Have you heard anything new about the item we discussed?"

Errol shook his head. "Not without knowing more. There is always a buyer for unique and exotic treasures although"—Mr. Craig paused to place the gold peacock necklace back into its tray—"not as quickly as one would hope."

"Everything I know of sacred treasures makes me think it would be a figurine of some kind." Darius eyed the necklace. "Something wearable and easily transported. My fear is that not all shop owners are as sentimental as you, Mr. Craig. If they melted it down . . ."

"Then it's an ingot in some rich man's vault, sir, or already reworked into a hundred brooches and rings. There's not a jeweler worth his salt that leaves aught to waste." Errol's brow furrowed then smoothed out as his innate optimism reasserted itself. "But I know of no mention of *sacred*, and as far as I know, you're the only one who comes to ask for such things. I've a note to my staff to keep an ear out for anything special or if someone's come to inquire so that we might discreetly alert you, sir."

"Thank you, Mr. Craig."

"Can I talk you into parting with another stone, then? That last." Errol sighed, his expression that of a man in love. "Ah, what a joy! I'd thought I'd seen good stone, but that opal made even the hard-hearted Mr. Cavendish cry it was so full of fire—and the size! A robin's egg of rainbows! It sold within three days after my partner set it in a pendant, and if you don't mind me saying it, eased my worries of old age."

Darius had been careful not to overuse any one dealer when selling stones for his friends. As a result, Mr. Craig knew him for opals while other dealers sought him for other gems. But all of them were quizzed almost weekly to see if anyone had approached them searching for a *sacred treasure* from India.

It was a weak and remote chance.

But it was a chance.

"I'm glad to hear of it. Let me bring you something next time and see if we cannot improve your retirement." Darius stepped back from the counter. "But I should warn you, Mr. Craig."

"A warning?" Errol straightened.

"My supply of smaller opals, such as you purchased, is limited." Darius bowed. "But I will do my best."

He turned on his heel, deliberately leaving a happily sputtering and giddy Errol Craig in his wake. Darius left the shop and found Hamish waiting by the carriage.

"Any luck today?" Hamish asked as he opened the door.

"Not yet." Darius climbed up to take his seat next to the packages of sundries and ready-made pieces they'd collected for Helen that morning. "Blackwell may be right and I may be wasting my time."

"Whatever it is, not my business of course, but my mother always said the patient and persistent angler eats, and the ones that stomp about and complain go hungry." Hamish touched the brim of his hat and closed the door, leaving Darius to stew with the proverb.

All well and good if I'm fishing but—

Darius sat up straight as if he'd been goosed. "Stomp about and complain . . . go hungry. Damn that's brilliant!" *If the villain who's been pressing us for the prize could be characterized as anything, I'd say he's more prone to stomping about. Hell, it's been his impatience that's caused us more headaches than anything else! If he were a coolheaded tactician, this would probably be over by now.*

Which means he's not looking for it here!

The traders would have conveyed it to me if he had—no

subtlety in the matter. He's the kind of person who would just strong-arm it if he needed to, and the only ones he's strong-armed are the Jaded.

Which means he's not looking for it anywhere but in our pockets. And we're the only ones who keep looking elsewhere since we're not convinced we have anything of a sacred nature.

How could I have missed that?

"All I need to do is figure out what it is and I can stop wasting my energy looking for him on the markets," Darius said aloud.

"What was that?" Hamish drew back the small wooden window between them. "Off to the next as usual?"

"No. Thanks to your mother's wisdom, we're done, Mr. MacQueen." Darius leaned back against the cushions, a more contented man. "Let's go home!"

* * *

Samson pressed his soft muzzle against her cheek, mussing her hair. Isabel closed her eyes and sighed, inhaling the comforting sensation and warmth of the stallion's gesture. She'd slipped from the house in the afternoon to come see him, disliking the emptiness and silence. Isabel had tried reading in the library but found herself missing Mr. Thorne's presence and was distracted by chess pieces and the sight of his makeshift bed against the wall. A velvet cushion still bore the imprint of his head, and Isabel had fled the room before a wave of restless heat overtook her thoughts. It was unseemly the way her body had begun to betray her as if some strange part of her clung to secret dreams her waking mind didn't understand.

Why? Why does the thought of him sleeping there make my chest ache with the desire to see him—and more shockingly—to touch him?

Darius had made every effort to act as a gentleman toward her.

She was simply frustrated at how much more effort it was taking her these days to play the lady.

I'm off the leash for the first time in months—perhaps in my whole life. I think running away and being at my own liberty is starting to play tricks on my better judgment.

Samson whinnied as if impatient that her thoughts focused on any other male.

He'd been a gift on her sixteenth birthday from her father. She'd taken one look at him and known several truths. First, that he was not the usual staid pony one gifted to a daughter, and the disapproving glare on her mother's face proved it. Secondly, that the reason her father had made such a purchase had everything to do with his love of horses, racing, and gambling and almost nothing to do with his remote pleasure at a daughter's birth. But the last truth trumped all.

Samson was hers. She was already horse-mad as most girls her age, but from the first ride, it was true love. She'd sung in his ears and cried on his neck with happiness, and Samson had absorbed every ounce of her adoration only to return it in his own fashion. He'd tolerated no other rider and made such a nuisance of himself that her father had counted him a loss and yielded him over completely to the wasted role of a lady's steed.

"There's my brave beauty," she crooned. "Did I thank you, dearest? For getting me away? Did I omit it, my darling?"

Samson snorted and nodded his head, as if eager to encourage her to praise his heroics.

Isabel laughed. "You poor thing!"

"The way you talk to that beastie . . ." Mrs. McFadden interrupted from the stable's large doorway. "I suppose it's all right so long as he doesn't answer."

Isabel reluctantly stepped back, her cheeks warming at being caught in an unguarded moment. "I often think he does."

"I meant to find you as the men are gone. I'd say it's a good chance for a hot soak, if you wished." The housekeeper crossed her arms against the cold. "I've got a lovely copper tub in the storeroom off the kitchens and it's all ready for you."

"Mrs. McFadden," Isabel said, a bit shocked at the house-keeper's thoughtfulness. "A bath!"

"Well, I'm not six young girls to be toting boiling water in buckets up those stairs a dozen times! The kitchen's good enough for the moment." Her tone was sharp but Isabel knew her well enough to recognize the tender flash of worry in her eyes.

"It's splendid of you, Mrs. McFadden, and very thought-ful. I'd love a bath." She stroked Samson's neck and left him to follow the older woman back toward the house. "Thank you."

Mrs. McFadden shrugged. "Well, it's not much. But I also wanted to tell you that my niece skipped by early this morning with some butter from my sister's and there's been no talk in the village, madam. No word of inquiries."

"However did you determine that? I mean"—Isabel rephrased her question carefully—"without telling her about me?"

"No worries! I just asked if there was news. Trust me, the village is so small, a cat can't have kittens without caus-ing a stir. If your—if anyone was asking for a lady such as yourself, the words would have tumbled out of her mouth before I'd taken the jar out of the basket."

It was a relief to know, but still . . . Isabel was certain that eventually her husband's agents would widen the circle and might just come across a farmer who'd seen her riding wildly across their field or a stranger who'd noted Samson's unique size and beauty.

The women tapped the mud off their shoes before cross-ing the threshold of the back door into Mrs. McFadden's warm, tidy kitchen. The curtain across the pantry door was pulled back and Isabel sighed at the sight of steam curling up from the large copper bath.

Mrs. McFadden took her coat and scarf. "Here, there's a hook on the beam for your clothes and you can take your time with it."

Isabel dropped the curtain and set about making quick work of the transition. Even with Mrs. McFadden's cast-iron stove blazing, it was still a chilly enough proposition before she climbed gingerly into the steaming welcome of the tub. The housekeeper had lined it with linens to add to her comfort, and Isabel gripped the sides and closed her eyes as she slowly slid down into the water.

Pain and pleasure warred at the contact of heat against her skin, but the stiffness in her back eased and Isabel let out a long, slow breath in relief. The sound of Mrs. McFadden returning to her work in the kitchen on the other side of the makeshift curtain was reassuring. She took a few minutes to inventory what marks she could see on her upper arms and shoulders, wincing as she twisted to try to see the worst of it.

"I forgot to set out the soap!" Mrs. McFadden said on the other side of the cloth. "Mind, I'll step in with it if that's all right."

"Y-yes, of course." Isabel pulled her knees up for modesty.

"Here you are." The woman held out a bar of soap the color of dark honey. "The soap's not as fine as you're likely used to."

Isabel took it from her and sniffed the bar in curiosity. "It's cinnamon!"

"I make it for the professor and did not have a dainty in mind."

"I love the smell of cinnamon."

"Your back looks better, if I can say it." Mrs. McFadden's voice was a bit brisk as she then deliberately made a show of looking at the ceiling to give Isabel a better measure of privacy. "Still as bright as a rainbow though. However you came by it . . ."

"It isn't very painful." Isabel soaped her arms, the awkward moment stretching out between the women.

"I'll leave you to it." Mrs. McFadden retreated again and Isabel slid down into the tub until the tip of her nose lapped at the water.

Isabel lingered as long as she could, long after the practical business of a bath had been concluded. The warmth enticed her to stay but she also felt shy about her inability to respond to the housekeeper's hints to share her story. It was natural for her to ask, but Isabel still wasn't sure what to say. She felt cowardly and small today. Darius had spoken of her bravery, but it was difficult to see it in the still and quiet of the house.

She closed her eyes and the memory of the chess lesson came back to her.

The queen is the most powerful piece on the board.

She believed it when he said it. Worlds of power and freedom opened up as Darius sat across the small table, as tantalizing as the electricity of his touch when she'd taken his hand.

She wasn't brazen enough for flirtation or unaware of the nature of her position.

I am a married woman.

But with the smell of cinnamon surrounding her, Isabel's heartbeat raced at the notion that his skin would carry the same scent, that there would be traces of it on her own, and that by merely breathing in, she was connecting with Darius in a very real and intimate way. For one fleeting instant, the memory of Darius in her room in the night with his shirt unbuttoned spun out in her imagination, and she wondered what her life would have been if he were the one who had the right to touch her.

She sank back down into the water to scrub her feet and toes, attempting to ignore the rebellious and impractical twists of her thoughts. A lifetime of dutiful obedience and a firm adherence to every rule and restriction ever placed on her wasn't something a woman overthrew easily.

Besides, I have already trespassed so far over the line there may be no chance for any sort of life. Richard swore to denounce me and have me committed before he'd allow a divorce. He said a thousand times that he would rather see me dead than give up a farthing of my dowry or be publicly humiliated in scandal.

There is no retreat to be made.

Mr. Thorne has already placed himself in harm's way.

It would be demeaning if he knew I'd repaid his generosity with sordid carnal thoughts involving his . . . person.

She finished quickly, washing and rinsing her long hair to pile it loosely on top of her head before climbing out of the water to dry. Abandoning the warm water for the cooler drafts of the pantry was a test of her resolve, but Isabel did her best to embrace practicalities and give Mrs. McFadden the free run of her kitchen for her work.

The dress she'd borrowed from Mrs. McFadden didn't require any help, as the buttons were placed in the front. It was a simpler design for women who would know nothing of a ladies' maid or the intricate fashions that dictated that a lady have assistance as she dressed. But managing the belt and refolding the skirt to make sure she didn't trip ended her illusions of independence.

"Mrs. McFadden. I . . . Would you help me with this?" Isabel asked as she stepped through the curtain.

"Of course." The housekeeper washed and dried her hands before approaching. "Let's see to you."

Isabel dutifully turned or moved as the older woman made quick work of it and straightened the back of the blouse to make sure the undershirt lay flat against her bruised back.

"Here. Let's get your hair combed and pleated while it's still wet. It's an old trick when you have hair as soft as yours, but I think we can manage."

"Thank you, Mrs. McFadden."

"It's practically white, isn't it? Like an angel's." The housekeeper sighed as she combed through it.

"My nurse used to tease me when I was little and said I was a ghost baby left on my parents' doorsteps." Isabel shrugged as she took a seat on the stool near the kitchen table. "But I never was transparent enough to get out of lessons or escape the blame for mischief."

"What child is?" Mrs. McFadden scoffed. "My brothers probably wished themselves invisible a thousand times for all the trouble they managed to get into! Worthless hooligans! All of them!"

"How many brothers do you have, Mrs. McFadden?"

"Three fools and a sister. All in the village still." The housekeeper's voice was muffled as she put a few hairpins in her mouth as she worked. "I see them market days each week and they come out to check on me sometimes."

She removed the pins from her mouth with a sigh. "Interfering matchmakers and gossips, that's what they are! But I've waved 'em off for the most part, my lady, so you needn't fear at being spotted. Not that I expect you to be dancing in the lane outside the house or making a show of yourself. . . ."

Isabel sat as still as she could while Mrs. McFadden played the ladies' maid, braiding and pinning up her hair. When she was done, she handed Isabel a small metal mirror and returned to her stove to see to the evening's courses.

Isabel reached up to touch the elaborate coils, admiring the woman's efforts. "You're a woman of many surprising talents, Mrs. McFadden."

The housekeeper puffed her cheeks in protest. "It's just braids. I'm no ladies' maid."

"Well, I'm grateful for it. Thank you."

"I'm one to speak my mind. I hinted earlier but now I'll just ask." Mrs. McFadden crossed her arms. "Was it truly your husband? That did all that?"

Isabel wasn't sure how to answer. She simply nodded and set the metal mirror back down on the kitchen table.

"Is he a drunkard?" the housekeeper said.

"I don't want to talk about it, Mrs. McFadden."

"Of course not! Who speaks of such things? It's a trifling business." Mrs. McFadden held her ground, her eyes kind despite her stubborn stance. "I had a cousin who endured a terrible husband. Of course, the way he told it, he suffered the worst in the bargain. She died in childbed, if that's a mercy, but he swears to this day she brought out the worst in him and blathers on whenever he's drunk about how he's a candidate for sainthood."

It was all Isabel could do to just blink in reply. It was the assumption of everyone who guessed at a wife's mistreatment that she had in some way earned her punishments. It was certainly the way her own mother had responded to her complaints.

Mrs. McFadden continued undaunted. "Some would say it's a woman's place and a testament to her character to stick no matter what. But those that say it haven't been on the wrong end of it, have they?"

"Have you . . . Were you—ever at the wrong end of it?"

"No." The woman's eyes darkened. "Ailbert was a dear, and you'd not know it by me now, but I was as meek a thing as ever walked this earth when Ailbert courted me. I *never* spoke above a whisper."

Isabel couldn't stop the smile of disbelief that crossed her lips. "Never?"

"A tale for another day, then."

"Oh, please! Won't you tell it now?" Isabel pleaded gently.

"Very well. In short, I was shy as a young girl. Ailbert's father had beef cows and we met in the market by accident one day and—that was that. He was so pretty! He won my heart in a single afternoon and I don't think I said four words, I was so overwhelmed. So he teased me and called me his . . ." Mrs. McFadden's voice trailed off, her eyes misting with the memories. "He called me his sweet dragon, which made no sense at all and made me laugh. He joked and said he was afraid of me and would dedicate his whole life to making sure I never frowned or fussed. We were married that same month and I had heaven in my hands for an entire year."

Isabel stood slowly from the table, hoping to offer her hand if the woman needed it, marveling at the changes that fate could bring about.

"Well, he died. Fever." The older woman's voice hardened, her words clipped and brittle. "And when he passed, I howled like a banshee. I yelled and roared to shake down the skies and I never stopped, and I never will. I frown and I fuss. Because . . . that, madam, is what dragons do."

"You aren't a—"

"Home, woman!" Hamish's gruff voice interrupted them from the outer kitchen doorway. "I've brought your precious

Englishman home in one piece. Now come complain about the state of him and tell me when supper is!"

"Get out of my kitchen!" Mrs. McFadden turned to chase the groom out. "You smell like horse sweat and worse! And she'll catch her death with the draft you're letting in, you big, ugly clod!"

The door slammed behind him and Isabel jumped away from the table, startled by the violence of the exchange, an icy knot in her stomach.

"They're early!" Mrs. McFadden was oblivious, cheerfully turning back as if all was right in the world. "I must see to the professor and make sure he's warm and settled. He'll sit in a cold, wet coat and ruin the furniture otherwise! Dinner's nearly ready and I'll ring for you to come down to the library if you'd like once I'm set on serving."

"Th-That would be lovely, Mrs. McFadden." Isabel retreated, warily eyeing the door where Mr. MacQueen had made his escape. "If you need an extra hand—"

"Pah! I can manage well enough! And a lady like yourself? In *my* kitchen? I'd go balmy before I'd allow it, madam. No fears on that account!" She ushered Isabel out like a small child, then bustled toward the other side of the house and the front entry to intercept "her Englishman."

Isabel had no choice but to retreat to her room and wait for the bell, feeling a bit useless and anxious at the abrupt shift, but she was excited to see Darius again and enjoy his company. It had been an empty, strange day without him, and now Mrs. McFadden's tale of loss spun around in her head.

Heaven in her hands.
Whatever does that mean?

* * *

Darius arranged the table before the fire and then added another pillow to her chair to make it seem more inviting. He stepped back to survey the scene before scowling at the notion that in all his studies and pursuits, he hadn't the foggiest idea of what appealed to a woman when it came to rose-embroidered cushions or upholstered chairs. He tried to remember the details of Mrs. Warren's lavender-hued parlor for reference and was faced with the real possibility that there was very little he could do to remedy things. He'd bought the house lock, stock, and barrel from a man who had died a bachelor, and now lived in it himself as a bachelor.

It's foolish to question the lack of lace at this point.
And I doubt she'd care.

Mrs. McFadden came in with the dinner tray and set down the covered dishes on his desk with a grunt of disapproval. "I'll let her know dinner's ready."

"You're a treasure, Mrs. McFadden," Darius said as solemnly as he could and was instantly rewarded with a fiery look.

"I'm not going to be turned by flattery, Mr. Thorne."

Darius took a short step forward. "Is something wrong, Mrs. McFadden?"

The woman crossed her arms. "I'm—not acquainted with many highborn ladies, and the few I've seen made me think I was a lucky woman to be out of their path. But . . . I'm going soft on her, sir."

"How is this a terrible thing?" he asked.

The housekeeper stiffened. "For a man who knows everything, you don't know anything, do you? Never mind. When this goes the way of a penny novel, I'm not the one that'll be sobbing in a mud puddle over it. You hear me? I'll say I told you so, and then I'm punishing you for the rest of your days for breaking my heart over that dear little lamb!"

He ducked his head, aware that if he smiled at her now he risked his safety. "Yes, Mrs. McFadden."

She growled in frustration and turned to leave. "I'm ringing the bell. I'll be back for the tray when you're done eating. I've a headache, so don't you dare keep her up late!" She closed the door firmly behind her and Darius shook his head.

Helen must have truly charmed her in his absence. He felt a stab of guilt at putting the prickly woman in a position to care, but there was nothing he could say to change things.

Mrs. McFadden doesn't like to risk the hurt because she's tasted the worst before.

And I'm the bigger fool because I know she's right. There is no happy ending for me. Even if I work a miracle and find a way to free her from her husband and restore her to her family or to some version of her former life—I'm that idiot left crying in a mud puddle.

Darius was intelligent enough to know all the signs of danger. He was already smitten. He'd taken pleasure in collecting all the items on Mrs. McFadden's list and added a few things he imagined a lady needed. When he wasn't with Helen, she dominated his thoughts. And when he was with her, for the first time in his life, Darius couldn't think at all.

But all of this self-pity hinges on the stupid notion that any of my actions are for personal gain. I don't need a vicar to point out that failed logic. It's for Helen. Helen's happiness is the only goal. Nothing else matters. I will protect her and see her to safety and then—then I can worry about mud puddles and Mrs. McFadden's feelings and the consequences to her cooking.

"Worst case, I can escape to the Warrens' for baked goods while awaiting forgiveness and—"

The door opened and Helen's appearance interrupted his monologue. She was wearing one of the new dresses he'd picked up for her in town. It was a simple, ready-made thing, but Darius had liked the pale blue print embroidered with tiny flowers. The shopkeeper's wife had convinced him that the ribbon edges were most desirable, and that even a country miss wished to have the "little touches" that made her feel pretty.

But Helen of Troy was no country miss.

In pale blue, she looked like an elegant dream. The cut of it was flattering and the simplicity of the design set off her figure and ensured that it was Helen herself that drew the eye and caught a man's attention. Her hair was up in a wreath of braids and twists, and eyes the color of white opals shone with pleasure.

"You're staring, Mr. Thorne." Helen smiled as she smoothed out the skirts.

"You look lovely." Darius cleared his throat and tried to recover his composure. "The color suits you. I only hope it's not too plain for your taste."

She shook her head and made a turn for him, a timeless and unconscious gesture to demonstrate her happiness and show off her skirts. "Your hidden skills betray you, sir." She faced him shyly and lifted her hem just an inch or two to give him a glimpse of the soft-soled shoes he'd found her.

"Are they more comfortable than riding boots?" he asked.

"Without a doubt!" Helen laughed, dropping her skirts. "But how did you manage it? They fit perfectly!"

Darius shrugged his shoulders and picked up the tray to carry it over to the small table next to the fireplace. "I'm tempted to make some insane claim of superior observation."

She moved to help him, shifting the chessboard over to make sure there was room for their picnic. "Resist temptation and tell me the truth."

He pressed his lips together, weighing it out. "Only if you never tell Mrs. McFadden."

Helen straightened her back, her expression startled. "I'll swear but . . ."

"I was going to borrow your boots after you'd gone to bed and trace the soles onto a paper for the sizing, but I couldn't find them and I certainly couldn't wake Mrs. McFadden to ask for them. So"—Darius lowered his voice conspiratorially—"I retraced events and found a muddy footprint in the stables that I knew wasn't mine or Hamish's. So I measured that and—there you have it!"

"And why can't I tell Mrs. McFadden?"

It was an obscure tangle but Darius did his best to keep Helen out of it. "Because I don't want her to know I was poking about the stables at such an hour. Just—trust me and let's not mention it to her, all right?"

"As you wish." She conceded gracefully and took her seat, allowing him to do the same. "The dinner smells delicious."

"It does, doesn't it?" He settled in across from her. "I'm not sure why, but the farther away you are from the dining room, the better food tastes."

"Does it?" she asked in astonishment.

"Absolutely! I first discovered it when I was in school after sneaking biscuits into bed. They were perfectly ordinary in the dining hall, but when ferreted up in that bedroom, they were ambrosia." He shared the story intending to amuse her but too late realized he may have just confessed to petty theft. *So much for that!*

"This is a theory you've tested often?" she said.

"Yes, I'm afraid so. But it has more to do with the eccentricities of a bachelor than anything else." He pulled one of the rolls apart. "Or an aversion to eating alone at tables that can accommodate eight people."

Isabel's eyes dropped to her plate and she recalled with clarity the ridiculous length of her parents' dining room table and the lack of intimacy and conversation. During her debut Season, she'd been giddy at the swirl of frivolous exchanges and cheerful banter at parties, convinced that there was nothing in the world so wonderful as the noise and distractions of a grand social occasion.

I was starving for all of it and measured my happiness in the number of ruffles on a skirt or the calling cards on a tray. God . . . what an easy slip of a thing for Richard to collect. . . .

"What are you thinking over there?" he asked.

"I'm thinking . . ." Isabel looked up, captured by the sincere concern in his forest green eyes. She was thinking of how she'd come to love the wonderful turns of his mind and how clever he was. But aloud, she was able to say only, "I was thinking I should see if Mrs. McFadden will let us wager a few biscuits on our game tonight. Then the winner can have the pleasure of ferreting them up to their rooms for a midnight snack."

He laughed. "There's a bet I'll take! Although"—he picked up his fork—"now that you know of my criminal past, there's nothing to say that the leader of the Black army might not just steal biscuits on account."

"I'll hold you to your professions of honesty!" she pretended to protest.

The meal unfolded in casual steps and before long they were both laughing at the turns in the easy conversation between them. Without any rush, the plates were set aside and the chess pieces were pulled out of their carved wooden box for another game.

"I warn you"—he sighed—"my soldiers are determined to recover their pride and take the field. I've tried to preach mercy, but . . ."

"I'm not afraid, Mr. Thorne." Isabel meant it as a taunt, but it rang with a clarity that made her breath catch in her chest.

Here. With him. I'm safe.

"Then it's your move, Helen."

She forced herself to study the board and not the beautiful masculine lines of his face and embarrass herself any further. She pushed one of her soldiers out, mentally giving them both an internal lecture on bravery on the field and the advantages of going first.

"Don't look so worried for him," Darius said. "He has an army at his back after all."

She smiled. "I was just thinking of telling him the same thing."

"Good. Because *my* men were about to remind him about the army in *front* of him." Darius made his first move in one confident gesture, matching her strategy as she squeaked in protest.

Once again, the game unfolded, still in a modified teaching rhythm that allowed her to catch her mistakes and learn from every effort that went into the battle. His patience never wavered, and Darius narrated his own choices to help her see how his strategies were formed and how he attempted to anticipate her moves to shape his own.

Isabel clapped her hands in triumph as her forces began

to encroach against his, her eyes locked on the prize of his lonely king.

Only to gasp when suddenly his knights were deep inside her kingdom and her queen was threatened.

"You! How?" she protested, fighting not to pout at the reversal in her fortunes.

He smiled and held up his hands in submission. "Scouts."

"Spies," she amended, eyeing the pieces with suspicion.

"Ambassadors."

"Assassins!" Isabel put her elbows on the table and perched her chin on her palms, surveying the damage. "Look at them! They are hardly innocent sitting there, eating off my best plate and upsetting my courtiers!"

"I assure you they are doing their best to mind the local customs and not frighten the natives."

She lost the battle to stay aloof and found herself pouting. "Well, my queen is determined to remove herself from this mess until her bishops can show your 'ambassadors' back out." She reached for her queen but Darius gently caught her wrist to stop her.

"Be careful, Helen. Don't retreat without thinking it through. See? See what's waiting for you?"

Isabel's heart was pounding so loudly she was sure he could hear it.

But it wasn't from fear.

The world narrowed to the touch of his fingers capturing her hand and the searingly sweet hold that was keeping her queen from harm. It was electric and unexpected, and suddenly all Isabel wanted was more.

She didn't want him to let go. It made no sense. But ever since he'd taken her hand the night before, Isabel had been faced with the illogical truth that, with this man, none of the rules applied. She wanted to be held, to yield control to this man and surrender herself to the consequences of the restless coils of hungry heat that began to unfurl inside her slender frame.

But he misinterpreted the change in her expression and released her.

"Do you see them, Helen?" he asked again, even more gently.

She forced her eyes back to the pieces, struggling at first to identify what he saw. But then she saw it. A black rook was sitting benignly to the side. A black bishop was nonchalantly standing near a small group of weary pawns. Her queen would have stormed off into an ambush.

"I see them."

"Are you all right?" He lowered his chin to look at her over the rim of his glasses, and Isabel smiled.

"I am. But my queen—is in a quandary. She cannot run and she cannot stay. Now what does she do?"

"She makes a new path." He tilted his head to one side to eye the board anew. "Ah! There! She isn't alone. Don't forget those courtiers, Helen. My ambassadors could easily be distracted by one of those rude bishops. Maybe you could talk one of your soldiers into stomping on my toes?"

"The reputation of my court might suffer after all this discourtesy," she offered with a sigh. "But it's good advice."

She leaned back in her chair, easing against the cushions, and found herself staring at the fire instead of her miniature army. "I wonder at all the ambushes I've walked into simply because I wished to be polite or adhere to social courtesies."

"I try to remind myself that not everyone sees the world the way I do," he said. "But I cannot look at everyone as an opponent or an enemy and abandon manners. I want to believe in man's better qualities."

Her attention turned to him, and Isabel made a study of her host and friend. "I don't know what to believe anymore. I don't know if I can trust my own judgment. What if no one is what they seem?"

"Don't mistake secrets for goblins, Helen. Everyone has something they'd rather keep private, but their character shouldn't be too difficult to discern. Not in ordinary circumstances." He reached up to take off his glasses, wiping them off with a handkerchief. "Only villains wear masks."

Only villains wear masks.

Isabel watched him work the delicate spectacles,

marveling at how the deduction of a single element from his face made him look so very different. Without his glasses, he was even more handsome—in a devil-may-care fashion. The firelight struck his features to golden flesh and shadows, a handsome mask that made her wish that there was nothing of secrets between them. He was a hero tipped in darkness and light, and she had to clench her fingers together in her lap to tamp down the desire to reach out and touch his face with the blades of her fingers to make sure that he was real.

"I am—like the queen on the board. I want to run but I . . . I'm afraid I'm going to just rush into a terrible trap. I've already moved without looking."

"In running? In escaping your husband?"

She nodded. "In running. In marrying him. In everything. I've apparently made a habit of it throughout my life, blindly believing that whatever was around the corner would be better. I was a shallow, silly girl that thought of nothing more than invitations and balls and when . . ."

He said nothing, the living essence of patience as she gathered her courage.

At last, she continued. "He was very attentive and flattering. He was handsome and . . . my parents approved of him. My father's title and estates are entailed to a distant male heir, and I think they were relieved to see me well matched. I imagined myself in love because that was the very next natural thing that I should be, after all. I was pampered and convinced that everything in my life would be . . . lovely."

He nodded, his attention unwavering.

Isabel sighed. "I never knew that things could be so ugly, that it could change in a single breath, and that a person could be robbed of the ability to say no."

"You never lost that power, Helen. You did whatever you had to do or told him whatever you needed to say in order to survive. But hear me now, from this moment forward, you possess the power to say no to anything and to anyone." Darius leaned forward, replacing his spectacles, and then deliberately knocked over the black king on the board and yielded the contest. "And there is no ambush here."

She nodded and stood, suddenly too anxious and restless to stay. His company was compelling, but she blamed the length of the day on the unruly turns in her thoughts and inability to focus on the game. "I should retire."

He immediately stood when she did, bumping the table and overturning a few of the pieces. "Of course! It's—I'm exhausted myself."

She started to go but turned at the last. "I wish to ask you something, Mr. Thorne. But it is terribly forward and . . . rude."

"Is it?"

She nodded miserably. "I'm afraid so. But—I have to know."

He smiled. "Then you should ask." He straightened his coat and kept his place by his chair. "There is no question out-of-bounds. My old teacher, Professor Warren, used to say that curiosity is a thing never to squander."

She took a deep breath. "Why are you not married, Mr. Thorne?"

"Ah," he said softly, "*that* question!"

She almost tried to take it back, offer an apology, and assure him that he needn't answer. But Isabel held her ground.

"Why do *you* think I'm not married, Helen?"

"That's not fair. You cannot use the Socratic method and turn this all around!"

He merely smiled at her and folded his arms. "Well?"

"Mrs. McFadden has hinted that it's all to do with your eccentric wish to spend every waking moment in your library and your inability to hear dinner bells."

"Hmm. That sounds promising," he said carefully.

"No, it doesn't! The love of books does not disqualify you as a husband."

His eyes flashed with something, a surge of hope—or heat—or . . . Isabel wasn't sure what it was in the quick betrayal of his expression before he ducked his head to examine the fraying threads on his shirt's cuff.

"I am not married, because I am not married, Helen."

"That hardly tells me why," she whispered.

"No, and I promised you could ask." He sighed and looked up, the vulnerability in his eyes sending a wash of aching raw electricity through her. "Don't mistake secrets for goblins."

"Is it a secret, then?"

He nodded. "It's not that I'm not inclined or interested. It's not that I don't envy my friends who've found their happiness in matrimony. But I'm . . . Marriage is for better men than myself. Let's leave it at that. Please."

Please. He gives me all the power and I'm so clumsy with it that all I can do is hurt him somehow.

"Of course." She turned and left to hurry upstairs without looking back.

The evening was definitely concluded and Darius stayed behind in the library as she retreated up to the sanctuary of her bedroom.

Why are you not married?

One day I'll tell her and be done with it. It's stupid pride that kept me from it tonight. Stupid pride and the hope of a fool trapped in a penny novel—I didn't want her to think less of me.

He had never allowed himself to get too close to anyone, terrified at the thought of becoming that monster he'd grown up with. A priest had told him when he was six that it was a family curse. "Your grandfather was a tyrant and your father . . . It's the way of it. Thorne men are handsome as the devil but known for their quick tempers and quicker fists." *Thorne men.* Even at six, he'd absorbed the worst of the implications.

He was a Thorne man.

That must mean he would grow up and become cruel like his father.

And so he'd set it all aside. All his energies had gone into a pursuit of a life that was not his father's. He'd drowned himself in books and avoided the company of women for fear that if he lost his heart, he'd lose his head as well.

Of all the women in the world, perhaps Helen would understand and respect my desire not to inflict harm.

Or see it as confirmation that all men are secretly base and unworthy.

At the moment, he felt extremely base. Every nerve ending was alert and alive, and there was nothing of pristine chivalry in the thickening weight of his flesh and growing demands of his body in her presence. Realms of intellect abandoned him and Darius sat down at his desk to face the truth.

He was losing ground quickly in his battle to keep her at arm's length.

Damn. I've sworn to protect her, but I never thought to worry about protecting her from me.

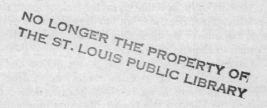

Chapter
8

The next morning, Darius was in his library penning a letter to Ashe about his revelations on the lack of leads amidst the Scottish gem dealers, oblivious to the usual noise of the house until the tone of the bickering drifting up from the kitchen seemed to change.

Darius stopped what he was doing and cocked his head to one side, listening to a new undertone of upset in their banter. With a sigh, he pushed back from his desk and headed toward the back of the house, his pace increasing at the sound of a scream followed by a great crash of metal and china against the floor.

Darius threw open the door only to freeze at the sight of Hamish laid out on the flagstones next to an overturned worktable, with Helen standing over him in tears, holding a cast-iron skillet upraised as if to strike him again. Mrs. McFadden was frozen with her apron held up to cover her mouth, her eyes wide with surprise.

Helen dropped the skillet and the jarring sound of it

hitting the stone floor made poor Hamish groan and sit up. "I'm . . . so sorry," Helen whispered.

"What happened?" Darius asked.

Mrs. McFadden looked as miserable as any creature he'd ever seen. "I . . . I . . ."

Hamish reached up to cradle his skull. "It's a goose egg but I'll survive."

Darius tried again. "What happened?"

It was Hamish who finally answered. "I found out your housekeeper's first name and . . . got clouted for it."

"Truly?" Darius asked, struggling not to smile.

"Here's a hint." Hamish moaned after running his hands through his hair. "It isna' Mary."

Mrs. McFadden nodded, her cheeks patchy with splotches of red betraying her embarrassment. "Margarida is hardly a good Scottish name, sir. My mother heard it from a Spanish gypsy and took a fanciful liking to it. I confess I've always been a bit sensitive over the matter and might have made a bit of a squawk. I believe madam thought to come to my rescue. . . ."

"A bit of a squawk?" Hamish scoffed. "Ye came at me like a Morrígan with that tongue of yours, you banshee!"

Mrs. McFadden crossed her arms defensively. "You *laughed* at me, you insensitive boor!"

"Well, here." Darius stepped forward to help the man to his feet. "Let's get you off the floor and get a cold cloth for your head."

"I'm so sorry, Mr. MacQueen!" Helen said as she offered him a cold, wet rag, her hands shaking badly. "I can't believe—I am truly very sorry, sir!"

The housekeeper took the cloth from her, folding it over expertly and stepping in. "Don't apologize to the brute, madam. It's his own fault and—mine. I should mind my temper. Here, I have him in hand. Why don't you take a glass of sherry in the library and I'll be in with some pies in a bit."

"Yes, a truce." He held out his arm to Helen. "Come,

Helen, let's leave them to patch things up. Mrs. McFadden can manage from here."

Helen meekly ducked her head and took his arm, allowing him to escort her from the kitchen. As far as Darius could tell, the sanctuary of his library had never been a more welcome sight. He showed her to a chair by the fireplace and then retrieved the sherry. He filled a small crystal glass with a generous pour and then knelt at her feet with his offering. "Here."

She took the glass, and Darius's stomach clenched at the fear in her eyes. "You have every right to be angry, Mr. Thorne."

"But I'm not angry."

"How is that possible? I hit Mr. MacQueen with an iron skillet and nearly killed the man."

Darius lost the battle not to give in to the strange mischief of circumstances and the comedy of his household. "Helen," he started, but had to stop as his merriment overtook him. Darius took the chair across from her as he laughed out loud. At last, he sobered enough to speak. "Anyone with sense would applaud your actions."

"Why?"

"Because you were being so brave." He watched her closely. "You didn't know that Hamish wasn't truly a threat, and yet you leapt into the fray and acted on Mrs. McFadden's behalf."

"I heard her screeching and then when . . ." Her blue eyes misted at the memory. "He—he called her a *witch* and was grabbing her arm . . . and I . . . made a fool of myself."

"Ah yes, a witch. I think it's a term of endearment in this instance. In return, she often calls him an idiot and something in Gaelic that I cannot translate in good conscience, but let's just say it's related to his profession and a certain fondness for cattle." Darius smiled. "But they're not enemies and Hamish would throw himself in front of a firing squad before he'd see a single hair harmed on her head. He adores her."

"Really?" she asked. "I didn't have that impression at all!"

"It's easy to misjudge that pair."

"Is he all right?"

"He'll live. It's just a small knot, and by the attention he's getting from Mrs. McFadden, I'm sure he'll thank you for it once his ears stop ringing."

"She *shares* his sentiments?" Helen asked, her expression rapt and serious as she wiped away her tears.

Darius nodded. "I knew it after I watched her one morning preparing a breakfast tray for the man after he'd taken ill. She drizzled honey on his porridge in the shape of a flower and strained his broth with the best linen—*twice*." He sighed, a touch of envy coloring his thoughts.

"But they are so cruel to each other. Is . . . all love . . . unkind?"

Darius's heart grew heavy as he realized the direction of her thoughts. "No. Never at its core should love be anything less than kind. It is the highest ideal for a reason, Helen. Their words are a false show. It's in our actions that we demonstrate our true nature."

"The honey flower in his porridge?"

"And a hundred other small gestures between them. I have a friend who is a zoologist, and after reading some of his works, I swear watching my housekeeper and my driver is like watching the courtship of porcupines." Darius smiled. "It's a prickly business but it suits them."

"So sweet," she exclaimed softly.

"When you—meet the right person one day, you'll know them by their actions. Your instincts will never betray you."

"Have you ever been in love, Mr. Thorne?" she asked.

He looked back at the tips of his shoes. It was such a simple question and the answer should have been readily given. But how could he say no without sounding like a heartless bastard? How could he reveal his worst fears and greatest hopes without letting her see how much he already stood to lose in her eyes?

Before he could compose an answer, she spoke again. "Pardon me, it is none of my concern and an impertinent question. Especially after last night. I promised you to leave the matter alone."

"It was another good question. It's the answer that would be imperfect." Darius leaned back against the cushions. He shook his head, shifting forward in his chair. "If you'd rather have tea or cider, I can get it for you. You haven't touched your sherry."

"No, please." Isabel sipped her sherry, politely watching the fire. When she'd heard Mrs. McFadden's screams, she'd been transported into a black panic where there'd been no room for logic. She'd simply taken action and grabbed the first weapon she could seize to save her friend—and when Mr. MacQueen had fallen into the table, it had been the worst catastrophe.

Because only then had reason returned in a miserable avalanche, and logic was an unforgiving mistress. Common courtesy dictated that a lady didn't overreact and murder her host's driver in the kitchens, no matter what!

Darius had said the two cared for each other, but the incident only further undermined her confidence in her ability to judge the character of others. She'd been so blind to her husband's true nature, so fooled by his civil courtship that it made her question everything—her instincts, her intelligence, even her sanity.

He stood to restore the decanter to the side table and she stood as well, wandering over to his desk. "The battle interrupted your work?"

"I'm pleased it did."

She eyed some of his notes, admiring the neat, firm lines of his handwriting and the graceful curves of his drawings.

"May I help you with it?" she asked. "I am very organized and have a fair mind. My tutors always praised my ability to master new skills very quickly. Perhaps—I could help organize your papers? Or . . ."

His expression was uncertain. "It's such a strange business. I don't wish to be indiscreet but—"

"Before you answer, I should admit that if I'm forced to

sit and stare at the walls of my bedroom all day, I might run mad, Mr. Thorne. It's . . . difficult to feel so useless as the hours pass and with nothing to do but think. . . ." She squared her shoulders. "Instead of being a charity case, I might act as your secretary, Mr. Thorne."

"My secretary?"

"Please. I know it is a forward suggestion but I'm not welcome in the kitchen, and after today, I don't think I have the nerve to offer, and cannot really leave the house. You said I wasn't a prisoner, Mr. Thorne, but I am very much confined."

"Then it would be unfeeling not to employ you." Darius squared his own shoulders to mirror her businesslike demeanor. "Helen, you've put your life in my hands, and if you helped me, you'd be returning the favor. My life and the safety of my friends might be in yours."

Isabel looked at him warily. "Are you deliberately being dramatic, Mr. Thorne?"

He shook his head. "I wish I were. I'd always prided myself on my ability to solve puzzles, but I think I've looked at this too long—or I'm living it and I'm too close to see the clues."

"Then, I could assist you. While I'm here." Isabel prayed she didn't sound as desperate to him as she seemed to herself. But if he could lose himself in his work, then perhaps she could learn the trick as well. She longed for a distraction.

"Very well. I'll trust myself to your discretion."

He sat Isabel at his desk and Darius began to lay out maps and drawings to underline his tale. He spoke to her as an equal and a trusted ally, revealing what little information he had in a puzzle that threatened the lives of the Jaded. Before long, Isabel was swept away in the dangerous world of sacred treasures, a mysterious character his friends had named the Jackal, lost Indian temples, and agents of the East India Trading Company, and for the rest of the day, she gave not a single thought to the "trifling business" of abusive husbands.

Chapter
9

The next morning, Mrs. McFadden came into her room with a pile of fresh bed linens. "Mr. MacQueen is recovered, madam."

Isabel turned from the wardrobe, where she'd been assessing all of Darius's purchases and admiring the joys of simple fashion. It was a brisk announcement, and after learning of the housekeeper's secret affinities for the driver, Isabel wasn't sure what to say in response. "I'm so relieved to hear it. Is he—quite angry with me?"

"Pah!" The housekeeper moved to strip off the sheets from the bed. "Not a whit! He was all spit and fire in my direction but I've got it managed."

Isabel blushed as she tried not to imagine the details. She fingered an ivory day dress before taking it down. "Well, I should apologize to him for the injury."

"Don't you *dare* apologize to that cretin! Laughing at my Christian name! He deserved what he got and worse if you ask me."

She stepped up to the bed. "Can I help you with that, Mrs. McFadden?"

"No!" the housekeeper replied. "You're a lamb to offer, but I'm not taking advantage of a guest and treating you like a scullery maid."

Isabel didn't want to argue with her, but helping to make a bed certainly didn't feel beyond the pale in light of her circumstance. She moved out of the way and tried to make a bit of conversation. "I think you have a lovely name, Mrs. McFadden."

The woman dropped the sheets as if she'd touched a hot coal. "It's a name suited to the theatre! And you mustn't—you're too kind!" She went back to the chore, her expression wavering between an awkward gentle sincerity and her usual grim determination. "It's a rustic house, isn't it? But I don't want to see you suffering for it. I know it's hard to make your way. But Mr. Thorne's made a vow to see you safe and away from whatever troubles you have. You'll see. He'll find a way to get you back to your family and your servants and everything you're missing."

Isabel shook her head. She wasn't missing any of it, and no matter how Mrs. McFadden worried over the rustic state of the country house, Isabel knew better. "I'm not suffering at a lack of servants. I've wanted for nothing since I arrived. Mr. Thorne is . . ." She hesitated, wary of giving voice to her feelings. "Most attentive."

Mr. Thorne is a dream, and when I look at him, I almost feel like my old self before Richard—I want to flirt and talk of little things and laugh and please him.

"Might be. If it's all to do with chess or books, I imagine he perks right up." The housekeeper turned the pillows. "I leave him to himself most often. He's not a hermit but he aspires to it."

"I'm to help him with his research. He was kind enough to allow it." Isabel lifted one of the sleeves of the dress, fidgeting with the cuff. "I find it fascinating."

I find him fascinating.

Mrs. McFadden's hands fisted at her hips as she surveyed the finished bed. "It's good to keep your mind occupied while you heal. You'll get no arguments from me, but—mind his toes."

"Pardon?"

"That's what my mother used to say when my brothers were too rough or my sister was more set on her nose than on where she'd lost her knitting." Mrs. McFadden continued as she gathered up the dirty linens from the floor where she'd dropped them. "At the end of the day, he's a lonely man no matter what he says about it, and you're—well, you're as you know."

Isabel's confusion grew. "I'm . . ."

"Very sweet, extremely pretty, and quite married."

"I am—not a child to be reminded of that last. I am a grown woman of nineteen, I'll have you know!"

"Nineteen?" The housekeeper looked at her with one thin eyebrow arched. "Still young yet though, wouldn't you say?"

"Yes, of course." The direction of the conversation became instantly clear. "Mr. Thorne has been very proper in his behavior."

"Of course he has!" the housekeeper replied, her expression mortified. "He wouldn't be otherwise! That man! That man would politely open the door for the devil if asked!"

"I—I am hardly the devil in this, am I?"

Mrs. McFadden's humor returned and she threw off some of her gruff posturing to take a seat on the bed. "You're an angel. It's ridiculous, but here we are. I only meant to say, it's exactly because he's who he is that you'll keep him at a distance and mind his toes, won't you?"

This is like having a conversation in a Gordian knot.

"All this talk of angels and devils is . . ." Isabel was at a loss for words. "I will mind his toes."

"That's a girl!" She sighed. "It's good for him to have company, don't misunderstand. I just feel better having spoken my mind on the matter. After all, he's not some blue blood like you're used to, and I was hoping you'd allow for it if he wasn't all polish and posh. I'm fond of him, as employers go, and I don't wish to see him crushed. His sort probably wouldn't have been allowed to walk in your father's front door and he knows it."

"I'm—sure that's not the case! Mr. Thorne is as true a gentleman as any and would be welcome in any house, no matter what his connections." It was a hollow protest but a sincere one. "There is nothing to object to."

Mrs. McFadden crossed her arms defensively. "Maybe so. But better to know the way of things than let a man hope." She stood up and took the dress from Isabel's hands. "Here, let me help you with this, madam. He's downstairs in the library if you're to help him today."

* * *

"Your housekeeper is—impossible!" Isabel said without a formal greeting as she entered the study. "One minute, I swear she's urging me to be kinder to you, and the next, I think she is worried that I am . . . capable of some great harm."

"She is a contrarian by nature." He stepped away from the windows with a steaming mug of tea in his hands, smiling at her appearance. "I think she's torn between an urge to chaperone us and a distinct desire to see me enjoying anything vaguely resembling a social life."

"You are *not* a hermit!" Isabel said, amazed at how close she'd come to stomping her foot. "I mean . . ." Isabel let out a long breath to settle her nerves. "Do you aspire to be a hermit, Mr. Thorne?"

"I've given it up," he said with an expression wrought with humor. "But please don't tell my friends."

"Your secrets are safe with me." She crossed her arms, her pride still smarting.

"I will speak to Mrs. McFadden. She has no right to lecture and fuss as she does, and I won't have her upsetting you." Darius set his tea down on the desk. "Would you like a cup before we begin?"

"Yes, please." She let go of her own elbows with a sigh. "But don't—say anything to her. It's not worth the stir and fuss."

He went over to the sideboard and poured her a large, steaming cup into a ceramic mug. He added milk and sugar out of habit, then looked up at her apologetically. "Milk and sugar, Helen?"

"Yes, please."

He laughed in relief and held out the mug to her. "I guessed rightly, then."

"Your instincts are uncanny, Mr. Thorne." Isabel took the warm mug, cheered in his presence. "Thank you."

There was nothing in his manner that bespoke overt seduction, but everything about him awoke her senses. His tousled brown hair invited her hands to push it back from his eyes. The strong lines of his body and the enticing juncture of his throat and shoulders made Isabel's imagination race in a direction she was certain led to ruin.

I just want to curl up against him and bury my nose in his neck, inhale the scent of his heat, and banish the world. What kind of woman have I become that adultery could ever have such a wicked appeal?

"—started?" he asked.

Isabel nearly dropped her mug as she realized that she'd been lost in a strange tangle of erotic fantasies involving her host. *This is ridiculous!* "I apologize, what was that?"

"I merely asked if you were ready to get started." He stepped back to the large desk at the room's center. "I pulled a few older notebooks I'd made when we first became aware that there might be some danger. In London, an Indian assassin with a knife went after a friend, and then another man with ties to the East India Trading Company made an additional threat, and we first heard something about a special object or sacred piece we'd taken with us. I starting writing down everything I could remember to see if it helped."

"Has it?"

He shook his head slowly. "Not yet. I've stared at these pages a thousand times and I don't think I'm reading them anymore. But you have fresh eyes, Helen."

She blushed and followed him to survey the materials he'd collected. Isabel picked up one sheet with a language in the margins she didn't recognize. "Decidedly British eyes, I'm afraid."

"Here," he said as he pulled out a large leather chair for her and helped her settle in at the desk. "I am grateful for those British eyes. Anything that isn't in English, I can translate readily enough for you."

"Can you?" She looked up at him in astonishment. "I mean—of course you can. I am . . . embarrassed to think that I barely muddled through a few French lessons and those only because my mother was convinced that a lady without any French isn't a proper lady at all."

His eyes flashed quickly with an emotion she couldn't identify. He stepped away from desk, shielding himself from her gaze as he busied himself with reordering a pile of books on a side table.

They worked quietly for only an hour or two, with Darius ending up on the window seat with a sketchbook and Isabel commanding a post at his desk. Time passed quickly for her as she scanned the strange notes and drawings, circled texts, and odd maps he'd collected. She was fascinated by all of it and drawn in to the allure of learning how his mind worked. Isabel turned one of the pages sideways to decipher yet another of his handwritten notes. "Mr. Thorne? Did you see this about a mask?"

Darius looked up from his book. "Mask? That doesn't sound familiar." He closed his pages and unfolded from the cushions. "Mask as in part of a ritual?"

"No, here. Does this mean your treasure is wearing a mask or that it *is* a mask?" Isabel laid the page back down on the desk next to a similar sheet from one of his first notebooks.

"Masks?" Darius shook his head slowly and crossed the room to take a look. "Where does it say masks?"

"Here," she said, pointing to the paper. "Well, that's what your translation says, does it not?"

He studied it for a moment. "That's odd. Of course, if it is a religious figurine . . . It has long been my theory that a sacred object would have to portray a local god."

"A deity wearing a mask?" she asked.

"Hmm, a god or goddess in disguise? As in the Greek and Celtic traditions?" he said quietly. "Where did I put that list of Hindu deities? Although it's still a dead end. We have no figurines in any of our caches and proving a negative to an enemy has been a bit of a challenge."

"Must it be a figurine?" she asked. "What of this?" Isabel opened an earmarked book and pointed to the text, standing to hand it to him. "Your handwriting is wretched, Mr. Thorne, but see where you wrote about Father Pasqual's accounts?"

Darius took the book from her hands and read the passage she'd indicated. "The priest said 'that a myth of demons gives a righteous man pause, but I give no weight to my host's claims that a mystic diamond in disguise has power.' " Dariu's brow furrowed as he read the priest's next quote. "Pasqual added, 'What foolishness to worship shiny paste!' "

"A mystic diamond in disguise," she repeated. "Was he not traveling in western Bengal, sir?"

"Damn," Darius whispered, then looked up in apologetic shock. "I'm sorry, Helen. I have the manners of a tinker. But how did I miss that? How could I have missed that?"

Isabel smiled, a woman triumphant. "Fresh eyes, Mr. Thorne!"

"How do you disguise a diamond?"

"By changing its color?" she asked. "Don't they heat some stones to change their color and make them look more valuable? Can you create the opposite effect with some kind of treatment to make a gem look dirty or . . . worthless?"

"Shiny paste . . ." Darius's eyes lit with inspiration, a man transformed. "Then it *could* be a stone! No matter what else—it *is* possible any one of us could have it in our pockets! It's not a figurine or a carving, and I've wasted far too long trying to prove that it had to be so that we would be innocent of its possession and better off! But"—he seized her hands in his—"we really *did* take a sacred treasure."

"You really did." Isabel echoed his words, caught up in the euphoria that flooded his face, and breathless as the heat of his hands warmed hers instantly.

"You're brilliant, Helen!" He pulled her into his arms with a laugh, for a clumsy and impromptu waltz around the library. His joy was contagious and Isabel laughed as well, giddy by the speed of the turns. It was a heady celebration that instantly taught her two things. First, that it was an amazing thing to be in Darius Thorne's arms with one of his hands splayed against her back and the other cradling her bare fingers in his, her face scant inches from his and the strength of his frame and broad shoulders wreaking havoc on her senses. And secondly, that Darius Thorne couldn't dance.

She laughed at the uneven rhythm of his steps, throwing her head back to revel in the dizzy tilt of the experience, and found herself looking directly up into his eyes.

Here. This is joy. Oh my. And I never thought to see it again.

He was humming a popular tune, the impromptu serenade making the moment even sweeter, and then something changed. The ache of her memories gave way to an awareness and acceptance of a new longing that pressed forward so quickly it took her breath away. Her laughter slowed along with his clumsy steps and Isabel had a few seconds to pray.

Please, Darius.

Kiss me and make me feel human again.

He stood looking down at her, his breath coming a little faster because of the exertion of their waltz, and then as if he'd heard her speak her wants aloud, he slowly lowered his face to hers. The descent was so gradual and polite, his expression an odd blend of fierce desire and caution, as if he were waiting for her to protest or step from his hold—even as his own hunger drove him to action.

Isabel held as still as a bird, her face tipped up to his to welcome his touch.

His breath mingled with hers and a tickle of anticipation sparked out across her limbs. She could hear her own heart roaring in her ears and wondered if he could hear it, too.

And then his lips grazed hers, as light as silk but so warm she gasped, an arc of delicious electricity skipping out across her skin, making her blush. Darius's touch redefined the act, and her soul surged with relief. His arms tightened around her, pressing her against him as the kiss changed from tentative contact to a feast of sensations as Darius took command. He kissed her harder, a moan escaping his lips that made her hips buck and spasm in response. She clung to him to maintain her balance, and her lips parted naturally to taste his, inviting him to do the same.

I'm no maiden, God help me. But this—this is new.

Richard had never kissed her like this. He'd never been tender, using his teeth until she'd feared his mouth as much as she'd dreaded his fists.

Darius's tongue teased the plump curve of her lower lip and Isabel trembled. Without thinking, she did the same to him and was instantly rewarded with a flurry of searing white-hot kisses that defied description. One kiss tumbled into another until she couldn't tell where one ended and the next began, only that she didn't want it to stop. The world dropped away and everything she knew of the workings of men and women was dashed into nonsense.

Shame fell away and Isabel leaned into him, eager, willing, hungry for more.

Isabel arched her back and was rewarded as he cradled her against his chest, but Darius lifted his face, a man fighting for air and composure.

"We can't . . ." he whispered. "*I* can't do this."

Isabel pushed against his chest, instantly freed to stand before him.

"I'm . . ." She stepped back to touch her lips, swollen and soft from his kisses, her cheeks blazing with a heat not entirely inspired by embarrassment. "I should—leave you to your—"

"I'm so stupid, Helen. That was—"

The front bell rang and both of them instantly froze.

"Helen, perhaps you should return to your room until I see who this is."

Terror made her agreement total. The kiss was momentarily forgotten. She fled without a single argument, moving as quickly and quietly as she could to regain the safety of her bedroom before the unknown and unexpected visitor was sorted out.

Once she had the illusion of the security of a locked bedroom door at her back, she marveled once again at the speed with which a person's life could change. He'd kissed her and a universe of longing and passion had opened up like a flower as effortlessly as any bloom. But before she could absorb what it meant, she was cowering in her room waiting for some ominous summons that would drag her back to her husband's cruel keeping.

It was a ridiculous impulse but her imagination immediately began painting a scene where her husband was standing at the gate downstairs with the constable demanding her return. He'd have brought his man with him and the carriage would be standing in the lane.

I won't survive the ride home. I don't think I can survive any of it again.

She sank down on the floor, her head tipped back against the door. Muffled male voices below did nothing to soothe her nerves.

I'll go mad.

She clamped a hand over her own mouth to keep from keening like a wild animal as the fear began to overtake her reason.

It's him.

He's come.

Tears flowed down her cheeks and she began to shake with the agony of her emotions. Every gain was stripped from her hands at the specter of pain awaiting her and the punishments her husband had always promised if she should ever dare to try to step beyond his reach.

The urge to run was so overwhelming, she lost her battle for control and cried out.

Can't. Can't reach the stables past them if they are downstairs. He'll have put a man into the stables and found Samson. Proof that I am here. No escape.

When her eyes fell on the window, she sobbed again.

Steps approached and the doorknob turned above her

head, the metal catching on the lock before it rattled back into place.

I'll jump. There's a window.

If it's him. If they've come, I'll just throw myself out headfirst onto the flagstones below and—

* * *

"Helen?"

Darius knelt in the hallway and spoke to her softly through the door. His heart was pounding but he made a conscious effort to sound almost nonchalant—as if the rending cries he could hear through the wooden door weren't tearing him to pieces.

"All is well. Helen, it was a messenger. A hired runner from a business I have dealings with in Edinburgh. Nothing to do with—there's no danger."

The sounds paused and Darius took heart.

Please, God.

"N-no danger?"

He could barely hear her but he could taste his own relief. "Not a sliver. It's probably just a lovely new piece of information for our puzzle, Helen."

He waited patiently, listening intently as she gathered herself on the other side of the door. The rustling of her skirts and the creak of the floorboards as she stood comforted him, and Darius mirrored her movements by getting on his own feet.

"No wooden horses, I promise," he added softly.

At last, the door's bolt was thrown back and she opened the door to face him, the confidence and humor she'd displayed throughout the day gone. Her beautiful face was ravaged with tears and her eyes didn't meet his.

"I'm a stupid child, yet again, Mr. Thorne." Her voice broke. "One ring at the front door and I'm . . . as you see."

"It was unexpected. It's only natural to feel fear, Helen. You are *not* a stupid child. You mustn't say such things." His palms itched to touch her again, to smooth away the tears from her pale cheeks. And then he wasn't thinking about restraint. It was her misery alone that could not be allowed to stand. Darius gently put a finger underneath her chin and lifted her face until her pale blue eyes fluttered open to look into his. "You are gloriously brave."

Her lips parted in a sigh, and every apology he'd meant to make for kissing her in the library was forgotten.

It was insanity to touch her again. But it didn't feel sane to stop himself.

Darius pulled her into his arms and affirmed that whatever had begun impulsively in the library was no illusion. His desire for her flared so quickly it was painful and made his heart twist into a knot of molten fire inside his chest. She was so sweet and eager against him, each kiss trailing naturally into the next, and he was ensnared by a tender lust for her that stripped him of intellect.

He had never kissed a woman before, never envisioned that such a simple act could hold such power. But there was more to it than flesh pressing flesh, and he was humbled at his own ignorance.

She was quicksilver in his arms, and every shockingly soft texture of her mouth pulled him into a spiral of need that made his body tighten and pulse. His arousal was immediate and the sensation of hot sand trickling down his spine and weighting his cock was so overwhelming he nearly cried out.

Experienced or not, his body didn't seem to be paying attention to anything his mind was advising of caution and restraint.

Which shook him to his core.

A lifetime of discipline, lost in the span of seconds.

Lost to Helen of Troy.

Damn. Here's a merry disaster of my own making. . . .

The sound of Mrs. McFadden's steps on the stairs ended it. He released her in a guilty rush, shifting his stance to shield Helen from view and praying the dim hall would keep his housekeeper from noticing the embarrassing way his pants were stretched taut.

"Is there a lunch, then, Mrs. McFadden?" he asked briskly.

"Of course there's lunch! I was going to bring it to the library and then noticed everyone had strangely scattered!" The housekeeper pursed her lips and gave him a searing look of suspicion. "What are you doing in madam's doorway this time of day?"

But before he could answer, Mrs. McFadden's eyes widened in alarm. "Is she unwell? Is everything all right?"

"I am fine," Helen answered as she peeked out from behind Darius's frame. "The bell upset me and Mr. Thorne came up to make sure that I was all right."

Mrs. McFadden's sober look was daunting. "I see. How are his toes?"

Darius squinted in incomprehension. "What?"

Helen's squeak of unhappiness only added to his confusion. "I'm . . . I shall eat in my room."

Damn it. I'm not apologizing with Mrs. McFadden standing there, and I'll be damned but I think I just missed a critical step—perhaps it's for the best!

"I'll be downstairs." Darius retreated without looking back, cursing himself for trespassing twice in a span of minutes and discovering that he was a man without control of any kind when it came to Helen. He'd dropped his guard in the library and sampled joy that had turned his entire world around more than once. Ashe had joked in India about getting drunk on a woman's kiss, and Darius had chalked it up to pure exaggeration and laughed.

He wasn't laughing now.

Touching Helen was a dream. Without warning, every cell in his body felt parched and Helen was cold, clear water. This was a longing so powerful and unexpected it made his knees shake. All the clichéd phrases he'd once dismissed about a man being *lovesick* or *swept away* came back to him in a symphony of internal mockery.

A few kisses and Darius was accepting that the deliberate gaps in his education had come back to haunt him and might be his undoing.

Perhaps if I'd dabbled a bit like Ashe, I'd be more immune. But it's too late to lament my choices now.

He drove his hands into his coat pockets and found the note. He'd completely forgotten it in his concern for Helen and gripped it like a lifeline now. "Back to work, Thorne."

At his desk, he examined the sealed note that the messenger had brought. He'd generously paid the boy, amazed that Mr. Masters would go to such trouble to send word. "Probably just in search of another gem or two and seeking a sale," he muttered, breaking the wax and forcing himself not to think about kissing Helen as he settled in to his desk to read.

Mr. Thorne,

As we did not see you this last Tuesday as usual, I was unable to pass along the following as I'd intended. From your many steady inquiries, I had begun to feel a sense of regret that I have never been of any assistance in your quest. But in the week prior, a startling bit of business came to my attention.

A foreign gentleman of Indian origins, wearing a turban, of all things, approached my son and asked to speak to me privately. I agreed in shock and will admit to a certain amount of curiosity. For he was very mysterious. He said that he knew of a sacred treasure in English hands. He said that I should warn its keepers not to trade or sell it. He said it was cursed.

"Sacred treasure" were your very words and so I took note if not credence to his statements.

He said that while it was distasteful to think of the treasure in English hands, some holy man of his region had prophesied that it would leave Bengal for a faraway land where it would fulfill its destiny. Then there was a bit about a deadly threat if the wrong hands touched it, and it was all I could do to nod before the fellow left! I assume he is making the rounds to several shops with his warning but I cannot say for certain.

Rubbish, I know.

*I had sworn to pass along anything I learned as expedi-
ently as possible. And as you were looking to acquire an
artifact, or sell it—it seems the turbaned gentleman was
warning against the attempt in either case.*

It is a tangle.

*All nonsense aside, I have had several inquiries for
another ruby of equal quality to the one you sold us last
year, so please keep in mind our honorable efforts to demonstrate our interest and support of your business (even in
the passing on of useless gossip from exotic characters)
and advise if you have any such stones on hand for sale.*

> *Yours sincerely,*
> *Walter S. Masters, Esq.*

"Damn it," Darius exclaimed and read the letter through
three times before the buzz inside his head quieted. He would
have to compose an apology to Helen later. He stood quickly,
crammed the letter inside his pocket, selected one of his
notebooks, and walked out of the room with long, hurried
strides. "Hamish! We're to Edinburgh!" He raised his voice
to make sure it carried up the stairs. "Mrs. McFadden! I'm
off to the city! Please see to Helen! I'll be home after
nightfall!"

He didn't wait for replies, swept up in the maelstrom of
the mystery that had haunted the Jaded for months. He
grabbed a winter coat and let the door close behind him to
make his way across the muddy yard to the stables to collect
Hamish for the dash to the city. He had to hear the entire
story directly from Masters and make sure that whatever
plans his friends were making in London weren't about to
set the worst in motion.

*That assassin—the first one—that attacked Galen all
those months ago! He spoke Hindi. Is it possible there are
two factions on our heels? Are we in the middle of something
bigger than ourselves?*

After weeks of careful thought and soul-grindingly slow

progress, Darius had the sinking feeling that time had just become a luxury he couldn't afford.

"See that?" Mrs. McFadden tapped her foot as she stood breathlessly in the front hall after a failed attempt to catch Darius before the carriage raced from the yard. "Forgot his hat and scarf. Let's pray the weather doesn't turn on him for it!"

Isabel could only nod mutely.

Mind his toes.

And let him go.

Chapter
10

At the breakfast table the next morning, Darius poured himself a strong cup of coffee. He was bone tired from his unexpected jaunt into Edinburgh, but it had been worth every grueling mile on muddy, icy roads. He was at once eager to share what he'd learned with Helen and dreading facing her after yesterday's intimate exchanges and his awkward departure.

She has every right to be furious if—

"You didn't return until well after midnight," she said softly from the doorway, a vision in a soft yellow day dress.

"Did I awaken you, then?" he asked, standing as she came in and pulling out her chair. "I tried to enter as quietly as I could."

She shook her head. "Burglars would have envied your skills, Mr. Thorne, but I was so anxious for your safety on the dark roads. . . . Mrs. McFadden felt compelled to bring up the threat of brigands and highwaymen more than once, and I lost the ability to sleep."

He smiled and returned to his seat across from her. "She's thinking of Hamish, then. I'll get an earful later for exposing him to the criminal elements."

"It was all to do with the note you received?" she asked.

He nodded and pulled the rumpled paper from his pocket. "It's a bit worse for wear but here is the original note."

She read it quickly. "Cursed? So now we must not only figure out which stone it is but . . . there is a curse of some kind?"

He shrugged. "I'm not exactly a believer, but clearly there is a player on the board who is. I questioned Mr. Masters more thoroughly and was able to get a better grasp of the story. Apparently, someone is making a distinction about who should have it, according to that prophecy, and I fear that my friends and I are the default *keepers* in this scenario."

"And the nature of the curse?"

"If we hand it over, and this is a direct quote, according to Mr. Masters, 'to the invading snakes and the Black Dog of the East India Trading Company,' all lives are forfeit." He picked up another muffin from the tray. "It's a wrinkle."

"And if you keep it?" she asked, beginning to fill her own plate.

"No blood will be shed." Darius held out the coffeepot. "Care for some?"

She shook her head. "So the mystery takes a turn. You have to keep it—whichever one it is."

He sighed. "Whatever or whichever one it is. We are back to square one. Except I'll need to go to London at some point. I only have my gemstones and we'll probably need to look at everyone's very carefully to make a proper assessment. I think pearls and opals are the least likely candidates due to their delicate nature and distinct essence." He ran a hand through his hair. "But I've already sold a few other stones on my friends' behalves, rubies and emeralds. It could be a diamond dyed to red or green and I only hope I haven't botched it already and passed the thing off. It's a stupid mess, isn't it?"

"It's worse than that. If you follow this myth's instructions, you have to keep your treasure. But—is not there some threat from the Company's agent for you to turn this item over? Wasn't that why we were trying to ascertain its appearance? So that you could satisfy this man and save your friends?"

"We might be between the proverbial rock and the hard place," he admitted. "The problem is that in Ashe's last letter, he wrote that they weren't going to wait much longer. I'm worried that they've cooked up a plan in London to try to move things along."

"Oh!" she gasped. "But they can't!"

"I'll compose a letter this morning to send by courier to Rutherford and put an end to it." He added more hot coffee to his own cup and set it down. "It is pressing but I've caught it in time so I don't want you to be anxious. Michael won't let them rush headlong into anything. He'll keep Blackwell in check."

"My goodness." Helen set down her fork. "We haven't even had time to come up with a test for our first theory about one of the stones being dyed or colored in some way. How in the world do you test a stone for its magical properties? Are you going to seek out some mystic textbook on the subject?"

"Rowan is the nearest thing we have to a scientist. I'll send a letter to Dr. West and delegate the task." Darius smiled. "I only wish I could be there to see his face when he reads it."

"You miss your friends." It wasn't a question but the care reflected in her eyes made him ache inside.

What would it be like to have a woman look at you like that, all the time? To fuss over each setback or smile at every glimmer of progress?

Damn it, why do I keep torturing myself by even asking such things?

"I do. They are family to me." He studied her for a moment. "Do you miss anyone?"

She shook her head. "No, which makes me sad. All those friends and acquaintances of my first two social Seasons vanished like so many ghosts, and I cannot say if anyone ever bothered to correspond after the wedding. Perhaps they did, but my husband never allowed me letters. As for my parents, all I can think of is the relief on my father's face and my mother's indifference once I'd made my debut."

"Well"—he tried to lighten the mood—"if you wish to aspire to being a hermit, I warn you, it has its drawbacks."

"Really?"

"For one, the conversations you have with yourself can be very one-sided." He took a sip from his cup, savoring the bitter warmth before setting it down.

"Ah, but I would win every argument," she countered mischievously.

"Helen," he said, pushing aside his plate. "I should apologize for yesterday. It was the worst betrayal of your trust. You are a married woman and I never—"

"Wait! I was the one who . . . I did nothing to protest what happened in the library. I encouraged you, Mr. Thorne. You cannot take *all* the blame."

"P-perhaps but I don't think that holds true for that second kiss in your bedroom doorway." He sighed.

"Then we are even," she said, surprising him at the defiant tilt of her chin. "I'm not—apologizing for my part. I won't."

Darius was stunned into silence. "I wouldn't have expected *you* to apologize. I thought it was generally the gentleman who took responsibility for any—"

"No." Helen stood from the table and stamped one of her slippered feet in frustration.

Darius had to bite the inside of his cheek to keep from smiling at the unexpected little flash of temper in her eyes as he also rose from his chair. "No?"

"I'm tired of moving blindly from one square to another or allowing someone else to decide my fate, Mr. Thorne. I—I wanted you to kiss me. I am . . ." She took a deep breath. "I am not helpless."

"I didn't mean to imply that you were." Darius forced himself to regain a bit of perspective. No matter how appealing, it was up to him to draw the line—for her own protection.

"But it was wrong of me to touch you. I promised you a haven and a sanctuary, Helen. I have no right to . . . trespass and will strive not to do so again. We must be practical."

"I'm grateful for the walls of Troy." Her bravado faded, the flutter of her eyelashes shielding her eyes from his. "Practical. I don't feel practical."

"It isn't a feeling, Helen. It's a dictate of reason."

She looked back up at him directly. "Can you do that? Separate the two so easily?"

"I've had to for a long time." Darius did his best not to flinch under her steady gaze. "I've tried to live my life with logic and intellect as my guides."

She shook her head, stepping back from the table. "You cannot have intellect without heart. The most perfect mind without emotion is devoid of compassion and capable only of conceiving cruelty and pain. Genius doesn't protect you from heartache. It isn't a refuge."

"I don't strive to live without feelings. I simply cannot let them rule me."

"Why not?"

"Because I don't trust them, Helen. When has passion served to improve man's circumstances? Or bettered humankind's existence?"

"It serves every day. Not all our emotions are basely driven. The heart can be a noble thing, Darius."

He shook his head. "I am in awe of you, Helen. To say such things after . . ."

"Don't be too quick to admire me, Darius. My knees are shaking."

"Why?" he asked, a twist of concern wrenching through him.

She smiled. "I've disagreed with you. I was a bit of a shrew just then and—" She broke off suddenly with a laugh that surprised them both. "I am still standing, Mr. Thorne. I am holding my own."

All hail the White Queen! Darius found he was grinning like a fool. "You've done more than hold your own. You've won the argument, if that's what it was. I did . . . enjoy the foot stomping."

She gasped and threw a cloth napkin at him, then laughed again at her own daring. "A lady does not stomp, Mr. Thorne!"

His laughter joined hers and he pressed the napkin to his mouth to try to stifle it. "As you say!"

"Well, here's a merry morning!" Mrs. McFadden chimed in from the doorway. She brought in a tray with a folded newspaper and a small bowl of apples. "My niece just stopped by from the village and brought these from the post, Mr. Thorne. I knew you'd asked for them." She set down the bowl and handed off the paper to Darius, who immediately opened it to study the front page. "Good morning, madam. You look a bit peaked! Should I make a spot of warm bread pudding for—"

"Damn it!" He pressed his fingers against the bridge of his nose to try to ward off a headache, then looked up to apologize at the distressed expression in Helen's eyes and at Mrs. McFadden's gasp of disapproval. "I'm sorry to curse. It's just . . . this paper is over a week old and . . . The meeting is set for four days from now." He threw it down on the table in frustration.

"The meeting?" Helen asked, her brow furrowing with confusion.

"The Jaded are set to meet with that mysterious figure we dubbed the Jackal. I can understand their impatience to move forward and confront whoever it is and get some answers but . . ." Darius let out a long, slow breath of frustration. "Mrs. McFadden, I'll need to pack for a trip to London. Can you see that I have the right clothes laid out and ask Hamish to get the carriage ready to take me to hire a carriage to the nearest inn for the post chaise? Although I might consider the trains. . . ."

"London? Good heavens! You just got back from Edinburgh last night!" she exclaimed but withdrew in a bustle to make preparations, apparently determined that this time he not leave behind the essentials in his haste to go.

"It's a week to London, isn't it?" Helen asked softly.

Darius turned back to Helen, shaking his head. "A week if you travel comfortably and make good time, but if I leave today, forfeit comfort, I might make it in time to stop them if I don't stop except to change horses or catch a train. The carefully crafted letter outlining our new conclusions that I was planning is useless if they make this meeting with the Jackal."

"You're certain? You trust Mr. Masters so completely?" she asked. "I mean, I know that you do, but it does seem odd to think in terms of curses and prophecies. After all, it's 1860 for goodness' sake! It is a modern world, is it not?"

He bit his lip. "Not entirely. And it doesn't matter how we view the world or this mythology. Prophecies have power when people believe them, and if the Jaded are in this one's path, then logic isn't the tool to apply. It's chess, Helen. They've developed a strategy and arranged for this confrontation, but they don't have a view of the entire board or all the pieces. It's an ambush!"

"You said yourself they don't have anything to give to this Jackal."

"True. But does the person behind *this*"—he held up the note from the gem dealer—"do they know that it's just a first meeting? That we have no intention of turning over anything after the threat to our lives?"

"I see what you're saying."

"Helen." He took her hands into his. "I don't want to leave you here. There's so much . . . Yesterday was . . ." He let out a long, slow breath of frustration. "I need you to trust me. I have to go to London and stop this meeting if I can."

Her eyes took on the sheen of unshed tears. "I know it."

"If someone could please explain to me why I am constantly rushing out of doors. . . ."

She managed a shaky smile. "For a scholar, you do appear to lead a very exciting life, Mr. Thorne."

"I would take you with me if I could, but I have to travel with speed, and if I'm worrying about your comfort or your safety—"

"No, I understand. You have to go, Darius."

"Helen, please. Don't look so stricken or I'm not sure I'll manage this with any dignity."

He watched her in a careful, compassionate study as she rallied, the fire in her pale blue eyes undampened. At last, she smiled. "Go."

Damn it. His own voice failed him and he turned on his heels to make his hurried preparations for the journey, despising the notion of abandoning her just when she'd begun to recover her spirits and regain her strength.

And just when I've discovered how much I've come to care for her.

* * *

Within the hour, he was standing in the entry hall and they were making their final farewells. Darius took her hands into his, pressing something small into the palm of her hands before folding her fingers around it. "Here, I want you to carry it in your pocket while I'm gone—to remind you."

She took it, gripping it possessively. "I want to be brave and not cry, but . . . I'm afraid I'm already failing." Tears spilled onto her cheeks.

"Mrs. McFadden will take good care of you, and Hamish will guard you like a lion in my absence."

"I know." Isabel felt small and slight but squared her shoulders. "I'll sleep with the skillet next to my bed."

"You're as strong a woman as any I've known, Helen. It's just for two weeks at most and I'll be back as quickly as I can." He hesitated. "Will you promise to be here when I return?"

She nodded, unable to speak through the miserable lump in her throat. She'd have promised him anything in that moment, but a wounded part of her curled around the strange hurt of his departure and pointed out the obvious.

I have nowhere else to go.

Isabel knew her next impulse was out of the question. But it didn't stop her.

"Kiss me good-bye, Darius."

He hesitated.

She did her best to smile. "Please?"

He dropped his bags and she was swept up into his arms and kissed so thoroughly she lost track of her toes. She cradled his face in her hands and entwined her fingers into his hair, savoring the glorious fire of his touch. A very unladylike groan of hunger escaped her lips and it heralded the end of their embrace.

He released her in an awkward move, stepping back to pick up his bags, and turned to go without a single glance backward. He ducked his head as he jogged down the stairs like a man running out of a burning building, and Isabel smiled. She instinctively knew that he'd meant no insult by it.

If he'd kissed me for one more moment, I'd have asked him to carry me upstairs.

It was only when the sound of the carriage and horses' hooves had faded down the lane that she opened her hand to see what he'd given her.

The white queen lay across her palm, her painted gaze as calm and unyielding as the stone she was carved from. Isabel pressed the chess piece to her heart, sat on the bottom stair, and gave in to her emotions to weep.

Chapter
11

Darius was forced to take a combination of a post chaise carriage and then a train to London. It was faster than struggling with carriages alone, and the issue with fresh change of horses at inns and posts along the way was solved with the train. He'd deliberately left Hamish and his own carriage for the women should they need them. He'd charged Hamish with keeping them safe in his absence and stressed again how important it was to hide Helen from prying eyes.

There was almost no sleep to be had on the long four-day journey in the jostled confines of the chaise and the requirement to change trains several times. Scotland's system wasn't as developed as England's, but neither had yet achieved the modern industrial miracle that allowed for the speed that Darius's fears requested. He rode first-class when seating was available, but during the last leg, only the second-class compartments had room and Darius was forced to sit atop a cushionless wooden seat crushed between other passengers. The weather turned foul on the trip, and the biting cold and snow stripped him of the last of his optimism.

By the time he'd reached London, he was exhausted, half frozen, and frustrated at the late hour. He'd had the good sense early in the journey to write notes to the Jaded redirecting them to stay away from the Thistle, so as soon as his boots landed on the street, he hired runners to get the word out to all of his friends. But Michael's note he kept in his hands. Darius decided he would deliver it in person.

If anyone would know what to do next, it was Rutherford. He'd been a trained soldier in the army in India, and there was no one better at tactics in their circle. Darius secured a hackney to take him to the Grove, only to fight a numbing exhaustion that began to creep up his limbs.

Come on, Thorne. You cannot let them down. Not now!

He'd been to the Grove Inn only once or twice before, as Michael was not one for entertaining friends in his rented rooms. So when he limped up the stairs, his memory faltered as he looked at the two unmarked doors off the parlor.

That one.

He pounded on the door, unceremoniously, and was rewarded when the door finally opened after a crash inside. But it was a young woman who answered and Darius had to struggle to apologize. "I'm looking for Rutherford. It is most urgent."

"His door is the next there." She firmly directed him toward Michael's apartment, and because of her youth, it took Darius a moment to reconcile the steely tone of a governess with the pert beauty tapping her toes impatiently in front of him.

God, I'm too tired for this. It was all he could do to mumble awkward explanations and deflect her questions.

"Is there something wrong?" she asked, and Darius had to force himself to try to see the scene from her vantage point. He was a half-frozen madman pounding on Rutherford's door in frustration, and if he wasn't careful, she'd not only call for the landlady, she'd start screaming for the watch.

"I'm a friend of Rutherford's. My name is Darius Thorne

and . . . again, I apologize for the disturbance. It's nothing to concern you, miss."

But when she introduced herself and then spoke of the Jaded and their meeting at the Thistle, Darius took note.

Eleanor Beckett. I can't see Michael sharing with his neighbor or . . .

"Is there any danger?" she pressed, openly fearful.

"No." She was a total stranger but it was clear that she had knowledge of the Jaded's business, and while he wanted to find out how this was possible, the urgency of the moment overrode his curiosity. "I can't believe I'm having this conversation, Miss Beckett." He checked his watch and saw that the time for the meeting with the Jackal was over an hour off. Rutherford would be there alone, waiting, since Darius had sent notes to everyone else heading them off. . . .

Stupid idea to catch Michael myself. I should have sent a runner but I wanted to be sure he knew about the new threat. Damn it!

He realized in shock that Miss Beckett was saying something else and he'd missed part of the exchange. "Everyone is safe and diverted. I'm confident I know where to find Mr. Rutherford since he's not here." He bowed and tipped his hat. "It was a unique experience meeting you, Miss Beckett."

He was too exhausted to argue and he couldn't think of what polite niceties were required in life-and-death situations when confronted by prim and feisty redheads and turned to leave without another word to race from the Grove.

I swear we are becoming the least-secret secret club in London's history at this rate.

Damn.

His legs were rubber as he stumbled out into the street, fear pushing him to ignore the protests of his body at the punishing pace. "To the Thistle!" he called up to the driver and fell into the carriage. "All speed!"

Any relief he might have felt in seeing the gambling hall was extinguished when the bar man directed him to the staircase and the second-floor meeting room.

More stairs? Am I the brunt of some great cosmic jest?

By the time he'd located Michael and, by surprise, Josiah in a room at the top of the building, Darius was nearly done in. But there wasn't time to complain. "It's off!"

"Off?" Michael was on his feet in a flash, his height and size no hindrance to speed.

Josiah Hastings was slower to stand. "Why would the Jackal call it off after all this effort to—"

"Not the Jackal," Darius began to explain, all the while waving his arms wildly toward the door. This wasn't the time for a sit-down lecture on ancient prophecies and why the Jaded's use of the public papers wasn't the wisest course of action, in Darius's humble opinion. He needed to get his friends out of the Thistle for safety's sake; the debates could happen later in the safety of Rowan's study. "I'll explain it in the carriage to West's, but we have a new problem to—"

He'd nearly gotten them to the door. Nearly. Screams and a commotion below stairs froze them all in place. "Fire!"

Darius's mouth fell open in shock and he very nearly said aloud, *If this is the curse that goes along with handing sacred treasures over, we are doomed, gentlemen.*

But his better judgment kicked in and he kept his surreal thoughts to himself. It was a staccato blur of events that followed and he was hard-pressed to absorb any of it. Darius found cloths on the sideboard and doused them with water to protect their lungs before they ducked out into the smoke-filled hallway. Josiah took the lead and they held on to one another's coats to make their way back toward the staircase.

He knew he should be counting doorways and trying to stay calm, but every thought was hundreds of miles away with her.

Helen. God, all I want is one more chance to sit across from her . . . one more chance to see her smile. . . . If I die here, what's to become of Helen?

The appearance of another person blocking their path in the narrow staircase and the presence of a pistol interrupted his melancholy. It was clear that the Jackal was just as confused by the fire as his friends but was in no mood for enlightenment about the nature of arsonists.

"To hell with you!" the man shouted over the roar of the blaze. "I should have known you'd trap me and play some trick!"

"No tricks!" Darius tried to explain. "We never—"

"Shut up! We'll meet on *my* terms next time!"

Rutherford wasn't having it. The Jackal's terms in the past generally involved trying to kill one of the Jaded, and none of them were willing to allow a murderer to hold the reins. But Darius had to close his eyes in frustration, since shouting matches in burning stairwells weren't exactly prudent either. . . .

Michael was furiously making threats to end the Jackal's life, and before Darius could catch at the ex-soldier's sleeve and remind him that guns were present, shots were fired point-blank toward them and all hell broke loose.

Josiah fell forward as he hit the Jackal's arm, and all three of the Jaded tumbled in a tangle on the steps. It was an ignoble effort to protect each other, and by the time their ears stopped ringing from the pistol shot and they realized no one was wounded, the Jackal was long gone.

The smoke and the fire, on the other hand, had not taken pause for the exchange.

"Gentlemen." Darius straightened up as best he could, helping Josiah to his feet. "May I suggest we keep moving? For men of action, I swear we're going to suffocate to death while we discuss how lucky we are not to be dead. See the irony?"

"The professor's right! Lead on, Hastings!" Michael agreed and their hurried exodus continued. It was all Darius could do to hold on to Hastings's coat and keep his wits about him as his lungs began to refuse to function.

When they reached the relative safety of the street, Darius could hardly believe it, but then watched in stunned shock as an apparently suicidal Josiah Hastings ran back into the burning building they'd just narrowly escaped.

Darius rose instinctively to stop him, or to go with him,

determined to help his friend, but the ground lifted up after three steps and Darius's chest seized up like stones. There was no air to be had and he landed on his hands and knees, spitting up black wet ropes of slime until he was certain he'd forfeited a lung.

It was humiliating, but Michael stayed with him, clapping one of his huge hands against Darius's back to try to help him through it.

By the time he could almost breathe again, he had the strange experience of feeling no shock at all when Josiah reappeared with the red-haired beauty from the Grove in his arms. Even the revelation of Josiah's blindness was muted by the haze of misery that shadowed his every breath.

Josiah's eyesight is failing. Miss Beckett is . . . My God, I've missed a bit of news, haven't I?

It was adrenaline and bravado, euphoria at surviving a gunman and an inferno in one go that sustained him on the carriage ride to Rowan's. But it was a ride he later couldn't recall a single detail about other than Michael's presence in the shadowy confines of the compartment, quietly venting to himself and whispering soft, deadly vows to see to the Jackal personally after the night's fiery end. It pained Darius too much to speak, so he just closed his eyes and let the man rail on. He knew Rutherford meant well. Michael's protective nature toward his friends was like a force of nature. And only a fool argued philosophy with a hurricane.

By the time they arrived at Dr. West's brownstone, Darius was sure he'd aged a hundred years.

"You two look a fright!" Carter exclaimed as he took their soot-covered coats. Rowan's elderly butler was usually unflappable, but their startling appearance made his voice shake. "My goodness! Dr. West! They've come!"

"Did you go?" Rowan asked as he came down the stairs two at a time with his lovely wife, Gayle, on his heels. "The note said we weren't to go and to stay away, but I haven't heard from anyone else yet and you're the first to arrive."

"Are you all right?" Gayle West asked, her violet eyes ablaze with concern. "You look like giant chimney sweeps!"

Michael held up a hand in greeting. "We're fine. We didn't exactly get Darius's note in time, but he arrived to warn us off and probably saved our lives."

Darius glanced at his friend in disbelief at the claim. He'd hardly managed anything except a mad dash from one end of London to the next, and as far as he could tell, it was Hastings who had led them out of the fire. Darius opened his mouth to say as much but no words came out.

Instead the marble floor of the foyer disintegrated in a shower of black sparks that crowded into his vision, and the last thing Darius remembered was a unique view of the chandelier in the central hall hanging over their heads.

From the floor, it looks like a perfect spiral. . . . I should sketch that. . . . Organic shapes in industrial . . . applications. . . . Where is Helen?

And then there was nothing.

* * *

He awoke in a bedroom he didn't recognize, fully clothed, lying atop the bedding. Darius reached up for his shirt buttons as if to touch the wet mortar that had filled his chest. He immediately tried to sit up, mortified that he'd fainted in front of his friends.

"Easy, there!" Gayle's hand restrained him, the pressure of her palm to his shoulder gentle but firmly keeping him in place. "Darius, please."

"What happened? Where are the others? Are—" He was defeated by another coughing jag and Gayle helped him sit up to relieve the strain.

"It's the smoke. I fear you took in more than your share, Mr. Thorne. Michael said you saved the others and—"

"He overstates it." He shook his head vehemently, unwilling to let the myth take hold. "I rode . . . in a carriage. I ran up steps. . . . It was hardly . . . heroic. And I was fine . . . before." His throat burned and it was all he could do to whisper, but he couldn't allow the misunderstanding to root. "Damn! I feel . . . like I'm breathing . . . through a dirty, wet cloth."

Gayle moved to retrieve a soft white cloth from a tray next to the bed. "Here. Cough into this when you have to, and I apologize for the indelicacy, but I'll wish to see it afterward."

He grimaced at the notion but sighed in obedience. "So much for . . . impressing . . . anyone."

Gayle smiled. "You raced from Edinburgh to London in record time, and warned your friends away from danger." She took a breath and amended her words when she saw him stir to argue. "*Tried* to warn your friends away from danger, and escaped a burning building. I, for one, am impressed."

"How long . . . have I been here?"

Rowan answered him from the doorway. "Not long enough! Just a few minutes from when we carried you upstairs. Rest, Darius. Mrs. Evans is boiling up a breathing treatment, and as soon as it is ready, we'll see about setting you up for a bit of relief."

Darius sat up on the side of the bed. "I'm fine."

Rowan nodded. "Of course you are. Care to run upstairs, then, to the study for a quick brandy?"

"You're . . . a bully." Darius gave in to the need to cough, wincing at the sensation of his lungs coming apart. When it had passed, Gayle gave him a fresh cloth and took the soiled one from him.

"Why do all my friends insist that they're fine when they aren't?" Rowan said calmly, his tone light even as he silently concurred with his wife over the black and bloody show on the white cotton and signaled her to see about hurrying Mrs. Evans's progress. "Is it a lack of trust in my skills? Or an aversion to admitting your mortality?"

Darius smiled. "It's timing. We have . . . better things . . . to do."

"That's what Michael said. But I've gotten those wooden splinters out of his face and restored his good looks all the same." Rowan came over to stand next to the bed. "We missed you. I know Edinburgh has become home for you, but Ashe relies on your friendship too much not to complain about your long absences."

"He has . . . Caroline now. But I'm . . . always at hand . . . for him." Darius shook his head. "I need to . . . tell the others . . . what I found. It's not . . . just the East India . . . not what we thought."

Rowan held up a hand to stop him, but Darius was punished for the effort and doubled over as his body fought for air and the room started to spin.

"Gayle!" Rowan's tone was all business as he seamlessly shifted into his role as physician.

She answered him from the doorway where she had stepped through to alert Carter for the need for haste with the treatment coming from Cook's kitchens. "I am here."

"Forget subtlety. Open the windows and let's get some cool air in here." Rowan bent over to put an arm around Darius's back and shoulders. "Believe it or not, I want you to come sit in this chair over by the window, Thorne. It's freezing out there and snowing, which is exactly what we're hoping for."

"You're going . . . to kill me . . . aren't you?" Darius teased him.

"I might," Rowan said with a wink.

Darius didn't have the breath for banter. He acquiesced without argument and did his best to walk over, leaning against Rowan until they reached an upholstered reading chair by the windows.

"I've a different approach to the use of temperatures, and there's some interesting studies to support my own theories— so, lucky you, Darius Thorne. You get to let me test a few things." Rowan took out a stethoscope and pressed the cold metal disk against Darius's back. "Talk of treasure can wait until tomorrow. The Jackal got singed tonight by all accounts and probably won't be up for any more mischief for a while yet. We have lots of time to go over it all." He stopped talking to listen and then shifted the disk to hold it directly against Darius's bare skin, bending over to concentrate.

Darius shook his head but said nothing. He'd promised to return to Helen as quickly as possible and it was unthinkable that he would linger in London an hour longer than he had to. He would allow Rowan to fuss and provide whatever treatments he saw fit. Darius would even rest for a day or two. But he would begin the journey back as soon as he could stand to walk without the room tilting to defeat him.

Rowan straightened, tucking the stethoscope into his large coat pocket. "All quiet for the rest of the night."

The front doorbell rang again and Darius almost sighed at the comical expression of surprise on his friend's face. *He hasn't experienced the madness of the evening firsthand yet, but apparently the Wests are getting their doses late.*

Rowan excused himself for a moment and Darius closed his eyes, listening for any sounds of distress below. He was worried about Ashe and hoped his cynicism wasn't the herald of more bad luck for his friends.

It's not like me to play the troll.

The cool air felt good on his face and amazingly began to ease the ache in his chest, allowing him to take even, shallow breaths without being reduced to hacking and coughing.

Gayle came in after a time carrying a large, heavy porcelain bowl. She drew a flannel across the windowsill and set down the bowl of steaming hot water. "Here, make sure this doesn't fall and try to inhale as much of its scent as you can."

Even over the lingering smell of soot and ash, Darius detected mint and anise drifting up from the water's surface, along with a few other ingredients he couldn't name. "As you command." He dutifully leaned forward, a winter's breeze delivering the treatment in a strange mist of home remedies. "Was it . . . a message?"

"Not a message exactly. Josiah sent his night guard, Mr. Creed, over for treatment. He was assaulted tonight and we've got him abed downstairs where Rowan is seeing to him." Gayle's violet eyes reflected fear. "Mr. Hastings's note said that no one else was harmed and that they're safe but— perhaps the Jaded should consider changing tactics?"

He nodded. "Agreed. May I . . . have paper and pen?"

"Of course," Gayle said, moving to retrieve a portable writing desk from where it rested atop a table. "Here you are."

"Thank you." Darius took the box from her, admiring for a fleeting moment its inlaid surface and clever hidden drawers. "No fear, Mrs. West. All this will be resolved . . . soon enough. And then we can all actually start quiet lives and one day lament that nothing exciting ever happens to us."

"That's quite a dream," she said. "I never thought I would long for boredom, but in this instance, I think you're right." She pulled a small bottle from her pocket. "You're to drink this."

"I need . . . to stay . . . awake."

"Then drink this," she said firmly. "And I'll leave you to your writing."

He smiled, unable to really talk more without fighting for air. The syrup was sweet with peppermint flavors and he detected no bite of a narcotic. Even so, there was something soothing in the cold liquid and it eased the ache in his throat. He handed her back the empty bottle and then pulled out the paper to set up the desk and begin his task. Gayle politely stirred the medicated water in the large bowl and then left him to rest.

Darius began to write out everything he hoped would be relevant for his friends, outlining as clearly as he could his theory that they'd stumbled into a larger puzzle than the simple shuffle of gems they'd long believed. He wrote until his hand shook from fatigue and the words blurred on the page.

And exhaustion finally overtook him into the darkness.

Chapter
12

For Isabel, his absence was very telling. Nearly two weeks
had passed in a crawl of time that had tested her mettle in
every way. Even sporadically broken by lively exchanges in
the kitchen between Mrs. McFadden and Mr. MacQueen,
the quiet of the house was suffocating. Every fear was ampli-
fied by isolation, but even the most rational part of her brain
was forced to admit that something had changed.

Her growing attachment to Mr. Thorne was undeniable.

In the brief span that she'd known him, it had been easier
to deflect her feelings and distract herself with conversation
and meals, board games and books. She'd credited her ease
in his presence with a natural need for social contact and
amusement. But never in her life had she been so obsessed
with the memory of someone's every word and gesture.

Over Mrs. McFadden's objections, she'd begun weeding
out the dead plants in the back garden whenever the weather
permitted. She'd borrowed work gloves from the housekeeper and a few garden tools to attack the project and
embraced the escape and distraction.

The tangle of the little wilderness slowly gave way to barren order and Isabel was shocked to discover that there was a lovely flagstone path that meandered through the small yard buried underneath unraked leaves. In a pattern of the symbol for infinity, the stones were laid out in gentle curves and Isabel began to see the space's potential.

"A few flowers and pretty hedges of lavender and it would be a dream," she said aloud. "I'll ask Hamish to find a bench to put in the shaded corner there and it will be lovely in the spring!"

There was no echo in the cold air and she shivered at how dead it sounded. "I'm a ghost in a ghost garden," she whispered at her pale reflection in a mud puddle. Isabel knelt down with her basket to continue her chore of pulling dead vines out of what appeared to be an abandoned water feature.

Spring was a few weeks away and she knew it was foolish to think of seeing his garden come to life. *I shouldn't be here by then. Samson will heal and I must do the right thing and free Mr. Thorne from his vows to me. He's been so kind and we've shut out the world beyond the walls of Troy—but if I remember my Homer, the world eventually came calling, and the price for one selfish act was the destruction of a kingdom.*

She had no desire to see anything happen to Darius's world. His orderly nest lined with books was an oasis Isabel wanted to protect. She wondered if his friends knew of his quiet ways and appreciated the heroic effort he was making on their part to solve mysteries and work out the dramatic and surreal puzzle involving sacred objects to help them. The Jaded struck her as an odd name, but if the men in his acquaintance had earned his loyalty and trust, then she did her best to dismiss her misgivings and trust them in return to take care of Mr. Thorne and make sure he was safe.

There is nothing jaded about Darius.

She envied that gift, to apparently skip like a stone over the worst that life could hold. Her back had healed but Isabel still jumped at loud noises and suffered from bouts of anxiety.

*But I am stronger. I'm not slipping into an abyss of bad
memories at every reminder of Richard. It's almost starting
to feel as if it happened to another woman.*

Isabel's life before she'd come to Darius felt more and
more distant. When she thought of it, it was like recalling
dance steps and watching a ball from a balcony. Every step
she had ever taken before meeting him was as choreographed
as a quadrille, and until she'd committed to marrying Richard, life held few surprises.

Suddenly an impulse seized her and Isabel gave in to it
without a single internal argument. She wrested off one of
her gloves and eyed the gleam of gold on her left hand. It
was such a simple thing, this plain band, but it signified the
tangle of pain and humiliation marriage had brought her.
She went over to the sword poking out of the dirt near the
rosemary and slipped off her wedding ring. She dug a good
hole next to the sword and made her own little offering to
the spirits of his garden.

*There. Buried unmourned. I shall claim what small free-
doms I can, and if there is the devil to pay, then I will point
him here and pay him in gold.*

"It's to rain!" Mrs. McFadden called out from the French
doors leading to the garden. "You're already a mess but let's
not have you soaked through!"

Isabel stood, doing her best to brush out the muddy wreck
she'd made of her day dress. She'd put on an apron under
her coat but it was just one more layer of cloth to suffer from
her efforts at being useful. She glanced up at the sky, startled
at the black tenor of the clouds roiling above. "I see that
you're right, Mrs. McFadden. I shall come in at once."

She gathered her tools and basket and dutifully headed
back to the house.

"Ach!" Mrs. McFadden wrinkled her nose in disapproval. "A fine lady such as yourself and you look like a
mud troll!"

"Yes, but look how I recovered the planting boxes for
your kitchen garden, Mrs. McFadden. Won't that be nice to
have again?" she asked.

The older woman's lips pressed into a thin line. "It will. I won't lie. But you'll catch your death out there sitting on that cold, wet ground, and how am I to enjoy it with you buried over there under that willow tree?"

"I'm fine," Isabel answered with a laugh. "The fresh air is doing me a world of good."

Mrs. McFadden crossed her arms. "Maybe so, but don't try telling me that dirt's good for my clean floors! Boots off here and then leave what you can on the floor by the door for a wash. I've got a clean blanket to wrap you in for modesty and Hamish is banished to the stables—so no worries on that lunk's account."

Isabel knew better than to argue. "You're so thoughtful, Mrs. McFadden."

She kicked off the caked mud from her boots before removing them to put in the wooden box set inside the doorway. Mrs. McFadden helped her with her coat, apron, and dress, but Isabel insisted on keeping her petticoats and underclothes. Even with Hamish safely out of the way, she was not about to make her way through the house wearing nothing but a quilted blanket.

As relaxed as I've become, there are some things a lady cannot consider!

She was also not about to let Mrs. McFadden catch sight of the white queen she'd tied around her neck with a ribbon to keep it close to her heart.

I'm not explaining my talisman! Nor will I take it off until he returns. . . .

She went upstairs to put on a fresh dress, and as she buttoned up the blouse, she realized that even in these intimate matters, Darius had thought of the details. Every dress he'd bought had been pretty but also practical to allow her to change with more ease and without the help of a maid. Everything buttoned in the front or allowed for her to adjust it comfortably.

It was humbling. His attentiveness and generosity. He thought of her in all things and omitted nothing if he thought it would please her or add to her comfort.

The honey in the porridge drizzled in the shape of a flower . . .

Is it possible?

He'd kissed her. That much was certain. And Isabel knew enough of the world to know that he desired her. Nor was she blind to the attraction she felt for him. Indeed, if he hadn't been forced to race for London that very day, she had no doubt that she would have shamelessly begged him to repeat the infraction.

Kissing Darius was like tasting sugar for the first time—and uncovering a craving for sweets that would not be quieted.

It's ridiculous but it is a truth I cannot deny.

It was a dangerous path to give in to passion, but a new rebellious voice inside of her pointed out that since leaving her husband would be publicly deemed the act of an immoral woman, she might have little to lose.

But . . . the heart is another matter, isn't it?

It was a terrifying proposition to trust her instincts entirely.

As much as Richard hurt me physically, I think having my heart so completely broken and betrayed was the worst of it. I loved him. I must have at one point. Or I imagined myself in love, didn't I?

Now she wasn't sure. She wasn't sure of anything.

Her feelings for Darius had no comparison. Where her affections for Richard had felt polite and "natural," there was nothing pale or polite in the hold that Darius had on her now. He occupied her waking thoughts and held her in her dreams. He'd crowded out most of her nightmares, replacing them with strange erotic episodes where he made love to her on the Oriental rug in his library before the fireplace or in a copper bathtub in his bedroom.

There was nothing soothing in her dreams of him but only an increasingly restless ache that spurred her to spend all her days wandering the house and yard thinking on what Darius had said about the distinctions between love and the semblance of love. She'd cleaned his library, dusting and straightening but doing her best not to actually move anything too far from its resting place. His system was a mystery but she respected him and knew that Darius saw the chaotic piles and odd notes in a different way than a casual observer. The maps looked mystical but his sketches were compelling enough to warrant frames.

Even so, she was running out of distractions.

Presently, she went down to eat her dinner alone in the library at his desk as she had each night since he'd left. Mrs. McFadden had allowed her to settle into the routine, as if instinctively aware of how comforting she found it.

Afterward she worked by lamplight, reading as much as she could in the hope that by the time he returned there would be no question of her value as an assistant. She'd found notes and sketches throughout the library as he tucked in pages to save his place in a book or to add his thoughts to the writer's. Isabel explored as discreetly as she could, ignoring the tickle of her conscience at invading his private work space by reminding herself that she had his permission.

Even so, when she pulled out the top drawer and found a green leather-bound notebook with his initials on the cover, she froze.

What if this one is personal? What if he finds out I touched it and is angry?

The old habits of fear and self-preservation that Richard had instilled in her warred with her new independence and the easy freedom that Darius had granted her. Ultimately, curiosity won the day and Isabel lifted the large notebook out to take a peek.

It was a more personal notebook, with an outline of his plans for the house and garden and research into improving the stables with Hamish's guidance. She was about to close it when a pencil drawing caught her eye.

It was a sketch of her with her cheek against Samson's and, in Darius's own hand, a bit of prose beneath it. He had an artist's skill but the words were what captured her attention.

A divine moment, so fleeting, but to be in her presence at such an unguarded moment of beauty, her heart's gentle nature revealed and the beast the lucky recipient of her caresses . . . I am humbled and enslaved, and will do all I can to see this goddess safely out of reach.

"Safely out of reach?" she whispered. "Of Richard's or his own?"

She put the notebook back where she'd found it, her ears warm with guilt and her hands shaking. Isabel had stolen a glimpse of his feelings and robbed herself of the ability to deny that he was equally affected by their situation.

She stood from the desk and paced the room, finally ending back at the wall of shelves to randomly pull down a volume on India. "Come on, woman," she chided herself, "mooning about him is getting you nowhere. Read and prove that you're more than some flighty thing in petticoats."

She retrieved his last academic notes on their new theory and made her way to the soft chair by the fireplace to sit with her legs tucked underneath her. Within minutes, she'd picked up the thread of their quest and was fiercely concentrating on the text to seek out the next clue to determining the magical properties of stones.

Isabel made her own notes in the margins of his, adding, as politely as she could, her opinion that seeking a scientific method to measure magic was innately contradictory and that perhaps they should be scanning religious texts or finding a Hindu holy man to assist them.

Is there a magic incantation to make it glow, like in the fairy stories I read as a child?

It was a fanciful notion but it kept her occupied.

She gave no real credence to the idea that any object inherently had power. *Father Pasqual and I are in accord on this one thing.*

But she understood that Darius's fears sprang not from vague spiritual superstitions about cursed stones or sacred rocks but from the very real and dangerous men who clung to those superstitions and would take action to protect it.

"So, if it's not in a book on the nature of stones and the geology of the region . . ." Isabel unfolded from her perch and went back to his desk where he'd left a translated section of the Code of Manu. Isabel opened it at random only to learn that, according to the ancient Hindu text, "a woman should never enjoy her own will. She must never wish separation of her self from her husband or father, for by separation from them a woman would make both families contemptible."

All the momentum she'd gathered died a little and she knelt soundlessly on the rug to try to take it in.

No will but a man's to supersede mine.

Is that the key to happiness or hell? I don't see a middle way. Isabel sighed. *England or India, I am condemned a failure. A fallen, scandalous thing to be avoided and shunned.*

Shame washed over her even as a part of her protested. The internal voice was stronger and clear enough to drown out self-pity.

I did nothing wrong.

The travesty of her wedding day and that first assault came back in a rush of chilly vindication.

I did nothing to deserve any of it.

From that day forward, he'd systematically broken her with isolation and punishments, rewards and assaults and vicious acts of calculated deprivation. He'd spend hours whispering insults and ungodly threats until she'd begged him to beat her and be done with it. Her soul had shriveled until the vaguest mention of a social outing was enough to render her hysterical with terror at the possibility of being exposed publicly as a failure and an abused wraith.

Honor dictated that she suffer in silence, and she'd tried to bear all of it, to find the path of behavior that would appease him and satisfy her duties.

How far did I slide down that dark, cold hole until I had no will of my own?

Until Samson intervened that day . . .

Isabel got up from the floor, leaving the manuscript pages on the carpet, and crossed over to the window to look out at the dark. Her reflection greeted her and Isabel studied the woman there for a moment.

Pale as always, with hair so blond it was nearly white, here was a familiar ghost. But this phantom's eyes sparkled with defiance. This woman's cheeks were fuller and touched with a faint swath of pink. Her dress was plain but pretty, and there was an air of self-possession to her.

It's Darius's Helen. I changed when I wasn't looking.

She turned back to survey the room and a new revelation struck her with the force of truth. *I have my own will to enjoy, and even if the law would override it, it is something that Richard can never take away from me. Never again.*

Isabel pressed a palm against her chest, amazed at the pulse of her own heart beating wildly. "I did nothing wrong. I am . . . entitled to my own will. And . . . I am free to love again if I choose."

She eyed the books lining the walls. *It couldn't all be pain and fear. Mrs. McFadden was right. Who speaks of such things? Who would write of them? Who would dedicate endless volumes in praise of anything as vile as Richard's actions, and how in the world would you coordinate such a vast conspiracy to create an untruth?*

So it must exist.

Mustn't it?

The hour had grown late so she carried her dinner tray back to the empty kitchen and left it, praying Mrs. McFadden wouldn't mind the trespass. She lit a candle and climbed the stairs, pleased to find that she might be tired enough to sleep.

In her room, she changed quickly and pulled the warm stone from the small hearth where the housekeeper had left it for her, wrapped it in linen, and tucked it into her bed. She was about to climb in when a light outside her window caught her eye.

Isabel moved cautiously to pull the curtains back only to

see Mrs. McFadden crossing the yard with a lantern. The clock in the downstairs hall chimed midnight and Isabel marveled at the strange sight of the housekeeper entering the stables at such an unlikely hour. In shock, she watched as the light moved up the stairs and then illuminated Mr. MacQueen's private apartment long enough to show a silhouette of the pair embracing passionately before the light was extinguished.

Darius said they were a match but—I thought he exaggerated or . . .

She suddenly couldn't stop smiling.

For there it was.

Love and desire, as real as the rain and the earth.

As intoxicating as any wine. One kiss and she'd accepted it that there might be more in a man's touch than pain. But fear had kept her from embracing a greater new truth—that love might also be within reach.

If ever she'd have consigned it to fairy tales and dreams, apparently even a sweet dragon like Mrs. McFadden knew better.

Common sense trumped Isabel's past experience.

Mrs. McFadden said that she'd held heaven in her hands. And when Darius kissed me, I began to understand what she meant. What would it be like to have such a man and be his completely? To be protected instead of punished?

Every woman in her acquaintance spent nearly all their efforts in achieving marriage. What woman would seek out pain if that's all there was to be had? If it were always as it had been with Richard, then no woman as strong as Mrs. McFadden would cross a dark, muddy yard to attain it.

Isabel stepped back from the window and climbed into the soft refuge of her bed, burying herself under the covers. It was not a convenient development or an easy admission to make to herself, acknowledging just how far she'd gone in her obsession.

But there it was.

She had fallen in love with Darius Thorne. Not as a

victim, but as a free woman, and now she would have to decide what to do.

The pieces are all on the board and it will be up to me to either forfeit my chance or try to win the Black King's heart and prove that I'm strong enough for the game.

Chapter
13

"You cannot leave! As your physician, I forbid it." Rowan stepped in front of him, attempting to block Darius from the door. "You need two weeks in bed before you travel, Darius."

"I *can* leave. Don't be a bully, West. It doesn't suit you." Darius held out the folded pages he'd drafted. "Here."

"What is that?" Rowan didn't reach for it.

"All I've learned to date. I wanted to compile my thoughts and make sure that someone else had the record."

Just in case you're right, Rowan, and my lungs fold in on me.

"And," he forced himself to slow down, unwilling to risk a demonstration of just how weak he was by running out of air, "as you said, the Jackal is off licking his wounds. There's lots of time."

"But . . . with everything that's happened—surely your place is here!"

Darius shook his head. "No. I need to . . . take care of something in Scotland. I'll return to London as soon as it's feasible."

"Your lungs are damaged, Darius. You're at risk for pneumonia—you're already on the edge of exhaustion, and two days of rest aren't enough to allow you to recover for me to let you go."

"I'll sleep for a fortnight when I get back but I cannot stay here."

"Why?"

"I can't tell you. I need you to trust me, Rowan, and then advocate on my behalf to Ashe. He won't understand and I don't want to add to his worries. He has Caroline to fear for. He doesn't need to add my concerns to the pile. None of you do." Darius pulled on his coat. "At least, not yet."

"We're not going to abandon you, Darius. No matter what kind of trouble you're in."

Darius smiled. "I'm counting on the loyalty of my friends, Dr. West. I'll call on the Jaded for help soon. I have no illusions of my self-reliance when it comes to—I'll send word as soon as I can."

Rowan crossed his arms. "I could physically haul you back to bed myself."

"And then what? Sit on me? Post a guard?" Darius began to button his coat. "Rowan. Please. I wouldn't insist on going if it weren't . . . I have a promise to keep and I won't be able to breathe, if you'll pardon the metaphor, until I've seen to matters at home."

Rowan gave him a searching look. "Matters at home."

Darius squared his shoulders. "Matters. At. Home."

Rowan's stance slowly relaxed. "Well, when you put it *that* way . . ."

"I'll take what precautions I can, *Dr.* West, and just for you, I will live to be a hundred." Darius did his best not to smile at the audacious lie and failed.

"I'll tell my wife you declared yourself immortal and see how that strikes her," Rowan conceded reluctantly. "I hope you appreciate the sacrifice of domestic bliss I am making here."

Darius gave him one nod before heading out the door.

He'd feared for his friends, but the minute he'd left Helen behind, he'd been a man torn and divided.

If only I could be in two places at once.

Before he'd reached the outskirts of London, Darius realized that Rowan hadn't been too far wrong.

His return was even more grueling than his headlong rush to reach London. The urgency to see Helen again ground against his soul and robbed him of his peace of mind. Darius battled a physical need to assure himself that she was safe and that none of the nightmarish visions of potential tragedy had befallen her in his absence. It was as serious a spur to speed as any.

He was so exhausted by nightfall, he almost gave up and conceded defeat, but the idea that Helen could be facing her husband undefended or simply afraid in the night without anyone there to comfort her—it was unacceptable.

Just get there, Thorne.

Prove to the woman that not all men fail to keep their word and that you're a true gentleman—and pray that she isn't regretting those kisses.

*   *   *

"My God, you look horrible!"

"I'm sending for Dr. Abernethy!" Mrs. McFadden announced, her lips pressed together so tightly they nearly disappeared.

"You're not," Darius countered firmly. "There was a fire in London and I . . . took in a bit of smoke. I need rest. I'm fine. I hurried back because I didn't want you to worry but—I'll admit that wasn't the soundest decision I've ever made."

"Ye coulda sent a note!" Mrs. McFadden screeched. "Why are men as dense as boards when it comes to—"

"Mrs. McFadden." Helen stepped forward, taking his arm. "Hot mint tea, please. I'll help Mr. Thorne upstairs. Get Hamish to carry up the tub and then draw a hot bath, and we'll get him settled as quickly as possible."

The housekeeper's eyes widened in astonishment as the

meekest of houseguests suddenly took charge with the calm authority of a true lady. "Y-yes, madam."

Darius smiled at the change and allowed Isabel to help him up the stairs.

Within minutes, the house was bustling at her command and the copper tub had been set up in the dressing room off his bedroom, awaiting the buckets of steaming-hot water that Hamish would bring up later. Darius tried to catch his breath, sitting in a chair by his bedroom window, and watched Helen confidently move about the room, pulling back the bedding and unpacking his things.

"You're enjoying this."

She blushed. "Perhaps. I've—never been one to give out orders and it was—thrilling to be obeyed so sweetly."

"I don't believe . . . you've *never* done it."

"Well, then, let us say I was out of practice," she amended, adjusting some cushions behind him. "The fire. Does that mean you didn't reach your friends in time? Did they give up the object without realizing it?"

He shook his head. "Nothing exchanged hands. But the fire . . . I have to believe it was an agent of the prophecy . . . seeking to stop us from making that mistake." His speech was halting as he fought off a coughing fit that would alarm her. He'd been spitting up gray bile for the last two days of his trip and feared he might never take a deep breath again.

"Thank goodness!" she exclaimed. "Well, we can talk of it later. I tried to study all that I could on the questions we'd uncovered before you left and—there is time enough for all of it when you're better."

He leaned back against the cushions and his relief at finally being home and in her presence again washed over him like a warm wall of fatigue, and then something on the table beside his bed caught his eye. She'd set out a single chess piece.

The black king.

She continued softly, "When you feel up to it, the rest of the board awaits you. I can bring it up if you'd like. . . ."

The idea of sitting across from the White Queen on his

bed and attempting to keep his mind on the strategic frames and gambits of chess transformed into thoughts of a far more physical contest, where Helen ruled the game—and him.

"I would like that very much." He closed his eyes for a moment, intending to compose a better answer, but instead drifted off to sleep without another word.

*　*　*

Isabel smiled and quietly walked to the dressing room door to wave to Hamish. "He's fallen asleep so we'll delay the bath for a time, if you don't mind, Mr. MacQueen."

Hamish ducked his head after dropping the linens that the housekeeper had ordered him to bring up and left through the opposite door into the hallway, leaving Isabel to attend to him as best she could.

She retrieved a knitted blanket from the bed and draped it over his shoulders and then added a piece of wood to the small fire in the corner fireplace. Hands on her hips, she surveyed the scene and found herself simply admiring the sight of him.

She agreed with Mrs. McFadden. His eyes had gray smudges of illness beneath them and he'd lost weight. His voice had been roughened by the smoke of a fire, and Isabel bit her lower lip to fight off the tears that accompanied the rush of terror that swept through her at the idea of her beloved Darius facing flames.

But he is here and whole and we'll make him well! And as soon as he is himself again, I'm going to kneel next to his bed and beg him to let me tell him how much I love him!

It was a romantic and foolish notion that banished tears.

I'm a giddy schoolgirl again, mooning over him and sighing at the sound of his breathing.

She turned on her heels and headed downstairs to the kitchens to find Mrs. McFadden and her nemesis sharing a cup of tea.

"He is resting," Isabel announced as she came in to sit next to Hamish. "Poor thing!"

Hamish shook his head. "He must've flown on the heels

of the devil from London! At best, I didn't expect him for another three or four days!"

"I fear he's made himself ill in his rush to return to—us." Isabel caught herself almost saying *to me* but knew from Mrs. McFadden's look that the woman hadn't missed it.

"Poor lamb!" Mrs. McFadden brushed her hands off on her apron. "I'm tempted to send for the doctor in any case."

"Ye'll do no such thing," Hamish said. "The man told ye no and he'll not thank you for interfering, woman."

"He'd be alive to argue the matter and I'd say that's better than—"

Isabel cleared her throat. "We must respect Mr. Thorne's wishes in this matter. We cannot overrule him unless he is truly deathly ill."

"He looks wretched," Mrs. McFadden said, her lips pressed into a tight line.

"He looks *tired*," Isabel amended. "And sleep is exactly what he needs."

"And the mint tea?" the housekeeper asked archly.

"I'll take it in the library, Mrs. McFadden," Isabel said, then lost her battle not to smile. "I'm so . . . relieved he's home!"

The housekeeper beamed back at her. "And so quickly!"

"He didn't race back with a lungful of soot for a hot bath, that's for certain!" Hamish growled as he stood to stretch his back. "Man's daft for her, but if you think he's killed himself to hurry back for another go at chess, ye're both mad!"

"Hamish MacQueen!" Mrs. McFadden squealed. "You've not a brain in your head, you bull of a man! Get out of my kitchen!"

He smiled, apparently used to being tossed from the house. "I'm going, woman. I, for one, am just glad not to be hauling buckets up those stairs!"

"What a coldhearted beast!" The housekeeper threw a wooden spoon at him, but Hamish caught it out of the air without a blink and set it on the table before he retreated with a wink.

Once the door closed behind him, Mrs. McFadden sighed and turned back to Isabel. "Rude creature, isn't he? He's just lucky I didn't have a skillet handy or he'd have suffered a real clouting this time."

Isabel hoped her cheeks weren't as red as they felt. She thought of the white chess piece tied to a ribbon lying against her heart and the king she'd set by his bed. It was a bold move, but if she'd learned anything from his lessons, it was to play with honesty.

* * *

The first few days and nights were rough, and Darius's hopes of hiding the worst of his infirmity from the women of the house ended quickly. He slept endlessly and lost hours until he finally awoke in the dark, unsure of how much time he'd lost. Every muscle ached from too many days of travel on cushionless benches and drafty compartments that did nothing to shield him from every rut and rock in the road, and Darius's ribs burned from the effort of drawing breath, but the pneumonia that he'd feared had never materialized.

He could hear the clock in the downstairs hall chime three and lay still, letting the quiet of the house soothe his soul.

Home.

I bought a house without seeing it, outside the city because I'd always secretly dreamt of a quiet living.

I'm such a simple man with my papers and books. Didn't Ashe laugh when I once told him that I was sure that the smell of a leather binding and fresh parchment was far more potent than any woman's perfume?

His opinions had changed. So much had changed with Helen's arrival in his life.

His academic ambitions seemed paltry now next to his need to see her safe.

In fevered dreams and the agony of his journey back to Scotland, Darius had clung to a new revelation about what a simple man was capable of doing when it came to love. *True love doesn't look for balance; it doesn't ask for rewards or happy endings. I can love her without hope. I can save her if I can keep my own selfish desires out of it.*

He tried to sit up, swallowing a groan.

As soon as his strength returned, he planned on telling her the truth about himself, certain that Helen would withhold her kisses and retreat from his affection.

And then he could act without distraction and dedicate himself to extracting her from her violent marriage and see to her financial and physical future, independent of any man's control.

And when we've waved her off in a carriage or delivered her to her new home, then I can return here and indulge in sitting in mud puddles and weep for as long as I like.

But I'll have earned my misery and there's a strange consolation in that.

For I'll have done the honorable thing and been honest with her.

Chapter
14

In the morning, he ignored his housekeeper's protests and announced that he would spend his days in his library and not staring at his bedroom ceiling. "Despite the appeal of cracked plaster, I can rest better reading in my study and in Helen's good company, if she'll bestow it. . . ."

"She will," Helen said firmly from the doorway.

Mrs. McFadden rolled her eyes. "Who am I to stop a man from killing himself?"

Darius smiled. "That's the spirit, Mrs. McFadden. May I have some more of that wonderful mint tea? I swear it works miracles in making my chest feel better."

The older woman's cheeks flushed and she crossed her arms, openly flustered. "I'll—fetch a pot, but the only miracle I can see is how you're still standing! Don't go flashing that soulful look at me and think I'll go soft!"

She marched off before he could thank her and it was Helen's laughter that completed the scene.

"You should be more careful!" Helen chided him gently.

"She'll put more than mint in that tea to teach you a lesson."

"I know." He sat down in one of the chairs by the fireplace and pulled the king from his pocket. "She was worried, I think. Barking makes her feel better. And this . . ." Darius held up the dark, crowned figure. "Thank you for the gesture. It was unexpected and I'll never forget it."

He set it on the board as she took her place across from him.

"Nor I yours," she replied, lifting the queen up from the ribbon at her throat and untying it. "I never took it off."

She added the white queen onto the field, and Darius had to clear his throat at the lump that formed at the sight of their armies back in place.

"Our talismans kept us safe," he noted.

"Are you revealing a superstitious nature, sir?" she teased him.

Darius shook his head. "Not at all. In all my studies, the only thing I seem to return to is a resounding belief that humanity is essentially the same, no matter where it is found. Palaces or mud huts, I think we are all more alike than we know."

She frowned. "But there are so many differences in the cultures we've encountered."

He shook his head. "On the surface, perhaps. But underneath, I think we all want the same things. Happiness, abundance, security, and family."

"It sounds like paradise. But all the harm and conflict—"

"Stem from our universal capacity for good or evil, depending on how we apply ourselves," he interrupted her, then leaned back in his chair. "No worse or better. Maybe it's the flavor of the local religion that colors our views. In India, Josiah thought the Hindu religion had its finer points."

"I don't like the religion of that region, Mr. Thorne." She shuddered. "That Code of Manu in particular was . . ."

"It was?" he pressed gently.

"Unfair to women!" she blurted out.

"Some if it but it's not all bad. There's a fair bit in there on self-reliance and telling the truth," he offered with a sad smile. "I had a long time to think about what I might say, if I saw you again."

"If?" she asked.

"Well, between spitting up my lungs somewhere outside York and the notion that you wouldn't wish to wait for my return—I had my doubts." He shrugged. "I'm only human, Helen."

"Before you say anything," she said, nervously smoothing out her skirts, "I have to know. Mr. Thorne. When you left for London, you . . . kissed me."

"I did."

"But you haven't since your return. You've been ill and asked for Mrs. McFadden to attend you. I would have gladly—seen to your comfort but . . . I didn't feel bold enough to push my way in. You're recovering and . . ." She looked at him directly, her pale blue eyes flashing with emotion. "Have your—feelings changed?"

"Not at all. If anything, I'm more sure of them where you are concerned."

"Oh! So how is it that we are sitting so formally, Mr. Thorne, with a chessboard between us . . . ?"

"Because I want to confess something—for there to be nothing I've hidden from you. I want you never to be able to accuse me of being less than truthful."

"Yes."

"You asked if I'd ever been in love, do you remember?"

"Yes."

"I never was. I never permitted anything in my sphere that threatened my inner sense of self-discipline, and love was not something I'd ever allowed myself."

"Why ever not?"

"My father . . ." Darius stopped himself, then squared his shoulders like a man about to face a firing squad. "I am the second son of a dockworker and a fishmonger's daughter. I suspect I am as far beneath you as a grass field to the moon."

Her brow furrowed. "Is love a question of the status imparted at birth? Is that what you're saying? That the second son of a dockworker and a fishmonger's daughter cannot love?"

He opened his mouth to answer and then closed it in shock, before he composed a response. Of all the reactions he'd braced himself to hear, *this* was nothing he'd anticipated. "No. I'm telling you because I thought it might alter your . . . perception of me."

She crossed her arms. "Are you a different man than the one who raced off to save his friends and nearly sacrificed his life to return to me quickly so that I wouldn't be alone?"

He shook his head, speechless.

"Then my perception is unchanged. Tell me why a man who is so noble and steadfast in his promises is not 'allowed' to love."

"I'm . . . It isn't just that my father was . . . rustic."

"No?"

"It isn't just that. It's because of the man I feared I might become." He took a deep, steadying breath. "My father was . . ." Darius tried again, finding it easier if he looked into the fire in the fireplace and not at her beautiful face. "He was a horrible man, the worst sort of man. When he wasn't beating my mother or looking for an excuse to beat his children, he was drinking until he couldn't walk. He was an ignorant creature and so sadistic I remember thinking that Satan must have sat at his feet in awe and admiration."

"Oh, God!"

"I overheard my mother crying to a friend that she couldn't leave my father because she *loved* him." Darius closed his eyes at the memory. "I hated her for it. I didn't understand how he could have such a hold on her that she would be willing to sacrifice so much—herself and her children—for love."

Isabel couldn't think of a single thing to say to comfort him.

Darius continued, looking back at her with clear eyes. "I'm an intelligent man and I'll forgive her her choices. But I am still faced with the legacy of *that man*'s blood coursing through my veins."

"But you are nothing like him!"

"No. I've dedicated my life to being nothing like him. He sent me into an apprenticeship when I was six and it was my salvation. It was a printing shop and the owner recognized that I was quick, and from there—I still don't know how I deserved the miraculous chain of events that led to my education and elevation from that murky, hopeless start."

"My goodness! You poor thing!" Helen reached out to put her hand on his arm.

"I'm not some character in a Dickens novel." He shook his head. "Volumes have been written about the question of the inheritance of character, Helen. Blood will tell, isn't that the saying? My father is long dead, but he haunts my every step. It's why I said marriage is for better men. I vowed never to marry because I didn't trust myself. What if I am doomed to repeat history? What if I'm no better than the monster you've escaped? You've run from a monster, Helen. But what if I am cut from the same cloth?"

"You aren't and you could never be that kind of man."

"You sound so sure. But Helen, of all the women in the world, I would rather die than ever hurt you. And after what you've survived, you don't need—you don't deserve any more ugliness. But here I am. So in love with you that I'm not sure how I'm still standing from the weight of it. I'm . . . a man with nothing but ugliness at his back, nothing but tragedy in his wake. You are a lady of fine quality and I am a product of an impoverished dockworker and the daughter of a fishmonger. How is it even remotely possible that you aren't repelled?"

"Wh-what?" she asked.

Darius's heart froze in his chest. Fearing a thing and experiencing it were two different things, and the strange expression on her face made it clear that he'd not really been ready to lose her. "It isn't possible then."

"Not that," she said, shaking her head. "Did you say that you *loved* me?"

He was a man trapped in a spiral of despair, but he forced himself to stay calm, standing from his chair, readying himself to leave the room if he needed to. "I did. I am in love with you, Helen. But I won't impose my feelings on—"

Helen stood immediately, matching his every move. "I don't care, Darius. I don't care about any of the—you aren't a character from a Dickens novel. It's meaningless."

"It—It isn't meaningless. And if I *were* a character in a novel, I'm sure this is the scene where the heroine says something complimentary about my selflessness and offers to shake my hand."

"You are reading the wrong books, Mr. Thorne."

"Am I?"

"I think you should kiss me."

Darius held his breath for a moment. "Mrs. McFadden will be back any moment with a pot of mint tea." Even as he spoke, his effort to look aloof failed completely as a grin overtook him. The entire conversation had become ridiculous and wonderful, and he was so completely out of his league that he found himself enjoying it. "God . . . what a thing to say when someone offers you your heart's desire!"

She smiled back at him, a fierce joyful mischief lighting her eyes. "Kiss me, Darius."

Darius purposefully walked to the library door and leaned out of it. "Forget the tea, Mrs. McFadden! I've changed my mind!" he shouted and then shut the door to muffle the sounds of the woman's complaints and the rattling of pans. He locked the library door and turned back, a man on a mission.

Helen laughed. "Your lungs are much improved."

"I would have walked through a dozen fires to reach you, Helen."

"I want to somehow prove that I'm as brave."

"You don't need to prove anything to me."

"Then—to myself."

"I'm not prepared to be some kind of test, Helen. I care for you too much to be a gauntlet that you run through. I'm flesh and blood, and while the exercise may strengthen you, I don't think my heart could withstand it."

"And I'm not merely flesh and blood?"

"Tell me what you want. Whatever it is, Helen, you have all the power in this moment."

"I don't want to be in power. I don't want to be the queen to move about the board."

"Then say it."

"I want you."

"Then I'm yours."

Darius closed the distance between them instantly, taking her into his arms and kissing her. Since the first time he'd trespassed in the library, the delicious feel and taste of her lips had haunted his dreams and sustained him along every agonizing mile from Edinburgh to London and back. He meant to be slow about this kiss, this singular kiss he'd longed for, but when her breath grazed him and her lips parted beneath his, Darius stopped thinking.

When kissing Helen of Troy, there was apparently no room for thought.

He lifted her up against him, so slight and warm in his arms, hungry for her touch, and driven by her own eager response. She matched his passion, suckling his lower lip, her tongue darting out to meet his own and give him all that he asked.

In a tender reclamation of all the ground he'd yielded, Darius kissed the corners of her mouth and drank in her sighs. She leaned against him and he felt somehow stronger and taller. She reached up to press one hand against his heartbeat, and with the other, splayed the soft blades of her hand behind his neck to wordlessly beg for more.

And in the space of a single breath, tenderness gave way to a blaze of desire.

Darius experienced a sensation like hot sand spilling down his spine to pool at his hip bones and stiffen his cock until he was certain the seams of his clothing would give way.

Not thinking may not be wise, professor.

"Helen, wait . . ."

"What is it, Darius?"

He was a man on fire but he still held himself in check. "I want . . . to keep my promises. I want to be gentle. I don't ever want to hurt you. But this . . . this isn't a soft passion or a polite affection I'm wrestling with—" He closed his eyes. "Damn it."

"I'm not afraid of you, Darius."

He opened his eyes, struggling with his warring emotions and the taut pull of his desires. "I'm no well-bred gentleman. I have only a vague idea of the rules of this game, Helen."

"I married a gentleman, Darius, and have suffered for it. Don't try to be a gentleman. Just keep kissing me. I feel alive, Darius . . . and I want so much to stay that way."

To hell with the rules. . . .

A lifetime of discipline and denial had only primed him for a feast of the senses and made him feel like a starving man sitting at a banquet.

He lifted her up again, this time high enough to part her thighs and part her skirts, savoring the sensation of her body even through all the layers that separated them. She instinctively raised one of her legs to make it easier for him, and Darius slid one hand up into her skirts to trace the smooth lines of her thigh through the lace and gathers of her underskirts. The heat from the juncture between her legs pulsed against his hips and his body responded, urging him to press forward and betray the unmistakable evidence of his arousal.

Her eyes fluttered open a little wider at the sensation of his enormous erection, even through the barrier of their clothing. And Darius knew they were at the Rubicon, so to speak. Because if she wished to stop, it would be now.

"You're sure?"

"I am certain."

He eyed the wide surface of his desk for a brief moment but dismissed it out of turn. Instead, Darius lifted her off the floor to cradle her against his chest and carried her over to the hearth of the fireplace, where he roughly pulled down every cushion in sight to make an improvised place to lay her down.

He wanted her to be warm and comfortable, and since he fully intended to deprive her of every stitch of clothing she had on, Darius hoped he'd made a good choice.

Her expression made him hesitate. "What are you thinking over there, Helen?"

"That I landed on those cushions that very first day . . . and here I am again. . . ." She gave him a shy smile. "But look how far I've come."

He pulled her into his arms and pressed her back onto the soft pillows, a surge of joy making his throat close. He'd thought her beautiful that first day, but now she was incomparable—a sensual goddess sweetly offering him a stolen taste of happiness.

Darius slowly reached up to tug at the top button of her dress, just under her chin, kissing her softly just once as if paying a small toll. The modest bodice had glass buttons all the way from her throat to her waist, and as he changed tactics and worked from the lowest fastening at her waist upward, he trailed light kisses across her lips and jaw up to the sensitive shell of her ear.

The back of his palms lightly brushed upward to caress the rise of her breasts and their peaks on his way to reach the uppermost round bob. Darius took his time over each little button, his eyes watching her face and the subtle changes in her color. The intensity of his gaze made her drop hers, but within seconds, she was peeking at him through pale golden lashes as her breath came faster and the work of his fingers reached her collarbone.

"I . . . could manage them," she whispered, and he smiled at the trace of impatience in her voice.

"You *could*," he conceded, "but I am enjoying the process."

"Darius!"

"Shhh. I want to remember every moment of this so that I can recall it on my deathbed when I'm a hundred and die happy," he said, thrilled to see her smile at the jest.

He'd never been with a woman before. Every inch of her was uncharted territory, and as he uncovered her skin, myth after myth was shattered. She was hot to the touch, not cold like the marbled Greek beauties he'd seen before. And where he'd thought of women as otherworldly and unfamiliar, here was flesh that matched his own, reacting as he did, and her humanity humbled and inspired him to love her more.

He pushed back her bodice, uncovering the simple lace of her chemise and lightly boned corset with its ribboned edges. The column of her throat was bared to him, and the gentle lines of her collarbone and the curves of her shoulders. It was a universe of valleys and rises that beckoned a man to taste and touch at his whim, and when he dipped his head down to trace the pulse of her throat with his tongue, he was instantly rewarded with her gasp and the telltale marbling of her skin.

She leaned into him and tipped her head back, and Darius accepted the invitation without a second thought. She fit against him as if made for him, and Darius reveled in the sweet trust of every stroke of her hands across his skin and every sigh.

Her corset proved a bit more challenging, but once he'd sussed out the fastenings, it came apart easily, like cracking the shell on a lobster. The comparison made him smile as the lovely feast of her body was finally bared for his enjoyment.

Her breasts were tipped in the palest rose pink, the same color as her lips, and he loved their size, like small apples he could cover with his hands. He caressed them, enjoying the heat and heft of her flesh against his palms, but more so, the way his touch incited Helen to wriggle beneath him.

Darius leaned back to move his hand over more of her. He traced the indent of her waist and marveled that his hands could span her and almost touch fingertips. She was at once delicate and fragile to him, but then vibrant and sensually commanding. He covered her ribs with his fingers and measured the planes and rises of her curves, doing his best to ignore the throbbing indignation of his cock at all the delays.

He made quick work of the tapes and buttons of her petticoats and was grateful for her help in kicking the cumbersome layers out of the way.

Her belly button was a small revelation, for he'd forgotten about such things, but spotting hers made him smile. It was a fascinating little well nestled on the rise of her belly, and Darius made a mental note to revisit it if the chance arose.

"Darius," she whispered his name.

He worshipped her with his hands and with his mouth, trying to take it all in. He skimmed his hands over the lines of a woman that fashion hinted at and art celebrated. Nothing had prepared him for the power of the heat of her firm flesh against his palms and the sacred sense of her power that threatened to overtake him.

The sight of the triangle of pale blond curls on her mons made him sigh at the beauty of her sex. He caught a glimpse of the pink petals beneath and slid his fingers into the silken folds of her body, marveling that anything could be that soft and perfect. He was enthralled by the mysteries of her form, but Helen's sigh recaptured his attention.

"Darius. I'm . . . You're staring."

"I was admiring. I am sure there is a difference," he replied, shifting back up to cover her body with his, hoping he hadn't trespassed too far with his bold curiosity. But he was reassured when she began to work his shirt from his body, her hands impatiently baring his flesh for her own touch.

It was a much faster process to shed his own clothes, and Darius lost no time with it.

The buttons at his waist gave way at the first tug, the pressure from within too great for much resistance. The movement made his breath catch in his throat, and when she caught his member in the palm of her hand, stroking him in her gentle assessment of his size and girth, Darius had to pray for control to keep from spilling himself right then and there.

"I'm not made out of porcelain. I'm—I won't cry."

"What? Why would you say that?"

"I'm . . ." Isabel blushed furiously. "I'm a married woman. I know all about . . . these matters and I meant to . . . reassure you that I'm used to the pain. You needn't worry about hurting me."

"Is it painful?"

She nodded even before words formed to properly answer him. "Of course."

Darius's brow furrowed in concentration as he summoned every hint and conversation on the subject he'd ever had with friends. Ashe was the least guarded in his opinions on the matter (or *had been* open about the topic before the beautiful Caroline Townsend had come into his life) and he had never spoken of tears, discomfort, or anything remotely unappealing in the act.

"Helen." Darius held his breath and addressed the inescapable truth of his own instincts. "I'm no expert but . . ."

Words failed him.

Painful? There is some discomfort the first time for a woman, that much is certain from what I've read—but always? Unacceptable!

"Helen, as a man of letters, I will have to ascertain the truth for myself and apply the principles of a good chess game."

She nodded. "As you wish."

"This is my opening gambit," he whispered in her ear.

He kissed a light trail along her jawline and then down her throat, his fingers barely touching her skin as he moved them over the contours of her body and circled her breasts. She writhed with pleasure and was rewarded as every path his fingers blazed was followed by his mouth to fan warm, wet, teasing kisses along every line of her being.

Her breasts grew taut and her nipples puckered until they truly resembled pert pink roses. Darius hovered over her to inhale their fragrance, and she arched up to try to capture his mouth and press it against one pebbled tip.

He traced the peak with his tongue and then suckled her gently, his hands never still across her skin. He shifted up, his bare thigh pressing against the searing wet of her sex and adding another sensation to her experience, determined to give her whatever she needed, to add layers of contact and texture and draw her out of her reserve.

His only guide was his own heart and its longing to bring her nothing but satisfaction. Using his hands, grazing the crests of each breast with his palms Darius lightly pinched the hardened peaks only to beg her forgiveness with more kisses.

Down between the valley of her breasts, he diverted his attention, even darting his tongue into the well of her belly button to make her giggle before he slid his hand down between her legs, delving again into the wet silk, ensuring that her body was relaxed and open for him. He teased the tiny bud at the crest of her folds and watched her closely to learn where his fingers gave her the greater pleasure, and then lingered on those lessons until she cried out.

He hesitated. "Yes?"

"Yes! Don't stop! If ever you . . . cared for me . . . don't stop!"

It was all the encouragement he needed.

He moved his fingers faster but lightened his touch, teasing her with friction that wasn't friction, and discovered that his queen's pleasure might be without limits.

She gripped his shoulders, her nails clawing at his upper arms, as the pinnacle of her climax unfurled beyond her control.

"My goodness!" she exclaimed. "Darius, that was . . ."

"The opening gambit," he supplied with a playful growl. "And now, on to the castling."

In chess, castling was a special move that the king was permitted only once in a game to shift over toward the rook and place the castle at his back. But in this instance, Darius hoped to redefine the maneuver for their purposes.

Darius nudged her thighs apart with his and then positioned himself above her. Once he'd achieved his safe harbor, he lowered himself onto his elbows and looked into her eyes. "I am castled."

"So you are." She smiled, linking her ankles around his waist to hold him captive. "Now what?" she asked playfully. "And don't say something about bishops or I'll take a nip at your nose!"

He laughed, then wickedly began to move his hips against hers. "Middle game."

She sobered as her expression warmed with renewed lust edged in wariness. "Middle game," she echoed in a whisper.

The head of his cock had swollen into a fierce dark knob the size of a plum, and the instant his sensitive head was notched against the slippery heat of her body, Darius had to bite the inside of his lip to keep from bucking his hips forward to take all that was offered.

Instead, he forced himself to move slowly into her, inch by measured inch, his breath coming in ragged hitches at the sheer delirium of the grip of her body on his cock. Instead of hindrances, he was pulled and drawn in, her hips lifting up to take him, rocking up toward him as her legs parted even wider to yield to him. He pressed in and then retreated, only to drive forward with greater speed and force, immediately grasping the implications of following one's primal instincts.

Oh my. I never thought to enjoy the middle game this much. . . .

Isabel didn't know whether to cry or shout with joy. All the pain she'd anticipated from her experiences with her husband never came to pass. Instead, his every touch had elicited a new understanding of the possibilities between a man and a woman. Darius's firm and gentle hands soothed and excited her in turn, sending her over the edge to experience the bliss of release and redefine what it meant to be a woman.

Even so, when the reality of his cock first pressed up inside her entrance, she felt a small jolt of concern. He was twice the size of her husband, and Isabel had learned quickly to hate the invasion of her flesh.

It was the moment of the truth she'd quietly coached herself to simply bear.

But dread evaporated before she had the chance to fully acknowledge it.

Because almost immediately, her body began to sing with a delicious tension that promised another climax as his cock stretched her taut flesh and slowly eased into the hungry recesses of her core.

She'd never felt so alive. Isabel closed her eyes and tipped her head back, clinging to him as her memories died in the fires of this delicious game. Her hips involuntarily rocked up to pull him farther inside. She embraced the fall, shedding any pretense of ladylike reluctance, and met him stroke for stroke until her every thought was swept away in waves of raw lust.

Isabel opened her eyes and leaned up to taste him, defiantly licking the salty sweet fire at the juncture of his throat, and kissed the path of his blood beneath his skin. She wanted to immerse herself in this pleasure and groaned as the white-hot coil inside of her began to tighten to an unbearable tension.

This.

This is a new and wonderful kind of torment.

Darius the kind.

Darius the strong.

Darius, her protector and friend.

Here was a physical shield against the demons of her past.

Here in his arms.

Here was Troy.

She framed his face with her hands to guide his mouth to hers, kissing him so passionately that he stopped everything he was doing to respond, to give her what she craved. She suckled his tongue and savored the wet velvet textures of his lips as he mirrored her movements.

Every kiss fueled the next, each satisfying sweep of his lips to hers only adding to her need for more.

End game.

His body was ranging beyond his control and her kisses whipped his senses into a wild storm that demanded release. His cock was so hot and heavy it was almost painful, but the grip of her wet channel against him was his sole relief—an erotic torment as her inner muscles held and released him in a primal rhythm that made him want to drive into her faster and faster.

More.

Suddenly it wasn't a desire but a need. As if his life depended on his obedience to the fiery sweet ropes of hunger that snaked through his frame.

More.

More of everything that was Helen.

Check.

She held him tightly, her ankles at his back, urging him to ride the slick friction of her core, to drive deeply into her until he couldn't tell where his flesh ended and hers began.

He shut his eyes and an ecstasy as sharp as wire broke free and his essence jetted inside of her body, wrenching from him a cry of sheer pleasure. Darius wasn't a child not to know the workings of his body, but this was a climax like none he'd experienced alone. She arched against him, her cry echoing with his and bringing him back to the present.

Isabel wrapped her legs around his waist, leveraging herself up to press her breasts against his chest, absorbed in the contact of her body to his, her nipples pebbling at the wicked friction of the patch of hair on his chest.

Check and mate.

"Do . . . you . . . yield?" he asked, gasping for air.

"That was . . . a wonderful . . . stalemate. . . ." She sighed. "I refuse to think in terms of . . . winning and losing . . . Darius."

He smiled at the ceiling. "A better philosophy and probably a sign of wisdom. Although it certainly *felt* like winning. . . ."

She playfully punched him in the shoulder and they both dissolved into laughter and ended up entwined in each other's arms in their nest. They lazed on the cushions for a time, covered by an impromptu blanket of shed clothes and a lap blanket from the window seat, and talked quietly, watching the fire.

"God, you're so beautiful."

"Do you think so?"

"Yes. I'm . . . I'm no poet, Helen. Don't ask me to describe you. I'll make a mess of it and you'll banish me—a punishment I have no intention of accepting, by the way."

She laughed. "I'd not banish you for bad poetry."

He levered himself up on his elbows, shifting to tuck her beneath him as if to shield her from the world with his body. "And the pain? Was there pain?"

She shook her head, blushing until her skin glowed. "No, quite the opposite, as I'm sure I . . . demonstrated."

He gently nipped at her earlobe and teased it with his tongue until she writhed beneath him. "Hmm. It *was* my first attempt." He kissed the sensitive indent behind the shell of her ear. "I'm sure I could improve on things with more practice."

"Your first attempt? Ever?" She squeaked in mock protest but tipped her head back to give him more access to the ivory column of her throat. "If you improve, I might expire with happiness, sir."

"You look pale. Are you sure you're all right?"

"I always look pale, Mr. Thorne," she replied, the corner of her lip pulling up into a quick smile that gave him a glimpse of the light humor she possessed.

"Helen, can you tell me . . . who he is? We've come so far down this path. If I know who your husband is, it might help me to resolve things."

She pulled away from him, her pale hair falling like a curtain that shielded her face from his scrutiny. "It might. But I'm . . . please, Darius. I need a little more time. I love being Helen. I love—*this*. I'm frightened that I'll have spoiled what little happiness I have once I speak his name aloud. We've carved out this sanctuary and I don't know if I'm ready to bring *him* into it."

"I understand," he said and shifted over to be closer to her. "But the rest of it, Helen. There is nothing you can't tell me."

"You've shared so much of yourself, I'm selfish to cling to my secrets."

"It's different. I asked because I must. But you are under no such compunction in revealing anything to me. When you're ready . . ."

"You asked me before about the nightmares," she began carefully.

"Yes."

"I was dreaming about my husband. In my nightmares, I am . . . being punished again."

"Punished?"

"If I displeased him, if I failed in some way to—I never knew what he wanted or what might set things in motion but the punishments were . . ." Her voice broke a little and she kept her eyes locked onto the bedding. "We were only married for a few months, but I didn't think I would live to see an anniversary."

"My God. Was there no one to step in?" he asked gently. "Not even a Mrs. McFadden of your own?"

She shook her head. "The servants lived in fear of him and I learned quickly where their loyalties lay. They were rewarded for keeping a close eye on me and disobedience was—out of the question. The worst was his bodyguard and valet, a horrible man. I hated the way he looked at me like some black raven eager to see me fall."

"What made you finally run?"

"I don't know. The last punishment was like so many others before it. He flogged me this time because I'd asked him to take me to London." Isabel rested her chin on her knees, drawing herself into a protective ball. "It was a stupid thing to ask. He caned me and then I spent the night on my knees in a cold, empty room to demonstrate my obedience. I even managed a pretty speech at breakfast about . . . my gratitude for his discipline."

Darius gasped but didn't interrupt. It was absurd to think of thanking a man for a beating, but nothing in a world of punishment and submission made sense unless you'd lived in it.

A ghost of a smile crossed her pale pink lips. "My apology was accepted and he rewarded me with a rare ride on Samson. The groomsman's cinch broke on his saddle. I was already mounted on Samson. He was pawing at the ground to go, and for one moment, I was holding him back. And then . . ."

"Then?"

"And then I wasn't." Helen tipped her head to one side, the curtain of her hair shielding the curve of her hips. "Because I knew he was going to kill me, sooner or later, and it didn't matter what I said or did to try to appease him. My husband was going to kill me, Darius, and I didn't want to die. So I gave Samson the lead he wanted on the reins and I spurred him into a gallop and I never looked back."

"Thank God."

"A smarter woman would have packed a bag, Darius."

"Not smarter at all. I can't see your husband letting you walk out with luggage for a morning ride, Helen."

She lifted her face at the revelation. "I never thought of it that way."

"Your departure was sudden," he repeated slowly, piecing it all together. "Have you not told your family, Helen? Should we send them some word of your status—if only so that they won't worry?"

She shrugged. "I'm not sure what they would say. I tried, when I was first married, to write to my mother about . . . my husband's temperament but her reply was . . ." Isabel's eyes filled with tears. "Less than assuring."

"I'm sorry."

"It was a brief reply, as if my mother was convinced that I'd done something to offend him and that I apparently just needed to learn to rely on my husband's guidance and accept my new responsibilities, however challenging they might seem." Isabel picked at the ribbons on the quilt's edge. "As if it were my fault."

"Could she have misunderstood?"

"Perhaps." Isabel was as still as a porcelain statue. "I wasn't brave enough to write again and ask. And then I realized that my husband was monitoring my correspondence and I abandoned the effort."

Darius gritted his teeth, trying to hide his fury. *God, I hate this man. I don't think I hated that raja in India as much as I hate her husband.*

"And you?" she asked, interrupting his thoughts. "Besides your parents, do you have family, Mr. Thorne?"

Damn, another dark topic for me to botch!

"What little is left is estranged from me."

"Estranged?"

"Not entirely by my choice. When I left home to that apprenticeship, my older brother was extremely angry. He argued that he was older and should have been the one to go, but I was the lucky one with the gift for letters."

"He was jealous?"

"He was as desperate to escape as I was and I understood why he hated me for leaving him there."

"You were six! You were hardly abandoning him willfully!"

"You're looking at it with the fair-mindedness of an adult, Helen." He caught her wrist and traced her pulse with gentle, phantom strokes of his fingers as he talked. "Over the years, I sent home money whenever I could but I never went back. I never wanted to brush up against the poverty and cruelty that had crafted me."

"It's only natural."

"Perhaps."

"Can things be mended between you?"

Darius shook his head. "One hate-filled letter from my older brother reached me before I left for India, advising me that despite our father's passing, I was unwelcome at my mother's table for my 'cold nature.' After I returned to England, a local vicar from the seaside town where my family had lived sent word that there'd been an epidemic that had taken my mother on to 'her heavenly reward' and my brother had immigrated to America without a word of farewell."

"Oh no!"

"I'd have shared all that I have with them if I'd had the chance. But now, it's all I can do to muster relief that he's gone, that my mother is at peace and my father is likely enjoying a special corner of hell reserved for men like him."

To his best friend, Ashe Blackwell, alone he'd previously confessed his lack of grief when it came to his relations. Now as he looked into Helen's eyes, he saw no judgment.

"It doesn't matter. My friends are closer to me than any blood relations, and as dear."

She arched up to kiss him with one tender sweep of her lips against his. "You've made your own way, Darius. I admire you for it."

"I'm not worthy of that compliment—or of you."

"Don't say such things, Darius!" She put her cool fingertips gently against his lips. "When you touch me, I feel whole again. I don't want to imagine myself beyond this moment."

"I don't either. Helen, we have each other. Let us say that it's enough."

For now.

Enough for now.

Chapter
15

At the University of Edinburgh a few days later, in the Old College's library, Darius was using a magnifying glass to study a detailed map of Bengal. His notes from his own travels were long gone but his memory was inviolate. He opened a small leather-bound journal and set it down on the table, taking notes of potential areas that could be temple seats.

If the prophecy is tied to a specific temple, then there might be examples of sacred objects unique to it—and when we know what kind of stone the diamond is disguised as, we can secure it somehow and avoid the worst.

"Ah! I had a feeling when Professor Douglas said he'd seen you this morning that I'd find you with your nose pressed against some old parchment," Mr. Harold Pughes called out as he strode toward him with another man in tow. A third figure stayed outside the large double doors and made no move to follow.

Darius straightened immediately, subtly closing his journal and folding the map. "It *is* my occupation and Professor Douglas has been kind to allow me access to the archives."

"Here! Here, Mr. Thorne, is one of our university's great friends I wish to acquaint you with!" Mr. Pughes said, his hand clapping his friend on the shoulder in a very public show of familiarity as they entered the library. "Lord Netherton."

The room was primarily deserted, but it jarred Darius's scholarly sensibilities to be greeted as loudly as if they were in a coffee shop. Darius rose and nodded respectfully, answering in a hushed tone, "It is a pleasure to meet you, Lord Netherton."

Lord Netherton was Darius's equal in height but much broader in build. His features were aristocratic and chiseled, his expression one of practiced boredom that men of his station seemed to favor. He was a contemporary in age, if not slightly older, but Darius knew that dissipation played a role in most gentlemen's lives and could make it hard to guess at their true age. Overall, his first impression of Lord Netherton was that this was a man with the warmth of a stone.

"Darius Thorne is one of the most gifted translators I have ever come across." Mr. Pughes continued with his introductions. "You asked me to keep an eye out for talent! Thorne is the fellow I told you about. Remember?"

Netherton's eyes widened in recognition and he held out his gloved hand. "Yes, I remember. You may be just the man I've been looking for!"

"Am I?" Darius took his hand, slightly bemused at all the sudden attention and the change in Lord Netherton's countenance.

"Thorne has no patron that he speaks of, Lord Netherton, for all that we speculate on the source of his carriage and horses," Harold added.

Darius ended the handshake with Netherton and ignored Pughes. "How can I be of service?"

"I am questing for a man who speaks Hindi and can read Sanskrit or whatever this scrawl is, who might be interested in a private commission to work on some very specific translations," Lord Netherton said.

"The work *could* lead to a permanent post at the

university, Thorne," Pughes added. "What do you think of that?"

Darius had to blink at the unexpected proposition. A fleeting daydream about his acceptance into the elite circles of British academia after all his years of hard work coalesced briefly in his mind. Darius pushed it away to focus on the matter at hand. "A private commission?"

"An entertaining commission as well, if I may be so bold." Netherton's smile was a sly thing, and the icy gleam in his eyes almost made Darius take a step back.

"Entertaining?" he asked.

The smile on Lord Netherton's face lost some of its integrity. "Why do you repeat everything I say, Mr. Thorne? Or is this the way of translators? To say nothing original but act as parrots?"

Pughes cleared his throat at the awkward turn in the conversation. "I'm sure Mr. Thorne will be interested. After all, a generous patron of the university could have his pick of men for his projects." He gave Darius a barbed look over the peer's shoulder. "It's an honor to be asked."

Darius put his journal into his inside coat pocket, unaffected by Pughes's glare. "Undoubtedly, but I would have to understand the nature of the work before I even considered it. No matter how entertaining it might prove to be."

"A man of principles," Netherton said softly. "An exotic find."

"Thorne is notoriously principled," Pughes said wryly.

"Not *too* principled, surely?" Lord Netherton said. "You're not a puritan, are you, Thorne?"

Darius chose not to address the question, affronted at the vague notion that either puritans were *too principled* or that any man would deny having principles for the sake of banter.

It was Pughes who picked up the thread of conversation. "Thorne has traveled the world and seen too much to be a shrinking violet. But he'll never get a wife or tenure if he doesn't stop sacrificing opportunities."

Netherton nodded. "Then I am happy to give him another chance to improve his fortunes, even if he will waste them on acquiring a wife." He completed his speech with an odd sneer, and Darius watched the two men exchange knowing looks.

Pughes grinned. "Netherton's recently married very well and he was extremely generous in his pledge to my next expedition. I would thank the new Lady Netherton, but I've not had the pleasure of making her acquaintance."

"No need to thank Lady Netherton. You can thank *me*, since providentially, her money is mine to dispose of as I wish, and as you know," he said with a conspiratorial wink, "I've always aspired to be associated closely with great discoveries."

Darius's brow furrowed, unsure of the direction of the wink. Pughes had always been one of his least favorite people. He was openly ambitious and socially aggressive but had achieved funding for his pet projects with his charming good looks, and he made no secret of his disdain for anyone who disapproved of his methods. As for Lord Netherton, Darius was experiencing an instant loathing that was making it difficult for him to concentrate on the conversation.

How to tell him to bugger off without offense . . . that's the large question, isn't it?

"I'm flattered, Lord Netherton," Darius began. "But I'm currently committed to other work and couldn't take the time away to travel to see your collection or—"

"My man, Mr. Jarvis, has a few examples here." Lord Netherton interrupted him, raising a hand to signal the man in the doorway. "I brought a few tempting pages from my recent acquisition, so you can take a peek without infringing on your schedule to see if the work entices you."

His man came forward, a scarred and surly gentleman with black eyes as indifferent as a shark's. "Your lordship." He handed over a portfolio case and withdrew without a single glance at Darius or Mr. Pughes.

Darius watched him retreat like a black raven to his perch beyond the library and fought the urge to shudder. *The sooner this conversation is concluded, the more content I'm going to be.*

Netherton set out the leather portfolio, untying it to lay out the papers within. "Look your fill, Mr. Thorne, and tell me what you think of my beauties."

Darius turned his attention to the texts and immediately surmised the source of Lord Netherton's "entertainment." The illuminated drawings were erotic and lewd, without much artistic merit. Darius struggled to find something diplomatic to say. Even for a man familiar with the contents of the *Kama Sutra* and *The Perfumed Garden* and who had seen countless exotic depictions in his travels, Darius was having trouble glancing at the meticulously detailed drawings. They were nauseating in their portrayals of obscene and unnatural acts involving every combination of sex imaginable, including apparently the use of children.

Across the table from him, the men made small talk as if Darius no longer existed, and Darius's world came to a grinding halt as he became an unwilling witness to the conversation one overheard in nightmares.

"You jest, but I meant what I said. I wish to meet your lovely new bride, Richard."

"You can't, old friend. In confidence I must tell you that it seems my lovely wife has taken a bit of a holiday without me. She's been gone for over two weeks."

"Oh?" Pughes's voice lowered to a curious whisper that naturally carried even better across the room. "A winter holiday? Where?"

"I'm afraid I don't know. She neglected to tell me."

"The scandal!"

Netherton's sigh was overtly theatrical. "I know. Women these days . . ."

"What will you do, your lordship?"

Netherton chuckled. "Besides enjoying the quiet?" Netherton said as he put his arm around Harold's shoulders, then sobered. "Forgive me. My dark humor hides my heartache. Lady Netherton is skittish and hysterical, even for a woman, and I fear that I was duped into marrying a weak-minded and pale, sickly thing. What can I do? I must put on a brave face, Harold."

"Is there—infidelity?"

Netherton waved his hand dismissively. "Impossible! But I've already shared too much of this. I'm sure I don't need to even ask for your discretion, friend."

"Of course not!"

"Or yours, Mr. Thorne?" Netherton asked evenly. "I'm sure you couldn't help but overhear about my personal difficulties."

Darius shook his head. "Your business is your own." *It's you, isn't it? You black-hearted son of a bitch! You're deliberately planting all these seeds of misinformation about a "weak-minded and sickly" runaway bride only to cover your own tracks and give yourself carte blanche.* Darius wondered just how many of these "inadvertent" confessions about his unfortunate marital issues Netherton had been making since Helen's escape. His stomach clenched with nausea at the revelation that the villain of Helen's existence was the selfsame man smirking at him. He had to fight not to be instantly sick, praying that none of his distress was visible on his face.

"And the project?" Netherton stepped forward to the table. "Surely you find the work appealing? What red-blooded man would not?"

"These are . . . unusual."

"Aren't they?"

Darius lifted his gaze from the table and kept it resolutely on the man in front of him. "But not my area of expertise."

"Forget expertise!" Netherton laughed. "I would pay you to translate them, Thorne, not perfect the techniques they show! Hell, that will be for me to consider, won't it, so long as my mistress doesn't complain, eh?"

"Lord Netherton!" Pughes intervened. "He'll mistake you and miss the joke!"

Netherton shrugged, some of his mirth fading. "Naturally, my interests are purely *academic*."

"As a gentleman, I must decline." Darius took a step back, folding his hands politely behind his back.

"As a gentleman? What kind of *gentleman* are you, sir?"

Pughes's countenance shifted, openly uncomfortable at the turn. "Perhaps another—"

"Harold told me of your unfortunate family ties. Your father was a fisherman or something, wasn't he? Don't play the lofty soul with me!" Lord Netherton's eyes glazed over with ice, his civility gone. "You're as much a gentleman as my stable boy!"

"I may be. The word applies to any man who carries himself with honor, dignity, and with—"

"You'll not lecture me on the meaning of the word, you prig!"

"It wasn't intended as a lecture," Darius said, "so much as praise of your stable boy."

"Watch your tone! I could see you sacked from—" Netherton began.

But Harold touched his arm and stopped him. "He is not employed by the university, your lordship."

Netherton's face became red. "Nor will he be! If your conservative and narrow views keep you from seeing the value in these ancient manuscripts, so be it. But how dare you insinuate that I am any less of a gentleman than some lowborn book snipe without the common sense to mind his manners in the presence of his betters!" Netherton gathered his papers as he spoke, and Darius noted that Mr. Jarvis's silhouette filled the doorway.

"Thorne!" Harold hissed his disapproval. "Apologize to his lordship!"

Darius folded his hands behind him, deliberately keeping his voice level. "I would, if it were warranted. But Lord Netherton knows better. These are no ordinary pages hinting at positions or conveying ancient formulas for aphrodisiacs. He'd have taken them to the linguistic department or geographical society without a blink of concern if that were the case. But instead, he's ferreting them around and presenting them to someone who, by your report, Mr. Pughes, because of his humble background and lack of a formal position must need the work and would be desperate enough to take any-thing on the vague promise of a teaching chair."

"Well!" Mr. Pughes huffed uselessly, unable to argue such an obvious truth.

Darius kept his eyes on Netherton. "I meant no insult. I merely said it wasn't my area of expertise and that I must decline. I said nothing of your lineage, social standing, or character. My reasons are my own. If his lordship wishes to make a greater protest, then by all means, I can summon some of my peers and we can form an academic committee to review the pages and debate my choice."

Darius strolled over to a table next to the windows. "Shall I ring the bell for a runner?"

Lord Netherton's expression was one of frozen rage. "No need. It was meant to be a diversion, but Harold's misin-formed me of your character and there's an end to it." He held up the portfolio for Mr. Jarvis to step forward and take it from him, the maneuver almost choreographed in its smoothness. "Good day, Mr. Thorne."

He turned on his heel, and while Harold Pughes followed instantly, already babbling away his apologies and applying his skills as a sycophant to try to salvage his funding, Mr. Jarvis lingered for a few telltale seconds.

Darius held his ground, submitting to the scrutiny of Netherton's servant, ignoring the flashes of adrenaline that threatened to unnerve him. Darius made a subtle shift of his weight to the balls of his feet the way that Michael Ruth-erford had taught him and mentally tried to prepare for whatever assault Jarvis would make.

"No one tells him no," Jarvis said softly, his voice like gravel on a steel plate.

Darius smiled. "Are you sure?"

Mr. Jarvis's expression darkened. "I'm sure."

Darius waited. Either the man would seek to intimidate him further or make some point with violence, but he didn't care. Darius remembered the black of a dungeon and the deprivation and pain he'd suffered and survived.

One man in a black wool coat just doesn't compare.

"I wonder why not," Darius said. "His charismatic charms, perhaps?" he added sarcastically.

Jarvis's look took on a touch of surprise. "Good day, Mr. Thorne."

"And to you, Mr. Jarvis."

It was only when he'd turned his back and left that Darius allowed himself to exhale. "Shit."

It could be another man. Pure coincidence. Another horse. Another missing wife. Another heartless bastard . . .

Shit.

Chapter

16

Darius directed Hamish to make one more stop in the city before the journey home. There was a gentleman's social club that he was acquainted with and he didn't want to leave Edinburgh until he'd asked the questions that crowded his mind. Hamish pulled over to wait and Darius climbed out unassisted.

Inside the foyer, the club's butler stepped forward to greet him.

"May I help you, sir?"

"Is Mr. Carrick available?"

The butler answered coolly and Darius submitted to the man's subtle inspection of his coat and shoes. "Do you have an appointment with him, sir?"

It was clear that Darius was no member, but he held out his card with as much confidence as he could muster. "No, but here is my card and if you'll explain to him that it is an urgent matter . . ."

Mr. Carrick didn't keep him waiting long. The older man sauntered out of the club with the elegance of Beau Brummell, evoking an age gone by. "Thorne! Did I forget a meeting? I have not seen you since last summer when you presented that brilliant paper to the Architectural Society."

"May we talk?" Darius asked, awkwardly omitting any small talk.

"Of course. Here." Carrick directed him to a formal sitting room off the main entry hall. "I would take you into the central card room but . . ."

"I'm not attired for the private rooms of your club, sir." It was more of a statement than an apology. "If you'll pardon the intrusion, I won't take up too much of your time."

"Not at all." The men sat on a long sofa set in the round room's center. "Warren charged me with keeping an eye out for you, but I've utterly failed. I cannot lie. These days I am so easily distracted and cannot seem to keep any task to hand. The years are catching up with me, Mr. Thorne."

"Professor Warren always said you were too clever to grow old."

Carrick laughed. "God, I love that man! But come, you are his protégé and let's hear this business of yours."

"I am a scholar, sir, and no expert on Burke's lists." Darius shifted on the cushions and went directly to the heart of the matter. "Are you aware of a Lord Netherton? Richard Netherton?"

"The earl? His estates are northwest of the city," Carrick replied in confirmation. "He inherited from his father just eight years ago. Odd fellow. Spends all of his time in London, from what I understand."

"He recently married."

Mr. Carrick nodded. "Last spring. A good match to Miss Isabel Penleigh. Her father is a marquis, although with no male heirs, it all stands to shift off to a distant cousin, sadly. Even so, her dowry was substantial and it has allowed Lord Netherton to recover his good credit and pay his tailors, from what I've heard."

"So, he is—well connected."

"Without a doubt. He has quite the social profile in Town,

and while I am not a personal acquaintance, it is my understanding that he has shaped up quite nicely after a raucous youth." Carrick shrugged. "A common enough story. Marriage often reins a man in once he tastes the joys of domestication."

It was all Darius could do to nod. *Shit. Netherton? Is it really possible I've trespassed that far from my sphere?*

"A quick engagement so there was a tiny whisper that he'd rushed her to it, but no one blamed him for being eager." Carrick went on, "I saw her at a party a week before the nuptials, and I must say, it is the reason I remember all of this as well as I do. Isabel Penleigh was the most stunning woman I have ever laid eyes on. She was like a slender slice of moonlight—so pale a beauty that I almost thought her hair white! But eyes like . . ."

"Opals," Darius whispered without thinking.

"Yes, opals!" Carrick clapped him on the back. "You read that in the social pages, did you?"

"Yes, the papers were . . . very complimentary, if I recall." He recalled nothing but decided the lie was understandable. "Well, I should be going. I've taken enough of your time."

Darius stood and Carrick followed suit, his confusion apparent. "B-but your business! Surely you did not just burst into my club just for—whatever was that?"

"Lord Netherton has approached me for a commission, but he struck me as insincere and I—wanted to hear your impression of the man. I trust your judgment, and since I know as much of English lords as I do of North American savages . . ."

Carrick smiled. "I'm flattered. But my best advice is to always trust your own instincts. Not that I've heard anything off on this gentleman's reputation! I'm sure he is a fine gentleman and in no way untrustworthy!"

"But you said he was odd. What did you mean by that exactly?"

"I spoke rashly and without thought." Carrick straightened his coat. "I've been casual in my remarks, Mr. Thorne, forgetting myself a bit. You caught me off guard with your sudden appearance, but I hope I've conveyed what you needed. Lord Netherton is a peer of the realm and above reproach, I'm sure."

Darius nodded, stepping back to end the exchange. "Thank you, Mr. Carrick. I'll let you get back to your cards."

Darius left without another word, his legs numb and his head pounding.

He caught himself and closed ranks but it's all the same. I have my answers.

The chances of being able to offer Helen's husband money enough to avoid a scandal had been slim, but now—it was a pipe dream that faded in the icy air that enveloped him as he walked back to where Hamish was waiting with the carriage.

He felt like a fool.

His fantasies of Helen being just a shade wellborn or her husband nearly his equal so that the path would be smoother ahead all turned to dust.

The option of just slipping away and changing her name also evaporated. He'd learned that her father was the Marquis of Penleigh and her debut in London was memorable, as was her quick engagement and marriage to the charming Lord Netherton. His Helen was well-known and scandal seemed inevitable.

The daughter of a marquis.
The wife of an earl.

Helen was Lady Isabel Netherton. And if he was not extremely cautious, he could end up swinging from a rope from any number of trumped-up charges, including being a horse thief or a kidnapper. But it wasn't his own life he feared for; it was hers. His determination to see her free and safe had taken on a new urgency.

The question was, would Isabel be strong enough to face it? They'd whispered endearments and fallen into each other's arms, but the implications of not knowing her station had made it all seem more tangible.

It hadn't felt as much like adultery when her husband was

no more than a nameless, cruel shadow. But now, he'd met the man and absorbed that this was no phantom to conveniently fade away and allow for fairy tales.

On the ride home, he chased the circular arguments for and against loving her before he finally abandoned the notion that it was a decision to be made.

I love her. There's no choice to be had. All I can do is love her and find a way to free her. For better or worse, the monster in the dark has a name.

Netherton.

And once she was free, Darius accepted that the only way to guarantee her happiness would be to sacrifice his own.

* * *

When he walked through the front door of his house, Helen was waiting for him on the stairs.

"Was it a good day? Did you find the temples that Father Pasqual referenced in the university's archives?" she asked eagerly. "I found an old recipe in one of your geology books on how to dye stones red like rubies so . . ." Her words trailed off as she came closer. "Is something wrong?"

"No. Not really. Not . . ." It was his turn to lose the thread of his thoughts. "I accidentally encountered your husband in the city, Helen, and I can now say without any doubt that I personally detest him. Not that I didn't loathe him before on your behalf, but after meeting him, he is—vile."

"Y-you met . . . Richard?"

Even knowing it for certain, to hear her say his first name and confirm all made his stomach churn. "Lord Netherton was at the university looking for a translator to work on some bit of exotic pornography he'd picked up somewhere."

What little color she had in her cheeks vanished instantly at the news as she shook her head. "S-so vulgar and bold of him, wouldn't you say?"

He nodded. "Tell me what you're thinking."

"I'm terrified that you will have weighed it out and decided that I am not worth the risk of crossing such a man." She kept her place on the last step, her grip on the banister so strong he could see her arm shaking. "I'm . . . certain that I'm supposed to say something noble about releasing you from any promises you've made to spare us both the—"

"I love you."

Her eyes filled with tears, and he caught her as she fell forward into his arms, relief robbing her of her balance. "Oh, God! Darius, I'm so sorry!"

He stroked her hair and held her close as she sobbed against him. "There now. It's all right. He's no more or less of a threat than he was yesterday, and we are just as happy, are we not?"

She buried her face in his neck, her cries rending his heart.

He simply waited, unwilling to give in to despair, caressing her cheek and warming her against his body. "Don't worry, beauty. This time, the walls of Troy will hold and we'll find a way."

She lifted her head, a woman bereft of hope. "H-how?"

Darius looked at her and knew that she loved him. But he also knew that after all that she'd been through, her spirit was too fragile for the blast and shrapnel of a publicly detonated marriage.

Damn.

"*I'll* find a way."

"It must be wrong to touch you, to want you, to love you as I do when I'm—his."

He shook his head. "You're not *his*. Whatever claim he had as a husband, I have to believe he forfeited it the first time he hurt you."

"Perhaps that's right. Because it doesn't feel sinful to love you, Darius. It doesn't feel wrong."

"Then let it be. Let's simply take what happiness we're allowed for as long as the fates allow it, Lady Netherton. To hell with the world!"

She gasped at his language, coloring beautifully at his boldness. "Call me Helen, again. I love it when you call me Helen, Darius. I can pretend to be someone else. Someone more brave . . ."

He smiled and lifted her into his arms and began to carry her up the stairs. "My Helen."

Now it was truly a game of chess.

And Darius was just the man to figure out how to win the day and save his White Queen.

Chapter
17

Thorne left her abed and walked the house into the wee hours of the morning, wrestling with an impossible problem. *How can we end a marriage without creating a scandal? How do I destroy the ties that Netherton legally holds without also hurting Isabel in the process?*

The moon was full enough to light the rooms and guide him through the halls. Darius tried to consider everything, even pondering what Netherton's view would be. The man was making it known that his wife had deserted him but then underscored it with complaints about her disposition and health. He'd put himself in a position of power so that no matter where she surfaced, she would either be hounded back to him for her immoral flight or branded as unstable and give him grounds to put her in an asylum or lock her quietly away somewhere.

The clock over the mantel in the library struck four and a possible solution came to him before the echoes from the chimes had ended.

Netherton is no angel, and while the law protects him, there are limits.

As wicked as he is, no one knows the depths of his depravity, or that protective shield that Carrick and his kind uphold would fall instantly. Odd isn't a crime. But if he's gone too far, then no one will defend him.

If the scandal he's threatened with has nothing to do with his wife and everything to do with his own personal proclivities . . .

He might let go of her to protect himself from exposure.

If I can research the man and uncover any tangible proof of wrongdoing, I might have the leverage I need to free Isabel. I just have to keep her clear of it and out of Netherton's hands until I've succeeded.

Darius went back up the stairs as quickly and quietly as he could, eager to rejoin her for a few hours of sleep before telling her in the morning of his idea. But he found her standing by the bedroom window, a sensual ghost in her white nightgown with the curves of her body revealed by the bright light of the moon.

"Did I keep you up?" he asked. "Stomping about the house?"

She turned to him with a smile, keeping her place. "No, and you weren't exactly stomping. I had another dream but when I awoke I thought I saw something outside."

"Did you?" He walked over to share her view of the courtyard in between the house and the stables, already suspecting what she'd spotted.

A light from a lantern moved across the stable yard toward the house. "Is that . . . ?"

Darius winced. "Shhh! Mrs. McFadden would be mortified if she knew we'd seen her returning to the house."

Isabel blinked at him innocently. "The arrangement seems to suit them both."

"You're not shocked?" he asked.

"You said they were a match, but I—somehow it never occurred to me that you meant it truly until I saw her cross the yard one night while you were gone. . . ." Isabel reached up to press her fingers to her cheeks. "I'm such a ninny! That's why you didn't want me to mention you getting that footprint from the stables! Isn't it?"

He nodded and folded his arms around her. "I was trying to protect their privacy. Mrs. McFadden would be mortified if she knew her secrets were . . . not her own."

"And Hamish?" she asked. "You—might have overheard them. But if you know, wouldn't they be relieved not to have to hide and sneak about?"

He laughed softly, reaching out to push a strand of her hair back from her face. "Hamish knows of my awareness but I'd do anything not to spoil the illusion of my ignorance. It probably adds to their relationship to guard their affairs."

"What other clues did I miss?" she asked, playfully pushing against his hand.

"Not many. I thought it was more telling that Mrs. McFadden never came when you had nightmares. I was hoping that you wouldn't notice that my dear housekeeper isn't on hand in the night."

She was irresistible in the moonlight and Darius stepped closer to inhale again the fragrance of her skin and the faint musk of her arousal at his nearness. "Come back to bed, Isabel."

It was the first time he'd really used her true Christian name, and the power of it affected them both.

She turned in his arms, her eyes filling with tears that shone like diamonds.

"Darius."

He led her back to the bed, sitting on the edge, and then guided her to stand in front of him. Without a word between them, she read the stark need in his eyes and began to fulfill his unspoken wish.

She took one small step back and started to untie the ribbons at her throat and then slip the nightgown off her shoulders to drop it around her feet. For long moments, it was all he could do to stare at the woman that had so completely overtaken his existence. She was naked before him like a living statue, and Darius barely stifled the urge to kneel at her feet.

For there was his Galatea.

Although he made no claim to her creation. His contribution to Isabel's beauty was hardly a wisp, perhaps only the energy of a true follower at the feet of a goddess.

"God, I want to map you!"

"Darius!" she protested with a laugh. "I am not the Congo."

Darius smiled. "Perhaps not, but I fully intend to explore this territory and claim it for my own."

He caught her hand and pulled her onto the bed, spreading out her limbs and even arranging her hair to survey this "territory" he intended to take.

"Darius," she whispered, "please."

He indulged in another moment or two to take in the sight of her, laid out before him, ripe and fertile, the beautiful, glistening petals of her sex open to him, her small breasts high and firm, and everything about her was the beckoning call of a siren. Here was his shy goddess, suffering the worship of his eyes and begging him with her gaze for the worship of his body.

He made quick work of shedding his robe and knelt at her feet, a sly smile coming over his features as his strategy unfolded. He lowered his mouth to taste her ankles and then deliberately worked his way upward to the prize he sought—the honey coating the swollen soft flesh between her legs.

He didn't hesitate to lower his mouth, deliberately exhaling over her to elicit her cry of want. At last, he touched his mouth to her, the sweet play of his mouth against her making him long to extend the game. He used the tip of his tongue to trace her folds and then circle the distended nub of her clit, flicking it gently and driving her beyond her fears.

She was salty and sweet and it was addictive, this contact. To kiss her so intimately and deeply shook the foundations of his soul and made him wish that he truly had the power to send the world away. He imagined himself connected to her very soul as she began to buck and writhe beneath him.

He increased the speed of his tongue, and her fingers wound into his hair, gripping his head and holding on, her breath coming in jagged gasps at each movement of his mouth against her tender skin.

She'd accused him of promising too much, but her release was all he desired now.

Isabel threw her head back, and he knew she was losing control.

He boldly slipped a finger inside of her, pressing upward while his tongue laved the taut jut of her clit to push her over the edge.

Her taste was so intoxicating he wanted to savor every drop of her climax, forfeiting his own reason as the sound of her cries drove him beyond logic. He sat up and tried to catch his breath and was frozen at the sight of what his touch had wrought.

In the moonlight, she was transformed into a creature of pure magic, and with her eyes heavy with the spell of her own unfolding orgasm, Darius knew he would have given his soul to join her.

Without thinking, he climbed between her thighs and drove his rampant erection into the warm well of her body, gently impaling her with one stroke. Wishing to share her climax, to feel her come on him and around him, Darius pumped his body into hers, mercilessly chasing the ecstasy that encircled them both in its spell.

Deeper. Deeper. A spiral of touch, taste, smell, and sight ensnared him until she was perched in his lap with her legs wrapped around him, until there was nothing between them and neither could move without setting off a ripple of ecstasy through the other.

Isabel reveled in it. Her breasts felt heavy and ripe as they pressed against the firm, hot wall of his chest. The swirl of dark hair on his chest only added to the sweet friction of flesh on flesh, and her nipples pebbled against him, and she could feel him swelling and growing even harder inside of her, spurred on by her touch.

At last, he came inside of her in searing hot splashes of release and she almost laughed with the strange joy of it.

Darius called out her name and lost a part of himself irrevocably in her, imparting his heart and soul into the body of this woman that he had no right to claim.

And accepted that no man had ever loved a woman more. *Married or not.*

* * *

"Where is your wedding ring?" he asked.

"I buried it." She pushed the hair back from his eyes. "I couldn't wear it anymore once I realized my feelings for you." She studied him for a moment. "Tell me what you're thinking, Darius."

"Two things." He sighed. "Firstly, that I may never get used to calling you Isabel and may just insist on using Helen as a term of endearment."

"Rightly so," she agreed and kissed him on the cheek. "And the second?"

"I'm thinking about what I told you about the queen on the board."

"And?"

"I'm wishing life were that simple. That it were squares of black and white and that the path ahead could be measured in a few careful moves."

"Please." Her voice broke and he instantly turned back to take her into his arms.

"Isabel, I would do anything for you."

"Don't give up, Darius. Please don't—abandon me."

"It was never an option."

She shook her head. "He'll destroy you. I don't want to lose you, but I don't know if I can face—"

"Chess." He interrupted her, the one word a calm invocation.

"Wh-what?"

"The game isn't over until the king is defeated. I wasn't lamenting that I couldn't win, Isabel. I was just expressing my regret that it won't be easy. But hear me," he said, reaching up to push back one pale lock of hair off her cheek. "Netherton's no match for us. We'll find a way to outmaneuver him and free you."

"You've thought of something already, haven't you?"

"I have. The obscene texts were a clue to his—treatment of you. I suspect he has more than one twist to his nature, and if I can find proof of it, without any reference to his marriage, it isn't the most ethical idea but I think I can talk him into a divorce in exchange for avoiding a very personal and pointed scandal."

"A divorce? Is that . . . possible?"

Darius thought of the strange glimpse he'd already seen of her husband's tastes, and suddenly the image of Harold Pughes standing behind the man anxiously lodged in his mind.

"I'll see . . . but not until I start looking in earnest." He sat up, gripped by the idea that the last person he wanted to talk to would in fact be the first.

"What is it?" she asked.

"I'll have to go back into the city in the morning but not for long."

"So soon?"

He pulled her gently into his arms, enfolding her in a protective embrace that allowed him to absorb her sweet warmth and inhale the scent of her skin. "One more quest for information and then I'll have what I need to corner Netherton when he least expects it."

"Darius! No!" she protested, but Darius kissed her until there was nothing of talking, of schemes, and most importantly, of a single thought of Richard Netherton between them.

Chapter
18

"How exactly are you acquainted with Netherton?" Darius asked as he pushed his way into Harold Pughes's private apartments near the university. He wasted no time with civilities and decided that if ever a man needed to use the lessons that Rutherford had drilled into him, it might be now.

The element of surprise and a decisive first blow. Come on, Harold, give me what I want.

"What business is that of yours?" Harold sneered. "And good afternoon, by the way! If you're thinking of crawling back to him with an apology to chase that commission, you can forget it. He left for London this morning and I'm told he has no intentions of returning to Scotland anytime soon."

"He leaves for London? What of his wife? Won't it cause a scandal if he arrives in London missing his bride?"

"And now you are an expert on etiquette and scandal?" Harold looked at him in disbelief. "I'm sure it's nothing to you! Frankly, I'd say he's going to London to get away from the matter and will avoid a breath of scandal by telling people his wife prefers the countryside to the city in winter."

"Has he no intentions of finding her?" Darius asked.

"Are you balmy? It's none of our concern and I imagine he has every intention of recovering his wife! He may jest to say otherwise but I'm—damn it! Why am I even conversing with you?"

"Because," Darius countered with a smile, "a part of you is still trying to figure out why Douglas gives me free rein in the archives and how it is I have my own carriage and fortunes enough to tell your friend, the earl, to bugger off."

Harold's brow furrowed. "How *is* that possible?"

"Tell me everything you know of Netherton and his interests in London and I'll let you ask me anything you wish of my circumstances and the secrets of my wealth."

"Your wealth?"

"Netherton is not the only rich man in your acquaintance, Pughes. You may think about casting a wider net and improving your circles as a result."

"Should I?" Harold shot back, all bravado and swagger, but Darius sensed he'd hit a nerve. "Are you offering me a bribe, Thorne? It's a bit unexpected, considering your blasted personal integrity."

Darius just stared back. "Netherton. What do you know of the man?"

"I am not the man's bosom companion."

"No. But he confided in you about that sordid little bit of translation he was after and you seemed close enough. As you say though"—Darius shrugged and moved as if to leave—"I've probably overestimated your connections."

"I know him better than most!" Harold offered, openly offended. "My father was his tutor growing up although I only just met him when he was at university. He spends as little time as he can at his estates in Scotland and prefers Town. I admit I was—surprised to hear he'd brought his bride north and then acted as if they intended to settle in." Pughes shrugged. "But who knows the mind of the nobility? Certainly not you or I, Thorne."

"And what did your father say of his pupil?"

Pughes walked over to a small cupboard and pulled out a bottle of liquor. "Very little. Richard's a bit—cold. But he can be very charming. My father encouraged me to stay on his good side if I could."

"And so you have."

Harold filled his glass without offering any to his guest. "It's not a sin to stay in good stead with one's betters, Thorne."

"Lord Netherton *isn't* my better. But that's a debate for another day." Darius sighed. "So forget the boy. What about the man?"

"In what regard?" Pughes asked evasively.

"What draws him to London so suddenly? What interests him? Where could I find him in Town?" Darius held his ground. "Come, Pughes. You said you knew him better than most, so let's have it. I need to know whatever you can convey. All of it—every filthy secret or strange obsession, because I am bound to uncover it, with or without you. Tell me and I'll keep my promise. Refuse and I'll find another way and you can continue to play lapdog to the worst kind of men, all in the name of your science."

"You're a prig, Thorne. You know this, right?"

"Good day, Pughes."

"Wait! All right!" Harold downed the contents of his glass, the strong smell of scotch tainting the air. "You must swear you'll never reveal that we've spoken."

"You have my word."

"You saw the papers he bought. The last couple of years, I've kept an eye out for unusual texts to offer him. He used to be a generous buyer and then, for a time, simply took things from me 'on account.' Of course, since his marriage he's been . . . more free spending and I was happy to give him what he wanted."

Darius tried to hide his disappointment. "It's not an uncommon vice."

"I don't think he's limited to the page."

"In what way?"

"H-he asked about certain entertainments in the city and I . . . had to disappoint him at our lack of variety in sport."

"What kind of sport?"

"Private clubs for . . ." Harold hesitated and Darius waited as the man weighed out his curiosity to learn a rival's secrets and the risks of angering Netherton. "Sport with ladies."

Darius crossed his arms. "There are prostitutes aplenty in the city and a few gambling houses with . . . lovely women on hand. How exactly was he disappointed?"

"I took him to a house. Hell, it was far out of the comfortable confines of my purse and they only admitted me because I had a member of the peerage in tow. But apparently it didn't meet his expectations." Pughes poured himself another drink. "We were shown the door because one of the girls complained after Netherton took her upstairs. He was furious and said she lacked training. He said a scullery maid at the Velvet House could have warmed him better."

Darius nodded. "What was the girl's complaint? Did you hear?"

"No, but it was clear that the madam of the house took the girl's side of it without hesitation. Apparently, he— marked her in some way."

"Damn."

"In the carriage, he said that a little rough play was nothing. He said that the rules of common men didn't apply to him. He rattled off a few clubs or houses that catered to it in London and I—I just agreed with him as if I had any idea of what he was talking about."

Darius pulled a notebook from his inside pocket. "Write them down. Any reference he made."

Pughes froze. "I . . ."

"Here, I'll make it easy for you." Darius located a pen and ink and set them down on the desk. "The Velvet House. And then you said he rattled off a few clubs or houses that catered to him in London. Write, Harold. Restore my faith in you."

Harold took up the pen with a growl and then bent over the paper. His scrawl was measured by his temper but Darius counted each line a triumph.

There's the trail. Somewhere in that list, I'll find another madam who's had enough of him and secure proof of his depravity so strong that Netherton will do anything to keep it hidden. Hell, he may have done her a favor by spreading a few lies about his wife preferring the countryside. If an annulment is possible, it might make it easier if Lady Netherton is beyond the reach of the gossips' claws for their next feast.

Pughes finished and set the pen down in disgust.

Darius grabbed up the paper quickly, unwilling to wrestle the man for it if he changed his mind. He folded it and put it in inside his vest without looking at it. "Thank you, Harold. I'm sure you'll understand if I don't linger for your delightful company."

"Wait! You said you would tell me the truth of your circumstances! If you've a path to wealth, you promised to share it!"

Darius shook his head. "I said I would let you ask. I never said I'd answer. But trust me on this, since I've proven that of all men in your acquaintance, I always keep my word—breathe one word of this, Harold, and I'll make sure Netherton knows what a slick squirrel you are and how quickly you betrayed him on the slight promise of a bit of gossip and a show of coin."

"You heartless bastard!" Pughes hissed. "You're not going to get the better of me. I'll say nothing to Netherton but that won't keep me from reminding anyone I know with any influence at the university that you have the breeding of a chimney sweep. Let's see how far you rise, Thorne! Let's see who secures a teaching post at a prestigious college or earns honors for their research! For I'll be damned if you'll get beyond tutoring village idiots in the Highlands if I have anything to say about it!"

Darius took a step back. "Do what your conscience dictates, Mr. Pughes." He bowed formally to the sputtering red-faced man. "And I'll follow the dictates of mine."

Darius left without looking back and let out a long breath.

He's a blowhard but I think I might have just traded in my academic future if he makes good on his threats.

Oh well. A hollow sacrifice since there wasn't much of a chance in any case. . . .

And she is worth any sacrifice.

* * *

The rest of his outing went quickly. He stopped at Craig & Cavendish to sell three more of his stones to finance his plans and pick up a few things. Once again, he marveled at the value and remarkable returns he was able to easily secure for the gems.

Let's pray my luck holds as well in London.

The ride back to the village closest to his home was relatively smooth, although they had to stop twice to clear the mud from the wheels, and by the time they reached the constable, Darius feared he looked a bit more rustic than usual, with mud on his coat and even in his hair.

"Mr. Thorne!" The constable greeted him as the carriage pulled up outside the man's offices. "I was off to home, but if you needed anything . . ."

"Just a word, Mr. Pritchard. I won't keep you long from your dinner table," Darius said, climbing down to converse with the man.

"No trouble, I hope! We see you rarely enough but my wife is always pleased to hear of you, sir." The constable patted his broad middle, his smile genuinely warm. "She's certain you'll expire so isolated out there and has announced a grand plan to turn matchmaker on your behalf!"

Darius allowed his horror at the notion to play on his features, eliciting a laugh from his good acquaintance. "God, no! Tell her my health is sound but I'll move to Iceland before I'd play along. Now is—not a good time, Mr. Pritchard."

"It never is," Mr. Pritchard agreed, shaking his head. "I'll do my best to deter her, sir. But it's like asking the tide not to come in! They do have their schemes! But what was it you wished to speak to me about?"

"I just wanted to mention that if anyone has lost a horse, I've just come on one in my garden. A dark-colored thing but apparently happy to be warm in our stables. He's terribly lame and no good for riding, I fear."

"Shall I come to fetch him for you?"

"No," Darius said, keeping his tone casual. "Hamish is working on his recovery and I'm putting out notices to find the owner. Probably just someone's lost pet the way he eats, but if someone asked, you'd know where to inquire."

"You're a good man to take him in! Winter oats aren't cheap!" Pritchard said.

"It's the least I could do." Darius leaned forward, lowering his voice. "Hamish is falling in love with the beast, I fear. So if you would, do me the favor of making it clear that I'd be willing to buy the stallion if the owner comes forward and might be interested. MacQueen's got a soft heart for all his noise and I'd love to gift him with the animal."

Mr. Pritchard shook his head in amazement. "You're too kind!"

Darius shrugged. "If it spares the creature a painful long walk back to where he came from, saves his owner the cost of his appetite, and makes my driver growl a bit less, I can't see that it's not an easy choice to make." Darius held out a folded slip of paper. "Here's a copy of my consent to allow Hamish to negotiate a cash price on my behalf if it comes up."

"That's well and proper, sir." Mr. Pritchard took the document. "But wouldn't you rather handle the matter yourself and limit the expense?"

"I'm to London on business and I just didn't want to leave any loose ends."

"You are a wise man, Mr. Thorne. No worries. If anyone reports a horse missing, we'll see if your man has him. And in the meantime, I'll just keep this on file."

"Thank you, Mr. Pritchard." Darius held out his hand and shook the constable's hand to end the matter. "Enjoy your dinner."

"And you yours," the constable said with a wave, stepping back as Darius climbed up into his carriage. "Ah, the quiet of a bachelor's life!"

"Good day," Darius hailed him before closing the door and signaling Hamish to pull away.

It was risky to bring Samson into it, but riskier to leave without covering his tracks. With Isabel safely hiding in the house, there was no need to keep anyone from his doorstep if they inquired after the stallion. Lying would draw only more attention. This way, if one of Netherton's agents did show up to ask, Darius would have seen to it that there'd be no grounds for accusations of thievery or demands to search further. He imagined that they would ask questions as to whether anyone had seen Isabel but would have no valid excuse to physically search the property, and English law would prevent the trespass. And now there was even a remote chance of buying the horse to secure him for Isabel's happiness.

He decided to say nothing of the matter to Isabel, for fear of reminding her just how close a pursuit could be. One glance at Harold's list had been enough to send his own fears careening.

It was a short list.

Five names of obscure establishments in London with no addresses.

Ridiculous.

Impossible.

Her future rests on what I can uncover behind these five doors.

Hell, that's if I can find them. . . .

Darius closed his eyes, summoning the strength he would need for yet another headlong journey to London. He'd just begun to feel like himself again, and the lure of simply staying in Isabel's arms and shutting the world out was no fleeting temptation.

*   *   *

"Were you successful?" she asked.

He nodded. "Your husband has returned to London. Unfortunately, that's where the trail leads if I'm to get any proof of his misconduct. I was able to get a few leads, Isabel, but I don't want you to lose heart. I'm going to dedicate every waking minute to figuring out a way to prove his depravity and cruelty. If I'm successful, the last thing he'll want is a public divorce, and he'll consent to a quiet annulment to avoid the scandal."

"I'm going with you."

"Isabel, you are—"

"Darius, before you say no"—she touched his sleeve—"hear me out."

He nodded, doing his best not to compose his argument against it beforehand. "I will listen as impartially as I can."

"Whether I am confined here or there, there is little difference. I can stay out of sight, Darius, and no one need know that I am in London. I'll stay in whatever lodgings we secure and never see the light of day if need be, but I am more likely to be able to stay hidden in the labyrinth of Town, am I not? And if I am with you, then it is one less distraction of worry, is it not? You need not fear the not knowing if Mrs. McFadden's niece has let it slip that she has seen me in the garden—"

"She's seen you in the garden?" he asked in alarm.

"No, but who is to say she wouldn't?" she countered solemnly.

"You're making my heart race, woman."

"Hush. What say you to my logic so far?" she asked.

"It's terrifyingly solid."

"Then may I add one more thing?"

"You may." He sat down slowly, in awe of the turns of her mind.

"Well, I will avoid using the obvious emotional ploy of bringing up how precarious our time is together and how I should hate to forfeit a single second that I did not have to—should the worst ever come to pass. . . ."

"That's very kind of you," he noted, completely bemused.

"And instead I will tell you that I can be packed and ready to go within minutes." She crossed her arms, as resolute as a judge. "And that if you don't take me with you, I'll . . ."

Her words trailed off as she obviously reached the end of her prepared remarks.

"You'll . . . ?" he prompted.

"Resign as your secretary? Throw a temper tantrum? Walk to London on my own?" she said, then sat next to him with a sigh. "I am not one for threats. I will beg you on my knees not to leave me again in this house without you. It's too quiet and too empty, Darius. Before—I didn't even know you as I do now. How could I face it after what's passed between us?"

Darius looked into her eyes and acknowledged that he felt the same way. Leaving her before had been hard enough, but now . . . it was an impossibility.

"Come to London with me, Helen."

The joy that flooded her eyes was an instant reward, and he knew there was no turning back. He would bring her and make the best of it.

And ask Michael and the others in the Jaded to understand.

* * *

Isabel made good on her promise to pack quickly, once again appreciative of her small wardrobe and few personal possessions. Mrs. McFadden loaned her a valise and a small trunk, and within minutes, all was tucked away for the journey. The housekeeper was openly miserable at their departure but masked it by fussing in the kitchen and packing a hamper of food for the journey.

While Darius rushed through his own more chaotic preparations in the library to organize a few of his papers, Isabel slipped out to the stables one last time.

Samson's head lifted the moment her feet crossed the threshold, and his loud neighing summoned her to his side. She hugged his neck and then leaned back to look into his soulful dark brown eyes. Isabel did her best not to cry, but it was as if he sensed her purpose, nuzzling her neck and hair and snuffling his soft nose against her skin.

"I know, dearest. But you cannot carry me any farther. Not today." Isabel reached up to ever so gently cup his ears and stroke the firm lines of his neck. "Hamish will take good care of you, and as soon as I can, I will send for you!

Or I'll be back. Would you like that, my warrior? Shall we live here forever and replant the garden? Ride the Scottish countryside and see what the villagers make of us?"

She smiled. It was a sweet daydream to think of a simple life with Darius, playing secretary and drying flowers or doing whatever was required of a country wife. She had no real grasp of it, but even the vague promise of just being with Darius each day and sharing his bed each night seemed too good to hope for.

"We have to defeat the dragon, Samson, before I can have my prince."

He whinnied again, jostling her as if to remind her that he was ever ready to fight on her behalf, dragon or no.

Chapter
19

The journey was unorthodox as he "smuggled" her back to London without a single soul seeing her. Trains were too public, so they'd secured a post chaise and Darius had paid for all the seats to make sure that they had the cramped interior of the carriage all to themselves. Even so, Isabel wore a veil over her bonnet, her hair tightly braided and tucked up whenever they stopped for fresh horses and meals. Darius addressed her as Helen Stewart if there was anyone within hearing and made a point of leaving no trace of their identities behind them.

The pace was not as dreadful as his previous journey's, and Isabel's company made it all bearable. He liked the intimacy of their private meals and shared hardships, and strove to make things as comfortable for her as possible.

As the city loomed closer and closer, Darius pushed away the growing feeling that he was leading her like a lamb into the slaughterhouse.

God, if her husband finds us now, there'll be no escape.

As they transferred to a hackney, he signaled a runner

and handed off the note he'd already prepared to send word to the Jaded that he was back in London and needed to see them at Rowan's right away. He included no explanations but knew his friends would trust the summons and come without question.

The questions will come later, no doubt.
I just pray they won't mind the answers.

After long days, the Grove was a welcome sight, and Darius paid the driver to wait with Isabel hidden inside the carriage while he went in to see about rooms.

He took off his hat as the landlady approached. "I'm not sure if you remember me, Mrs. Clay, but I am a friend of Mr. Rutherford's and—"

"Mr. Thorne!" Mrs. Clay interrupted him cheerfully, setting down a large tray of pewter cups. "Of course I remember you! You have been here once or twice, and from Mr. Hastings's account of that dreadful night at the Thistle, why you must be one of my favorite persons!"

He shook his head. "Josiah is prone to exaggeration but I thank you for that."

"Have you come for Mr. Rutherford? He's out today and I've got Tally up there pulling linens and doing all he can to clean the room. It's a good chance to see to matters without bothering my dear giant!" Mrs. Clay beamed. "Will you stop for a bit of tea?"

Darius struggled not to laugh. Mrs. Clay's enthusiastic and friendly manners were legendary in their small circle, but he marveled at how much a woman could convey in so short a time. "I was wondering if the apartment that Miss Beckett had occupied is available?"

"Oh no!" Mrs. Clay sighed, then instantly cheered. "I've brought a young girl in, an acquaintance of Miss Beckett's— I mean, the new Mrs. Hastings, as you know. She introduced me to her young friend by the name of Margaret Beecham, and the girl has been a godsend. Maggie's such a sweet thing and so eager to please and learn the business. I needed another pair of hands, and in exchange for her place, I'm giving her room and board along with a modest wage." She smoothed her hands over her apron. "It's tough times and a young woman without family . . . I just couldn't allow it. There's a pure little bird who just needed a warm nest and a mother's care. And I don't allow any grabbing or nonsense in my common room so she's safe as churches here. Although, I fear Tally's losing his heart again!"

Darius tried again. "Then another pair of rooms perhaps? I have a friend looking for discreet accommodations. I know she would be safe here, under your good care. And I need a place to set down my luggage."

"Of course! I pride myself on maintaining a respectable inn and allow no rough trade here." Mrs. Clay stepped forward, lowering her voice. "Discreet, you say?"

"You are someone I trust entirely, Mrs. Clay. She is a respectable lady, and I would never willingly bring trouble to your doorstep, but I cannot leave her in just any public house, and a hotel . . ." Darius took a deep breath. "A hotel would expose her to too many eyes."

"Oh," Mrs. Clay exclaimed softly, nodding as if she were instantly aware of all. "I've a good room for her and another to suit you. But I don't allow—" Mrs. Clay pressed her lips together. "If you're calling on her, you can use the private first-floor parlor for meals and conversation, but I don't allow a gentleman into a lady's room for social visits. Even men of good character, so no getting around me, Mr. Thorne!"

It made perfect sense, but it ground against him to be parted from her. Even so, he knew he had no other choice. They were exhausted from traveling and Isabel needed a haven. The Grove was perfect, and with Michael on hand for security and Mrs. Clay's protective wings, Darius couldn't imagine a better choice.

"No, Mrs. Clay. No getting around you. I swear it."

"Lovely! The common room's fairly deserted at this hour, so no worries coming through to the west stairs. I'll ring Maggie to show you both up, and let me get a boy to help you with your things." Mrs. Clay retrieved her tray. "And may I say, it's a pleasure to have you as a guest, Mr. Thorne!"

"You're too kind." He gave her a half bow and made his way back out to Isabel and the waiting carriage.

He hailed the driver just as one of Mrs. Clay's burly male employees came out for the luggage. "If you'll give him a hand with our things, sir."

The driver touched his hat brim and climbed down as Darius opened the carriage door. Even at such a moment, she was a sight of delicate beauty that made his chest ache. "Mrs. Clay has a room for each of us and will see to your privacy, dearest. If you'll pull up your hood and use that sheer scarf, we'll make the most of it and get you safely upstairs."

Isabel complied, giving him a saucy smile. "The landlady must think me a scandalous guest!"

"Mrs. Clay thinks only that I'm to respect the sanctity of your rooms so that she can mother and spoil you, from what I can gather." He held out his hand to help her down. The gloved hand that slid into his was trembling but Darius did his best to pretend not to notice.

"I don't want to be alone, Darius."

"I know. Let me see what I can do." He guided her up the walk, and as promised, a young woman was coming down the stairs to meet them.

"I'm Maggie Beecham and I'm to welcome you to the Grove," she said, then added an awkward curtsy. Her dress was modest and pressed, her bright eyes spoiling her efforts to appear serious. "If you'll follow me."

She led them through the main dining room and common area and then up the west stairs to the first floor. "Mrs. Clay wanted me to tell you that anything you need, you just ring the bell. Good and hard so that Tally can mind it as well. He's deaf and mute but a lamb really."

They reached a door near the end of the hall, a good quiet distance from the stairwell. "Here we are," she announced and opened the door with a key before standing aside. "I hope it meets with your approval. I'll send Tally up with coal for the fireplaces and that will cozy it up for you."

Isabel stepped inside, a mysterious woman with her face

concealed by the sheer scarf and the cowl of her cape. "It's lovely."

It was a good-size room, with dark green drapes and bedding that might have seen better days, but it smelled of sunshine and beeswax and every surface gleamed with the care of its landlady's hands.

Maggie set the key down on a side table. "It gets good light considering it's February, and there's a lovely sitting area."

"And my room?" Darius asked.

Maggie nodded. "This way, sir."

He gave Isabel an encouraging smile before he followed the young miss out, anxious to map the route to his room so that he could retrace his steps back to Isabel at the first opportunity. So when they only went ten steps, Darius nearly ran over Miss Beecham. "Here?"

"Yes, sir." Maggie pushed the door open and Darius immediately realized he was looking at the room directly next to Isabel's, with drapes and bedding the color of pomegranates. "There's a window seat, and as I said, I'll have Tally cozy it up for you. And there's . . . that."

"That?" Darius asked, following her gaze to the paneled wall.

Maggie blushed. "I'm to say again how respectable the Grove is and how proud Mrs. Clay is of her reputation." The girl moved to the wall and, even as she spoke, demonstrated how the hidden door between the rooms worked. "And well I know it! She took me in from the streets and has given me a chance to truly make something of myself, sir. This is a good place. So," Maggie said firmly, "I'm to give the lady the key that locks the other side. So it's all square."

"Understood. Thank you, Miss Beecham."

"Would you like something from the kitchens sent up, sir? If you've only just arrived in London, you must be famished and ready to set for a while."

"You're an angel, yes, thank you."

Maggie blushed again. "I? I'm many things, but an angel is not one of my claims. But I do aspire to better things and I am lucky in my friendships of late. Well, Daniel will be up with your bags and will help you get sorted. I'll see what Cook has for you." She curtsied and scurried off before he could thank her again.

Darius walked over to the secret door, testing the latch hidden in the carved panel and admiring the workmanship. He was tempted to try it but knew better than to startle Isabel when her nerves were already on edge. Instead he went back to her open doorway and leaned against the frame, hoping to elicit a smile.

"So much for my worries about creeping long hallways in the dark," he said.

"Your room is there, isn't it?" Isabel pointed at the wall they shared.

"Closer than you know," he added. "Apparently, there's a secret door. Maggie was to give you the key so that I couldn't take advantage."

"Ah!" Isabel unfolded one gloved hand to reveal a large, ornate key. "I was wondering what this was. She just darted in to hand it to me and then rushed off without a word."

"It's there. If only to make you feel better that you can reach me if you need to," he said, then crossed his arms. "It *is* London. I would understand if you chose to leave it latched—"

"No! Are you insinuating that I loved you only when it was remote and easy, that my feelings for you might have changed because we're in the city and the danger of discovery is greater?" She laid the key on the mantel. "Or that here the rules of society apply differently?"

"I suppose not." He had to swallow the lump that rose in his throat. *I'm as guilty of trespassing here as I was there—but somehow with the weight of it all pressing in and the trust she's put in me by coming here—please God, don't let me fail her.* "Mrs. Clay is too astute to have fooled for long, so I'm pleased to think that the White Queen can summon me when she wishes."

The sound of the man bringing up their trunks ended the exchange, and Isabel nervously pulled her veil back into place to shield her unique coloring from view.

Darius helped them sort out the boxes and then paid the footman for his aid. "Please tell the driver I'll be back down and in need of his services for a while longer."

"Will do, sir." The man ducked his head and hurried back down the hall to the stairs.

"You'll need the carriage?" Isabel asked.

"I'm going to Rowan's to meet with the others."

* * *

Isabel nervously unpacked her trunk. It only took a few minutes to hang up the dresses she possessed and to put away her things.

She'd abandoned dozens and dozens of gorgeous gowns, a life of luxury that so many would have envied; the life that she had been raised to expect.

The life I would still have but for Richard. . . .

I would still be that spoiled and pampered pet if the man holding the leash hadn't turned out to be a demon in disguise.

It was like recalling someone else when she thought of Miss Isabel Penleigh.

I like being Helen Stewart.

Her eyes trailed around the room again, surveying every detail and fighting off the melancholy that nibbled at the edges of her mood. Because in her quest for freedom from her marriage, she'd become more and more confined. It was temporary, Darius had tried to reassure her, but it was harder to appear brave as she faced the reality of her return to London.

She would be unable to leave these rooms. Not even to walk down to the common room unless she wore her cloak and veil for fear that some guest would recognize her or notice her coloring to make a comment to the wrong person.

One whisper, one breath of gossip or speculation about the mysterious woman staying at the Grove and Richard could be standing on her doorstep and all would be lost.

I am a prisoner, just like Helen of Troy. I'm with the man I love but I'm trapped, too. God help me.

She pulled out the wooden box he'd set on the bed and lifted the lid.

It was the chess set.

Tears filled her eyes at the sight of it. All the love and patience he'd shown her was manifested in the neat rows of black and white carved figurines lying atop the red velvet, awaiting their next battle.

"I am the most powerful piece in the game," she said softly.

She pulled out the board from the hidden drawer underneath and slowly set out the elements on the table by the window, her nerves soothed by the ritual and the promise of Darius's return.

Chapter
20

The men of the Jaded met in Rowan's study, all of them present at Darius's request except for one.

"Has Josiah come up for air yet?" Ashe asked wryly.

"Don't make light of it!" Rowan jumped in defensively. "He's entitled to settle in to his life with Eleanor. I'm to send word to him of any news and he's as anxious as any of us for an end to this business, but his eyes are giving him trouble and I reassured him that attendance wasn't required."

Michael crossed his arms but said nothing.

Ashe turned his attention to Darius. "We are here, D. I, for one, am glad to see you back in London, but from the look on your face, I'm wondering if I should be more worried. Is everything all right?"

"I'm in a bit of an . . ." Darius's voice trailed off and he instantly regretted that he hadn't thought about the best way of telling his friends about Isabel. "There is a personal matter that I'm striving to address."

Ashe sat up straighter in his chair. "Is this the same personal matter that was keeping you in Edinburgh?"

Darius nodded.

"Is it a woman?" Ashe asked.

"Of course it isn't a woman!" Michael spoke before Darius could react. "This is Thorne we're dealing with. He's far too levelheaded for that business now! It's not as if . . ." Michael's speech faltered as he caught sight of Darius's expression. "It's a *woman*?"

"If we're oversimplifying things, yes. It's a woman," Darius said and calmly watched his friends' varied reactions. The married and matched men in the room appeared instantly supportive and welcoming to the announcement, but Rutherford's expression was disgruntled disappointment.

"Congratulations!" Ashe was on his feet and warmly shaking his best friend's hand. "Damn it! I knew you'd find happiness, despite all that show about being too smart for it! Or did she find you?" His eyes widened. "We aren't talking about that housekeeper you wrote me about, are we? Because she sounded . . . a little long in the tooth, Thorne. Not that older women don't have an appeal but—"

"Blackwell!" Rowan said, slapping Ashe on the shoulder. "The turns of your mind confound reason!"

"No! I am not in the company of my housekeeper Mrs. McFadden, who, by the way, I believe I can hear screeching in protest at the notion even from here." Darius rolled his eyes. "I should have braced myself better for this."

"Something's wrong," Galen said softly, the dark timbre of his voice quieting the room. "He'd have led with the news if it were good. And this wasn't an announcement of joy but a reluctant request for our help with something."

"He's right. Let's have it, Darius. You know we'll stand with you," Michael Rutherford vowed, and every man nodded in quick agreement.

Darius closed his eyes for a moment and then opened them to take the plunge. "In the midst of a winter storm, a rider stumbled into my garden and collapsed off of her horse. I took her in and quickly realized that she was in real trouble. She was attempting to escape a violent marriage and I—I have vowed to help her. I've brought her to London."

"Shit." Ashe blurted it out and sat as if his knees had given out.

"Her husband? Do you know him?" Michael asked.

"I've met him. He is a villain by any measure but he's also titled, and with his new wife's wealth, a man of influence. I am"—Darius took a deep breath—"facing a bit of a challenge."

"Darius," Rowan said as he sat back down, gesturing for his friend to join him. "It's a delicate matter, but if she'd be more comfortable, I can send Gayle to examine her if there are injuries."

"Thank you, Rowan." Darius took the seat. "She has recovered remarkably well and is now in perfect health. At this moment, it's her future safety that makes me wary."

"I hate him already but who is he?" Blackwell asked.

"Lord Richard Netherton."

"Lady Isabel Netherton?" Galen winced, drawing air through gritted teeth. "I'm not one to soak up the society pages, but I swear they had a duke or two at that wedding, Thorne. Her father is a marquis. I remember it only because Haley was mad for the wedding dress details last spring and raved about the woman's unique beauty. They'll boil you in oil if you're caught in this thing."

"Where are you staying?" Ashe asked.

"I've rented rooms at the Grove and—"

"You'll bring her to my house." Ashe stopped him. "I've got footmen the size of bears now and Rutherford had me hire night guards to walk the grounds after sunset."

"I don't want to implicate you or Caroline directly if a scandal erupts, Blackwell."

"Nonsense! I'm impervious to scandal and Rutherford's about to have an apoplectic fit over there if you don't agree to it. We'll smuggle her in and the incomparable Mrs. Blackwell"—Ashe paused as the very mention of his wife made his countenance soften—"will shower me with kisses for bringing her a friend to talk to and sparing her my incessant hovering."

Rowan rolled his eyes. "As if an army of houseguests will stop you from smothering that woman!"

"I cannot intrude to—" Darius began.

"Stop talking, Thorne!" Ashe crossed his arms. "You're bringing her. I'll give you a floor of the house to yourselves, and no one will say a word if I've asked my best friend to keep me distracted while my wife is 'in a delicate condition.'"

"That's one thing settled," Galen said before taking a sip of lemon barley water. "Where is Netherton in this?"

"He's in London." Darius leaned back in his chair, a man relieved to be defeated by his friends' generosity.

"Then why aren't you still in Edinburgh?" Michael asked. "You need to keep out of his path and keep her as far from him as you can."

Darius waved him off and stood to make his case. "No! If I'm to find a way out of the marriage for her, then I need to uncover his weaknesses and see if there isn't something I can use against him if it comes to the courts. I have to find a way and free her from a life of fear."

Michael cleared his throat. "The law . . ."

"I know the law, Michael."

They all knew the law. The wife held no rights of property or person, and so long as her husband wasn't guilty of incest, bigamy, cruelty, or desertion, divorce wasn't allowed. The definition of cruelty was elusive and nonsensical, and more than one woman had lost her life without meeting the law's standards. Even if her husband were insufferable, few women of rank would consider the destruction and humiliation of a public trial to prove the worst only to be rewarded with the life of a social pariah plagued with blacklists and judgmental gossip.

"What is your plan?" Ashe asked calmly.

"I want to find proof of his true nature. From what I've learned of him so far, he's prone to enjoying the edges of a moral degradation that would make Ashe nauseated. It's all rumor, but if I can actually prove it, I may have the lever I need to move this mountain. I have a few leads on some of the private houses he enjoys that cater to men with exotic sexual tastes."

"Blackmail." Galen shook his head. "Thorne, you are an unlikely villain to take this on."

"D's no villain!" Ashe protested.

"No, he isn't," Galen agreed, "which should make this all the more challenging for him. Darius"—he turned back to watch Darius pace across the floor—"are you sure you have the stomach for this?"

Darius nodded. "I have no choice. I could give her most of my fortunes and encourage her to head for the Continent, but what life is that? Living in exile and fear?" He stopped the restless turns about the room and planted his feet firmly. "No. Helen deserves to be happy, and so long as that animal has power over her, I cannot turn away. I'll find some scandalous secret he's harboring and drive him into the sea."

For a few moments, the men sat in stunned silence at the transformation of their quiet and scholarly friend into a man of determined action.

"Helen?"

"Don't ask!" Darius folded his arms. "It's . . . complicated."

"I take it back." Galen smiled. "I think Thorne has this one."

"If you're out sniffing after that man's trail, here." Ashe held out a small stack of his cards. "I'm not saying I was ever that far off into the dark woods, but . . . at least I once had a reputation for being a bit of a scoundrel. It might help you gain entrance somewhere. You can even lie and say you're scouting a bit on my behalf now that I'm imprisoned by marriage. I don't care what you say if it helps you bring that bully down."

Galen's emerald eyes flashed with venom. "Hell, throw out the bait of my title and see if that does it! I'm with Blackwell. I despise any man who strikes a woman because he thinks to make more of himself. Should we try to go with you?"

"No. This is where I draw the line, gentlemen." Darius kept his voice level. "It's one thing to offer us shelter, which I appreciate. But trust me, friends, not even the Jaded are jaded enough for the places I'll have to go. I'm not dragging your names into it. Keep your cards, Ashe, and for God's sake, keep your good name, Galen. I for one will be fighting to protect my own if I can."

Darius crossed the room to pour himself another drink. "I'll call on you if I need help, but for now, do me a favor and keep a close watch for the Jackal. I need some breathing room to attend to this matter and I don't think I can fight a war on two fronts."

"Very well." Ashe relaxed his stance.

"But only because you agreed to stay at Blackwell's. At least your safety and hers will be secured while you start your search," Galen conceded.

"Did I agree to the arrangement?" Darius asked in mock surprise.

"Don't quibble. Of course you did," Michael growled.

"We'll come tomorrow. That should give you time to either prepare for guests or change your mind," Darius said to Ashe with a wry smile.

"Tomorrow!" Ashe seconded. "Well, is that everything on our silly club's agenda?"

"Not everything." Galen raised a hand. "Haley's coming to London. Her last letter made it clear that she's had enough of the country, misses Caroline and Gayle, and has no intention of being parted from me for anything as nebulous as her 'safety.'" Galen's emerald eyes darkened defensively. "And I'm not stopping her."

Michael shook his head. "This is getting out of hand. We have no idea what to expect, and every time I turn around, someone decides it's time to go to a ball and play the dandy or lose their heads and get married!"

Galen gave him a dangerous look. "I'm not living apart from my wife for the foreseeable future simply because you'd rather have us holed up in a fort somewhere! No offense, Rutherford, but I've already spent my time in prison.

We're free men, and by God, I'll live freely and have what joys I can carve out—and this Jackal can choke on his sacred treasure! Prophecies be damned!"

"Here, here!" Rowan agreed softly. "Did anyone else notice that Lord Winters nearly sounded like an optimist ever so briefly?"

* * *

They put on their coats and Darius climbed up into Blackwell's waiting carriage for the ride back to the inn. The cold night had a stale scent that clung to their clothes and made Darius nostalgic for his country house and the green, fresh "wee bit of wet" of Scotland.

"What aren't you telling them?" Ashe asked quietly in the shadowy confines of the carriage.

"You are all so eager to lend a hand and aid me toward my 'happy ending.' . . ."

"But you're not heading that direction?"

Darius sighed. Only with Ashe did he feel safe enough to speak the worst aloud. "You heard Galen. There were dukes at her wedding. Even if I free her and end this, it's—impossible. If it doesn't create a scandal, then her choice of a lowborn unemployed scholar would do the trick. As my housekeeper kept pointing out, I've not taken in a stray kitten, and as much as I love her, I know that I cannot condemn her to a life with a lesser man."

"Snotty bit of blue blood, is she?"

"She is not! She doesn't care about my pedigree! She doesn't even mind—any of it."

"So your problem is imaginary."

"It is not imaginary! My father was a dockworker, Ashe. I may have elevated my mind with education and shed the accent of a Bristol street urchin, but that doesn't make me the Earl of Utopia!"

Ashe grunted. "Well, you look like a *wealthy* Earl of Utopia from where I'm sitting, D. Money makes up for a lot when it comes to bloodlines, and if it's that rot about becoming your father—I've never seen the smallest hint of it. Hell!

When you're furious, D, and I mean *furious*, do you know that you get quiet and start quoting the classics?"

"I don't quote them randomly, Ashe. Some of the best insults are found in the—"

"See? You're missing the point, friend. You were in an inferno in the Thistle that night and you were politely asking them to move a little faster, by Josiah's account. We were in hell in Bengal and you were as civil as a judge after they dragged you out and beat you for trying to speak to the guards in their native tongue to get more water for us."

"If I was civil, it was only because that seemed like the best option."

"D, we were in a dungeon chained together, you and I, and there were moments when you were the slice of humanity I clung to when I couldn't remember what it was to be human anymore. Darius, forget your father. He's as relevant to who you are as"—Ashe leaned forward to point out a lamplighter on the street as they passed by—"that bloke."

"Thank you, Ashe." Darius pushed back against the cushions. "We'll see."

She loves me now. But it's an affection spawned by circumstances, and once she's free, it could all change. I already look like a man with a great rusty chain, and at the other end of it sits a butterfly. It's ridiculous.

Chapter
21

Isabel stared at the blank page and then back out the long window looking down into the garden courtyard below. In the week since their arrival in London, she'd felt even more useless, as Darius had taken on most of the burdens of seeing them settled and shielding her from the challenges ahead. But the transition to move their quarters to the Blackwells' home had been a highlight.

She'd balked at the idea of intruding into a private residence and risking the involvement of his friends in her predicament. Mrs. Clay had been so kind, Isabel didn't want to forfeit her room. Darius had finally convinced her that safety and security carried more weight than Mrs. Clay's hospitality. Even so, he'd kept the rooms to give them a place to go to if they ever needed a quick escape or spot for an emergency rendezvous.

They'd smuggled her in through the servants' entrance, and Isabel had gotten a little tearful with embarrassment at her state of disgrace. But she'd had only seconds to wallow in self-pity before the surprising warmth and welcome of the house took hold. Mrs. Clark had bustled forward and offered dinner and a hot bath in one breath, to Ashe's amusement.

The butler, Mr. Godwin, a more serious man as befitted his position, made an effort to calmly review all the extra security features of the house and restated the commitment of the entire staff to ensuring that the utmost discretion was applied during Mrs. Stewart's visit. He'd revealed a hidden tender nature by adding to her directly that if she had any anxieties, "on any matter great or small, you must ring your bell without hesitation!"

"Godwin ordered extra candles because Mrs. Clark told him that it would please your spirits to be in a brighter house," Ashe teased.

Godwin's harrumph of protest was a thing to behold. "I ordered extra candles because we *needed* them."

"Of course, Godwin! Of course we did," Ashe said with a smile. "Now come meet my wife, Mrs. Stewart. You will be doing me a great favor, staying here. My Caroline is confined, thanks to the tyranny of Dr. West, and she'll be thrilled with company."

With a wink from Darius confirming all, she'd been shyly whisked up the stairs to meet her hostess and to make a new dear friend. Within minutes, Isabel had discovered that Mrs. Blackwell was wonderfully sweet and candid about her current condition and her approval of Isabel's attachment to Darius.

"Ashe! Tell me you didn't just kidnap this poor girl to provide me female company!" Caroline protested half-heartedly.

"I did," he admitted solemnly. "I will undoubtedly hang for it, but it was worth it."

Isabel gasped. "He is jesting, Mrs. Blackwell!"

"I know," she assured her, holding out her hands in invitation to a chair by the bed. "Please don't mind him. Ashe shared your situation, so you've no fear of us. He just—says these things to make me blush. What shall I call you?"

"Helen. Helen Stewart," Isabel said hesitantly as Ashe

came forward to adjust his wife's pillows. "But if you are unwell, I should—"

"I am completely hale and hearty!" Caroline interrupted her, swiping playfully at her husband for his attentions. "Mr. Blackwell is deliberately taking advantage to linger and will make you swear to keep an eye on me but it's ridiculous to think I'm to stay in bed for weeks and months yet." Caroline pouted. "I feel perfectly fine!"

Ashe lifted her hand to kiss his wife's fingertips. "My defiant colonial wife. You feel fine, dearest, *because* you are resting as you should. We must yield to Rowan's better judgment and do all that he asks."

Caroline rolled her eyes but blushed at her husband's touch. "Go away! I want to meet Helen and talk without you hovering and spoiling the conversation."

"Does this mean I'll be one of the subjects of the discussion?" he asked.

"It is guaranteed at this point! Now go!" she commanded, and her husband bowed and dutifully retreated from the room. "There, now we can converse freely."

"You're American." Isabel sighed in open admiration, then blushed as she took the chair Caroline had offered. "I mean . . . how wonderful that you're American. What an odd thing to say!"

Caroline laughed. "Please! Always say what you're thinking! For I'm eternally guilty of blurting things out and being the oddest woman I know."

"May I ask why you're to bed? Is it common to be so restricted so soon for . . . your condition?" Isabel asked. "Because you're expecting?"

Caroline placed her hands on her growing belly, blushing a little. "Not common but I suffered a mishap early in November, and Dr. West felt it wise to take precautions. Have you met him?" she asked.

"No, not yet."

"You'll love him, and his wife. Gayle is studying to be a physician and works with her husband now." Caroline shook her head. "They are a formidable pair if you dare to so much as get a head cold within their sphere."

Isabel's mouth fell open. "A woman to be a doctor? How extraordinary!"

"And why not?" Caroline said with a confidence that awed her new friend. "There is very little a man can accomplish that a woman cannot match. She simply needs the right tools and opportunities for education that—I'm sorry. I am a bit of a reformer. I dream of creating a college solely for women, and my husband and his grandfather have supported my ideas."

"Are all the wives of the Jaded so . . . forward thinking?"

Caroline bit her lower lip as she considered the question. "I never thought of it. I suppose we are, each in our own way, a little unique. Even Lady Winters has insisted on a profession of her own as a designer, and the new Mrs. Hastings, whom I had just met, said something about helping Josiah with his paintings. So we are apparently an unconventional ladies' club." Caroline shrugged. "But it makes the meetings more interesting!"

"Undoubtedly," Isabel agreed, her pale blue eyes growing sad. "Although I would hardly add to the circle. I've an education that included nothing more than playing the pianoforte, wearing dancing slippers, and making bonnets."

"I am *glad* to make your acquaintance, Helen Stewart," Caroline said firmly. "You are part of our circle now and you add to it simply by being yourself and for the happiness that you bring to Mr. Thorne. You have nothing to prove."

Caroline's generosity was a bit overwhelming and Isabel's eyes dropped to her hands. "Thank you for that." To alleviate her embarrassment at compliments, she attempted one of her own. "Your . . . home is beautiful, Mrs. Blackwell."

"Caroline. You must call me Caroline, and thank you. Ashe has good taste and I—" She laughed again, merriment making her large brown eyes brighten. "I knew better than to add a single lamp pull and spoil the effect!"

Isabel nodded in sympathy. "Because he forbid it."

Caroline's laughter ended quickly, her look of shock price-less. "Forbid it? *My* Ashe? No. I meant because I have the innate taste of a mud wren when it comes to fashions and furnishings. My impossible husband—I cannot think of a thing that man has ever forbidden me to do!"

"Die," Ashe corrected her from the doorway. "I forbid you to die, remember?"

Isabel stood awkwardly, unsure of the macabre turn in the conversation and Mr. Blackwell's return.

"Ashe!" Caroline protested with a squeak. "What a thing to say! You're going to make Helen think you're an arrogant creature out of a gothic novel, Blackwell!" Even as she chided him, she lost the battle and smiled. "I'm the picture of rosy health. Leave me alone!"

"I apologize for interrupting so soon, for I can tell you were in the midst of forging a lifelong alliance. . . ."

"We were!" Caroline assured him quickly, and Isabel's cheeks colored with pleasure. Even a premature declaration of friendship was so desirable to her she wasn't sure what to say.

"Yes, we were," Isabel echoed softly.

"Mrs. Clark insisted that I come up and make sure that no one was hungry. Cook's made a fresh tray because"—he paused for effect—"*someone* did not touch her lunch despite the inclusion of her favorite gingerbread cakes . . . so there's a bit of an uproar in the kitchens below stairs, and I overheard plotting to rival any military coup to figure out how to trick *someone* into eating."

"Do you see, Helen?" Caroline turned to her friend. "Why I'm so glad you've come? I'm already plump as a dinner hen and they're conspiring against me!"

Isabel read Ashe's expression out of the corner of her eye and knew where her loyalties lay without being prompted. "Not *against* you, surely! But *for* you, don't you think? Besides," she said, "I'm sure I would love to sample some gingerbread cake. Will you not join me?"

Caroline crossed her arms but nodded with a sigh of defeat. "Very well."

Ashe's relief was obvious as he took his leave again and Isabel watched him go. "He is—so . . ."

"Bossy?" Caroline supplied.

"Attentive," Isabel amended. "It is clear he adores you."

"We are ridiculously in love." Caroline beamed, hugging her elbows. "I still can't believe it's possible to be this happy. Especially when I think of our contentious beginning. . . ."

It was all Isabel could do to nod. She had never expected to speak of such things so directly, but her new friend's manners made the impossible matter-of-fact.

Caroline leaned back against the pillows. "Ashe hasn't told me too much, only because Darius has said very little to him. But one thing is clear. Darius will do everything he can to resolve things and end . . . your current predicament."

"He's already done so much. I hate to think that all I've done in return is disrupted all his plans and brought him to ruin. If anyone finds out that he has taken up with a married woman . . ." Isabel shuddered. "The gossips will twist it into something so vile I cannot hope to keep him from—"

"You worry too much." Caroline interrupted her gently. "No one is ruined, and if ever a man was set in his decisions and plans, it is Darius. He won't plant one foot without thinking through the entire journey, and despite the circumstances, we both know he is the most upstanding and moral of men. He just wants to protect you and there is nothing nobler."

"No, nothing nobler." *Than my wonderful knight.*

"But to serious matters at hand!" Caroline's tone changed. "I have a desperate problem and I am hoping you can provide some relief."

Isabel had instantly shifted her attention, alert and wary. "Anything you need, you have but to ask."

"Daisy is my maid, but she's a bit lost since I'm not exactly dressing for social calls or doing more than changing night-gowns and bathing for excitement these days. Do you mind if I have her attend you? I can tell just by looking that you're far more elegant than I could ever aspire to be, and Daisy is so eager to learn to be a proper ladies' maid."

Isabel nodded. "It's so kind of you to offer. Although, confined to the house myself, I'm not sure if I'll prove to be much of a distraction."

"If you've a better understanding of hats and ribbons, then you are bound to be an improvement for her." Caroline's cheeks reddened. "I'm a terrible disappointment for her."

"I could not take your maid."

"Then just share her, won't you? Please?" Caroline asked sweetly, and Isabel accepted that she'd been deftly outmaneuvered.

"We'll share her."

"It's perfect! Between the two of us, we can make her happy, and she's a sweet girl, Helen. Very discreet." Caroline took her hand. "They all are. Godwin and Mrs. Clark run a tight ship and you're safe here."

"I feel safe already."

It was true.

From that first conversation onward, she felt inherently secure under Blackwell's roof, and Darius had encouraged her to make the most of it. She had a true friend in Caroline and a vicariously watchful older brother in Ashe. But best of all, she had Darius. In a strange limbo between her past and her future, they guarded each moment together, sharing meals, playing chess, reading, or locking their doors and refusing to leave the bed.

It was all bittersweet because Isabel knew that no matter what anyone said, it could never last.

One way or another, Richard would have to be faced, and despite Darius's assurances that her husband would see reason if he were threatened with exposure of his worst secrets—she wasn't nearly so confident.

And here I sit, idly by, like a helpless child, waiting for Darius to solve my problems and save the day.

Frustration raged inside of her and she remembered how Caroline had described the wives of their circle and all of them had sounded so independent and strong. Instead of pouting about her situation, Caroline was vivacious with plans for her college and her pursuit of its accreditation.

There is very little a man can accomplish that a woman cannot match.

"I wonder what I can do?" she asked herself aloud.

He'd lamented that there was no simple path to take, but Isabel wondered if she'd missed something obvious. It was true that her first attempt to tell her mother of her troubles had gone awry.

But I was so shy of it and it was such an incoherent ramble to send her. Perhaps Darius is right and my mother's advice was misdirected.

It was a small, frail thread of hope but a tantalizing idea.

Her parents could be powerful allies for her and potentially apply great pressure to Netherton to release her quietly. The daydream of a mother's comforting arms fueled her resolve. Isabel finally began her letter with the determination of a woman with little to lose.

I only asked my mother once for help. And I was so terrified to name the details of my situation—if she misunderstood, then I may already have the resources I need to resolve this quickly. I can spare Darius the nightmare of blackmailing Richard and stand up for myself.

I can prove myself Darius's equal and demonstrate that I'm not just a porcelain doll to sit by while others make sacrifices on my behalf.

"It is time for me to make a move of my own," she whispered and began to write.

Chapter
22

Red purple velvet brocade wallpaper and overly ornate furniture created an atmosphere of opulence and overt strangeness that jarred Darius's sensibilities. Men in evening coats relaxed at card tables in a large room on the ground floor, surrounded by young women in garishly bright silk dresses who fawned over them and encouraged each bid. The theatrical touches of their feathered costumes and immodest cut and fit of their dresses turned them into exaggerated versions of their respectable counterparts—a mockery of the Victorian ladies Darius had long idealized.

A chill trickled down Darius's spine. The idea had seemed so straightforward. He'd felt so brave confronting Harold to get the names of Netherton's haunts. But faced with the reality, his confidence faltered. Under the smell of cigar smoke and perfume, there were traces of sweat and sex, unwashed linens and wine.

Darius forced himself to simply exhale and focus on the task at hand.

"What may we do for you, sir?" a woman purred as she

approached him, wearing the brightest red dress he had ever seen. "Name your pleasure and let the Velvet House provide."

"I have . . . an unusual request."

The woman barely reacted to his words. "We specialize in the unusual here."

"May we speak privately?" he asked, shifting his weight as he assessed that in the foyer there were at least a dozen interested audience members at this point.

Her expression became smug as she dropped a shoulder in a practiced gesture that allowed the beaded strap of her gown to slide down one creamy bare arm. She waved a fan toward another set of ornate doors almost hidden by red velvet drapes. "If you desire it."

She left the door open, and a man whose neck was as wide as his skull moved to stand at the curtains to shield them from the foyer. *And lend a hand if I prove to be an unruly or an unwanted guest.*

It was the moment of truth.

Darius had never been a good liar and so he'd decided on a very risky strategy that skirted as close to the truth as he dared.

"Well?" she prompted him, a small sign of impatience alerting him to the seconds he had left to make his case.

"I take it you're familiar with certain books on the subject of sexuality? Ancient texts that some enjoy a great deal? The *Kama Sutra*? The erotic tales of the Arabian nights?" he asked. "Some of your clients may seek out interesting pictures or books that hold a special appeal?"

She nodded. "Naturally."

"Well, I've been commissioned by one of your patrons to write such an illustrated book. An anonymous piece, of course, of his adventures, and he has challenged me to see what I can make of his thrilling tastes."

"Challenged you?" Her expression flashed with interest. "Is it a wager?"

And there it is. The lady has a weakness for gambling and there's my midgame.

"In a manner of speaking." He leaned in conspiratorially. "There's a purse to win if I can astonish him. But of what I know of the man, he'll be difficult to awe."

"A bit world-weary, your employer?" she asked. "But he's put up a bounty?"

"On his own story." Darius nodded, smiling as she openly warmed to the idea. "I think it's a bit of personal pride and a dash of patriotism that makes him resent that all the best erotic works of literature seem to come from outside of the country."

She smiled. "That's because English men are more busy having a go than wishing to sit back and write about having a go, in my opinion!"

"Which is what brings me here."

She crossed her arms. "If this is some ruse to get you a bit of free access to my girls without paying in the name of 'research' for some pamphlet, then you've mistaken me for a fool, sir."

"You're no fool. And I'll pay for the time I spend interviewing your girls. And please understand that no names will be used and there is no threat of exposure of your wonderful establishment."

She arched one eyebrow at him, openly skeptical but still engaged. "A proper book?"

"A masterpiece, if I complete the commission as promised. You see, my employer's ego would demand nothing less, so this isn't going to be a penny-novel slapabout. I'm to uncover the tales of his exploits and document his . . . tastes. He is convinced that he is unique and that his mastery of the arts of these secret houses will cause a very profitable sensation."

She uncrossed her arms. "Profitable, you say?"

He nodded. "You of all people have a grasp of the demand for certain 'entertainments.' And for every man who cannot afford or does not have the right connections to gain entrance to the Velvet House, a book like this would give them a glimpse of another world."

"I'm not sure I like the idea of the world peeking in my windows," she said.

"I would not name your establishment, madam, unless you desired the notoriety," he offered. Darius reached in his wallet and pulled out some folded notes. "Here, for the inconvenience."

She took the money smoothly from his hand, pocketing it in one graceful practiced maneuver. "What you do with the girls is your business. You'll pay for their time and I'll not forbid them to speak, but you must understand that . . . discretion is at a premium. What you can win out of them, I leave to you."

"Then I wish to see the women that Lord Netherton prefers."

The friendly expression on her face grew distant. "Netherton? He wants a book of it?"

Darius nodded. "Apparently, he does."

She shook her head. "You're on the devil's errands, sir. But if it's a big enough purse he's promised you that you would consider such a thing—who am I to argue against it?"

"Thank you," he said, bowing slightly as she stepped away and led him back out to the foyer.

"It's Nell you'd want. But she's occupied at the moment." The madam waved her fan toward another girl standing on the stairs, signaling for her to come down. "Charlotte's another of his choices, so perhaps you can start with her."

Darius held his place as a girl no more than fifteen or sixteen approached, wearing nothing more than a corset and sheer petticoats.

"Charlotte, take the nice man upstairs for a bit of *conversation*," the madam said with a sly smile.

Charlotte took his arm without a hint of reluctance, and Darius realized that no matter what he said, they didn't expect him to keep his hands in his pockets.

No matter.

He allowed himself to be taken up the stairs and into a small bedchamber halfway down the hall. Charlotte's flirtations were practiced but sweet, and Darius did his best to keep his eyes set on her face alone.

"What's your pleasure? A pretty and proper man like you . . . I bet you'd like to forgo the niceties, eh? Shall I give you a French kiss, then? To get you started?" She began to reach for the buttons of his trousers, kneeling between his legs, but Darius sidestepped her quickly and started to help her back onto her feet.

"Charlotte," Darius said, taking a deep breath. "I just wished to talk to you, if you don't mind."

Her eyes widened in surprise but then took on a knowing look. "I can sit on your lap and whisper all the filthy words I know, Professor, if that's your fancy. Or you can teach me what you'd like to hear." She leaned forward to whisper, giving him a wicked look through her darkened lashes. "I've a bit of Latin, sir."

"How enterprising of you," he said, biting the inside of his cheek to keep from smiling and inadvertently encouraging her. "No, please, if you'll just sit there and I'll take a seat over there and we can—chat for a time."

She bit her lip in confusion but sat where he directed her, a strange imitation of a lady with her bare knees showing but her hands neatly folded in her lap. "Well, I'll say it first. When Mrs. Scarlett said you wanted conversation, I was fully expecting to be on my back for it."

Darius lost the battle and smiled. "Would you like something to drink? Or eat?"

She sat up, instantly alert. "I'm famished! There's hardly time to eat once the evening starts and . . . even if a man orders himself a plate, well, they don't share, do they?"

He nodded and then stood to ring the bell, summoning a footman and ordering a plate of food and a bottle of wine.

"That's awful kind of you," Charlotte said.

"It's a small thing." Darius shook his head and returned to his chair. "While we're waiting, I must tell you the reason I'm here. I'm trying to learn a bit about a certain man's tastes and I understand you may have kept him company more than once."

"We aren't to talk about our customers," she responded quickly. "The house has firm rules on the matter."

"I spoke to Mrs. Scarlett and she gave me permission to talk to you on this very topic."

"Well, that's all right, then, but I'm not sure I'll be much help," she said. "One bloke blends into another in my mind, and no offense, but one poke is as much like any after a while."

Shit. I hadn't thought of that. . . .

"Perhaps this man would be different. Lord Richard Netherton?"

Charlotte held her place but grew a little less animated. "You are friends with Lord Netherton, are you?"

He hesitated and then went with his instincts. "No, not at all."

She tipped her head to one side, openly assessing him. "But you're asking after him?"

"I am." He didn't want to say more. He didn't want to lie about masterpieces of erotica and wagers of ruin.

For long minutes, she didn't say anything and then there was a knock at the door. Darius opened the door for the footman, who set down the large plate of meat, cheese, and bread and then left behind an opened bottle of wine with two glasses. Once the door was closed, Darius waved his hand to invite her to partake.

Charlotte lunged at the food with the gusto of a child, her hunger omitting manners. He simply poured them both a glass of wine and then sipped his thoughtfully while she ate. Her age was impossible to know, her painted cheeks and lips disguising her natural beauty, and she was extremely well-endowed, but her bones showed at her shoulders, and whatever baby fat she'd possessed had grown lean by the lifestyle and the trade.

Sixteen? Are you even sixteen?

She looked up with a mouthful of meat and caught him midstudy. Charlotte blushed and finished her bite. "Sorry. I guess I was hungrier than I'd imagined. The gin takes the edge off but I don't like the taste of it really. This wine is nice though," she said and lifted a glass in a jaunty toast.

He lifted his own glass in reply. "No need to apologize. You should eat your fill and we can order more if you'd like."

She pushed her plate away. "No one is this kind."

He laughed. "Why do all the women I know say that?"

"Because it's true," Charlotte said, then took a long draw from her glass. "I'd think you were just putting me on to get what you wanted, but for some reason I think you'd sit there, keep your hands to yourself, and feed me until dawn without complaint."

He shrugged his shoulders. "If you'd like."

She leaned back. "All right. Ask."

"How old are you?"

"Fourteen."

Darius's smile faded. For a fleeting moment, it had been a light game, ordering chicken and seeing her content. But this—this was bound to get ugly. Darius retrieved a small leather-bound notebook from his coat pocket.

"And what can you tell me about Richard Netherton?"

* * *

It was only his first interview, and in the nights that followed, Darius received a quick education in the dark underbelly of Victorian society, and acquired new respect for what Isabel had endured at her husband's hands. It was houses of sadism that the man frequented, and anything exotic or "forbidden" was apparently in demand by Lord Netherton's appetite.

Charlotte had calmly told him of her encounters with Richard, describing in graphic detail what made it clear that, while most of her clients melted into a pool of forgettable couplings, Netherton had made an impression with his use of leather straps and his gift for humiliation.

He'd put linen sachets full of salt and herbs inside of a fourteen-year-old to make her channel drier and tighter for his purposes. Netherton had deliberately made that child bleed to increase his own pleasure. . . . God . . . what have I gotten myself into?

Charlotte had mentioned another couple of girls in the Velvet House with an even better understanding of him, Nell and Laura, and Darius had been forced to realize that he would be spending more than one night in the Velvet House if he was to be thorough.

Every night afterward became what he dubbed "the worst night of his life"—as he talked to girls less than half his age about atrocities he'd never envisioned. Their stories were told with such emotionless calm that Darius was sickened at the damage their spirits had suffered. Even the most sporting of women shivered at the mention of Netherton, and when they pulled out the tools and toys he preferred or revealed the scars he'd gifted them with, it was almost too much.

After less than two weeks of it, it was harder and harder to return to Blackwell's home and face his queen. Isabel was all that was beautiful and good in the world, and Darius began to order scalding hot baths before he would head up the stairs and touch her. As if he could cleanse himself of the knowledge that corroded his sense of place and justice. As if until he scrubbed his own skin off, he wouldn't be clean enough to approach her.

Hell, and I'm just listening. . . . There are men that participate in it and cheerfully ride home to their wives and sleep like babies. What kind of man is that?

Netherton is twisting in my mind into something other than a human being, and it's clouding my judgment. I've never hated anyone so much that I couldn't see my way past it.

Darius poured himself a glass of brandy as the clock struck midnight and wondered if he had the courage to look at his own notes and make a run at looking for any usable threads.

I'd rather scrape my eyes out of my head, God help me.
"Darius?"

He turned to see her there, in her nightgown, standing in the doorway of the sitting room. "Yes, my love."

"I heard the carriage but then you didn't come up." She came toward him, apparently unaware of the picture she presented with her hair down and her sensual curves undisguised by the angelic white of her nightdress. "Are you all right?"

He started to nod and make light denials but something

stopped him. She'd endured the worst and given him her trust. The least he could do was repay her with honesty.

"I've filled two notebooks with interviews of the most vile sexual deeds on this earth." He tossed back the brandy in one swallow, savoring the heat of it and the soothing fire that coursed through his veins. "It's a wonder some of the girls survived his patronage."

"Is it enough?"

"No. It's twisted and sick but . . . what proof do I have of any of it? I can threaten him with scandal, but without leverage, he'll shake it off and I'll be exposed for having far too much interest in his wife's well-being for an ordinary outsider."

Her hands were clasped so tightly she couldn't feel her fingers anymore. "It's as he said. Hurting women is a sport. His friends will see nothing in it."

"It isn't a sport!"

"Isn't it?" she stood, openly upset and trembling. "Th-there are clubs that cater to it! And you said the other night how busy the girls were kept. You said none of the gentlemen there seemed concerned! What if all his sins are ordinary? Abandon this course, Darius. There is nothing but the agony of facing the worst of nature and I don't see his downfall—but yours!"

"I'm not at risk of finding anything appealing in this, Isabel. It evokes too many memories of my mother's suffering and I loathe—"

"Don't you see? It scars you. It has already wounded you. You've spent a lifetime separating yourself from the nightmares of your childhood. What will you do to erase the things that you're exposing yourself to? How can I see you deliberately destroy your peace of mind all for me?" She began to pace frantically. "Even if you win, what victory is there if you cannot sleep at night?"

He stepped into her path, her momentum carrying her into his arms. "Isabel. Look at me."

She tipped her head back, her cheeks streaked with tears. "I am not worth this."

"No. You're worth more." He kissed her slowly and tenderly on her cheeks, tasting her tears. "I'll go back out and interview every whore in London if I need to, and I won't stop until I find the lever it takes to move this mountain."

"Darius, I don't know if I want to see you hurt in this way. This isn't right." She reached up to mold her palm to the strong curve of his jaw, caressing his face. "Would it not have been better for all those poor men on the battlefield if Helen had seen reason and sacrificed herself, returned to her husband and allowed Paris to live out his days?"

He caught her hand in his and kissed her palm, the contact of his lips to the indent of her hand sending sparks of desire up across her skin. "No. For one, they'd already burned their ships and gone too far, and more importantly . . ."

"Yes?" she whispered, leaning against him more heavily as her joints grew weak with wanting.

"Paris couldn't live without her."

"Oh." She sighed.

Isabel's heart ached at the sight of him, so handsome and hurting. She knew what it was like to carry wounds that others couldn't see, and all she could remember was that when her world was overtaken by memories of her husband's cruelties, Darius had taught her to play chess and made her see her own power.

"Darius?" she asked, quietly waiting until he finally looked into her eyes. "May I teach you something?"

She'd surprised him, she could tell, but she had his attention. "What lesson did you have in mind?"

"It's a silly distraction, but I think . . . you should learn to dance."

His mouth fell open slightly. "Pardon me?"

She smiled and did her best to imitate an old instructor she'd once had, playfully trying to divert his thoughts and draw him away from his pain. "Now, you may think it's just a bit of social nonsense and all about footwork, but there is far more to dancing than meets the eye, Mr. Thorne."

"Is there?" he asked.

"Oh yes. There is strategy in the movement and purpose,

physical challenges and mental work to be done. But unlike games of battle"—she leaned in with a conspiratorial smile—"the goal is not conquest."

"Are you sure?" he teased. "For the one or two times I've tried it, I swear my partner proclaimed that I had laid siege to her toes."

She laughed. "If I had a fan, I would strike you playfully just *so* on your shoulder for being cheeky, Mr. Thorne."

"I apologize. What were you saying about goals?" he asked contritely.

"The goal is harmony."

His brow furrowed. "Are you sure?"

"Dancing is an elegant reduction of life and love. It is the art of moving together as one, of accepting and trusting each other, and it betrays a man's true nature to everyone who watches him."

"That cannot be good," he said firmly. "I'm not about to demonstrate that my nature is clumsy and hopeless to you, Isabel."

She laughed. "No, nor will you." She stepped closer and put his arm about her waist, setting his hand against her back, and then took hold of his free hand to guide him into position. "Shoulders straight. See? You will guide me with the lightest touch and I will mirror your steps. On the dance floor, you show your care of me by subtly seeing to my person and ensuring that you don't steer me into a wall."

It was his turn to laugh and she was glad to hear it again.

"Or the furniture," he added.

"Or the furniture," she agreed. "Ready?"

"Oh, God. I think so. Although, there is no music."

"Is there not?" She smiled up at him, full of mischief. "There is one more reason you should learn to dance, Mr. Thorne."

"And what reason is that, my Helen?"

"Because when you dance, the world falls away and it's just us. Nothing else matters, Darius. Here in this framework, I am safe. Inside your arms, I am protected. And you are invincible, my dearest."

She held her breath, watching the light rekindle in his eyes.

"Then we should dance."

The first steps were clumsy but Isabel didn't allow him to slow. She hummed softly and looked up at him as if dancing in sitting rooms in the middle of the night was as normal as porridge and far more fun.

Come, my love. Let the world fall away.

And then it was magic.

Darius's body caught the rhythm of the waltz and slowly took command of the steps to steer her about the room, in and out of moonlight, in and out of firelight, until Isabel forgot the lesson.

He must have stopped dancing to kiss her, but she couldn't remember stopping.

The kiss was an extension of the dance, and Isabel gave in to the dizzying spirals of electricity that coursed through her body. His tongue delved into the velvet warmth of her mouth, going deeper to taste her, and Isabel moaned at the echoing ache between her hips at the thought of him deep inside of her.

She tried to swim through it, determined to give more pleasure than she received, to heal his spirit and reassure him that what lay between them had nothing to do with the soulless acts he'd recorded in his notes.

She led him to their bedroom and gently guided him up onto the mattress, where she climbed in behind him.

"What are your intentions, Isabel?" he asked as she removed his glasses to tuck them safely onto the bedside table.

"Shhh. Tonight I am Helen." She kissed the back of his neck and then the sensitive point between his shoulder blades.

"That feels wonderful," he whispered.

"Then I shall apply myself to just that. To making you feel wonderful." Isabel trailed kisses across his back, dragging her lips across his skin and using her tongue to make him moan. Then she blew against his moist flesh and smiled as his skin marbled at the unexpected sensation.

"This is torture." He sighed.

"Shall I stop?"

"No. Never."

She massaged his aching shoulders, soothing what hurt she could. She used the heel of her hands to press along the furrow of his spine, seeking out the knots of tension and manipulating his muscles until the smooth warmth beneath her hands was too powerful a lure. She untied her own night-gown and slipped it back from her shoulders to press her breasts against him, the friction and sweet contact instantly making her nipples harden.

He gasped in surprise but leaned against her in approval, seeking more of her touch. "I like this."

She smiled and tried to gently drag her herself down his back to tease him further, but Darius turned as quick as a cat and pulled her beneath him on the feather-down mattress.

"Let me. Let me love you, Darius."

"As you wish," he said and released her to stretch out on the bed.

She straddled him playfully, exploring her new powers and continuing her lazy game of indolent worship as she kissed and tasted his body. She wished to seek out anything to please him, and at the unmistakable prodding of his erec-tion against her bottom, Isabel wondered if she hadn't over-looked an obvious choice.

On her hands and knees, she deliberately trailed her long hair across his chest on her way to the jutting column of his sex. She bent over, eager to taste him, mesmerized by the masculine beauty of his cock, so erect and beautiful, but he stopped her.

"Darius!" she protested but then forgot the argument as her small world turned into one of motion and the addictive work of his body against hers.

Her nightgown was bunched around her waist as he bared her legs and parted her thighs. Isabel looked into his face, unashamed of her need and aware that he could see how wet she'd become and how wanton.

"Middle game," he whispered, and Isabel stretched her arms open wide to welcome it.

"Yes! A nice, long middle game, if you please. . . ."

He lowered himself onto her and Isabel sighed with happiness as her beloved Black King obliged his White Queen.

* * *

Darius held her until her breathing evened out and she was asleep in his arms. He stared up at the ceiling and did his best to follow her, but his thoughts hammered at his peace of mind.

Even his desires for Isabel had been affected by his grim education. When she'd started to try to kneel between his legs, he'd had a sudden flashback to Charlotte in the Velvet House calmly offering him a similar service in the same tone one expected to be offered tea.

She's right. I'm taking on a bit more damage than I'd expected.

But his love for Isabel was inviolate.

She taught me to dance.

His eyes filled with tears and Darius did his best to blink them away.

No matter what happens, it's a lesson I'll carry with me for the rest of my life—please, God.

Chapter
23

"What is it?" Isabel found him the next morning sitting alone in the music salon. It was an odd location for a man who had no inclination toward music, but after a brief search, she finally spotted him sitting as still as a statue next to an ornately carved harp in the corner by the windows.

"It's . . ." He held up a folded note. "A letter from Mrs. McFadden."

"Is everything all right?" Isabel came into the room, her steps uncertain. There was something in Darius's face that warned her that something unpleasant was coming.

"One of your husband's agents came around and they recovered Samson."

"No!"

Darius stood to deliver the rest of the news. "They almost charged Hamish with being a horse thief except the constable knew we'd found the horse and were making every effort to locate its owner. Hamish fought them like a lion and was nearly arrested for striking one of the men, but Mrs. McFadden said the locals weren't about to take the agent's side in the matter. Not after he'd accused one of their own without cause."

"They t-took Samson?"

"By law, he is your husband's property to recover." He opened his arms. "Isabel, I'm so sorry."

She ran to him, throwing herself against his chest, blindly sobbing at the loss. "H-he was m-my friend."

He stroked her hair and enfolded her in his embrace. "I know. I would give the world to change it."

"H-he's gone!" she cried, her fingers entwined in his shirt, clinging to Darius as if he were the only thing tethering her to the earth. "Oh, God! And now Richard knows of you!"

"He knows almost nothing," Darius said, his voice calm and steady in her ears. "Mrs. McFadden could stare down the devil if he asked her where she kept her house keys, so I don't see her or Mr. MacQueen blinking and giving away a breath of your time there."

"Yes." She nodded, her tears slowing. "Mrs. McFadden isn't afraid of anything."

"Not with Hamish there. And since you've shown her how to wield a skillet properly . . ."

"Samson was all that I had in the world."

"No. Never. Not so long as I draw breath."

She managed a shaky smile. "Careful, Thorne. You'll make one promise too many and—I keep waiting for you to say, *Enough!*"

"You'll waste a lifetime, then."

"Kiss me, Darius."

It was easy to oblige her. He dipped his head to taste her lips, salty with tears and soft against his. He kissed her until the pleasure of it eclipsed her pain, each touch of his mouth another vow to keep her safe and find a way to restore her happiness.

* * *

"Will you be all right alone for a time? I promised Rutherford I'd attend him at the sports club for a fencing lesson. I think he's determined to see all of us prepared for some kind of battle."

"Darius. Swear to me that you won't—enter into some duel or challenge with Richard. I don't care about anything else. Swear you won't risk your life in any of this plan—not for me!"

"Isabel, I—"

"On your honor, Darius Thorne, I need your word."

"Then you have my word."

"I hate this."

"What do you hate?" he asked, an anxious edge to his voice.

"Being so helpless. I am nothing more than a spectator in all of this and I . . . hate it." She reached up to press her fingertips against her temples. "I'm truly a ghost floating alongside the living but barely here."

"Your coloring suits the image," he teased, drawing her against his chest. "But I can assure you that you are very corporeal, Helen. Shall I demonstrate how much you are physically grounded to this world, my dearest?"

"N-not here!" she protested weakly. "Our hosts are very accommodating but—I'd rather not give Mr. Godwin a heart attack, Mr. Thorne."

"Nonsense. He's lived with Blackwell too long to be shocked by anything," Darius countered, but he gently let her go. "Very well. A small reprieve but I warn you I may lock the dining room door and interrupt your breakfast with a wild and desperate tangle if you don't object."

"Will you be home tonight?"

He shook his head slowly. "If Michael doesn't bruise me too badly, I'll stay out and try to make the most of it."

"How . . . many more on the list?" she asked.

"Two."

"And if there's nothing?"

"I can't think of that now. I can't allow myself to think of failing you."

"But you're staying safe? You've promised me."

"I'm as safe as churches." He kissed her again. "And so are you."

* * *

After he'd left, she walked the salon alone, pacing through the slants of pale sunlight that cut across the room, an ivory sprite unaware of the dance of light and shadows that made her all the more striking as she moved in and out of the beams.

Every memory of Samson was a sharp pain in her body, and Isabel knew that she would grieve for a long time for the loss of her only true friend. But watching Darius go and once again being left to sit and wait . . . it was too much.

"You've a letter, madam." Daisy greeted her as she crossed the room. "It came by a runner. And Mrs. Clark said to ask if you had any opinion on whether to expect Mr. Thorne this evening."

"I . . . I don't think he'll be home tonight. I'll take my dinner in my room alone unless Caroline wishes company."

Daisy blushed. "Mr. and Mrs. Blackwell are having a private dinner this evening and are not to be disturbed."

Isabel nodded, pleased for her friend and her happiness. "Very well. Thank you, Daisy."

Daisy handed over the letter and curtsied before leaving Isabel with her thoughts.

Ashe Blackwell was one of the most attractive men Isabel had ever seen, but what made him even more remarkably handsome beyond his golden looks was his singular attention to and adoration of his young wife. It was as if he'd dedicated his life to pleasing her, and Isabel knew that his existence hinged on Caroline. No one had said anything overtly, but anxiety over her condition and the impending arrival of the child in the summer was impossible to miss. The household was holding its collective breath and it was easy to see why. Isabel prayed for her friend's safe delivery and the health of her unborn child, out of love for Caroline and for Ashe.

Theirs is an example of what a marriage should be. I am

privileged to have been invited into their home to see it for myself.

It's what life would be like with Darius, I think.

She indulged in her recurring daydream of such a marriage with her beloved scholar. Their passion for each other hadn't waned in the slightest, and she knew that as his wife, he would treasure and protect her like no other man.

But I am already married. . . .

Her attention returned to the letter, and Isabel instantly recognized her mother's elegantly measured hand.

"Please, mother," Isabel whispered as she broke the seal and opened the note. "Please."

Isabel,

I was shocked to receive your letter and to learn of your situation.

As your husband has already written us of your scandalous behavior and inexcusable actions, along with his fears of your mental weakness, I can only conclude that your letter is proof of his fears. Lord Netherton has expressed his heartbreak at your callous choice to run off with another man and has assured us that, if you return to your senses, he will magnanimously forgive you and credit this folly to your youth and inexperience. All will be as it was.

So long as the scandal does not become public.

I am astonished at his generosity. Any other man would see you horsewhipped as a whore, Isabel. As your mother, I refuse to take any blame for this failure in your character and order you to see reason.

You were married before God and took a sacred oath to your husband.

You will return immediately to Netherton's care and spend the rest of your life striving to be his dutiful and obedient wife or we shall never speak to you again.

> *In earnest,*
> *M/P*

*I have given Lord Netherton your letter in the fervent hope
that it will help him find you and bring you back from the
pit of hell you seem content to wallow in.*

Isabel's knees gave out and she sat on the floor with her
skirts fanned out around her. In one morning, she'd lost her
Samson and the last hope of her parents' love.

And Richard had her letter in his hands.

*   *   *

At the sports club, Rutherford's fencing lesson was exactly
the kind of distraction Darius craved. Physically and mentally demanding, when you stood across from an intimidating
fighter like Michael, there was no room for any thought
beyond survival.

"You're improving. But you still get winded too quickly."
Michael stepped back, dropping his foil. "It's the fire."

"It's nothing. Rowan said to give it time. Besides, if it
does come down to a fight, I have the growing suspicion it
will be a very short battle—so who needs stamina?" Darius
jested, trying to divert Rutherford from the usual grave bent
of his thoughts.

"You need to be ready for anything." Michael gave a nod
toward the bench next to the practice area, and the men
retreated to catch their breath. "All right. Let's have it. How
goes the dark quest?"

"Michael. I'm nearly at the end of my short list of leads
for houses that Netherton prefers. Three out of five have
yielded nothing but horror stories to give me nightmares
and make me sickened by the trade. What if I've sacrificed
my peace of mind for nothing?"

"What are your other options?"

Darius tipped his head back in frustration and groaned.
"None of them are very good."

"Humor me and list them."

Darius straightened himself, unwilling to look weak in
front of Rutherford. "We can leave the country. Disappear
with new identities into the wilds of North America."

"From Caroline's descriptions, you might like Boston," Michael offered calmly.

"Or we could take up residence somewhere in Europe."

"The Mediterranean is very nice. A villa on the sea perhaps?"

Darius dropped the towel from his neck, scowling, and leapt to his feet. "Are you having a bit of fun at my expense? This isn't a jest, Michael! If I take her out the country, it's tantamount to kidnapping. I'd be stealing another man's wife, and while it's the right thing to do to protect her, it doesn't feel very honorable to slink off under false names and live half a life where I might be hired to tutor someone's children and she spends her days hiding inside a house like a phantom! We'd live in fear every day of our lives, and if her husband's agents ever found us, he could make every immoral claim imaginable and she'd have no grounds to fight him! If we're discovered at any point, I'm either dead or imprisoned and—it's worse for her!"

"So don't run," Michael said softly, his expression calm.

"You . . ." Darius stared at his friend with renewed respect. "You're good."

"I was just testing your resolve, Thorne. If you want to win this, then you'll have to win it here. And until every last rotten stone he's ever touched is overturned, you know what to do."

Darius sat back down, his knees a bit unsteady. "Why did that make me feel better? It makes no sense that I should suddenly feel better."

"Sometimes knowing that you have your back to the wall just gives you clarity and the will you need to keep fighting." Rutherford shrugged and then stood to wipe his own face and put away the equipment. "It's when you think you've overlooked a strategy or missed a clue that you'll drive yourself in circles."

"There's a truth." Darius moved to help him, retrieving their protective gear.

"Don't forget to ask for help when you need it, Darius."

Michael took his mask from Darius's hands. "We're all holding back only because you asked us to stay clear."

"I know," Darius said. "I promise. I'll ask. Soon."

The men walked out of the exercise hall toward the changing rooms and Darius was unable to stop smiling.

"What?" Rutherford asked.

"You know, for a man who swears against the ills of being overeducated, I think you'd have made a hell of a teacher."

Michael ducked his head, his face flushing with embarrassment. "I'd have been a great many things in another lifetime. But that's done. I am what I am." Rutherford picked up his bag and left without another word.

That touched a nerve!

Darius contemplated the puzzle of the self-appointed guardian of the Jaded for just a few seconds until his own fears for Isabel resurfaced and proved far too distracting.

My back is to the wall.

No retreat.

It's clarifying to realize it, but why do I still have the feeling that I'm turning in circles?

Chapter
24

That evening, at the next narrow little house on a dark, crooked street on his list, one of Darius's worst fears came to pass.

"Ah, here's the bloke who was mentioning your lordship!" The wizened older woman running the house made a cheerful introduction just as Darius was crossing the doorstep.

Lord Netherton turned in surprise, his arrogant face flushed with drink. "What's this I hear? Are you shadowing me, Thorne? And spinning tales?"

Darius shrugged, handing off his hat and coat as if Richard's presence wasn't in the least unexpected. "And you're not flattered?" He turned to the woman. "A bottle of your best port."

She hurried off, happy to accommodate them, and Darius made his way into the salon where Netherton was holding court, ignoring the scantily clad women with their hardened expressions or the way they nervously eyed Richard.

"Are you buying me a drink?" Richard asked.

"I'm buying a bottle. If you care to share it with me, you

are more than welcome. Our first meeting was awkward, and I'm assuming you're curious about what you've heard, so I'll leave it up to you."

"Why aren't you afraid of me, Mr. Thorne?" Richard asked as Darius took a seat next to him and accepted the glass he was offered.

"Should I be?"

"My man Jarvis found a stallion of mine in *your* stables, sir. Just a few days ago."

"Did he?"

"You heard me mention that I'd lost an animal when we met in the archives at the university that day! Yet you said nothing."

Darius shrugged. "I failed to make the connection."

"And my wife? Did it not occur to you that the two might be connected? That if I'd known the direction the horse had taken I might be able to conduct a better search for her?" Netherton picked up the cards in front of him. "If they find her dead in a ditch with her neck broken from a fall when the snows melt—how will you face it?"

Darius sat up as if he'd been prodded. "Do you think she's dead?"

"How would I know?" Richard rolled his eyes. "Your groomsman could have thought to keep the beast for his own profit and strangled her himself!"

Darius smiled. "*My* man? You'll have to come up with a better tale than that. If he meant to play horse thief, he was certainly taking his time disposing of the animal, and as to the other nonsense . . . Is your wife that odious that every man who encounters her would think nothing of murdering her?"

"It is a dangerous world we live in, Thorne."

"It is indeed." Darius set his drink down for a moment. "Someone may have found your horse in my garden, your lordship, but that's fairly circumstantial evidence to say I've also managed to find your wife. But by all means, call the authorities and explain to them exactly how it is that you've lost her and now weeks later can claim she's hiding in my stables in Scotland. I should warn you that my driver, Hamish, lives in the rooms above and will be extremely put out if your wife has been trespassing there all this time!"

"What game are you really playing, Thorne?"

"No games. I've every right to be here, if I choose."

Netherton's look was openly skeptical. "After you played the prig with me in Edinburgh, I'd not have guessed that this was your kind of entertainment. Or—that you had the purse for it!"

"It was Pughes who told you I was poor, did he?" Darius sat back, doing his best to channel the look he'd seen Galen use to put any peer in the realm running. "He'd say anything to get you to look away while he picks your pockets."

Lord Netherton smiled. "Good thing I had Jarvis close at hand. Nothing gets past my man."

"Really? Not even wives?" Darius threw out the taunt and held his breath.

Netherton's expression became icy. "Do you take delight in angering me, Mr. Thorne?"

Darius shrugged and retrieved his glass to take a small sip from his port. "Not really. But in the brief time I've known you, you've insulted me and insinuated that my station is one or two steps above a stable boy's, thrown a temper tantrum because I wasn't interested in looking at your Chinese pornography, and accused me of being a horse thief. I'd say I'm handling it all beautifully, wouldn't you?"

For a single moment, Darius had to wait to see if he'd read his opponent correctly.

Finally, Richard burst into laughter. "Damn! You're not such a stuffed shirt, are you, Thorne?"

"Oh, but I am. I'm a dusty bore, Lord Netherton." Darius picked up his cards. "I've seen too much and now I'm unshockable. It's a sad state of affairs but there you have it."

"Unshockable?"

Darius looked up at him with an unsubtle challenge. "I take no pleasure in the claim."

"Even here? How can you not be amused? Look around you!"

Darius looked again. It was a shoddier version of the Velvet House but the concept was identical. Gambling tables were set out in a back room where men smoked and drank as they played cards, and women milled about, flirting and making overt invitations for a turn to the bedrooms upstairs. Except here, the women wore collars like dogs and some of them had bruised and mottled flesh visible where their immodest dresses didn't hide their skin.

And now faintly, I swear I can hear a woman screaming. . . .

And no one was reacting at all.

"It's all very sweet but—"

"Sweet?"

"Would you like to hear a confession?"

Richard leaned forward, his eyes alight at the prospect. "Let's have it."

"After meeting you in Edinburgh and that disastrous conversation, I wanted to see what a true gentleman enjoyed. I have been attempting to follow in your footsteps."

Richard's brow furrowed. "Like a spy?"

"More like a disciple." Darius sighed. "But it's been useless. Your secrets are your own, your lordship. I'm a man starving at a feast, but you—you had the appearance of a man who knew how to satisfy his appetites. I dismissed the erotic works you showed me out of pride and a misguided attempt to show up Pughes. But I've wondered about it ever since, and when he said you'd gone to London, I decided I'd see if a man like yourself might have the answers I'm seeking."

"What answers?" Richard asked, openly intrigued.

"To discovering the secret to true gratification and to experiencing the ultimate pleasures. After hearing Pughes brag about how you were no ordinary gentleman and that you alone knew how to enjoy life, I had hoped to learn what he meant, but it's a lost cause. I'd since given up the guise of trying to match you."

Richard's mouth fell open and then he grinned. "And this tripe about writing a book?"

Darius shrugged. "*If* you'd proven a worthy subject, I was considering it. It would be a work for the ages, and if nothing else, an anonymous book about the exploits of Lord X might have made the pages written about the Marquis de Sade look like nursery rhymes. And made an interesting profit."

"Which you'd have shared with me," Netherton said, his eyes narrowing.

"Naturally." Darius sighed. "But it's a moot point. I've learned almost nothing and was considering yielding the chase."

"A work for the ages." Richard drained his glass and refilled it, his eyes conveying all the warmth of a cobra's. "I'm not sure I believe you. Why not just come to me directly?"

"You'd already left for London and we are not exactly friends for you to reveal your best secrets." Darius took one small sip of his own drink. "I might have made a better case for it once I had a manuscript worth consideration, but as I've said, no one is talking and your private exploits remain your own. But there's no need to fear. It was a foolish idea."

Richard held up one hand. "Not so fast. It's not a completely terrible notion. Much like the horse, I'm thinking you've just come at it wrong."

Darius shook his head. "Undoubtedly. Well, I'll leave it to you to write your memoirs one day and I'll accept my own limited fate."

Damn. That felt ham-fisted at best. But his ego is a sight to behold. . . . Look at him torn between preening about his sexual prowess and the urge to punch me in the face for not kowtowing to his every whim.

"It is an art form, Thorne. A balance of pain and pleasure, punishment and reward. Did you find the Velvet House?"

Darius nodded, swallowing bile at the memory. "I did."

"Be honest. Did you try something young? The fresher, the less rehearsed, Thorne." Richard signaled one of the girls to bring more port. "I like them unmarked. Then it's for me to decorate them as I wish."

Decorate. Dear God, he's talking about the welts and bruises he inflicts on those children.

"Don't you tire of it?" Darius asked. "It's all so . . . empty."

"Nonsense! Pain merely serves to warm a whore, and they secretly love it. When I take charge of a woman like that, when she doesn't even breathe unless I allow it, there is nothing like that power. And they don't mind the lesson. Especially when I drop a few extra coins on the floor."

Charming. I don't believe there's a demon anywhere who would wish to be your companion.

"I suppose." Darius yawned. "It's a tragedy to be this jaded. After tonight, I'll blaze my own trails, your lordship."

Netherton snorted and withdrew something out of his inside coat pocket. "Here! Take this token to the address on this card."

"What is it?"

"A very special place that is guaranteed to awaken even *your* dull and dreary senses, Thorne. It is extremely exclusive and a personal favorite of mine for many years now." Richard drank his port in a single swallow and stood. "I'd take you myself but I'm too well-known there."

"I thought to go to Gray's." Darius boldly tossed out the last name on the short list.

Richard's expression changed, his eyes icing for a moment before he shifted his stance. "Don't bother. It's not worth your time. Its glory days are long behind it."

Darius stood and held out his hand. "Very generous of you, your lordship."

"It is," he reaffirmed shamelessly as he prepared to go. "But here's a bit of advice to augment that good opinion. Next time you find one of my horses, confess it sooner!"

"Any chance you would sell the animal to me?" Darius asked.

"Never! I have plans for that animal."

"Plans?"

Netherton's eyes glittered with malice. "I'll use him to teach my wife a lesson when the time comes."

Shit.

"Where *is* your wife, your lordship?" Darius kept his

gaze steady as any man would when standing next to Satan incarnate.

"In Town, I just learned," Richard replied with a cold smile. "Mr. Jarvis is giving the matter his full attention, so I expect it won't be long now." He set his top hat on his head and touched the brim in a mocking salute to Darius. "Enjoy your evening, Mr. Thorne. And if you still feel nothing after a visit to *that* house"—Richard nodded at the card still in Darius's hands—"then give the whore the whip and see if that doesn't do the trick."

Darius waited as long as he could to make sure that Netherton had truly gone, paid the madam for the port, and then made it as far as the lamppost next to his waiting carriage before losing the contents of his stomach in the gutter.

* * *

"He knows you're in London."

Isabel looked up as he came into the room, jolted from her chair by the fireplace. It was just after dawn and the sounds of the house coming to life made things strange as she struggled to read Darius's mood. "Richard knows." She repeated the knowledge, still trying to take in what it meant for them both.

Isabel shuddered but she was too quiet.

"Why aren't you more surprised?" Darius asked, moving toward her. "What aren't you telling me?"

A wash of shame so potent it made her breath catch in her throat swept through her, and Isabel slowly sat back down. "It's my fault."

Darius went down on one knee in front of her and took her hands into his. "Tell me."

"I . . . found out yesterday after you'd left that he'd been alerted to my presence in the city. Not this exact address, but—" She let out an unsteady, hitching exhale as her anxiety mounted. "There was a letter. From my mother."

Isabel could see the quick turns of his mind as he began to put the puzzle together. "Your mother wrote to you *here*?" he asked.

She shook her head. "I used the Grove for the return address. I shouldn't have. I see that now. Mrs. Clay gave the letter to Mr. Rutherford . . . and I think he sent a runner." Tears threatened but she fought them back. "I wrote to my mother because I thought maybe there was some chance that if she really knew—if I told her the worst—they might support my cause and help us."

Isabel fished the offending letter from her skirt pocket and handed it over to him with trembling fingers. He scanned its contents quickly, his eyes sparking with anger and disgust. An icy spike of dread drove into her stomach at the change in his countenance, and she braced herself for the lecture and punishments she'd earned. But when he looked up at her, there was nothing but concern in his face. "It is an unchristian thing to say, Miss Isabel Penleigh, but I dislike your mother very much!"

Isabel felt a strange laugh of relief bubble up and she pressed her fingers to her mouth to keep from giggling. "I forgive you."

Darius kissed her hands. "I'm so sorry, Isabel. It's nothing a daughter should ever experience."

"I've put you in danger, haven't I? I—I was afraid you'd be angry." Isabel lost her battle with the tears and they spilled down her cheeks. "I wanted to help and not just sit idly by."

"It's done. And I'm in no more danger today than I was yesterday. Nor you, hopefully. I'll have to talk to Michael and make sure he's aware of the threat, but if the trail ends at the Grove, then Netherton's man can stew there until he's an old man."

Oh, God. Mr. Jarvis at the Grove!

The idea of the very sweet and accommodating Mrs. Clay being subjected to that man's presence made her heartsick and added to her misery. She hadn't thought of such a possibility, hadn't considered how quickly the demons would enclose everyone she had ever come in contact with.

Darius spoke aloud as he thought it through. "Your mother must have told him she had word from you and summoned him to give him your letter. How did you send your note to her?"

"I gave it to Mr. Godwin to send via runner."

"That would be the telltale clue you're in the city. . . ."

"I didn't say that I'd run off with you. I just said that I had found a Good Samaritan who had offered me his protection and . . . was a great comfort. But apparently, my mother made her own interpretation of my words."

"Proof of your rebellion." He shifted forward, encircling her waist with his hands. "I'm glad I've been a great comfort to you, my dearest love."

She shook her head. "And to what reward? I am so sorry, Darius."

"No more of that," he said and kissed the tip of her nose to make her smile. "I need to sleep and recover. Perhaps a game of chess this afternoon? What do you think of that? Before I leave tonight and I'm gone for God knows how long this time?"

"Caroline is having tea this afternoon at four with the other wives and wished me meet her circle but . . ." She nodded, then stopped herself. "Wait! How did you know that Richard had discovered where I was? You announced it when you came in before I said anything of the letter."

Darius groaned and lowered his head onto her lap. "God, you're clever, woman."

"Just tell me in a rush."

He answered her without lifting his head, obstinately enjoying the soft feel of her silk skirts and the warmth of her thigh against his cheek. "I ran into Richard, managed to bluff my way past him and pretend to admire the bastard. It was like stepping over a sleeping tiger and I'm not sure I managed it with any actual grace—but I lived to tell the tale."

"Well, that's an accomplishment."

"He's pieced nothing together, Isabel. I'm just an annoying acquaintance who found your horse and whom he assumes shares his penchant for the worst sexual games."

"We're running out of time, Darius. The demon is almost on our doorstep."

"We'll get you out of England if we have to but he's watching me now, and if I run, he'll know I have cause. If I stay and make a show of staying, he'll second-guess his instincts and we'll have more time. Perhaps the time we need."

"I won't leave you."

"We don't need to decide anything today." Darius groaned and shifted back to see her face. "Did I mention that I hate your husband with a loathing that has no equal in the history of man?"

Tears filled her pale blue eyes but she smiled. "It's one of the things I love about you, sir."

"My loathing for Richard?"

"Your passion for me," she amended and then leaned over to cradle his face in her hands and kiss him.

The velvet of his lips to hers was a soothing balm to her frayed nerves, and Darius responded by delving into the soft textures of her mouth, tasting and teasing her until she was sure the room had tilted her out of her chair and into his arms. All her grief and fears transformed into a need for the comfort of Darius's touch, and Isabel melted against him, sighing as his strong arms pressed her close.

Each kiss linked to another, a sensual chain of desire that blurred the lines between giving and receiving. Isabel moaned as her senses came alive, arching her back to ride the waves of wanton fire that rippled through her body and pooled between her hips.

"Come take me to bed, woman. I'm exhausted but I need you. I need you to love me until I fall asleep." His eyes blazed with raw hunger, and her own hunger leapt up at the knowledge that she alone had inspired his lust.

"Yes."

He swept her up into his arms and carried her toward the four-poster bed.

Isabel buried her face in his neck and inhaled the delicious smell of his skin. He was still slightly damp from bathing in the room off the kitchens, and it reminded her of his rituals and the occupation of his nights.

He was doing everything he could for her and she had

no illusions of him taking any pleasure in any of these vile clubs. She knew him better. She knew without a breath of doubt that he was nightly sacrificing more than any man should—and all for her.

It was unacceptable.

But what choice do we have?

Isabel kissed the pulse at his throat and knew the answer. *No choice but to love him for as long as I live.*

*　*　*

As Darius still slept, Isabel indulged in the rare experience of female companionship and the light joy to be found in a simple social gathering. The ladies of the Jaded had gathered in the large dressing room connected to Caroline's bedroom, transforming it into an impromptu picnic and high tea. Mrs. Clark had brought in extra chairs and added flowers from Bellewood's hothouse to make it perfect for the women's meeting.

"I love this room!" Lady Winters exclaimed. "It's so bright and cheerful!"

"The flowers are a lovely touch," Mrs. West added. "Although, I'm sure we'd have been just as comfortable in your bedroom. . . ."

Caroline squeaked in protest and rang the bell. "Don't say it! It took a week to negotiate this 'treacherous journey' of thirty steps, and I for one am glad to see a different pattern of wallpaper!"

Mrs. Clark came in with the tea trolley, bursting with pride at the abundance of delicacies on each silver platter. "Good afternoon, ladies. If you need anything at all, you're just to ring. Shall I pour?"

"Oh no." Caroline waved her off gently. "We can manage, Mrs. Clark. Thank you! It's a feast. Please tell Ellie she's outdone herself and that I'm . . . overwhelmed."

"I'll be sure to tell her, madam. Thank you." Mrs. Clark curtsied with a huge grin and left them to their conversation.

Lady Winters eyed the cart. "Gracious! I'm not eating for a week after this. Are those your cook's famous chocolate tarts?" She bit her lower lip. "I'll ask for the recipe later, but if you care for me at all, don't give it to me."

Isabel smiled. She liked Lady Winters's easy manners and recognized the universal struggle every woman seemed to have with her figure. Although, it was apparent from the lady's cleverly tailored dress and lithe, balanced figure that her fear of chocolates was ungrounded.

I wonder why we do that? No matter how perfect we are . . . why we worry so?

"Helen, would you help me serve?" Caroline asked.

"With pleasure," Isabel answered. The opportunity to pour gave her a chance to busy her hands and steady her nerves. It had been a long time since she'd been out amidst company and she wasn't sure if her social skills hadn't faded from a lack of use. And this was no ordinary company. She was surrounded by some of the most beautiful women she'd ever seen, each striking in her own way. She had never felt more self-conscious about her lack of coloring than this moment as she surveyed the mahogany silk of Lady Winters's hair, Mrs. West's black tresses, and the ripe gold of Caroline's curls.

It's ridiculous, but I swear I look like a powdered white pastry by comparison.

Gayle smiled at her as she took her cup, refusing sugar. "Thank you so much."

"Did you want milk, Mrs. West?" Isabel asked.

"Gayle," the woman replied, eyes the color of violets flashing with humor. "You are well in it, now. I know I speak for our informal little club when I say anyone who has been so kind to Caroline and won her approval—"

"Has the love of all of us!" Lady Winters finished merrily. "And you must call me Haley. We don't stand on formalities in this company."

"Oh," Isabel exclaimed softly and nearly overflowed Haley's cup. "I'm . . ."

"Whoa!" Caroline laughed. "I should have warned you, but I'm sure I said something about the unique nature of my friends."

Isabel nodded. "You did, but I wouldn't have presumed to instantly be so . . . welcome." She blushed. "After all, my circumstances are . . . awkward at best."

Gayle shook her head. "We are not always the mistresses of our surroundings and circumstances. There's not a woman among us who doesn't admire your courage."

Haley nodded. "My Aunt Alice isn't discreet enough for confidences, but even when I mentioned a hypothetical version of events to her—well, I believe she advocated something involving hanging a certain peer up by his . . . Let's just say she was in total support of your defection."

The women laughed, and even Isabel managed a smile.

"Besides," Gayle interjected, "we love Darius, and to see him happy is a true delight."

"I just wish Ashe would stop teasing the man!" Caroline sighed. "Why do men feel compelled to give each other such a hard time over the—"

A knock at the door interrupted their conversation and there was a small flurry as another lady arrived. Isabel was astonished at her fiery red hair pulled back into intricate and modest braids and her face a striking composition highlighted by eyes the color of a tropical rain forest against skin like cream. Or what would have been cream but for the blaze of embarrassment on her cheeks. "I'm late! I'm so dreadfully sorry! Did I miss anything?"

They all stood to make room for her as Caroline did the honors. "Mrs. Helen Stewart, may I introduce the newest member to join our odd clan? This is Eleanor Hastings, newly married to Josiah Hastings, the artist."

Eleanor nervously smoothed a stray curl back into place and held out her gloved hand to shake Isabel's. "Mrs. Stewart, I am honored and hope I've not insulted you by coming late. I . . . was delayed." Her blush deepened as she made a study of removing her gloves.

Isabel shook her head. "Not at all, Mrs. Hastings."

"First names, remember?" Caroline corrected her, then turned to Eleanor. "And you are a newlywed and expected to be late to everything."

The women exchanged knowing looks as Eleanor primly took her seat. "There is no excuse for tardiness," Eleanor amended, then laughed in spite of herself. "But it's true that I am still navigating just how late a man can make you when he applies himself."

Isabel sat back as the rest of the visit flew. The women jested openly about their beautiful husbands and the strange twists of fate that had brought not only the original circle of men together, but now this next tier of feminine company. All but apparently Mr. Rutherford had forfeited their bachelor state—although, out of respect, none of the women probed too directly about the nature of her relationship with Darius and its questionable future.

Instead, they spoke of Haley's new dress designs, of Gayle's progress with her medical studies, of Caroline's preparations for her baby's arrival, and of Josiah Hasting's reluctant agreement to show a painting publicly during the summer season.

"It's to be in June," Eleanor announced. "*Lady in Red* has caused a stir but I'm hoping his next painting will also make a splash."

Caroline sighed. "I'll miss it, then. I'm already desperate to see it! Ashe is still raving over it and it's simply not fair, but I suppose it won't be any less lovely by the time Gayle consents to my release."

"Complain all you like, Caroline Blackwell," Gayle countered, "but when you have that sweet babe in your arms, you'll bless every cautious measure you've taken and thank me for the fuss!"

Isabel held out a plate of gingerbread cakes to Caroline with a conspiratorial grin. "Here. Eat one and placate her."

Caroline waved away the plate. "I've no room for another bite, but thank you."

Haley shook her head vehemently. "As to the art show, I'd say we can solve that problem for you, Caroline. The boys can bring it here and we'll have a private showing all our own. Ashe isn't going to allow you to miss the fun!" She turned to the other women for support. "Am I right?"

Eleanor pressed her hands to her cheeks. "I'd prefer to view it just with friends. The thought of the public terrifies me."

"That settles it," Haley announced. "We'll bring the show to you a month before the public gets a peek and make a small party of it."

Gayle crossed her arms. "A very small, quiet party of it, ladies, and Caroline will be abed or I'll put my foot down and forbid the venture."

They all obediently agreed, and before long, the tea was at an end.

Isabel helped to gather plates and cups, discreetly admiring her new friends. *This. This is what normal felt like once. Friends and laughter, social calls and silly conversations. God, what a blessing to be this version of myself again. . . .*

She bent down to retrieve a napkin and regretted it instantly. The room tilted in a strange electric wash of sparks, and before she knew it, Isabel was staring up from the couch, where she'd magically landed with the ladies' help.

"Cold lemon water, Mrs. Clark," Gayle commanded softly, startling Isabel into realizing that she'd lost a few minutes if the housekeeper had materialized, if the tea trolley had vanished, and if the furniture had been moved.

"I'm fine." Isabel pushed away the hands that would have restrained her. "I moved too quickly and the blood rushed to my head."

"You're terribly pale," Caroline whispered.

Isabel smiled. "I am always terribly pale, dear friend." She sat up, embarrassed to be the center of attention. "Please. It's nothing at all and I'm perfectly fine."

"It's the stress of . . . circumstances, Helen," Haley offered. "We should leave you to get some rest. *Both* of you," she added to include Caroline and spare Gayle the fuss. "Before Mrs. Clark returns and chases us from the house with a broom for causing trouble."

The ladies disbanded with quick hugs and gestures of affection that underlined Isabel's amazement at her newfound membership in their circle. But Gayle West lingered, seeing Caroline to bed over her protests, and then returning to sit with Isabel alone in the dressing room for a few more moments.

"May I ask you something very directly and very privately?" Gayle asked softly. "As a physician and as a friend?"

Isabel nodded.

"When did you have your last monthly courses?"

Isabel gasped. "I . . . for . . ." She forced herself to stop and think calmly, despite the strange question. "Sometime early in January."

"It is March." Gayle folded her hands in her lap. "Is it generally a regular occurrence? Your time of the month?"

"Yes, I suppose so. Am I . . . ill?"

Gayle shook her head. "No, I think not. It's fairly soon but it may be that you're pregnant. If you wish, I can arrange for an examination here and we can know for certain."

Isabel was speechless. She wasn't entirely ignorant of the process but naïve enough apparently to have missed the obvious. "Gayle. Please don't—say anything. I'm . . . until I'm certain, I cannot . . ."

Gayle reached over to touch her hand, her eyes full of sympathy and support. "I take professional pride in my discretion, Helen. I'll say nothing, not even to Rowan. And don't worry. Everything has a way of coming right. Even when it seems impossible—or perhaps, *especially* when it seems impossible."

"Thank you."

Gayle left her alone with her thoughts and intercepted Mrs. Clark in the hallway to give her more time to absorb this latest twist of fate.

A tendril of joy curled up inside her, but the nightmare of adding more pressure to Darius's already stressful existence drowned it out. Not to mention her own precarious position in life . . .

A married woman who takes up with another man.

What do they call such a woman? A wicked voice in her head that sounded like Richard immediately answered. *They call her a whore, my dear.*

Oh, God.

And what do they call her when she is carrying her lover's child?

It was her own internal voice that answered this time with equally quiet cruelty.

They call her a fool.

Chapter
25

"Out for a bit of sport, sir?" The hostess of the house came forward, her ample bosom barely covered by a low-cut gown in black satin. "Welcome to Gray's."

Unlike all the other clubs, there wasn't a single working girl visible and no patrons in sight. Only the hostess in her garish dress and one surly bear of a bodyguard who'd suffered himself to wear nothing more than a loincloth and be painted head to toe in silver paint. He'd have been mistaken for an ugly statue except for the obvious glare on his face and change in his position when Darius came through the inner door. In a small foyer with several doors ornately carved and painted gray, Darius fought a touch of uncertainty. It was the last name on the list, and when Richard had tried to warn him off it, Darius had decided not to waste any time.

Now that the bastard knows I'm lurking about, he might be out covering his trail by bribing the women in his wake to silence.

Or threatening them to hold their tongues.

Or paying that silver gorilla to break my neck.

"I am somewhat."

"What flavor?" she asked smoothly.

"I want Netherton's favorite, if she's available."

"Ah." She eyed him up and down as if assessing him with new eyes. "That's an expensive flavor, sir."

"I will pay whatever it takes. But only for Netherton's favorite."

"His true *favorite* isn't in tonight, but Julia knows him well enough and can provide you the same pleasures."

Damn it. So much for my luck.

"I'll take her for the night." He held out a small purse, and once she felt its weight, her smile broadened.

"Yes, the night!" She stepped back with a ridiculous little theatrical flourish of her hands. "Middle door. Top of the stairs. Last door on your left."

"Brilliant," he muttered and headed through the door, ignoring the gray velvet cut wallpaper and silver embellishments everywhere. For an establishment that Netherton had described as past its prime, there was nothing that didn't gleam and bespeak wealth in the house.

God, what a waste! Another secondary player who's going to show me a few scars and make me wish I hadn't been born . . . which means another trip back to try to meet his "true favorite," whatever the hell that means, and then I think I'm at my wit's end.

He counted the identical gray doors and flinched at some of the muted sounds of distress coming through the walls. Even after weeks of his exposure to the inner workings of these clubs, it never failed to shake him to hear a child crying or the screams of a woman in agony.

He hurried to the last door and knocked twice before entering, not actually waiting for a response to turn the knob and escape the hallway.

"Ah!" a woman spoke in surprise. "In a hurry tonight, darling?"

He shook his head, then had to blink in confusion at the tangle in front of him. She was a petite blonde wearing black lace skirts and a black leather corset, but instead of sitting in a sexy pose or preening, she was sitting next to the bed openly fighting knotted leather straps that connected her somewhat painfully to the bedpost. The straps were on so tightly that he could see them biting into her flesh and starting to draw blood.

"May I . . . help you with that?" he offered carefully.

"Would you?" she asked. "My last customer left without doing me the courtesy of freeing me and I . . . seem to be . . . losing feeling in my toes."

He knelt next to her and began to tackle the Gordian knots as gently as he could. "A common hazard, this?"

The question won him a smile. "The least of them. Most gents just make a show of the restraints, but I'd say a few are a bit overzealous."

As he worked, he noted the scars at her ankles and wrists and even around her throat from the repeated use of straps and shackles. There was blood on her thighs from several shallow cuts, and her skin was covered in signs of abuse. He shuddered but did his best to maintain his composure.

She eyed him closely as he worked. "You're new. You going to be kind to sweet little Julia, then? Or am I to be punished for being such a naughty, wicked creature?"

He sat back on his heels and exhaled in frustration. "I'll have to cut this last bit off. Do you have a knife? Or scissors?"

She nodded. "There's anything you need in the drawer there, next to the bed."

He went to the drawer and pulled it out, only to freeze at the sight of its bloodied contents. Knives, razors, tweezers, and metal clamps of every size lay in an unordered jumble.

Shit.

I think Dante missed this for one of his circles in hell. . . .

He retrieved the most innocuous knife he could see and returned to her, making quick work of the last of the leather and freeing her. She cried out in relief and rubbed her wounded calves.

"Thank you, sir."

He held out his hand and helped her to her feet. "It was the least I could do."

She sauntered over to a small wardrobe cabinet in the corner and opened it to reveal a hundred more thin strips of leather hanging at the ready, alongside several odd harnesses and tools of the trade.

She turned back to him with a smile. "All that effort to be free, and here we go again."

"Not tonight." He held his ground. "I just wanted to talk to you and ask you a few questions."

Her brow furrowed. "You paid to talk to me?"

He nodded.

"Well, this *is* new!" She sat playfully on the edge of the bed. "I'm not much of a talker unless I'm tippled."

Darius nodded, displeased to discover that he was becoming an old hand at this game. "Is there a bell to pull to ring for some refreshments, Julia? Or do I call down the hallway to that oversize gilded cherub to ask for a bottle?"

She giggled and slid off the bed to yank on a bellpull on the wall hidden by a embroidered cloth in silver thread portraying several satyrs raping a shepherdess and her flock.

Before he could ask for her preference, there was the sound of a bell and she pulled back a wooden panel to reveal a bottle of red wine and two glasses.

"Clever," he commented.

"You're not supposed to see anyone else at Gray's. It's all like ghosts," she explained. "Makes our clients feel very safe here."

How could anyone feel safe here?

She filled one glass to the brim and started to pour another but he waved her off. "None for me."

Julia didn't argue but greedily settled in to enjoy her wine, sitting back onto the bed with the open bottle in hand. "You are an odd bird, sir, but I think I like you."

He pulled up the one chair in the room and sat next to the bed. He made small talk, asking her the usual questions about her age and her history, and true to her word, her answers began as terse little syllables that gave him almost nothing. But after her fourth cup of wine, she was far friendlier, and at last, Darius began to think he might have some chance at one or two slips of useful information.

"Netherton?" She bit her lip. "What a horror that one is! He pays well enough and well he should since it takes a week to recover from a single session, and he's been known to end a career or two if you don't know the game well enough."

"He comes here often?" he asked.

"Not so much anymore."

Darius could feel his heart slowing as his hope faded. "No? Not even to see his favorite?"

Julia took a huge swallow and then brayed with laughter. "He doesn't come because he doesn't have to if he wants to ride that mare!"

He forced himself to smile to try not to spoil her happy mood. "Why ever not? Is she not here?"

"He's stabled her, for sure and certain! And thank the gods for it! It's been a few years now since he came regular, and I won't lie. We talk amongst ourselves, we doves, pondering what tricks she had to capture and keep a man like that black-hearted beast. But it was different between them, I think."

"Different how?" He refilled her glass himself, upending the bottle and then heading over to the bell to get her another.

"She liked it! Every brutal moment I suspect. Not," she tried to backtrack, "not that I mind my work, of course!"

"Of course," he agreed as sympathetically as he could, handing her the new bottle. "But she kept him interested. . . ."

"More than interested! Not that I envy her the bloke—just her carriage and four-in-hand."

"He still has her keeping? How do you know?"

"Her keeping? More than that I'd say!"

"How? How more than her keeping?"

She bit her lower lip. "I shouldn't have been so free. . . ."

He summoned a smile, hoping to coax her. "Not *free*. But I won't lie—I have a penchant for a good story. The better the story, the higher the price, yes?" He leaned forward. "Is it a good secret, Julia?"

She nodded, a conspiratorial smile tugging at her lips. "It's a very good one, sir. I'm not giving it over without a reward to match. No matter how tippled I am, you rogue!"

"Is it true? This secret?"

She was quick to squeak in protest. "Of course it's true! What good is a grand bit of gossip if it's not true?"

He shrugged. "Let's have it, then."

"And my reward?" she asked with a pout.

He leaned back in his chair. "Name it."

Her eyes widened. "You're having me on!"

"Name your price, Julia."

"A hundred pounds!" she crowed and then held her breath.

"Done. If it's good, I'll give you two."

"Truly?" Julia swayed, hugging herself in happiness. "Two hundred pounds?"

He stood. "If it's good. Let's have it."

Darius braced himself for disappointment, but he'd have paid a thousand pounds to uncover what she knew quickly and escape the stifling confines of her bedroom.

"She's more than his mistress! He married her!"

"What? Wh-why would he marry . . ." Darius had to stop himself from babbling with the shock of it. "He married her."

Julia nodded again, openly happy to have doubled her earnings by his reaction. "It was all hush-hush, of course. I don't think he wanted his family to know he'd settled on a woman like that, and who knows?" Julia shrugged her shoulders. "I heard her say that when he was drunk, Netherton had confessed that he'd hated his father enough to marry a pox-covered scullery maid, just to spite the old man."

"Then why keep it a secret?" Darius asked.

Julia laughed. "What a man says bravely when he's drunk, he rethinks in the light of day! Besides, I think it suits them both to keep their wicked little game to themselves. And"—Julia leaned in slowly—"I think it lets them both play whatever games they like on the side. She still comes round, every once in a while, when her husband's away." She lowered her voice to a whisper. "She misses the sporting life and Madam Peaks doesn't mind the game. It's all masks and fun, ain't it? And if it keeps her fresh and ready for that black-hearted eel, who's to say he minds?"

"She still . . . sports here?"

Julia looked at him through her lashes, a practiced expression. "Excites you, does it? Maybe I'm a fancy lady, too. Maybe I've some great man at my beck and call but I'm left wanting. Does that warm you, sir?"

He ignored her offer. "Her name."

"Have I earned two?"

"You'll earn more if you keep talking, Julia."

"Jane. Jane Chambers."

"And her lodgings? Where can I find her?" he asked, praying she couldn't read the excitement in his eyes.

"On Market Street over near the theatre," she said with a pout. "How much was that worth, sir?"

Darius didn't know whether to laugh or cry. "You have no idea."

He emptied his wallet over her in a shower of notes and coins as she held her hands as if to catch a mystic rain, and Darius closed his eyes at the flood of relief that threatened to unman him.

And the walls of Troy held! This time, they held!

Chapter
26

"Are you ready?" Michael asked.

"I am." Darius looked past him at the two men that Ruth-erford had enlisted to aid their cause, marveling at how authen-tic their costumes appeared. He'd sent Isabel a brief note at first light begging forgiveness for his absence but he'd not wished to waste any time before seizing this opportunity. He'd warned Isabel it might be a day or two before he could return to Blackwell's. He hoped that that wouldn't prove to actu-ally be the case, but his instincts told him he was in for a marathon.

Even so, it was still early the next morning after dear Julia's revelations, and Darius hadn't slept a wink. *I'm ready. Because if Netherton finds out I was at Gray's and spoke with Julia, he can move this woman and I'll lose my only chance for Isabel's freedom.*

"And you're sure?"

Darius shook his head. "I'm not sure of anything any-more, but I'm certain I'm not willing to give up."

"Then let's make a call on the lady. The detective I hired

said there's no man on the premises, so let's hope that's right." Michael signaled the men. "Off we go."

Darius hung back behind them as Michael led the way up the stairs and banged on the door until a maid finally cracked it open.

"What is—" Her voice failed her at the sight of Michael Rutherford glowering down and the uniformed men behind him.

Michael pushed the door open and the men filled the foyer. "Tell your mistress to come down. We have an official matter to settle, and she either comes down those stairs in two minutes or we shall go up to fetch her."

"B-but . . . she is . . . still asleep and . . ."

"Then we'll go up." Michael swept past her as she started to screech in protest, and Darius tried to give the poor servant a small reassurance.

"You'll not be charged with her crimes," he said calmly only to see the girl drain of color in response.

Instead of denying the remote possibility that her employer were guilty of any crime, the girl immediately began to blubber. "I ain't in it! Please! I'm a good girl!"

The commotion at the top of the stairs cut the exchange short and Darius hurried up to try not to miss anything.

"What is this?" a woman's sharp voice demanded. "How dare you barge into my house and my bedroom?"

"We dare." Michael crossed his arms and Darius stepped around him to enter Miss Jane Chambers's private apartment. He ignored the garish decorations better suited to a Turkish brothel and focused on the prize. Jane clutched at a lace dressing gown, her face haggard from a lack of sleep and a bit too much liquor. Darius toed an empty gin bottle on the floor as he stepped forward.

"You're to be charged with fraud, miss. We have a report that you've claimed to be married to a certain English lord and made free with his name to gain credit at various establishments," Darius told her. "I'm afraid it is a crime of libel and fraud that cannot go unpunished."

"What? I don't *claim* anything! I am a legally married

woman and whoever says otherwise is a liar!" Jane was practically spitting at them in her shocked rage. "And I don't make free of anything! Who accuses me?"

"The peer that you're pretending is your husband. He's pressing charges and offered a reward if we can reclaim some of his property he said you've stolen in the guise of a jealous mistress."

Michael nodded and began reaching in his pocket. "I have the list of 'gifts' here." He handed a folded paper to one of the uniformed men. "Make a search. If you find anything on the list, we'll add theft to the charges as warranted."

"Netherton! That bastard!" Her face was practically purple with emotion. "He's sold me out! That pile of putrid sh—"

"Unless you have proof." Darius cut her off quietly and was immediately rewarded by a hiccup of silence and the desperate grip of her fingers on his coat sleeve.

"I do! I can prove it!" she said and promptly burst into tears.

Rutherford rolled his eyes. "You're a known prostitute and an actress, Miss Chambers. Let's have off with the show and get you down to the station."

"No!" she cried out, recovering some of her composure with a feral growl. "It'll be in the registry at St. Bride's on Fleet Street. It's there!"

"What's the date?" Darius asked, praying his voice didn't betray how his life hung in the balance.

She pursed her lips together, a small part of her instinctively reluctant to yield.

"It's a wild-goose chase." Rutherford sighed. "Come on, miss. Ring for the maid to dress you or we'll take you as you are."

"That's *madam* and I married Lord Netherton on November the twelfth in fifty-three. As for that goose, you can stuff it! I'm no weak puff to blow over just because Richard has decided to make off without me!" She grabbed the bedpost as if preparing to make a last stand. "It's a secret marriage but it's legal, and God knows, I've earned every *gift* that man has ever given me! He's the one needs hauling off! What's the Crown's take on bigamy?"

Darius pretended to be shocked at the revelation. "Are you insinuating that Lord Netherton would knowingly commit such an egregious crime and besmirch his good name by—falsely marrying twice? To what end?"

He knew to what end. But hearing her say it made it all the more satisfying.

"His good name? That's all he had! He lost his money overseas in a stupid scheme in Egypt and he'd have married anything rich and kicking to keep us afloat. I allowed it because . . ." Some of her fire faded and Darius's stomach churned at how disgusting she looked attempting the part of the wounded innocent. "I knew Richard truly loved me. It didn't matter what the pigeon looked like. He'd use her up fast and bury her, and we'd go back to it being us. So you see, it's Richard you want. I was never smart enough to think past the edge of my petticoats."

To Darius's horror, her hands dropped to clutch at her dressing gown and slowly slide it up. "What say you men forgive and forget all this? Good ol' Jane could make your day and you can tell Richard I wasn't home when you came to call. I never could keep my skirts down when there's rough sport to be had."

Darius didn't wait for the finale of the show. "Not if Hades were serving iced lemonades. Let's go. We've more work to do than hours allotted, gentlemen."

Michael took a quick step back, for all his height, shrinking away from her reach, and nodded. "Time to retreat, boys."

As quickly as they'd come, the men withdrew from the house with even more commotion as Jane howled with indignation and a whore's stung vanity—and the growing realization that she might have capitulated her future without much of a fight. But even Michael wasn't completely heartless. He turned back and tossed her a small purse full of money.

"Run, Jane. Run as fast and as far as you can, woman. Netherton'll want revenge and you don't want to be here when that gutless excuse for a human being comes around for it."

Chapter
27

White's wasn't the sort of club to allow anyone to just stroll in to bother one of its members. But Darius wrote out a short note and waited in the entranceway, confident that he'd get just such an invitation. He'd spent the day after meeting the real Mrs. Netherton in a strange marathon of activities and fallen asleep on Michael's sofa well after midnight. But all his preparations were made and it was midafternoon when he arrived at the gentleman's club to wait one last time.

I wonder what portion of my life I've spent on the edges of these clubs? Good enough to run some rich man's errands or research some academic society's projects but never good enough to take my place inside.

After only a few minutes, the butler returned to show him up to a small private room off the main club's first floor.

Netherton's face was so red he was nearly purple as he came through the doors. "What game is this? Let's have it, stable boy, for I'm moments away from calling for the authorities and demanding your arrest. I knew that bit about the book was a ruse but I was too distracted to squelch you like I should have. So what is this now? Is this—a new hoax?"

"Is it? I have a certified statement from the bishop at St. Bride's, Lord Netherton. It seems many of your friends missed the occasion and I thought you'd want to show off your lovely wife. I thought you'd be pleased. Didn't you say you'd lost a bride? But I've found her for you. Shall we order a toast?"

"You son of a bitch! I'll see you dead before you—"

"Really? That's your counter? As if I uncovered it alone or didn't think to make sure that enough of my friends are aware of the situation? You'll just kill me and it will all magically go away?"

"What do you want?"

"What I want and what I'm going to ask of you are two different things. What I want is for you to suffer every torment imaginable in a slow, icy dark that guarantees that you'll never harm another human being again. But what I'm going to ask is that you annul your marriage to Isabel Penleigh. It is, of course, technically not a legal match, but things are so much simpler if you are the one that petitions for her release and we avoid making your true marriage to Jane Chambers known to the papers. It would be quite the splash, don't you agree?"

"*Annul* my marriage to Isabel?"

"Here." Darius held out a set of folded legal documents. "I've drafted everything with the help of an experienced attorney and I have a carriage waiting to take you to see the archbishop."

"On what grounds am I *supposedly* annulling this marriage?"

"On the grounds that you were impotent and unable to consummate the marriage."

"Screw you!"

Darius slowly smiled. "I wonder what your peers will make of the *first* Lady Netherton. She seems like such a delightful creature. And I'm sure they'll be ever so forgiving about your fraudulent scheme to take a second wife for her fortune and, what was the phrase? 'Use her up fast and bury her'?"

The look on Richard's face was terrifying as it calmed into an unreadable quiet rage. "She is hardly a reliable witness."

"She doesn't need to be. We have your signature and the word of a bishop. And there are other witnesses. You'd have to murder every whore you've ever touched at this point, your lordship, and I'm not sure you have the stamina or the time."

"I *can't* annul the marriage. There are . . . reasons."

"Ah, the money." Darius's tone betrayed his disgust. "Keep it. In exchange for your agreement, the contract states that there will be no retribution or effort made to sue you for repayment of her fortunes. Off the record, nor will we expose your true wife to the public eye. So you see, you get what you wanted all along and I'm the one who must live with the disappointment of thinking you're still somewhere rich and happy."

"Why?"

"Because I don't want you to have a reason not to let her go. Because even with prison and scandal hanging over your head, you might just be vindictive enough to make the wrong choice. Because as much as I hate you, I love her more."

"You? You *love* her? You think the daughter of a marquis is going to—what? *Marry* you? Is that what this is about? Did she come to you and beg you to save her?" Netherton laughed. "You're a fool! Her parents will cut her off without a penny for this no matter what that paper says—involving herself with some mutt of a bookworm after fleeing the match that they endorsed and promoted? You gain nothing! Not a farthing!"

"Then you agree to let her go."

"Cheerfully! You've saved me the trouble of snapping her neck and kicking her body down a flight of stairs! I have everything I wanted from the exchange and my freedom back to boot! But Isabel will have nothing but ruin! By all means, tell her I said that I wish her every happiness in her newfound poverty and exile. Annulment or divorce, the consequences are the same. No one will take her cards and every door in London will be shut against her."

"I'll meet you at the archbishop's within the hour. There must be witnesses to the signing and no question of the legalities," Darius said as evenly as he could, holding out the address to the church.

"Fuck you." Richard snatched the card from his hand and threw it on the ground. "I know where it is!"

Darius pointedly ignored him, blinking as if he were listening to a horse bray. But before Netherton stormed off, he caught his sleeve. "One more thing."

Netherton's look of rage and astonishment was unparalleled. "Besides the insanity you've already enforced?"

Darius nodded calmly. "The horse. Samson. How much?"

Netherton's expression changed to something akin to a cobra's before a strike. "I'll see him shot and ground to paste before I sell him to you, Thorne. But if you'd like, I can send him to her in a box with my compliments."

"Pardon the interruption." Galen Hawke's voice was level but there was no mistaking the look of contempt on his face. "I didn't realize this room was occupied."

"I apologize, Lord Winters." Darius turned away from Netherton in surprise.

"It's a private conversation," Netherton growled at the unexpected intrusion. "But one that has come to an end."

"Has it?" Galen asked with a cold smile. "Did I hear you refuse to sell a horse?"

"Yes. As I said, a private conversation to—"

"Sell it to me," Galen said softly.

"What?" Netherton's confusion was complete. "You don't even know if it's a pony or a sorrel, sir. Why would you make such a ridiculous offer?"

"If it galls Thorne, I'd pay any price." Galen cast a single look of brutal loathing in Darius's direction and Darius immediately knew the game and played along.

"Winters, you bastard! Keep out of this!" Darius protested.

Netherton's eyes lit with pleasure. "I see you've made a

habit of angering your betters, Thorne." Richard gave Galen his complete attention, dismissing Darius. "It's a fine horse, a stallion, and I'll give him to you for a mere twenty pounds."

Galen arched one eyebrow. "Twenty pounds?"

Netherton laughed. "To make it all the sweeter knowing the bookworm could probably have afforded it and will still be denied the beast! There'll be no parting gift to his ladylove and I'll have the satisfaction of the last blow."

Darius started to protest but Galen asked, "Where is this creature?"

"In my stables here in London. Send a man and you can take possession of him today."

Darius shuddered, thinking of just how close Samson had come to destruction.

Galen shrugged and immediately pulled out his wallet and the two men stepped over to a side table to draw up a quick bill of sale for the stallion as Galen secured a card with an address where the horse was being boarded. "I am happy to oblige and put a little salt in the wound if I can."

Richard signed it with a flourish and pocketed the twenty-pound note. "Tell me, Winters, what did Thorne ever do to you to make an enemy?"

Galen's emerald eyes darkened dangerously and he stiffened his back. "I will never tell a living soul."

Netherton smirked and looked over at Darius standing by the windows. "I leave here a wealthy man, unencumbered and untouched, Thorne. Oh, and one twenty-pound note in my pocket that guarantees the whore *never* forgives you for not securing her darling's keeping. I'll see you shortly at the church, Thorne, and insist that you smile while I make the better bargain. Good day, gentlemen!"

Netherton walked out with the jaunty walk of a man who had won the day, and only when the door closed behind him did Galen speak again.

"Tell me why I can't strangle that man, Darius."

"There's an inconvenient law forbidding murder . . . but don't ask me to quote it because at the moment I'm struggling to remember it myself." Darius knelt down, his hands shaking, to begin to gather the papers.

Galen immediately knelt next to him to help. "And I bought a horse. . . ." Galen shook his head in disbelief. "I'll send a special courier for him right away since I have the feeling that Lord Netherton might decide he'll enjoy carrying out his grisly threats more than that ridiculous bit of money."

"You overheard that? However did you manage to be here? I mean—I'm so grateful I'm having trouble speaking, Hawke."

"Rutherford. He sent a runner as soon as you'd arrived. Said you might need a bit of titled help inside White's and I was the man for it." Galen held out the sheets he'd collected. "Here."

"Thank you, Galen." Darius took the papers and let out a long, slow sigh of relief. "And may I say, you are quite intimidating when you set your mind to it."

"And when I don't try, if my wife is to be believed," Galen agreed with a smile that softened the saturnine cast of his features. "Haley seems to find it charming when I try to growl her out of things."

The men stood and Darius folded the precious documents he'd sacrificed so much to get. The bargain was struck, and if Netherton kept his word and met him at the church . . .

Almost there.

"You look like hell, Thorne." Galen eyed him cautiously. "When's the last time you slept?"

"I have to go. I have to take the documents and see this thing through. I'll sleep later when Isabel is free."

"Let me come with you," Galen offered.

"No." Darius stepped back. "You can't play the role of my enemy and then show up to demonstrate moral support. Everything hangs by a thread and I can't risk it. Please just get Samson."

"Samson?" Galen's brow furrowed.

"Your twenty-pound purchase."

"Ah! Forget the courier. I'll see to it personally and meet you later."

The men shook hands and Darius left quickly to find Rutherford outside with the carriage, awaiting the final leg of a journey that Darius at once longed for and dreaded. Every step he took was fueled by pure adrenaline and the bright hope that after all the feints and false starts, his endgame strategy was about to pay off.

Check and mate, Netherton.
May you rot in hell!

Chapter
28

Isabel pressed her fingertips against her temples and sighed. Daisy was patiently trying to weave a rose-colored ribbon through her curls, and offering what comfort she could.

"If it's a headache, I'll bring up a treatment, madam," Daisy offered softly. "Mr. Godwin keeps a locked cupboard of remedies he gets from Dr. West. Doesn't trust an apothecary to any of it! I know for a fact there's a lovely syrup for headaches since Dr. West suffers them terribly! Poor man."

"No." Isabel straightened her back and smiled. "I was just . . . thinking."

"You worry too much, if you don't mind me saying. Perhaps a breath of fresh air? It's a touch of spring today and as blue a sky as a heart could ask for to—"

There was a soft knock on the door and then Caroline slipped in.

Isabel gasped in shock at the sight of her friend roaming about with her swollen belly. "Caroline!"

"Mrs. Blackwell!" Daisy squealed unhappily. "If Godwin hears you out of bed, he'll skin us all!"

Caroline rolled her eyes. "Mr. Godwin is as gentle as a lamb and it's not him I'm worried about. I just need a moment with my friend alone, please. Daisy, please go and keep watch for—"

Mrs. Clark's knock was brisk and unmistakable before she came into the room. "Madam! Are you trying to give me a heart attack? Out of bed and risking the stairs in your condition?"

Caroline groaned in frustration. "Mrs. Clark. What a bother! I feel hale enough to skip up and down all the staircases in London if—"

Isabel caught at her sleeve. "Please, Caroline. Indulge your husband's love of you and your physician's caution and don't get me into trouble. Lamb or no, I'd rather not face Mr. Godwin."

"Very well. I just needed to delivered this note and I'll tiptoe back like a child caught in the kitchens." Caroline held out a small ivory square of folded paper. "It was an excuse to escape and the exercise has done me a world of good. I apologize for the broken seal but it was misdirected to me thanks to Mr. Thorne's horrible handwriting. Apparently *s* and *b* are too wretchedly close for the upstairs footman."

Isabel took the note from her, smiling. "It takes some practice to discern. Thank you, Caroline."

Caroline left without any further protest, with Daisy and Mrs. Clark escorting her back to her nest on the second floor. Isabel shook her head as she listened to Mrs. Clark's gentle chiding echoing down the hall before opening the note to read.

Mrs. S—

Meet me in the back garden.

—D

Isabel pocketed the note and ran down the stairs, anxious to see Darius and discover what such a summons might mean. He'd been gone for nearly two days and it was unlike him. Her fear had been palpable, and despite his assurances that she'd not done irreparable damage by writing her mother, she couldn't help but worry that some great harm had befallen Darius.

Just as Daisy had described, the day was bright and the sky a limitless blue, but Isabel took almost no notice of any of it as she lifted her skirts to hurry across the garden path to find him against the far wall near the entrance to the stable's courtyard.

"Darius! Is something wrong?"

He shook his head slowly as she came closer.

"You're free." Darius's chest ached at the words, at the sight of Isabel running toward him, a vision of elusive beauty and incredible survival.

"My God. Is that possible?" Her steps slowed as she reached him at last. "Truly?"

"Truly." He folded her against his chest, inhaling the soft scent of her hair and skin. "You are no longer his wife."

"How?" She pushed away gently, eager to understand. "I know it's been weeks but this seems sudden. Did you uncover scandal enough to convince him? How did you make him to relent?"

Darius nodded. "I wish I could say it was through sheer brilliance, but I stumbled onto a solution to surprise us all. He'd secretly married his mistress years ago, and his alliance with you was some kind of twisted greedy game to refill his coffers. He married you for the dowry and intended to . . . get you out of the way before long."

Instead of growing even paler as he'd expected, her cheeks flushed with roses at her fury. "He is the worst villain of all men!"

"He is." Darius sighed.

"So he's agreed to divorce me." She squared her shoulders as if preparing to take on a great weight. "There will still be a scandal but I don't care."

"No, no divorce. The marriage is to be annulled. The archbishop agreed and Netherton swore before witnesses just an hour ago that the marriage was invalid and that he never touched you."

"N-never . . ."

"I forced him to say he was impotent and incapable of fulfilling his duties."

Isabel's eyes widened in shock. "It's—miraculous! I cannot believe he would readily agree to say such a thing, even if you had a knife to his throat!"

"He didn't cheerfully surrender. Even with the threat of exposing his bigamy, he didn't go down without exacting a price."

"A price?" she asked softly.

"He's to keep your dowry, Isabel." He squeezed her hands in his, doing his best to anchor her against the blows. "If I didn't concede, he could have dragged it out endlessly and you'd have been the one to suffer from the worst of public scrutiny and exposure. I couldn't allow it. I couldn't imagine allowing you to be—violated and wounded like that. You are not a woman to be pitied, and I knew you didn't want to ever be seen like that."

"You cannot protect me from . . ." Isabel's eyes lowered to look at her hands in his. "People will think whatever they want but I'm beyond Richard's grasp. Even penniless, I am better off."

"You aren't penniless." Darius pulled out one more folded document and pressed it into her hands. "Here is an estimate from Mr. Cavendish on a set of stones I left in his trust. The money is yours."

"No. Absolutely not."

His brow furrowed. "If it isn't enough, you are welcome to all I have to—"

"I cannot simply take your money! Are you . . . paying me to step aside?"

"God, no! I just . . ." Darius took a deep steadying breath. "I want you to have the means to have whatever life you choose. Independent of anyone, even me."

"If I take your money, I hardly see how that makes me

independent!" Isabel crossed her arms. "You've somehow gotten Richard to agree to an annulment and now you wish to provide for my financial future?"

"I wanted . . . you to have as many choices as possible for your future."

"Choices." Isabel reached out to touch his face. "Why do I have the feeling that you are stepping back?"

He captured her hand, pressing her fingers against his cheek to savor the contact of her flesh to his. "I've never loved you more."

"But? Why do I hear hesitation in your voice?"

"Because I can see the whole board. Because I can see all the pieces in motion." Darius kissed the palm of her hand, his lips lingering against the warm well of her skin. "I love you so much it makes my bones ache. But my life . . . the quiet of libraries and the smell of books. Where is the music? You're so young. I'm afraid you'll miss the dancing, Isabel. Perhaps not right away, but in time, when the dullness of a scholar's existence cements like walls around you, and you'll remember all those glittering balls and sweeping social engagements and regret that you settled for a humble man who is terrified of even simple country dances."

"I've already walked away from all of that!"

He smiled. "For a time. But you could recover that world, if you wanted to. Even without your parents' blessing, you are a celebrated beauty, and with a little bit of strategy, you could have the Ton at your feet." He let out a long, slow exhale. "You didn't think you would have that chance, Isabel. I don't want you to throw it away before you've genuinely considered all your options."

She pulled her hand from his, her eyes snapping with fury. "Stop counseling me like this is some game!"

He shook his head. "You are the queen on the board, Isabel. You must look before you move. I don't think I could survive it if later you thought you'd run blindly from one situation to another and forfeited your future. I want you to be sure that you haven't mistaken gratitude for something more."

"Gr-gratitude? You think that gratitude is the basis of all that has passed between us?"

He shook his head slowly. "No. God, no. But everything I've said about respecting your will, about embracing your independence—I can't ignore all of it when it suits me. You're free. Free to do whatever you want, not just to do what I want you to do."

"So that's it. You end my marriage and offer me a fortune. You'd give me your home and pay for my care—and where are you in this? Where is your heart? Now that you are finally free to do so, where are your declarations of love?"

"I love you so much I'm willing to let you go."

"You don't want me anymore?"

"I want you! But I want you to use your head. If you choose me, be clearheaded. I'm an unemployed academic with a pedigree the village baker could best! On the heels of this annulment, you could avoid the worst of scandal. Your parents may yet amend their stance and apologize for all the harm they caused you. For their own pride's sake, they may wish to make quite a show of their acceptance and sympathy. Genuine or not, it would be all the support you needed to rewind the clock and begin anew."

Isabel's look wavered between astonishment and anger. "You're impossible, Darius Thorne! Pushing me around and making foolish pronouncements about your worthiness! You think you're the only one clever enough to have any perspective? To see beyond the surface of things and to understand what's at stake?"

He slowly shook his head but was unable to speak.

His silence only fueled her fury.

"You think nothing of my happiness! I may not worry about class and blood, but it's clear to me now that you are the one trapped by prejudice and preconceptions!"

Darius cleared his throat. "I'm not trapped. I'm just more familiar with the ways of the world, Isabel."

"I don't care if your parents were pig farmers, you prat of a man! I don't care! And I said I loved you! Which apparently is also a fact you've dismissed in your survey of the

game! Well, I don't wish to play! I'm not a pawn to be protected or ignored! I've learned the lesson, Mr. Thorne. I am
the most powerful woman on the board and I don't need you
or any man telling me what is best for me or wh-what . . ."

Her tirade suddenly lost steam, a faint confusion clouding
her eyes as the sound of a horse's whinny interrupted her
thoughts. "B-but that's impossible. . . ."

She turned on her heel and ran toward the stable adjoining
the garden only to be confronted with the sight of a very
impatient and anxious Samson demonstrating to Ashe's
grooms that he wasn't about to be pulled or pushed anywhere.

"Samson!" she cried out and, ignoring the fearful warn-
ings of the stablemen, ran forward and threw her arms
around his great black neck, sobbing in relief and joy. The
stallion's reaction was equally remarkable as he lowered his
head to enjoy every wet kiss she offered him and accept the
worship that he considered his due.

Darius watched the scene, pleased to see her happy and
miserable at the return of his unreasonable jealousy of his
equine rival. He watched them until he couldn't bear the
sight of his beautiful Helen for another second and turned
to go.

"Wait."

Darius froze and Isabel's hand on his arm pulled him
back to face her once again.

"You secured an annulment, negotiated my freedom,
took care of all of the legalities, and . . . somehow managed
to get Samson in the bargain?" she asked in astonishment.
"How?"

"A stroke of luck," he conceded. "Pure luck."

"Darius?"

"Yes."

"It's the most amazing and thoughtful gesture that anyone
has ever made to me. How is it possible that you can solve
complex puzzles, master foreign languages, and wield such
intellect and then be so blind when it comes to love?"

Darius studied her for a long moment. "I just want you

to be happy, Isabel. What if you had everything you ever wanted and it was my selfish desire to be a part of your life that ruined it for you?"

"And what if you're wrong?" she asked.

"How wrong?"

"*Completely* wrong," she said with a smile. "How can anyone still think themselves selfish when they've sacrificed everything for someone else? My happiness isn't going to be found at a ball. It isn't about the balance in my accounts or ribbons and hats and ridiculous parties."

"Perhaps not but—"

"No. You cannot have it both ways, Darius Thorne. Am I the queen? Yes or no?"

"Yes."

"Then stop overriding my wishes. I'm telling you that you are my happiness. I will forfeit anything to have you, Darius, and I will never know a moment of regret."

"You're sure?" he asked, a blaze of hope overtaking him.

"I am sure that I tire of living in sin, sir. I am sure that we should marry quickly and here so that my best friend, Mrs. Blackwell, can be in attendance and so that our child can bear the name Thorne with all the pride and pomp it is due."

"Our child?" he whispered.

"Let's be clear, Mr. Thorne. I am marrying you because I love you! Not because of . . . circumstances."

He nodded wordlessly, then finally managed to speak. "But you *are* marrying me."

Isabel smiled. "Yes."

"Then that, my dear Helen, is what is known as man's ultimate victory."

Chapter
29

At Rowan's brownstone, every seat and corner inside his eclectic study was filled with the Jaded and their wives, all gathered in a quiet evening's revelry.

"I cannot believe it! Thorne is tethered, and by such an elegant hand!" Galen smiled. "Welcome to our odd family, Miss Penleigh. I'd always thought that Darius would be the last in our company to find a willing wife."

Isabel blushed. "Thank you, Lord Winters. But I cannot believe such a thing of Darius. He is too appealing to go unnoticed or to be neglected by the fairer sex for long."

Rowan held up a small tray full of glasses of sherry for their toasts, which his wife promptly took from him to avoid spills. "We don't doubt he's pretty," the doctor teased, "but we had worried that he wouldn't look up from his books long enough to even notice the fairer sex."

"I swear, I would think you men would be kinder to each other," Gayle chided as she graciously ensured that everyone had a glass of their own. "Poor Darius."

Isabel sighed and stepped closer to her fiancé. "There is nothing poor about Mr. Thorne."

Darius took her free hand, tucking it into the protective harbor of his bent elbow. "Don't mind them, my darling. They are mannerless oafs and it takes some time to accustom yourself to their idea of jealous compliments." He shot his friends a cutting look over the rim of his gold glasses, and the men sobered as best they could, especially in the presence of ladies.

"We were fools not to use our heads as wisely as Thorne and find our wives by hiding in libraries," Galen conceded, raising his glass of lemon water to initiate the festivities. "A toast!"

"Yes," Haley concurred, rising from her chair in a lovely dress of ruby raw silk. "I think a toast is definitely called for."

Michael stood from his chair in the corner, joining in the gesture. "To a friend's well-deserved happiness."

Rowan lifted his glass. "To you both!"

"To Darius and Isabel! May the difficulties of your beginnings mean you'll have nothing but ease from this day forward!" Ashe raised his glass even higher.

"You're not taking her back to the wilds of Scotland too soon, are you?" Galen asked.

"Stay long enough for a new trousseau!" Haley added. "My gift to wish you well, Isabel."

"Thank you, Haley!" Isabel said, her eyes filling with tears at the generosity of her friends. "You are too kind."

"Not to Scotland too soon," Darius said. "Not for a while yet. There's too much going on here, and Caroline has asked Isabel to stay for her confinement. I hate to be the one to point out the obvious, but a feminine coalition has been created behind your backs, gentlemen. The Jaded have been outflanked."

Michael's eyes darkened. "Not *all* of the Jaded. At least one of us has to keep a clear head during troubled times."

"Your turn is coming," Rowan said firmly, but Michael's look was uncompromising.

"Never." Michael put down his glass, his gray eyes darkening with his vow.

"Enough!" Isabel swatted at Darius's shoulder. "No one is outflanking anyone. It is an innocent friendship among the wives and I am grateful for it. Leave Mr. Rutherford alone. Besides, my promises to Caroline aren't the only reason we're staying." Isabel turned to address the circle, her voice laced with quiet pride. "My husband-to-be has accepted a formal position as head of the new women's college at Bellewood. Mrs. Blackwell has asked him to run the academic programs and see to the certifications!"

"The formal academic position you always dreamed of!" Rowan cheered. "Ashe! Why didn't *you* think of it?"

Ashe shrugged his shoulders. "I was still befuddled by my beautiful American's insistence at hiring *female* professors as well as male instructors for the venture. Besides," he said in mock defense, "I assumed Darius was already occupied. I've never met anyone so buried in books and paper in my life."

"A terrible recommendation if ever I've heard one," Darius said with a smile.

"There's still a certain prophecy to resolve and a wounded Jackal on our heels," Michael stated flatly. "We'll need that keen mind of yours if we're to move ahead."

Gayle stepped forward. "Yes, but that is for another day. Tonight, we are celebrating the joy we have and not lamenting unknown shadows on the horizon. Gentlemen, please. For one night, let us pretend that our greatest worry is coming up with a better name for your club."

There was laughter all around at her jest, and hearty protests defending the Jaded "to the end."

* * *

Darius pulled Isabel from their midst and retreated to the quiet of Rowan's first-floor landing to take his fiancée into his arms. She was a vision in a pale blue silk, wearing the peacock necklace he'd sent for from Craig & Cavendish's. The opals of a raja gleamed at her throat, their opulence muted and outshone by her delicate beauty and the love shining from her eyes. The necklace had been his engagement gift to her, and Darius knew it had somehow been fashioned for her alone.

Isabel blushed. "What are your intentions, Mr. Thorne?"

He carefully placed one hand at her back and lifted the other level with his shoulder. "I'm going to dance with the woman I love until the world falls away."

"Oh!" She smiled at him in the candlelit hallway. "There is no music, Mr. Thorne."

"Since when has that stopped us?"

He swept her into a turn, and Isabel laughed, giddy with the euphoria of finding her place in his arms, protected and safe.

And invincible.

From *New York Times* bestselling author
of *Sinful in Satin*

MADELINE HUNTER

Dangerous in Diamonds

Outrageously wealthy, the Duke of Castleford has little incentive to curb his profligate ways—gaming and whoring with equal abandon and enjoying his hedonistic lifestyle to the fullest. When a behest adds a small property to his vast holdings, one that houses a modest flower business known as The Rarest Blooms, Castleford sees little to interest him . . . until he lays eyes on its owner. Daphne Joyes is coolly mysterious, exquisitely beautiful, and utterly scathing toward a man of Castleford's stamp—in short, an object worthy of his most calculated seduction.

Daphne has no reason to entertain Castleford's outrageous advances, and every reason to keep him as far away as possible from her eclectic household. Not only has she been sheltering young ladies who have been victims of misfortune, but she has her own closely guarded secrets. Then Daphne makes a discovery that changes everything. She and Castleford have one thing in common: a profound hatred for the Duke of Becksbridge, who just happens to be Castleford's relative.

Never before were two people less likely to form an alliance—or to fall in love . . .

Enter the rich world of
historical romance
with Berkley Books . . .

Madeline Hunter

Jennifer Ashley

Joanna Bourne

Lynn Kurland

Jodi Thomas

Anne Gracie

Love is timeless.

M9G0610

Discover Romance

berkleyjoveauthors.com

See what's coming up next from your favorite romance authors and explore all the latest Berkley, Jove, and Sensation selections.

See what's new
~
Find author appearances
~
Win fantastic prizes
~
Get reading recommendations
~
Chat with authors and other fans
~
Read interviews with authors you love

berkleyjoveauthors.com